The Zoo

BOOK ONE

The Zoo

A novel of intrigue and deception on the East African coast

KEITH BROWN

...out of Africa

There is always something new out of Africa,

Pliny the Elder, "Natural History"

The Zoo
Copyright © 2019 by Keith Maurice Brown

All rights reserved. No part of this publication may be reproduced, distributed, or transmitted in any form or by any means, including photocopying, recording, or other electronic or mechanical methods, without the prior written permission of the author, except in the case of brief quotations embodied in critical reviews and certain other non-commercial uses permitted by copyright law.

This story is fictitious, with a few half-remembered local tales and imagined scenes blended together like the delicious ingredients of an African stew. One might picture some people dwelling in a mysterious community, The Zoo, close to the fictional Monkey Island.

How did the characters develop? Simply, a familiar gesture, a memorable phrase; plus, perhaps, a fragment of an unguarded late-night conversation.

The opinions expressed in this novel are the author's alone.

Graphics by the author.

Tellwell Talent
www.tellwell.ca

ISBN
978-0-2288-1333-0 (Paperback)
978-0-2288-1334-7 (eBook)

Dedication

To the Kenyan people who, for sixteen years, shared their lives, struggles, and joys with our family. They taught us many things.

Their beautiful country has seen much suffering, but the resilience of the people gives hope for the future.

Contents

Acknowledgements xi
Maps xiii
Prologue xvii

Part One: Mysteries

Characters in Part One 2

Part Two: The Wall

Characters introduced in Part Two 88

Part Three: The Attack

Characters introduced in Part Three 172

Acknowledgements

The editorial advice and critical input from Pauline W., Linda Whittome, and Marie Jordon-Knox were invaluable, and aided in the streamlining of the initial text. Sue De Vries, Laura W. and Pauline W. provided a careful reading of the final script and supplied many helpful insights. Their countless hours of careful review are very much appreciated.

I am thankful for the advice and support of many friends. The following people provided encouragement and valuable information from their own areas of interest and expertise: David Anonby, Erik Anonby, Tim Block, Patricia Boswell, ADB., Richard Cavalier, Don Craig, Marion Fuller, Jim Fuller, Randy Hoffmann, Peter Mitchell, John Potts, Jen R., Tom Rathjen, Pierrette Scott, Paul W., Richard W., and Cliff Warwick.

However, they bear no responsibility for the words or opinions written in this fictional account of some imaginary characters dwelling in a mysterious community near the mythical East African town of Mwakindini.

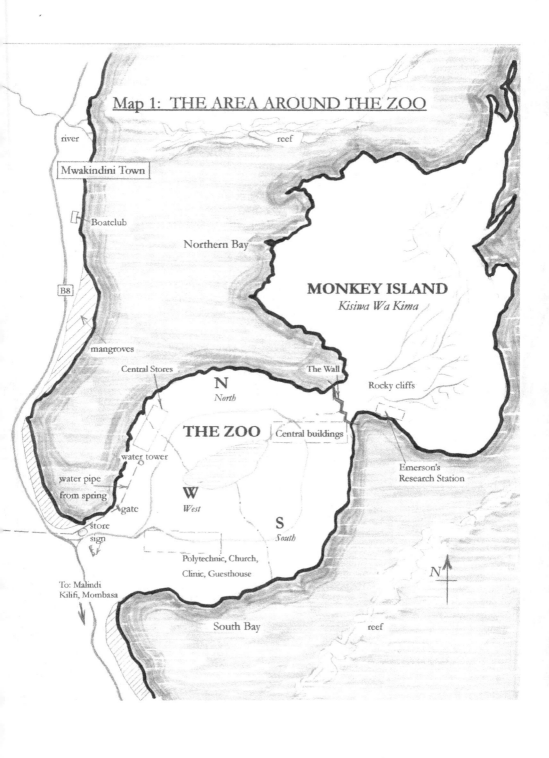

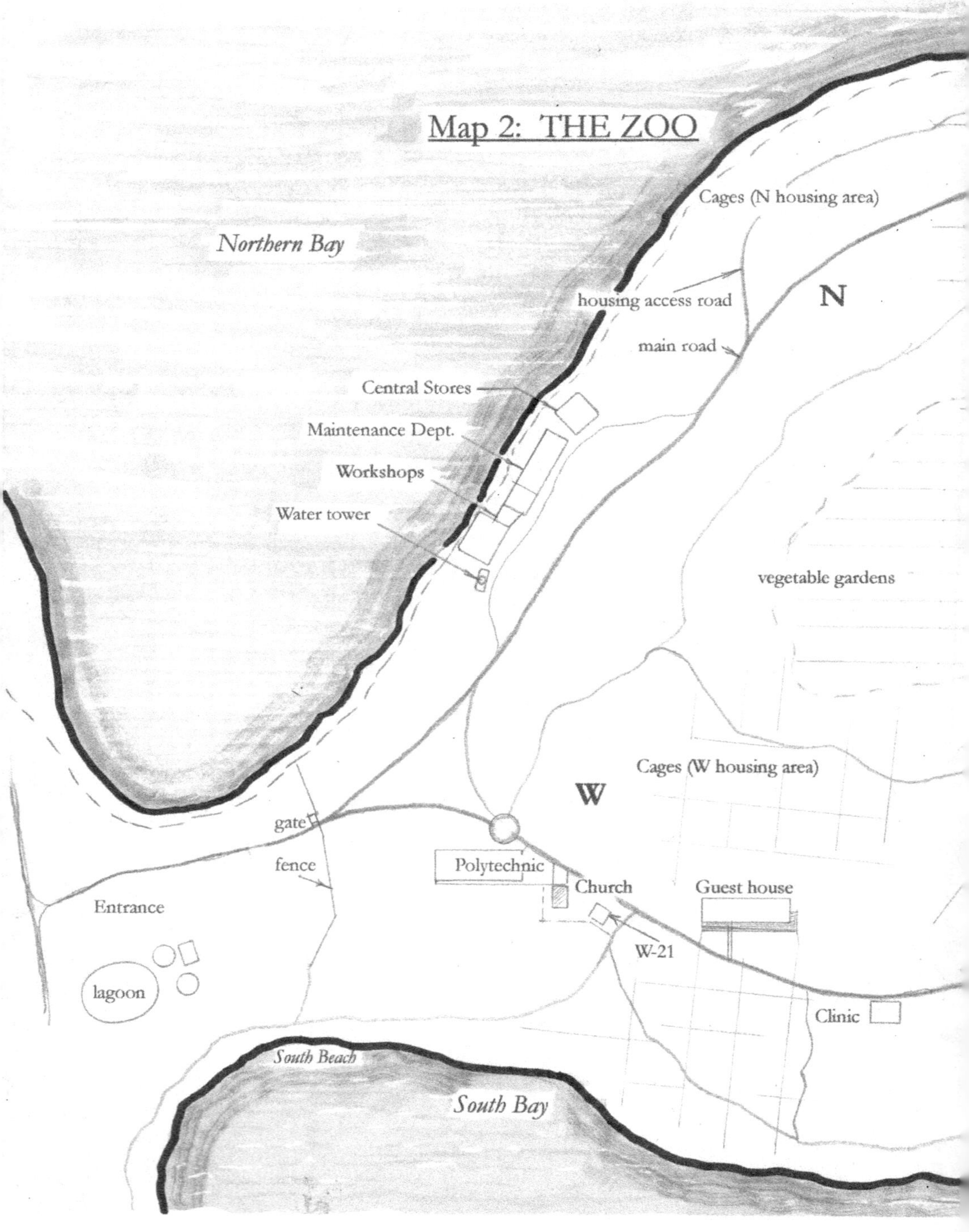
Map 2: THE ZOO
Northern Bay
Cages (N housing area)
housing access road
N
main road
Central Stores
Maintenance Dept.
Workshops
Water tower
vegetable gardens
Cages (W housing area)
W
gate
fence
Polytechnic
Church
Guest house
Entrance
W-21
lagoon
Clinic
South Beach
South Bay

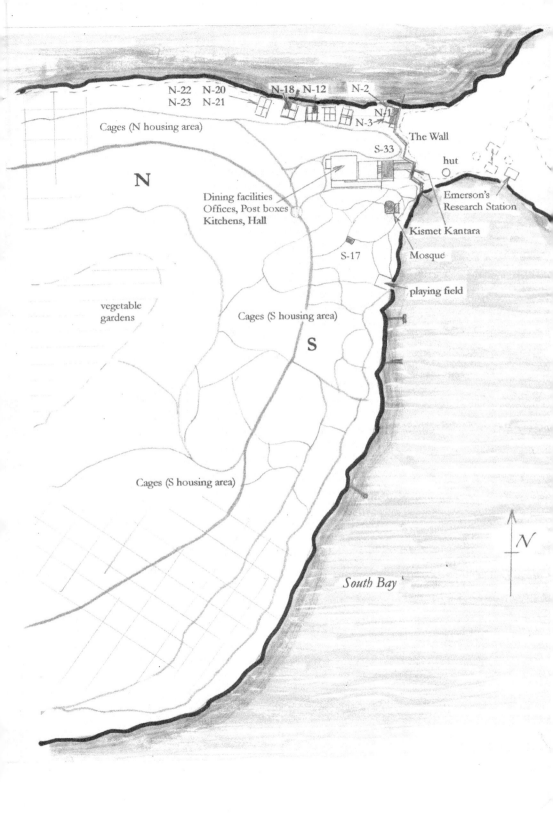

Prologue

The surge of pain left him gasping. Through a blur of agony, Brett saw two men dart out of his front door. The first blow had sent him reeling. The second punch caught him off balance. He had spun to his left, catching his leg against the jagged metal edge of the frame. That had cut his leg badly. Now he lay below the table, desperate to recall the intruder's words…"Be careful and keep your mouth shut…" There was more. What was it?

He winced at the stabbing pulses down his leg as he struggled up on his right knee. His mind was a turmoil of thoughts…*What was that all about?*

He noticed his bloodied leg. He grabbed a towel and tried to wrap it around his leg to pull the cut closed, and stop the bleeding. "This is going to need medical attention," he told himself. "Clearly, those thugs were sent to give me a message. What was it? A message from someone I know. Someone I know?"

He agonized over who had sent the two men. *How can I have made such vicious enemies in less than a year at the Zoo?* The attack, and the warning it conveyed, were obviously a direct consequence of his foolish actions and persistent enquiries. Only three people knew what he had found out: Chengo, Peter, and Louise. They had all urged him to say nothing, but they may still not trust him, and they may have felt he needed a further indication of their seriousness.

Now he had it!

The fictional characters in Part One
(in order of mention)

Brett, Bretton Morris James, mechanical engineer, teacher
Tony, Reverend Anthony Colburn, Alliance Community Fellowship, UK
Brett's parents in Guildford, UK
Jane Colburn, Tony's wife. Reading, UK
Dr. John Phillips, of Resource Data Imaging, Nairobi
Steve, Reverend Steven Brandon, Anglican priest, CPK, Church of the Province of Kenya
Coreene Brandon, Steve's wife. Expert on world religions
Jim Gossard, Brett's friend in Nairobi, retired optician
Mary Gossard, Brett's friend in Nairobi, retired teacher
Henry Emerson, Zoo founder. Retired intelligence officer
Louise Emerson, Henry's wife. Nurse
Peter Lancaster, Zoo founder. Retired from military and police activities
Miles, Miles Tiffin Jolly, retired colonial administrator, investigator
Simion Katana, Principal of polytechnic
Ruth Brandon, Steve and Coreene's daughter
Andrew Brandon, Steve and Coreene's oldest son
Graham Brandon, Steve and Coreene's youngest son
Khadijah, housekeeper in guesthouse
Tili, Brett's maid. Khadijah's sister
Hamud Sita, accounts clerk
Boniface Chengo, Executive Officer
Store owner, eccentric local man who dresses like an English lord
Brigadier Thomas Ridge-Taylor, retired brigadier and farm manager
Vi, Violet Ridge-Taylor, Thomas' wife
Len, Leonard Moore, retired water engineer
Marie-Anne Moore, Len's wife
Kaleem Butt, supervisor of Central Stores
Mr. Maina, government official in Dr. Phillips' office in Nairobi
Muzhere, Miles Jolly's maid
Grace, in accounts office
Ochieng, Malindi police detective

Kinyanjui, Mwakindini police sergeant
Faiz, assistant Imam
Joram Mwangi, Peter Lancaster's man
Jed Walker, former resident, outspoken writer and artist
Matthew Fletcher, retired sheep farmer
Tili and Khadijah's mother
Mjuhgiuna, the Emersons' manservant. Tili's uncle
Onesimus Njuguna, the Ridge-Taylors' man
Esther Fletcher, Matthew's wife
Harmless old man beside fence

1

"Several years ago, I concluded there are some things we are not given to understand, and the local accounting procedure is one of them!"
Steve Brandon

The flickering of the cabin lights woke him. The captain's voice over the intercom announced: "Good morning ladies and gentlemen. Our flight is on time and we should be landing in Kenya in just under two hours. The weather in Nairobi is clear…" Brett did not listen to the rest of the announcement. He glanced at his watch. It was 5:05am. He was pleased he had managed to get almost five hours sleep. He looked to his right, across the empty middle seat, and saw that his fellow passenger was still asleep, a man, perhaps in his mid forties. The previous evening, they had exchanged brief greetings as the flight got underway but neither had felt like talking then.

Brett was pleased to have reserved a window seat as he hoped to see the land as they flew into East Africa. He slowly raised the window shutter. The sky was still dark, with the waning crescent moon rising in the east. A few stars were shining clearly. There was a narrow band of orange light across the sharp horizon. This glow was reflected in the thin winding ribbon of the Nile River, snaking across the valley far below him.

He was distracted by the stewardess handing him a warm, moist towelette. What a wonderful invention! It helped to relieve some of the sting in his eyes from the cigarette smoke in the cabin. He concluded that he would have to put up with the discomforts until someone discovered a better way of getting from London to Nairobi in nine hours. He closed his eyes and allowed his thoughts to drift back to his last few days in England.

The previous day, Brett's old friend Tony had picked him up at his parents' home in Guildford to give him a lift to Heathrow airport. On the one occasion when they were alone together during the last year, Tony's wife, Jane, had confided in Brett that she was concerned about Tony's health – his persistent cough and general lethargy. Brett had known Tony and Jane for about twelve years, having worked with them in youth ministry. Tony, or the Reverend Anthony Colburn, was eleven years older than Brett. Jane and Brett had been close friends since their late teens at the church fellowship. Tony and Jane had married in the spring of 1974, and Brett had been with them recently when they had celebrated their tenth wedding anniversary.

In the intervening years, the three had remained in touch and their church had helped to support Brett's educational work in Kenya. During his ten months in England, they all met several times and Brett had given two presentations to their social outreach group, describing his life and previous work among the Kikuyu people in the highlands of Kenya.

The meal cart had arrived at their row and his fellow passenger had woken and put on his glasses. While the breakfast trays and coffee were being distributed the two men nodded to each other. As his neighbour tasted his first sip of coffee he said, "That's wonderful. It certainly helps overcome my fear of flying."

"Are you afraid of flying?" asked Brett.

"No. See how effective it is!" quipped the man. He reached his hand across to Brett, saying, "Good morning, my name's John."

"Hello, I'm Brett. Pleased to meet you."

"What takes you to Nairobi?" asked John.

"I'm returning to Kenya to continue teaching."

"Oh, where were you?"

"I was in Nyeri for about five years. How about you? Do you live in Kenya?" asked Brett.

"Yes, I work in Nairobi. I do resource exploration using satellite imaging."

"You must work with maps," said Brett. "Are you a geologist?"

"My background is in geology, yes. So maps do play an important role."

"The reason I wonder about maps," said Brett, "is I have been trying to get a detailed map of the area where I am going to live and it's proving incredibly difficult."

John smiled. "Yes, the Kenyan government has severely restricted map distribution these days. But, aren't you going back to Nyeri?"

"No, I'm moving down to the coast. I'll be living in a place called the Zoo. It's a cross-cultural community near a conservation area on the coast, north of Malindi."

"Are you involved with animals then?"

Laughing, Brett said, "No, not at all. I'll be teaching at a village polytechnic in that small community: the Zoo. Apparently, that's the name the development was given when they established that unique neighbourhood."

"I've never heard of it," admitted John. "How big is it? Why do you need a map?"

"Maps of the local area show footpaths, trails, and forested areas. I find it helps when exploring a new place. I'm not sure how large this development is, but it's on a kind of peninsula projecting out into the Indian Ocean. It's close to a small town called Mwakindini. At least, that's how it appears on the road maps I have."

John was silent for a minute and then said, "I'm not permitted to supply maps – or even sketches – but I'll have a look at the images I can get of that area and try to give you a general description if you like. How long will you be in Nairobi?"

"I will not be staying, because the chap who is meeting me at the airport in Nairobi plans to drive straight down to the coast. But I'll have to come back to Nairobi within a few weeks to pick up my vehicle and airfreight boxes."

"Okay, get in touch with me when you are back, and I'll see what I can come up with." John took out his business card which he passed across the seat. Brett took it and studied it carefully. He noted that John Phillips Ph.D. was described as a Technical Advisor in the Satellite Surveying Division. His company was called Resource Data Imaging.

John said, "As I say, I'll get you some information if I can."

"I appreciate that. I'll give you a ring when I'm back in Nairobi."

Part 1: Mysteries

"Fine. The phones work in our office some of the time! Now, where is this community that you are going to, exactly?" John asked.

"It's right on the coast. I was told it's about 200 miles south of the equator, and directly north of Mombasa."

"So that would be latitude about 3° south and longitude around 40° east. I'll remember those coordinates," said John.

Brett noticed a reduction in engine power which indicated that they were beginning their gradual descent. Looking out of the window, Brett saw some mountains far over to the east, including the two snow-covered peaks of Mount Kenya. They were both so familiar. It felt strange to be looking down on the area where he had spent several years, and imagine the places and the people that had become such an important part of his life. He saw the sparkling Rift Valley lakes, and small patches of shadow drifting below tiny clouds.

The stewardess passed out immigration cards. The first question was easy. Date of Arrival in Kenya: 21 August 1984. Brett completed his form, and then flipped through his British passport. In fine handwriting in distinctive turquoise ink, he read: Name of Bearer: Mr. BRETTON MORRIS JAMES. The section 'Accompanied by his wife…' was blank, as was the 'Children' section. The Description page said it all: Date of birth: 30.8.1954. Place of birth: Guildford, Surrey, England. Profession: Mechanical Engineer. Height: 5'11" Eyes: blue. Hair: brown.

His ears began to hurt as the plane descended further. They flew through a scattering of wispy clouds which rushed past the window, and then they drifted silently above the dry plains below. Brett saw two giraffes and some zebras grazing. A few squeals from the tyres, several gentle bumps, a bit of swaying side to side, and he was back in Kenya! He felt a flutter of excitement. Or was it tension?

The process of clearing immigration, though slow, was very smooth. As he was standing beside the baggage carousel, he glanced at his passport and noted that it had the arrival stamp with VP/3M written on it. From bitter experience he knew it meant he had a visitor's permit, valid for only three months. In the arrivals hall, after clearing customs, Brett saw his friend,

Steven Brandon, smiling at him. He was casually dressed, and greeted Brett with a warm hug, "How was the flight?"

"Great, thanks Steve. How are you and Coreene, and the kids?"

"Fine, thank you."

Under a deep blue sky, they walked across the parking area to Steve's car. The path took them alongside beautifully manicured gardens and familiar frangipani and hibiscus shrubs. Brett took a deep breath of the fragrant warm air and felt grateful to be back. "Kenya is still as beautiful as I remembered!" he said.

Steve asked, "Have you made any arrangements with the Gossards?"

"I arranged to collect my pickup and the other things they are storing for me in a few weeks. I'd love to just get going down to my new home, as you had suggested."

"Right, let's hit the road then," said Steve as they both heaved Brett's heavy cases into the back seat of the ancient Toyota Corolla. The temperature was comfortable, but Brett knew it would get much hotter during the 490-kilometre journey, as the elevation dropped from nearly 5,500 feet to sea level.

They spoke about Brett's time in England and recalled Steve's visit when he was also in the UK recently. "So, how are things with Tony and Jane in Reading?" asked Steve.

"They are fine."

Steve thought for a moment. "How is Tony's health? I felt he looked unwell."

"Yes, that's how it seemed to me; but if there is anything wrong they are both playing it down. They are praying for the healing of his throat pain, though," said Brett.

"And Jane, how is she?" asked Steve cautiously.

"She is very supportive of Tony and his work. She's a lovely young lady."

"You have all known one other for a long time," said Steve, glancing at Brett on his left.

Brett nodded in silence, and then said, "I am anxious to hear more details about the Zoo."

"What do you know about it already?" asked Steve.

"Only what you've told me...that it's a special community set up to enable people to live in their individual groups if they wish, but structured to nurture common community activities. You mentioned that the houses are called 'cages' and the organization is run like a zoo, whatever that means."

"At least it's not a circus!" said Steve.

"No, but I don't like the description of a zoo, or the idea of living in a cage!"

"I know it sounds strange at first. We just accept the terms now – and the concepts behind the Zoo."

"Which are what, exactly?" asked Brett.

"When he originally set up the village, old man Emerson had noticed that things were more peaceful when the different communities and sub-groups kept to themselves, but there was contentment and community spirit when they joined together in mutually supportive activities. For some reason, he likened this to a zoo where the animals are grouped by kind, in individual cages if necessary, but with a central control to provide protection, care, and the essentials for healthy and happy lives. The layout of the Zoo, and its management, reflect his original ideas, although over the years there have been many adaptations."

"How do you think I will fit in?" asked Brett.

"I'm sure you will do well there, once you get used to things. At first you will be housed in the guest wing until you have your interview with the committee – and then they'll assign you a cage."

"Okay, a cage," said Brett.

"That's a flat, of course, but they are very small, deliberately, in order to encourage folks to use the common areas for as many activities as they can – entertainment, meetings, dining, and social events. It's hard to explain, but you will enjoy the people at the polytechnic, and I'm sure you will appreciate the church community we have."

"How is that going, Steve – your ministry?" asked Brett.

"Generally, things are good. Over eleven years, I have adjusted my approach. After all, we are a simple community chapel in a unique situation."

They surrendered to their own thoughts as they watched the endless ribbon of road weaving ahead of them across the yellowing plains. Brett had met Steve and his family at a church guesthouse in Nairobi four years earlier. They each had an interest in educational development. Steve had suggested Brett consider joining the Zoo upon his return to Kenya. When Steve was visiting England, they had worked on establishing a relationship with the village polytechnic, which later issued a formal invitation to Brett to assist there. It was under the auspices of the NCCK, the National Christian Council of Kenya. Brett looked at Steve. He was about 38, he recalled, and his wife Coreene was two years younger. "Remind me, how long have you and Coreene have been married."

"We were married in 1968 so it's coming up to 16 years now. It seems like a long time."

"And I have forgotten the ages of your children," said Brett.

"They are twelve, nine, and seven. Our place is pretty crazy sometimes. They are on their August holiday now, so I'll try to spend more time with them in the next couple of weeks," Steve said, "Look, we are not too far from Hunter's Lodge. It's nearly midday, shall we stop for a bite to eat?"

"Good idea. I'll try to phone Jim or Mary Gossard from there."

After lunch, Steve said, "I'd really like to push on as soon as we can. We still have a long way to go and I don't want to be driving in the dark."

"Would you like me to drive for a while? I still have my Kenyan licence as it's valid for 3 years."

"I'd appreciate that, thanks. I'm feeling quite tired after my early morning, but how about you? You had a long flight."

"I feel okay at the moment but I expect it will hit me later. At least I can give you a break."

Brett drove out of the parking area onto the main Mombasa Road. Steve said, "Remember, animals can run across the road unexpectedly. We might see antelope, possibly elephants, and definitely baboons along the edge of the road. You won't see any others of the Big Five from the road, though."

Brett said, "Ah yes, the Big Five. I've seen four of them: Elephants, Black Rhinoceros, Cape Buffalos, and African Lions. But I've never seen an African leopard."

They fell into silence and soon Brett noticed that Steve was asleep. He was grateful for the strong Kenyan coffee he had enjoyed at lunch as he felt alert enough to drive, always conscious of potholes, oncoming traffic, and police checks. He thought about the last few hours since he landed: the contrasting sights and conflicting emotions. Every aspect of Kenya had multiple facets, with positive and negative elements at each level. No doubt he was going to be facing these again. He had appreciated his stable and predictable life in England.

Within two hours, Brett noticed a cluster of petrol stations and shops that marked the half-way point on their journey. As he slowed down, Steve woke up. "We've reached Mtito Andei," said Brett. "Shall we go to Caltex?"

"Yes, all the petrol costs the same because the government controls the prices."

They stopped briefly for breaks and drinks from a warm water jug, but otherwise pushed on steadily. After Voi, they encountered a sparsely populated desert with its dry plateau of low thorn trees and stubby baobabs. Steve had been thinking about Brett's situation and said, "You must feel suspended between two conflicting realities."

"It's all a bit confusing and overwhelming at the moment. Tell me about some of the people at the Zoo."

"Our family lives in the African area, to the west. Coreene has developed good friendships in the southern Muslim community, but you'll be living in what we call the North zone. Those cages all have the prefix N. Ours is W-21 in W for West, and the Muslim section to the south starts with S."

"Interesting," said Brett. "You mentioned Mr. Emerson. He must be quite a character. Tell me about him and some of the others."

"Henry Emerson and his wife Louise, yes, they were the founders of the Zoo, along with Peter Lancaster. Actually, Henry Emerson is a bit of a recluse now, but he still has enormous influence in the community and chairs some of the meetings, I believe. He holds the whole place together. He's not that old, but he has serious health issues, and some disfigurement, so he does not like to be seen in public. In fact, I haven't seen him for a long time. His wife, Louise, is a very pleasant lady, although she prefers working in the background. She and Coreene have a common interest in the Muslim community as the Emerson's cage, S-33, backs onto the Muslim village.

"Peter Lancaster is our Mr. Fix-it. He's in the UK at the moment. His military and police background in Kenya means he has friends in high places. Then there's Miles Jolly, with a quirky sense of humour. You'll like him, if you can stand his jokes. That's just a few of the English personalities. Also there are some wonderful Kenyans. We work closely with those at the church and through our different outreach ministries. I'm sure you will get on well with the staff at the polytechnic, particularly the Principal, Simion Katana."

It was almost dark. Brett looked at the sisal plantations and cashew-nut farms they were passing as they headed north of Mombasa. He asked how the Zoo project was funded.

"It was set up to be totally self-financing, of course," explained Steve. "There is no external source of funding. Much of the initial infrastructure was paid for by the Emersons. I don't get involved with the finances. Several years ago, I concluded there are some things we are not given to understand, and the local accounting procedure is one of them!"

"What about security; do you have any problems there?"

"No. We are blessed in that respect because most of us feel totally secure. We have two or three police families living there which helps, I'm sure. We have a fence and gate at the front entrance with two guards on duty all the time. The eastern section is where the nature reserve is. It is walled off so no one goes in there, other than the Emersons. That's where Henry does his research." Steve explained that Henry was trying to protect some of the unique animals in that area. "In fact, I heard it was a sick monkey that attacked Henry and eventually caused the serious disability he has now."

With their intense conversations, the time had gone by quickly, and they were soon approaching the Zoo. "Another five minutes and we'll be there," said Steve. "It's well past supper time but Coreene will have saved us some food. Come in and eat with us and then you'll be settled in the guest house. Tomorrow, I'll introduce you to the staff in the office, and we'll see what arrangements they've made about accommodation for you. You'll have most of your meals at the restaurant until they decide which will be your cage."

My cage, thought Brett, feeling a slight flutter of anxiety. *This is going to be interesting.*

Part 1: Mysteries

Driving in that first evening, the watchman's friendly smile and wave indicated what lay ahead of them. They were then greeted by Coreene and the children, Ruth, Andrew, and Graham. Steve took Brett to the guest house, where he met the housekeeper, Khadijah, who explained how things would work until he had his own cage. The accommodation was basic with gritty cement floors and thin stiff towels, but the warmth and the sound of the rustling palms enchanted him. He found the humid air oppressive, but knew he would learn to take things at a slower pace.

The next day, Steve introduced Brett to a short British man with an appealing smile, and sparkling jet-black eyes. "I'd like you to meet Miles." They shook hands, with what Brett felt was a rather awkward handshake.

"Miles Tiffin Jolly at your service, sir! That's what it says on all my arrest warrants. The middle name is not my fault; my parents had a sense of humour." Everyone laughed. "Welcome to the Zoo. You look a bit too normal for this place, but you'll adjust. Very happy to meet you," said Miles sincerely.

The rest of that afternoon was a blur of introductions, heat, mandatory handshakes, bewildering instructions, humidity, embarrassing confusion, warm ocean breezes, smiles, and the signing of papers. After meeting with the facilities committee, Brett had chosen cage N-12 because it afforded a view through the palm trees to the Northern Bay. Steve and Coreene lent him some basic bedding and linen until he could collect his belongings from Nairobi. They suggested the name of a woman who lived locally, Tili, who was looking for work. She would work part time every day to cook, clean, and do the washing. Brett felt blessed and thankful for the wonderful welcome. He paid deposits for keys, security, and the food services. A cheerful Kenyan accounts clerk, Hamud Sita, collected the cash and issued his receipts. He explained that a spare set of keys was kept in a locked cabinet in the central office in case he lost his or they needed access in an emergency. Sita assured him that only one senior member of staff had access to the key cabinet in the central office, Mr. Boniface Chengo, the Executive Officer. Mr. Chengo collected the post every day from Mwakindini and it was distributed to the individual pigeonholes outside the office in the central building, along with any official notifications or announcements.

The physical appearance of the Zoo surprised Brett, as it contained a much richer diversity of vegetation than he had expected, with a magnificent flamboyant tree and an ancient baobab in front of the main buildings. The cages in the Northern area were arranged with single-storey dwellings along the shoreline and two-storey buildings inland, towards the centre of the compound. Between the buildings, there were narrow pathways which allowed everybody access to the beach and provided a channel for the sea breezes to keep the centre of the peninsula comfortable. The Muslim section occupied the southeastern region, and butted up to the wall that separated off the nature reserve to the east of the peninsula.

Brett found it difficult to visualize the overall layout of the Zoo, or its size, so after a week he began to draw a map as he learned new pieces of information. Many areas were still a mystery, particularly the inaccessible region beyond the solid dividing wall. This structure fascinated and unsettled him. The wall zig-zagged north-south across the peninsula. A few spiky shrubs were struggling to survive in the angled recesses. The wall was about ten feet high with sagging barbed-wire along the top, supported on vertical steel posts. It was forbidding and was clearly intended to signal 'keep out', with *Hatari* and *Mbwa kali* painted in large red letters at intervals along the wall, warning of Danger and Fierce Dog. The lettering was faded, but the messages were clear. There was no development or structures for about ten feet from the base of the wall, just a wide gravel pathway across the unwelcoming, grey-brown dead coral. He knew this gravel base was often referred to as *murram*.

Steve Brandon and Miles Jolly both explained that the impenetrable wall was designed to protect the natural environment within the reserve area. Security cameras were visible from the upper corners of the buildings which faced the wall. Apparently, dangerous dogs patrolled the other side of the wall along a cleared pathway matching that on the western face. He learnt that the dogs were caged at either end of the wall near the shores beside cage N-1, and near the Emersons' dwelling, S-33. He heard dogs barking in those areas. In addition to the warning about the dogs, it was rumoured that there were some dangerous animals on the rugged headland: in particular, deadly snakes and large agamas – the so-called African dragon. Someone had also mentioned dangerous groups of vicious monkeys, and hinted at wild bush-pigs. All of these warnings ensured that the Emersons' research projects, and their privacy, were protected.

Brett had not yet seen Henry Emerson, but he met Louise one day as he walked across to the college. She was an engaging lady, about 5' 8", appearing to be in her mid sixties, with sunglasses and silvery-grey curly hair. She wore a pale blue dress and held a large woven basket. Mrs. Emerson seemed to be interested in his work in Nyeri. She made comments, and asked follow-up questions, that indicated to Brett that she had a detailed knowledge of that part of the Central Province.

As they parted, he mentioned that he was looking forward to meeting Mr. Emerson, but he wasn't sure if she heard him. Entering the polytechnic, he saw Coreene and told her he had met Mrs. Emerson. Coreene said, "A wonderful woman. She did amazing work during World War Two. She received a prestigious award." Brett decided to look for an opportunity to ask Louise about it.

For his 30th birthday at the end of August, Brett had celebrated with a small cake and tea at the Brandons' cage. Coreene had baked a round, iced cake and introduced Brett to a few more neighbours. He was particularly pleased at the warm welcome he had received from the Principal of the polytechnic, Simion Katana, and the committed staff there. Brett appreciated Mr. Katana's kind welcome and the way he took time to introduce him the staff and explain many details of the running of the college. They had some good conversations over drinks and snacks during his first few days. The term was due to start the following week. He needed his teaching materials that were stored in Nairobi and he missed having his vehicle, so he was planning to visit the Gossards as soon as it could be arranged.

Mr. Katana explained that Mwakindini means something like 'the place in the centre'. It was located approximately halfway between the Tanzanian border to the south and the Somalia boundary far to the north. One Saturday morning, Brett tried walking into Mwakindini town from the Zoo, but found the two-kilometre journey draining in the humidity, so he took a local minibus, a *matatu*, on the way back. It dropped him just outside the Zoo gate. An eccentric-looking black man stood outside the small shop near the entrance. He greeted Brett enthusiastically. He was dressed in a top-hat, wore a tie, a formal black jacket, and trousers even in the heat. Later, someone explained that he was perfectly rational, but he fancied himself as an English gentleman, so he dressed, and acted, the part.

Brett was slowly learning how the Zoo was managed. There was a multilevel committee structure, with representatives from the main ethnic groups. Above the committees, there was the council of leaders, referred to as The Elders, or sometimes, jokingly, The Keepers. The buildings near the cafe, canteen, dining hall, bar, and restaurant were affectionately termed the Feeding Centre. The central area, inside the main road loop, contained many vegetable gardens which were carefully maintained and watered. The whole area was a luxuriant green. He had seen groups of people working in their gardens, digging, cultivating, sowing, weeding, and watering. There always appeared to be a happy atmosphere, and occasionally some good-natured comments directed towards him as he passed.

To the west of the compound, beyond the Central Stores towards the main entrance, there was a cluster of small workshops, and outdoor garages. These were the informal repair shops where machine-minded wizards laboured in the open air, keeping everything mechanical running well beyond its expected life span. Local people from the area obtained employment in the Zoo in a variety of capacities, utilizing their natural gifts for assiduous enterprise and diligent service. Several simple modes of transport, from bicycles to minibuses, ensured that people moved smoothly, and noisily, in all required directions.

Everything appeared to run efficiently; but, on a couple of occasions, Brett had sensed a slight undercurrent of tension, as though someone was playing the same melody but in a minor key.

2

Miles replied vaguely, "In Kenya, things are seldom the way they appear."

On his second Sunday at the Zoo, Brett attended the small chapel where about fifty people were seated. Steve's sermon stressed that people could always call on God during times of need. After the service, Brett was introduced to several people, including Brigadier Thomas Ridge-Taylor and his gracious wife, Violet. They lived in cage N-1 beside the wall. He heard Thomas say to Steve in a booming voice, "That was a heck of a good sermon, I don't know how you do it."

Steve laughed modestly and replied, "Thank you, Thomas. I tried to make it clear, using short sentences and simple words because I knew Brett was joining us today! Just kidding, Brett," he said patting Brett on the shoulder. Steve continued to greet other people as they left the church, while Brett walked out with the Ridge-Taylors. The brigadier was walking stiffly while using a cane.

Brett heard Violet admonish him, "You shouldn't use the word 'heck' in relation to a sermon, Thomas. It's disrespectful."

"Oh, did I say that? Must have slipped out," said Thomas with surprise.

As they climbed into their Range Rover, Violet called to Brett, "We must have lunch together sometime. We will take you to a nice restaurant we know in town when you are fed up with the Zoo grub."

Thomas saw his opportunity, "You shouldn't refer to food as 'grub', dear. It's disrespectful." He handed his walking cane across to his wife as he adjusted his seat in the Range Rover. They drove off leaving Brett smiling, on the dusty murram driveway.

One day during the following week, Brett walked to the central building. Miles directed him into the cafe, towards a man sitting inside. He said, "Brett, I'd like you to meet Len Moore."

The stranger stood, extended his hand to Brett and said, "Hello, I'm Len, pleased to meet you."

Brett shook his hand and said, "Brett James. It's nice to meet you."

Miles said, "Len's a retired water engineer. He often explains that his dry wit comes from his work in the water department!" Miles waved Brett towards a chair at their little round table.

Len said, "Let me get you a drink. Coffee, tea – or something stronger? My account is looking a bit sparse these days. Needs a few more entries."

"Enjoy this, Brett, a rare display of generosity from old moneybags here," said Miles.

"Nice to have friends, eh?" retorted Len.

"I hope you realize, Brett, you are in the presence of wit and genius with Master Len sitting there."

"Look Miles, you provide the wit, I'll supply the genius, okay?" Turning to Brett, Len said, "How are you enjoying life in the Zoo? A bit of a zoo sometimes eh? If there's anything I can do to help, just let me know."

"The first thing he needs is a ride to Mombasa. When will you be driving down there next?" asked Miles.

Len corrected him, "The first thing he needs is a chance to get a word in edgeways. We haven't allowed him to speak yet!"

Brett laughed, "To answer your questions, I'd love a cup of tea, I am enjoying the people I've met so far, and I do need a lift into Mombasa to catch the night train up to Nairobi. If someone could help me with that, it would be wonderful."

"Marie-Anne and I would be happy to drop you off at the station in Mombasa," said Len. He went to the counter to get another coffee and ask the server to bring Brett's tea.

Miles nodded towards Len, "A visionary. Internationally recognized pioneer. But, you know, he's too modest." Len was a slender man, about 5' 7", Brett estimated. He had thin greying hair combed straight back. He looked the typical, retired, elderly European with his burnished skin, long shorts, and sandals.

As Len returned, Brett said to him, "Miles has been telling me about your energy-conservation projects. They sound interesting. I was looking at some of the structures you have along that jetty by your cage."

Len was sad as he said, "It's all looking a bit weatherbeaten these days."

Miles stood up to leave, "I'll leave you two to talk your technical jargon. He's a mechanical engineer you know, Len."

Len said, "Is that right? You're not a teacher?"

"I became disillusioned with the business pressures, so I volunteered to teach in a high school in Nyeri, and now at the polytechnic here. I will continue with my original profession eventually, I'm sure."

Len nodded in understanding. "I was a civil engineer most of my life, involved in water installation projects here at the coast."

Brett said, "So, your interest in energy conservation stems from your work with water projects?"

"Water, energy, sunlight, wind, oil, petroleum, and gas, they are all interrelated. I try to take a wholistic approach. I spent many hours studying it all. What I mean is, I devoted hundreds of hours sitting on the beach in the shade of waving palm trees, watching the waves, and the wind, and the effects of the sun!" Len explained that his ideal system was to have a self-sustaining energy-generating project which required no external inputs.

"How has it worked?" asked Brett.

"It's had its small intervals of complete success and long periods of disappointment. Yet, I feel the concepts are valid. Come along sometime and I'll show you what we did manage to accomplish."

One day, after his afternoon class, Brett wandered over to the Zoo's Central Store. He met the supervisor, Kaleem Butt. He explained how the Central Stores operated, including instructions if Brett wanted to borrow tools. On his way home, Brett was passed by Miles Jolly in his unimpressive old green Volvo. Miles asked when Brett was going up to Nairobi, and offered to keep him company on his way back as he was flying there the next week to attend to some business matters. "Do you have any idea how long you'll be staying up there?" asked Miles.

"I'll probably need 4 or 5 days. I'll let you know when I plan to drive back," said Brett.

Len dropped Brett off at the Mombasa railway station, and he caught the 7pm overnight train. Jim Gossard was waiting in Nairobi when Brett arrived the next morning. After warm greetings, Jim said, "Your pickup is looking good. The tyres have lost a bit of pressure but they have all held well. Oh, you'll need a new battery." They made their way in Jim's VW van, up the hill to Hurlingham Neighbourhood, where Mary welcomed him with a hug. "Everything is in the spare room where you left it last year," she said.

"What's on the agenda?" asked Jim. "Do you have any paperwork to do, or shall we try to get your airfreight boxes cleared through customs?"

"I'd like to get those soon, if possible," said Brett. Eventually, they collected his three boxes and loaded them in the pickup.

The next day, Brett made his way to Church House where the offices of the National Christian Council of Kenya were located. The NCCK staff had been helpful in the application for his three-year class-EX4(3) re-entry permit, based on his development work with the polytechnic. He also needed to update his Alien Registration book. Later, back at the Gossards, Brett made two phone calls: the first to John Phillips' office to set up an appointment for 11:30am the following day, Wednesday; and a call to Miles Jolly at his hotel, confirming the arrangement they had made for Brett to collect him on Thursday.

The following morning, Brett located the office of the man he had met on the plane – John Phillips at Resource Data Imaging. He walked up the stairs into a small reception area with a secretary at the desk. She disappeared to find Dr. Phillips, and Brett saw an African man standing in the corridor. When John Phillips came out, he manoeuvred so he could introduce Brett to the man, whom he referred to as Mr. Maina. Recognizing the Kikuyu name, Brett tried his polite Kikuyu greeting, which produced the expected warm smile from Maina. "Let's pop out for a spot of lunch," said John. Once they were out of the front door, he said, "I didn't want Maina to join us. I'll explain later. Let's try the Samosa Basket; it's quite close."

As they walked over to a quiet restaurant, Brett said, "Let me buy your meal, John, as I am taking up your precious time."

"Not necessary, but thank you. I'll take care of the drinks and the tip, then," replied John graciously. In answer to John's questions, Brett described the things he had experienced at the coast, and explained that he was curious to learn more about the physical layout of the Zoo. John said, "It sounds fascinating. I've seen it from the air, in a sense. I'm sorry I am unable to supply you with any maps, photos, or sketches, but I can describe what I remember seeing, if you like. Also, I have the map reference if you would like to try ordering one from the Ministry office while you are here. As I told you, map distribution is very restricted now, so I wouldn't hold out much hope. From above, the peninsula looks a giant hourglass with the narrow piece in the middle being less than a kilometre across. It's almost like separate islands but connected to the mainland by a fairly wide causeway," explained John.

"That matches what I have seen. I am interested in the area towards the east, out into the ocean, which is now off limits and is designated as a nature reserve," said Brett.

"There's nothing to be seen, except some features at the south-western corner. I saw some narrow paths or trails, but nothing much."

"The structure you saw in the reserve must be the Emersons' dwelling and research lab."

"Well, they must live very modestly because it didn't seem much of a house from above."

"Well, they do call them cages! Are there any high points or other prominent geographic features?"

"It's a big promontory and the reef is very distinctive, all around the area. Parts of the rocky headland extend well out into the Indian Ocean. Along the central ridge of the headland there is some evidence of a high rocky outcrop because the vegetation is clear where the cliffs drop off steeply. You should be able to see some of that with binoculars from the mainland." John took his cloth table-napkin and bunched it up. "This is how it probably looks," he said, pinching the cloth to indicate high ridges and cliffs.

"Were you able to get any idea of the overall dimensions?" asked Brett.

"I'd estimate each of the two areas, west and east, to be about two kilometres across, maybe slightly more on the undeveloped region tapering out into a long promontory. That area looks remote and untamed."

"That's interesting, thank you. I want to try windsurfing around the edges of the shoreline, so I might be able to see more from the water. It would be fun to explore along the shore but the central dividing wall is extended into the water, north and south, by a high, solid chain-link fence right out past the low-tide points. No one is allowed beyond those two fences," said Brett.

"That's odd," said John, frowning, "because I thought the foreshore, the strip of beach between low and high tides levels, was public property and anyone was allowed access to it. There must be some special arrangement that permits the shoreline to be fenced off like that."

As they completed their main course and ordered pancakes and a fruit bowl, along with coffee, Brett said, "Tell me, John, what was the point about Maina? Is he one of your staff?"

John's brow furrowed. "No, he is a government representative, a kind of liaison officer, assigned to our office, ostensibly to provide input and share his expertise. He is intelligent and pleasant but he always seems to be sniffing around and asking for details that can be confidential. We have to preserve the privacy of our clients' data. We are not doing anything illegal, just delicate and private investigations of potential resources. The government, naturally, does not want maps or data of their sensitive areas being shared. Maina's job is to ensure that we stay within the guidelines, but it is sometimes frustrating having him breathing down our necks all the time.

"He asks a lot of questions, which we don't mind; but it's when he is silent, and just stares, that I get uneasy," confessed John. "It's a fine balance: being open and willing to share things with him, but at the same time withholding information we feel he has no right to. But that's our problem, not something that I should be discussing with you, so please forget what I said."

"Of course, I shan't say anything," agreed Brett.

As they completed their meal, John gave Brett the details of the official OS map he should order. "I think the sheet you want is 154/111 but tell them it is centred on Mwakindini and they should be able to identify the exact map." Brett thanked John profusely as they left the restaurant. They agreed to keep in touch, possibly when John was at the coast sometime.

Brett walked south towards the distinctive Kenyatta Conference Centre, appreciating the cooler Nairobi air compared to the humidity of the coast. He stayed on the main routes, avoiding narrow or confined places, while clutching his small bag close to his chest. He felt more secure that way, and remained alert the whole time.

In the survey department, he filled out a long document requesting the map he wanted. The form asked a lot of questions about his address, profession, and reason for requesting the map, its intended use, and his employer. *It's only a map; they are asking for my life history,* he thought as he waded through all the questions. He paid the fee in cash, was given a receipt, and told to return the following week. That was frustrating, but he knew he would have to be in Nairobi again sometime, or he might ask someone from the Zoo to pick it up when they were in the city.

Brett wanted to be ready for an early start the next morning, so he and Jim loaded his boxes of stored items in the back of his pickup, behind the three large airfreight boxes. Mary had prepared a box of special items for him to take to the coast, explaining that friends in Europe had sent them imported delicacies – including cans of German sausages, Canadian salmon, Dutch cheeses, a specially wrapped box of Belgian biscuits, and some English chocolates. Jim wondered how long the chocolates would last in the heat. Brett answered that, in his experience, chocolates did not last long at any temperature. They enclosed all his boxes with a tarpaulin, roped it together tightly, and left it in the Gossards' covered carport, with instructions to their night watchman to guard it well.

The rest of the evening was spent enjoying Mary's cooking and good discussions with her and Jim. Brett heard more details of their current retirement activities, particularly the work they were doing in several small communities west of Nairobi. "We see this as a wonderful chance to share love with the Kenyans, and take social outreach programmes closer to where they live," explained Mary.

Brett had arranged to collect Miles at the Livingstone Hotel in the centre of Nairobi. Miles carefully lifted a corner of the tarpaulin cover and wedged his small suitcase in the back of the single-cab pickup beside Brett's boxes. He opened the passenger door, "Hello Brett. Thanks for picking me up. How are you?"

"Great thanks. It's just after eight so we are in good time. Thank you very much for coming along with me on this journey. I didn't fancy the long drive on my own, and I wouldn't want to break the journey and park the pickup at a hotel on the way with all that stuff in the back," said Brett as he drove slowly through the morning traffic.

"That's a huge pile of boxes you have there. Did they all arrive safely?"

"Yes, all three of them, I'm thankful to say, along with the boxes and cases that the Gossards stored. How was your time in Nairobi?" asked Brett.

"It was good, thanks. I cleared up a couple of dental problems and had two meetings with a few old colleagues. I also dealt with some paperwork – messy stuff with banks, insurance companies, and other rodents. I am more than ready to return to the coast now."

They both felt relieved to be on their way. However, they saw several vehicles stopped on the road ahead of them. "Looks like a police check. This one seems serious as they are stopping all vehicles in both directions, with those awful spikes. I wonder what they are checking for," said Brett. Two thin, uniformed police officers, with distinctive white hats, approached them. There was an exchange of words with Miles that Brett did not follow. Soon, the officer directed them forward through the narrow gap between the rusty spikes, and they were on their way again.

"What was all that about? I couldn't follow any of the Swahili," Brett asked with a hint of admiration in his tone.

"No, we were talking in the Kikamba language. He looked Kamba, so I greeted him in his language and he responded favourably. I find it often works well during encounters with the police. I generally try to politely ask them where they are from — their home area. It defuses any potential tension. Then I try to switch into their tribal language if I can remember a few phrases, the greetings at least."

"You're a regular little polyglot, aren't you?"

"Yes, but I'm trying a new ointment and I think it's helping," laughed Miles. "I'm glad they didn't make us uncover all that stuff in the back."

"Especially the hamper of snacks that Mary Gossard has prepared for us!"

"Those two cops were obviously not just after 'something little', to supplement their meagre wages. By the way, I am happy to help with the driving when you are ready for a change."

"Great," said Brett, "I'd appreciate that. Maybe we'll change at Hunter's Lodge. I don't know how some people do this drive on their own." After a few kilometres, he said, "You must have lived in the Zoo a long time, and made an important contribution to the community over the years."

"I first went there in 1972 when I retired from the government work. Peter Lancaster was the person who introduced me to the Zoo and facilitated my getting in there. I have tried to get along with everybody, although not all the residents appreciate my flippant humour," admitted Miles. "But I've refined it over the years. I made a study of humour."

"What do you mean?" asked Brett.

Miles was silent for a couple of minutes and then he explained that, in his early teens, he was bullied a lot, particularly over his appearance. He described how he was short and fat and had a childish grin on his round chubby face, which attracted the bullies: he was an easy target. His name did not help. He was called jolly-Jolly, jolly old Jolly, Smiles Jolly, Jolly Miles, Miles per hour. He added, "They got good mileage from that one! You can learn to roll with the punches, but you are still being punched!"

In school, he realized that other boys enjoyed laughing at him in a superior way. He managed to exploit that, along with his natural clown-like joking which matched his comical appearance. He sometimes got the older and bigger boys to accept him by demeaning himself with laughter, and boosting their prestige. After a while, he accomplished that in a skilful manner. Having ingratiated himself with the toughies, he maintained their acceptance with his self-deprecating humour. In the process of refining his technique, he acknowledged that it had involved an element of manipulation, bordering on deception. He accepted that, and even enjoyed exploiting it to some degree. "I became a keen observer of people, especially when they did not realize I was watching them. There's an irony here: I actually felt superior, and in control, the more I degraded myself and absorbed humiliation from others. Does that make any sense, I wonder?" Miles looked up at Brett who said nothing as he moved his head slightly in a non-committal way.

Miles continued, "I survived grammar school, which completed my less-than-stellar academic career. My parents were very poor so I never had an opportunity for higher education. I have always wished I had more money, and the security it brings." His voice became quiet as he said, almost to himself, "Security. That's what I yearn for. Security. It is very important." Looking at Brett, he confided, "Things were difficult at home so I had to get a job. I worked for the town council in Bristol. My aptitude for observation, and attention to detail allowed me to appear more capable than I actually was. I can still fool some people into thinking I am intelligent!" Brett smiled and shook his head. He noticed how dark Miles' eyes were, almost black, and strangely piercing.

Miles looked ahead and spoke distinctly, "Anyway, I rose up through the ranks, so to speak, and later joined the colonial service in a quasi-military, administrative function. I deliberately refined my listening skills. It has helped me with language acquisition too. I was involved in investigation work with several branches of the government, including military and police activities occasionally. A lot of people don't listen carefully, as they tend to hear what they expect to hear. They will often appear to be listening, but they are simply waiting for their chance to speak."

Brett nodded but did not interrupt. Miles was expressing his thoughts aloud as they came to him: "I found it a useful strategy to play the likeable buffoon. People feel comfortable with a court jester who is willing to be the butt of their jokes. It can make them feel safe and superior. Then, they will open up and sometimes reveal things. We investigators like that. We just sit, and watch. And listen."

The sun had risen higher, with a few wispy clouds in the bright sky, but the air temperature was still comfortable with all the windows open as they drove. Travelling with Miles was enlightening because he knew so much about the places they passed through; he was familiar with the region and

Part 1: Mysteries

the varied geography they were experiencing. He had many stories relating to the scenery or towns signposted off the road.

Miles added another thought: "I spent some years in Accounting. I soon realized that the people who control the money, control the whole operation. Money, control, and information. They are all interlinked."

"When did you come to Kenya?" asked Brett.

"1954, and I got involved with the colonial administration at a critical time in the country's history when the aroma of independence was wafting across the African continent. Discontent in the economic and political sphere was becoming heavy, and it was obvious that the stability and growth since the war was likely to be threatened soon," said Miles.

"That was at the time of Mau Mau, right?" said Brett.

"Yes, it began in 1952, and it was rough, up until independence in 1963. You wouldn't believe what went on during that time; there were incredible atrocities committed – on both sides. We were all up to our eyes in it and were grateful when it came to a conclusion, I can tell you. But you must have heard some of what went on, having lived among the Kikuyu for – what was it? – five years," asked Miles.

"Yes, I was in Nyeri from 1978 to 1983." They fell silent for several kilometres and Brett sensed that Miles wanted to say more but chose not to. They discussed the places they passed, the scenery, and the increasing heat as they drove southeast. They look for a suitable place for a brief break and a change of drivers.

"I know this road so well, I could drive it backwards," boasted Miles, "...and blindfolded."

"I'd rather you didn't!" Brett retorted as he noticed another roadblock ahead. "Police checkpoints are stressful enough for me as it is!"

After their short break, Miles got in the driver's side, adjusted the seat forward, and they continued their journey. "We're making some progress," said Miles, "Sa-fari so goodi." Then he said something that took Brett aback. "The people I met in Nairobi were some of the bogey-bogey men. You know, Masons."

Brett hesitated and then said, "Masons?"

"Yes, Freemasons. You never joined them, then?" asked Miles.

"No, never. Are you a member?"

"Oh yes. Have been for a long time."

"That's interesting, I thought you had a strange handshake," said Brett.

"So, you know about that…that's our initial point of contact with members."

"Yes, I know the handshake and some of the words, and a little about the organisation because several of my friends in England were members, but I was never interested in joining a secret society, especially one with men only!" said Brett.

"Not a secret society, just a society with secrets," retorted Miles. "There's a difference."

"I don't see much of a difference," said Brett. Miles looked at Brett in sullen silence. Brett continued, "Sorry, I don't mean to be critical. I'm just trying to explain why I have never felt attracted to a closed organisation with such secretive control over its members. But I have always felt totally comfortable with my involvement with Christianity, because it presents completely open and available information, accessible immediately to anybody, at any level. There is no controlling hierarchy which relies upon progressive revelation according to how high you rise in the organisation."

If Miles was uneasy at this rejoinder, he did not reveal it. He said, "Yes, well, everyone must follow what he feels comfortable with. I'm not religious myself, but we have a wide range of religious views and practices represented within the Zoo, and nobody tries to push their own ideas or agenda." Brett responded in a neutral way, sensing that the deep part of the discussion was over. He thought, *I must seek to learn more; I just want people to know the truth of practical faith in everyday situations.*

Miles asked: "Who have you met so far at the Zoo?" Brett mentioned several of the people, including his nearby neighbour Len Moore who Miles had introduced. Miles thought for a while and said, "Watch how Len behaves in a group. He's very interesting to observe. He'll sit quietly, listening to the discussion, and then occasionally lob a pun into the stream of conversation like a grenade, and wait for the explosion of laughter. If people don't get the joke, he'll just smile silently to himself. If Marie-Anne is there, she'll be totally tuned into his signals." Brett laughed. Miles added, "Len is a super person, one of the best. Absolutely dependable. He and Marie-Anne make a wonderful couple. She is a charming lady. If I ever had a wife, that's how I'd like her to be."

"Were you ever married?" asked Brett.

"No, I managed to avoid that trap, but it came dangerously close once. That was a long time ago. In recent decades, I've come to realize that women find me cute, but unattractive. Their loss, I'm certain! How about you? Any serious relationships?"

Brett thought, *He's shared a lot of personal details with me; I wonder if he's angling for me to reveal some confidences?* "No, I'm still waiting for the right time, and the right person. I was close to a girl in my late teens – Jane – but she married someone else, and I have accepted that God has other things for me to do at present – different areas in which to devote my time and energies." Miles was listening carefully, so Brett added, "Jane and I never went out together because she made it clear that she would not get romantically involved with someone who was not a deeply committed Christian – which I wasn't at the time." That was all that Brett was prepared to reveal as he did not know Miles well, and he was not sure how far he could trust him. Miles had already confessed to his inclination towards guile so Brett simply said, "I'm content to wait and see what happens."

"That's wise," Miles nodded. "What about your interests and hobbies? I love deep-sea fishing when I get a chance. It's wonderful at the coast for that. But I have to be careful not to overdo things. The old heart has a bit of a murmur, they tell me."

"Sorry about that. Well, I like photography and painting, plus exploring out in nature. Kenya has been super for that too. I have my decent camera in the boxes, as I only carry the small one when travelling. And I enjoy sailing when I can rent a craft of some kind. I have all the sailing equipment at the back. Also I'm looking forward to getting out my oil paints again."

"Painting pictures, rather than interior decoration?" asked Miles.

"Both actually. I have done some house painting, and sign-writing. I taught technical drawing in Nyeri, and I like graphic design."

"Well now, that skill is much needed at the Zoo. All our notices and signs are getting pretty faded and tacky-looking. Everything needs sprucing up. Henry Emerson was keen on creating graphics and logos – and codes. But he doesn't do any of it now," said Miles.

"I noticed some of the signs are looking a bit tired. I can have a go at freshening-up some of the aesthetics during the holidays if the committee would like me to."

Miles nodded and said, "I'll drive through to Mtito Andei and then we'll stop for our picnic, okay?"

"Yes. We'll need a break and a cold drink by then. It's getting hotter."

"There is a murram road across to Malindi. But I wouldn't risk it in this vehicle with the load we are carrying. Peter Lancaster has travelled it in his Land Rover."

Brett said, "Tell me about Peter. I haven't met him yet. He's been in Kenya for a long time, hasn't he?" asked Brent.

"Since Noah was a boy, I think! He's had quite a bit of involvement in this country, actually. He was 'Military' too, as Brigadier Thomas says it. There's not much to tell. He's in England at the moment, trying to sort out the ongoing mess with his family – also some medical issues I think. I don't know any details. He doesn't discuss his affairs with me." Brett glanced at Miles who was staring across to the dry, yellow scrub in the distance. "Goodness knows why he needs to go to England for medical treatment; we've got plenty of good doctors here." Brett thought Miles sounded abrupt, so he gently enquired when Peter was coming back. Miles shrugged, "I'm not sure. In the next week or two, I heard."

They appreciated the break, and Mary's delicious picnic. They wrapped up the remaining food and stored it near the cold water containers where the ice had melted. Brett drove south towards Voi. Miles dozed off for about half an hour. He woke up just as they were approaching Voi, saying, "Let's stop quickly for a coffee. My caffeine level is getting dangerously low, and, if you expect me to navigate or drive again, I'll need waking up."

Later, Brett picked up on an earlier conversation point. "It's interesting… when you get to know individual Kenyans well, and you have a chance to speak frankly, how they will open up and reveal the inside view of all that has happened over the years. I asked an elderly man about The Emergency, as they call it, saying that, to me, Kenyans seemed very gentle, so I couldn't understand why the Mau-Mau rebellion developed, and became so violent."

"And how did he explain it?" asked Miles in a low voice.

"I can remember his exact words: 'You have no idea how bad things were, Brett. Something had to be done. It could not continue the way it was'."

Miles stared at the road ahead. After a long pause, he said, "It's hard to look back now and draw any conclusions. Only those who experienced it know what it was like…"

It seemed to Brett that Miles was about to say something else. He asked, "Only those who experienced it?"

"I can tell you from personal…" and he stopped.

"What were you going to say?" prompted Brett.

"Nothing, I forgot what I was…I just lost my train of thought there," replied Miles vaguely, adding, "In Kenya, things are seldom the way they appear."

They drove quickly, noticing the increasing heat. They stopped for breaks and long drinks from their water jug, and a quick rinse of their dusty faces. They were each wearing loose shirts and slacks with open sandals but they agreed that they should have worn shorts. They pushed on, feeling the pressure of the pending early sunset around 6:30pm.

"How are you getting on with your housekeeper?" asked Miles out of the blue.

"Tili? She's a sweet lady," said Brett, "and we seem to have worked out a good routine. She is Mijikenda, so we speak in a mixture of my limited Kiswahili and the English she knows. We are each anxious to learn the other's language so it gets a bit amusing at times as we struggle to communicate. She calls my yogurt 'sick milk'! I asked if she would like some and she said, 'No please'. The other day, I had the radio tuned to a local station and she said, 'Oh, your radio speaks Swahili!' She only works in the mornings, as she has two children to look after. Her mother takes care of the children when Tili is working. She is very pleasant, and a good cook. She prepares my lunch, and I have told her to make enough to take some home for her family. She's had experience being employed by *mzungus* – us white people – before. Also, she used to work in the Zoo kitchen."

"She's a close relative of the manageress in housekeeping isn't she? Khadijah. A sister or cousin, I can never quite determine the relationships."

"Yes I think so. How about your maid?" said Brett. Miles explained that he had an elderly Muslim woman as a maid, Muzhere. "She is excellent; she treats me like a child, which suits me. She's old enough that there is no chance of any rumours developing. She calls my classical music, 'songs without words'. Working with me gives her some self-worth and recognition. There's no risk of me getting into her religion, I can tell you. Louise Emerson knows a lot about their lives as the Emersons' cage is right beside the Muslim section at the Zoo. Also Coreene Brandon is an expert, having studied various religions for a long time."

Brett said, "I have heard that she is knowledgeable about world religions. I know very little about them, so I'd like to learn more."

Miles responded: "I'd be interested in a faith that is open and treats everyone as equal: One that recognizes the worth of individuals and their rights to free choice."

"Ah, something that promotes loving relationships within a community and preaches love for one's enemies and a deep relationship with a personal God?"

"You're not baiting me into becoming a Christian, are you?" joked Miles. "If I went to church, God wouldn't recognize me."

"He certainly would recognize you because He loves you, and He'd welcome you, and tell you He's been waiting for you for a long time!" teased Brett.

"Enough! God's not interested in an old sinner like me. I've blotted my copybook and made far too many mistakes, right?" said Miles, half jokingly.

"Wrong! I think you'd better have a serious chat with Steve before it's too late. You're not getting any younger you know," joked Brett.

"Oh great, that's just what I need to hear!" laughed Miles.

As they travelled, they admired the beautiful terrain along the high ridge above the coastal plain, particularly as the scene was illuminated by the vermilion orb of the sun glaring in the sky behind them. Miles said, "This is the country of the Mijikenda people. It is the Giriama who live mainly in the region near the Zoo. They were known as formidable warriors in the past, led by some fearsome and charismatic women. Worth remembering when we speak with our maids!"

They descended onto the muggy coastal plain and joined the main coastal road, the B8. Miles observed, "This area around Kilifi is notorious for its ancient witchcraft. Even today, there are sometimes strange stories and accusations of sorcery." Then he muttered to himself, "That's just what I need with all the hocus-pocus I'm already involved with." As they drove past Malindi, it suddenly became dark, as it does in the tropics. Brett had taken over the driving on the last leg of their journey. "Take it easy now, Brett. You can expect lots of vehicles without lights. When we get to the Zoo, it will be too late to unload, so I suggest you don't park the pickup at your cage. Let's get the key from the watchman and put it in the enclosed compound in front of the main store. Then a guard will be watching your boxes all night."

"Thanks, good idea. I can't face all the unpacking now; I'm so tired. I have a couple of cars trailing me in total blackness," said Brett, glancing in the rearview mirror.

"I noticed that. Their lights are not working, so they are using you to guide the way. They'll follow you, and pretty soon, you'll have a few more I expect."

Within ten minutes Brett was the bright leader of an invisible snake of assorted vehicles winding its way north along the coast road in total darkness.

3

Brett was feeling some anxiety over the increasing background tension in this, otherwise perfect, tropical paradise.

Once he had unpacked his boxes, Brett was delighted to have access to his teaching equipment. He enjoyed teaching the polytechnic students, as they were highly motivated to learn. He taught mathematics, science, and technical drawing classes to support the workshop instruction. The students knew that practical training in artisan skills would allow them to obtain employment and contribute to the development of the rural areas. Their parents and older relatives were making huge sacrifices to pay the tuition fees.

Work was still needed in his cage to get things the way he wanted. Near the front entrance door, there was a shelf, a rail with hooks for coats, and a ugly, heavy, metal umbrella-stand just inside the front door. Brett noticed the sharp edges and planned to grind them down when he could arrange some time in Len's workshop. During the rainy seasons, he often used umbrellas, so he could see that the stand would be useful. Having his pickup made a tremendous difference to his life, as he was able to purchase larger items and transport things easily. He often drove it across to the polytechnic to teach in the mornings, but tried to walk when he was not carrying a heavy load. That way, he met more people, and felt part of the community.

When the Zoo was set up in the mid 1960s, the goal was to establish clear behavioural guidelines without a lot of restrictions in the areas of social conduct. Common decency and respect for others were paramount, but there were no restrictions placed on smoking or alcohol consumption.

However, there were strict rules against drugs or weapons of any kind, apart from the bows and arrows that the guards had at the gate, and any guns needed by the policemen who lived in the Zoo. The layout of the core buildings had been planned with great care. The bar, cafe, and the adjacent lounge with comfortable chairs and tables, was affectionately, and slightly pejoratively, referred to as the Old Boys' Club. This in no way restricted young females from attending; in fact they were welcome. The dining facilities included a restaurant which provided informal meeting places for all the residents, including families.

It was a Tuesday afternoon when a few residents were having tea and cakes together. Len and Marie-Anne Moore were there, chatting with Louise Emerson. Brett had joined them. He noticed Coreene entering the building, looking distressed and concerned. She came over to speak with the group. "Boniface Chengo told me that Hamud Sita has been arrested!" she said. Everyone expressed astonishment. "Apparently, he has been accused of embezzlement of our funds. Mr. Chengo seemed very worried, partly for Sita, but also I suppose because any irregularities will reflect badly on him as the Executive Officer." Those at the table asked what Sita had done wrong. Coreene replied, "I don't know many details, but Grace in the office had said something about his using two receipt books. I need to go now, and tell Steve. We must pray that Hamud Sita won't be mistreated, and he will be released soon."

News of Sita's arrest spread quickly through the Zoo. Everyone was in disbelief. Brett had met him only a few times, but he had seemed a helpful and efficient young man. Three days later, there was still no official word about Sita, but one of the policemen who lived at the Zoo told Executive Officer Chengo informally that the evidence was strong against Sita, and he would be put on trial soon.

Later that week, about ten minutes before Brett's lecture ended, the office messenger appeared at the classroom door, saying he had two important visitors. Brett quickly gave the students their homework assignments, and went back to his office. On the way, he was told there was a blue car at the front of the college with GK, Government of Kenya, registration plates. Brett suspected this may have something to do with Sita's arrest.

He entered his small office and saw two men in civilian clothes seated in front of his desk. The shorter man, wearing glasses, introduced himself as Ochieng. He pointed to the taller man with a round face, saying, "This is Sergeant Kinyanjui." They both appeared very serious, almost sullen, until Brett greeted Kinyanjui in Kikuyu, as he shook his hand, placing his left hand on his right elbow to signify respect for an older person. Kinyanjui smiled appreciatively. Brett shook Mr. Ochieng's hand the same way. They returned to their seats while Brett moved around to his chair behind the desk. Brett was relieved that his Kikuyu greetings with Mr. Kinyanjui had broken the ice slightly. He had greeted Mr. Ochieng in Kiswahili as he guessed that Ochieng was a Luo name from the western province, and Brett did not know any words from the western tribes.

Ochieng took out a notepad from his briefcase and started to question Brett, without explaining who he was, or why they were there. "You requested a detailed map of this area. How do you intend to use it?"

Brett concealed his surprise and replied calmly, "Yes, I would like to get familiar with this area and try to explore some inland trails…and the shoreline…around the reef, and so on."

"For what purpose, please?" said Ochieng in a flat voice.

"Just for my own interest. I enjoy visiting the beauties of your wonderful country, and I always found that maps enrich that experience. That's all."

"Why are you here?" That abrupt question came from Kinyanjui.

"I was invited to come here and teach—"

"Invited by whom?" interrupted Ochieng.

"By the board of this polytechnic, through the NCCK."

Ochieng flipped back through several pages in his notes, read something in silence, and then looked up at Brett. "Who pays your salary?" The direct line of questioning annoyed Brett. It was so unlike the Kenyan way of conducting discussions. He wondered what business it was of theirs, but he said, "I am not sure that it is appropriate for me to discuss this with people I do not know." Some of his suppressed irritation must have shown in his voice, because, immediately, Kinyanjui stiffened and glared at Brett.

"Mr. James—"

"Please call me Brett."

"Thank you Mr. Brett. We are here to establish that you are a very good person who can be allowed to continue, here, in this place. You are on a short visitor's permit, you understand, Mr. James."

"No, that is not correct. My visa has been re-coded to a three-year re-entry permit," Brett replied to Kinyanjui, with a small sense of satisfaction. Ochieng laid his pen on his pad, adjusted his glasses, and glanced out of the window.

Kinyanjui leafed through his papers and nodded discreetly to Ochieng who said, "It could be helpful for us if you would kindly outline the manner in which you meet your expenses – what it is you have to pay out each month. The rent here, in what is called the Zoo, must be very high, I think, Mr. James."

"Please call me Brett."

"Yes. Mr. Brett, it is somehow expensive, it seems."

"It is reasonable, considering what a beautiful place it is, and the wonderful community we have here. As Mr. Katana, the Principal, will explain, the college provides my housing, but otherwise my monthly expenses are covered from overseas in two ways. Do you need the details?" They both nodded. "Half comes from voluntary giving of individuals in a church in England which provides regular support. The rest is supplied from a grant issued by an African educational foundation in London, which is very supportive of my involvement in technical education. It is the African Educational Fund which also supports several technical colleges and institutes in Kenya." He decided that was enough information as he was not going to tell them about the gifts from his parents, or his personal savings that he was drawing on each month.

"Are you paid any cash in Kenya? Do you receive any income here?"

"No, I cannot receive any local funds. I am not permitted to earn anything while I am here," replied Brett. Ochieng's expression seemed to communicate: 'You don't need to tell me what you are not allowed to do', but he said nothing, while Kinyanjui simply nodded.

Ochieng wrote some notes while Brett was speaking. Brett watched and saw that he was about halfway down his list of questions. Over the years, he had learned to read upside down when explaining things to his students. Brett glanced at his watch, as he had another lecture starting at 10:30 and he needed a cup of tea before that. The atmosphere was becoming tense.

Ochieng's next question astonished Brett. "Mr. James, why did you meet with Dr. Phillips in Nairobi?"

Brett paused. "We had lunch together. He was interested in hearing about life here in the Zoo."

"Who paid for the food?"

"I did. But he–"

"You paid. What was he giving you in return?" interrupted Ochieng.

"Nothing. As I was about to explain, he–"

"Did he supply you with any maps?"

"No."

"Any photographs or prints?"

"No, none." Brett wondered, *What is this official up to? He won't let me explain anything.*

"Did he provide any sketches or draw a diagram?"

"No, nothing like that," said Brett, relieved to see that Ochieng had checked off the last question in that section of his list.

Then it was Kinyanjui's turn to ask a question: "What did he describe to you about this part of the coast?"

"Nothing more than what is shown on the tourist maps that we can buy at any curio shop, or see for ourselves at any point along..."

Brett was interrupted by a knock at his door and, to his relief, he saw the office messenger struggling in with a large wooden tray of tea and some bread. He placed the tray unsteadily on Brett's desk, and said, somewhat apologetically, nodding towards the kettle, "The cooks have already applied sugar." They all looked appreciatively at the much-dented aluminium kettle and the three large plastic mugs.

The interruption eased the tension, as each person poured a steaming mug of sweet, milky tea. Brett offered his guests the slices of white bread spread thinly with Blue-Band margarine and red plum jam. As the three of them sipped their tea and took a piece of bread, Brett watched the reactions of the two officials. He gave an appreciative thought for the secretary who probably had taken the initiative to order the snack from the canteen. As the two visitors munched their way steadily through the bread, and enjoyed their tea, Brett sensed a relaxation in the tone of the interview. He had accepted that he was going to be late for his class and assumed that Mr.

Katana knew about it. The official vehicle at the front of the polytechnic was probably sufficient explanation.

Kinyanjui smiled at Brett and joked, "I hope you will give Detective Ochieng the bill for this feast."

To which Ochieng responded, "You wouldn't expect an uncircumcised man to pay for this, would you?" They all laughed at that, Brett having heard from the Kikuyu that the western tribes do not circumcise their men. Once the snack had been gratefully consumed, the serious questioning continued, but with a more friendly tone – at least, at first.

"Why did you arrange to travel from London with Dr. Phillips?"

"I didn't."

"You travelled together on the same flight."

Brett wondered where they got all this information. "We only met on the plane. We didn't arrange to travel together."

"You were sitting together. How long have you known Dr. Phillips?"

Brett thought things were getting ridiculous. "Our seats were in the same row, yes, and that is where we met for the first time. Honestly, this is strange…may I ask why you are asking me these questions? Why are you so interested in my brief acquaintance with Dr. Phillips?" Brett knew he was being outspoken, and probably displaying a degree of annoyance, so he added, "I am supposed to be giving a lecture now."

Ignoring his remark, Ochieng said, "Dr. Phillips is with satellite imaging and that is a sensitive area of technology."

Brett decided to be bold, "Yes I know. Bwana Ochieng and Bwana Kinyanjui, obviously you both have access to some important information, and it has been a pleasure to explain some matters to you. May I ask if you are with the police force?"

Kinyanjui looked uncomfortable, but Ochieng appeared quite relaxed, as he replied, "Our activities do involve police work, yes. You have been honest with us, which is a good thing, so I can tell you openly that we have been asked to investigate some small things about what is happening here… to conduct a bit of research on some matters, let's say, here and there, and you being in this Zoo place, and why. Some small things like that. There is no need for concern because everything seems to be in order. So, we thank you Mr. James for agreeing to meet with us, and thank you for the tea and *bleds'*." Brett smiled inwardly at the local description of slices of bread.

They stood to leave and, with more handshakes, were soon out of the door, through the entranceway, and in their car. Brett was waiting in the doorway, watching them leave, when Simion Katana came out of his office and asked, "What was that all about?"

"I'm not sure. They were asking questions about a map I requested, and my salary, and a friend I met in Nairobi. I am not sure…it was a bit disturbing. But they enjoyed the bread and tea. The secretary deserves credit for arranging that, bless her."

"She also sent some over to their driver who stayed with the car."

"That's good. Excuse me, I need to get to class," replied Brett.

That evening, Miles found him at the clubhouse and asked about the police visit. "I hear you had a visit from the rozzers."

"How do you know?"

"I saw the cops' car. What have you done wrong now? Have you made a blunder, or what? At least *you* managed to avoid arrest! Were they police?"

"I'm pretty sure they were. One called his boss a detective. It was nothing serious. They just asked about the map I requested, and wanted to know why I met Dr. Phillips. I told you about that, didn't I?" said Brett.

"Yes. I remember."

"Is it a crime to sit next to someone on a plane, or ask for a map?"

"Generally, no. But in your case it obviously could be! They like to check up on new arrivals, especially criminal-looking types like you! I'm relieved that I don't have to visit you in prison. I'm a bit busy at the moment, you know."

"Busy? What do you do all day long?" teased Brett.

"I have my responsibilities…watching palm trees wave in the breeze and the tide go up and down twice a day…continuous demands on my time," said Miles, wandering away leaning on a stick, chuckling to himself.

In spite of the joking, Brett felt uneasy. The atmosphere was changing. Maybe the usual elated feeling of being in a new place was fading and, after a few weeks, the emotional letdown was setting in. He needed to start having some fun. He had heard that Len Moore had a windsurfer at his cage. Maybe it was time to wander along and show a bit more interest in his energy-conservation project.

Part 1: Mysteries

It was late in the afternoon on Thursday when Brett met his maid Tili's mother as he was leaving the polytechnic. She was worried about her grandson who had a high fever, and Brett had expressed sympathy, and promised to pray. She seemed to appreciate that. He was tired, and feeling hungry, so he walked over to the restaurant to treat himself to a nice supper. As he entered, he noticed Miles Jolly and Louise Emerson in serious conversation at one of the tables. When they saw him, they appeared to hesitate, but then Louise beckoned for him join them. Miles got up to leave, "You can continue to entertain her, Brett, until she remembers which way it is home." He winked, nodding towards the Emersons' cage. Brett sat down. "I'll be off then," said Miles. "I wonder who I'll meet next. As the taxi driver said, 'What I enjoy about my job is the interesting people I run into'."

From her indrawn breath and slightly raised eyebrow, it seemed to Brett that Mrs. Emerson did not find Miles Jolly's humour amusing. "I've finished my meal," she said, "but please fetch me an orange juice and ask the waitress to bring over a glass of cold, plain water."

"It's on my bill," Brett said, "because I have a question for you, Mrs. Emerson." Brett went to the self-service counter and collected his main meal, a wicked-looking dessert, and a cup of coffee. Louise was impressed. "They have been working you hard at the college – given you an appetite I see. Oh, to be young and slender again." Sensing danger, Brett ignored her comment. After a few mouthfuls, he explained to Louise that he had heard a little about her wartime experiences, and he was wondering if she would mind telling him about them, adding that he thought that she had received an award.

Louise said nothing for a moment, but she was obviously thinking carefully as she watched Brett enjoying his food next to her. She seemed reserved, but he acknowledged to himself that he had asked a quite personal question, and he was new in the Zoo. Eventually, Louise responded. "Yes, I did receive the Commander of the Legion of Honour award from France. I still have the medal. It was quite a ceremony, and a great honour, of course. I never felt like a heroine. We all just did what we had to do. Sometimes we just got through the next hour, and never thought about the wider picture, or the future. It was day-to-day survival, that's all."

She paused, and seemed a little distant. It was several moments before she continued. "I was born in Norfolk in 1918. At the start of the second war, I was just 21. I'd completed my training with the Queen Alexandra's Royal Army Nursing Corps in London before the war broke out. In 1939 we had just been through the 'phoney war', as it was called. I put my name in, thinking it would be over by Christmas. We all thought that. I was sent to North Africa as a junior theatre nurse with the French troops. Like everyone, I simply tried to stay alive and do what I could under terrible conditions. I cannot possibly describe to you what it was like, Brett.

"In 1941 and early 1942 we experienced disastrous losses during the North African Campaign, but once Monty took over as commander of the Eighth Army in the desert battles, things changed. By early October 1942, Rommel and his tanks were in retreat, and we were seeing successes against the Germans, starting with Tobruk. But our hospital was told to expect many casualties. I imagine you have heard your parents talk about Tripoli, Benghazi, El Alamein, Alexandria, and other places. They were household words for those back home who were following the desert war."

"Yes, my parents and my uncle mentioned them," said Brett.

"One day, a badly injured German officer was brought in. The French doctors successfully treated his serious wounds, but while he was still under, they carved a fleur-de-lis on his buttocks. The incisions were quite deep and I was furious with them because it was unethical and their stupid action gave us another injury to treat after he came around from the anaesthesia. Poor fellow, he would carry that scar for the rest of his life. I wonder, though, if he was grateful for the reminder of the surgeons who saved his life."

The people who were at the other tables were gradually leaving, and they nodded to Louise and Brett as they passed by. Louise continued quietly, "I expect you have heard about the bombing of London, the Blitz, which completely devastated some areas of London in 1940, particularly the East End where my parents were living at the time. Our house was bombed and both of my parents were killed. It was many months before I could get back to England, briefly, to see the damage, and look into the bomb crater. Everything was difficult then…" She looked across at the flamboyant tree outside the window, glowing rich and red in the rays from the setting sun. "Everything was difficult then," she repeated, very softly.

"Over the years I was promoted to Senior Sister. That carried a military equivalent rank of Captain. Not that it means much to anyone now. In

1943 and 1944 we followed the Italian Campaign. Experienced nurses were in high demand." She paused, "Some did not survive." She hesitated, and added, "Many did not survive. After the war, we were able to return to England but, for me, there seemed to be nothing of importance left. England was in shambles and it was obviously going to take a long time to rebuild. I suppose I could have had a contribution to make there, but I was exhausted from the wartime traumas. I had a nursing colleague who felt the same way. Her brother had settled in Kenya after the war and he invited her to join him. With nothing else to keep me in Britain, I came along with her. It was a stressful boat journey, through the Mediterranean and the Suez Canal, because Europe was still in chaos. It was eerie seeing the coast of North Africa again, but this time from the ship.

"We eventually arrived in Kenya but, as it turned out, her brother had already left for Ceylon. We both started working with the colonial government in its attempts to put Kenya back on its feet after the casualties and losses it had suffered from its involvement with the war effort. After about six months, my friend returned to England, but by then I had met Henry and we were becoming close friends."

"I am looking forward to meeting your…" Brett started to say, but just then, Louise noticed Miles Jolly lurking in the corridor outside the restaurant. She waved slightly and he came back over to the table, but did not sit down: he just hovered. She appeared as though she wanted to ask him something, but she simply said, "I was just telling Brett about the war."

Miles looked a little taken aback and replied, "A bit before my time, I'm afraid…well, actually, I was stuck in Old Blighty, pushing papers around on a desk due to the old ticker starting to act up in those days."

With that, Jolly nodded, and wandered away again. They watched him waddle towards the other end of the restaurant and start chatting with a friend near the bar. Louise gave a slight smile, shook her head slightly, and said, almost to herself, "What a character. What a slippery character."

"Don't you like him?" asked Brett.

"Like him? Oh, I've never thought about it."

"Everybody likes Miles," said Brett.

"Yes. Yes, I suppose they do."

They saw Miles walk back to the door. As he was leaving, he called over, "Still no news of Sita. It's not looking good." He paused, looked around at them again, and said, "By the way, Peter's back."

After Brett had finished eating, he and Louise left the restaurant. She walked along the corridor to the exit, and he went to check his pigeonhole for letters. As he took out the small pile, he noticed two with English stamps on them: one from his parents, and another from Tony Colburn. Walking towards the exit, he saw Miles and Louise outside, obviously deep in a serious discussion. He paused, wondering what they were continuing to talk about. As he left the building, Louise was making her way, in the fading light, through to the Muslim section; Miles walked, with his distinctive gait, along the road towards his cage on the north shore.

On the Friday morning, Tili did not work because she had to take her son to the clinic in Mwakindini. Brett had his lunch in the canteen. He did not have a class, so he decided to take the afternoon off, and do his lesson preparation over the weekend. He sat beside Faiz who was the assistant Imam in the small mosque on the south shore. They spoke about life in the Zoo, and Faiz described the operation of the Islamic centre based in the partly ruined mosque. He explained that they had just completed their Friday prayers among the small group of Muslim men who lived there. He invited Brett to visit sometime. As he wandered down the road to the Moores' cage, Brett thought about the Muslim community. He was finding it interesting having a Muslim maid, and seeing her faithfulness in daily prayers. He was impressed with Tili, and had agreed that she could continue working for him. She was pleased to have the steady income, as her husband had been killed several years previously in an accident at the sisal-processing plant located to the south.

Walking down the narrow laneway beside the Moores' cage, N-18, he saw their Peugeot in the carport on the right. The cage on the left seemed unoccupied but a lot of equipment was stored outside. The shining blue waters, stretching out to the white line of surf over the fragmented reef, looked refreshing under the hot afternoon sun. Viewed through the rustling palms, it was an idyllic scene. Once again, he felt blessed to be living there.

Approaching the water's edge, to his right he saw a roughly built hut, with various pipes and tanks stretching out over the water into the ocean. Turning and looking back at the low buildings along the shoreline, he noticed a figure sitting in the shade. He walked up and saw Len, in his shorts, his hat over his face, looking the very image of a retired settler appreciating an afternoon in tropical heaven. As he slowly approached, Len stirred and Brett said, "Sorry to disturb you Len, were you asleep?"

"No. Not completely. Let me show you what's left of my famous project," said Len sleepily, as he stood up and picked up his shirt. "Better cover up, I don't want the ladies getting too excited." Len slipped the shirt over his scrawny, tanned body.

They strolled down to the shoreline. A rock and coral-rag groyne or jetty projected out into the waves. On top of that, a series of metal stanchions supported a long, narrow wooden platform. "Here is where we had the little water-powered generator. We have up to a four-metre tidal height variation here. The generator was operated by the flow from the upper tank at high tide, and we could lower it as the tides went down to take advantage of the head of water stored in this big tank here," he said patting the side of the plastic containers.

"It's very ingenious, and I can see you put a lot of thought into developing it. How long did it work for?" asked Brett.

"Oh, a few years ago we had times when everything ran smoothly for a couple of months at a stretch. That was when we got the steady winds, but not the extremely large waves."

"You mentioned that there had been an article written in a technical journal."

"Yes, we documented our successes, and demonstrated that it is a workable concept. Now it just needs someone to pick up the idea, refine it, and address some of the corrosion issues," replied Len with a wistful look at the remains of his project. They walked under the overhead cables, strung between tall poles among the palm trees. As they walked back to Len's spot in the shade and sat down, Len was whistling softly to himself.

Marie-Anne's pretty, round face appeared at the kitchen door, asking if they would like some drinks and adding that she had heard Len's whistle as they returned. "What will you have Brett, a cold coke?"

"Yes please, that would be great."

"You too I suppose Len? Brett, I always know where Len is by his tuneless whistle," joked Marie-Anne.

"That means I can't get into trouble. But it's more convenient than a cowbell around my neck," said Len. He pointed to the west. "The two-storey cage, N-21, is where Mr. Butt from the Central Stores lives with his family. I rent N-20 as a workshop and a place for our man to stay."

"Who lives over the other side, in cage N-22?"

"That's Miles Jolly's cage. He likes to be near the beach."

When they were looking at the workshop, Brett had noticed Len's windsurfer board, with the boom and mast suspended under the eaves. "Oh, I see you have a windsurfer," said Brett, feigning mild surprise. "I enjoy windsurfing. Do you use it much?"

Len laughed, "You visit me, chatting for over an hour about trivial matters and, then, just as you are about to leave, you state the real purpose of your visit! You don't fool me, *Bwana*," he teased, gently hitting Brett on the shoulder with the back of his hand.

Brett smiled. "That's not totally true. I am interested in your project; but you're right, I did have an ulterior motive."

"That's okay, just kidding." Len chucked. "I bought the used windsurfer a few years ago from a hotel in Malindi. I can set it up for you anytime, if you would like to try it. Maybe tomorrow? High tide will be about an hour later than now. I can get our man to wash it and bring out the sails. The wind is getting steady from the north now. I would enjoy having another go myself. You have a life jacket and sailing boots?"

"Yes, I have kept all of my equipment," replied Brett.

As they turned to return to the beach, an old man walked along the road, from the main gate. He smiled at them. Len greeted him respectfully as old man, 'Mzee Mwangi' and introduced him to Brett. They chatted politely for a while and parted. "That's Peter's man: Joram Mwangi. They have been together for ages. He worked for Peter in Nairobi in the old days. I imagine he's getting things ready for Peter's return."

"I heard yesterday that he's already back," said Brett.

Part 1: Mysteries

"Mwangi will be pleased. He's such a sociable chap. No wonder Peter enjoys having him around, as Peter himself is a bit of a lone wolf."

The palm trees along the north shore provided welcome shade as Brett walked back to his cage. He decided to stroll along the beach, planning to walk as far as he could. The receding tide left the sand firm, and he met several other people ambling along the narrow band where it was comfortable to walk. Looking out to sea, Brett saw the white waves which defined the edge of the fringing reef; the roar of the waves provided a soothing sound. As his eyes drifted to the left, inland towards the coast, he noticed the open expanse of the Northern Bay with patches of dense mangroves along the shoreline, and up into the creeks which were reached by the high tide. The other evergreens, coconut palms, grew all over the humid coastal plain. Striding past his cage, he decided to continue east until he reached the large fence which he knew would bar him from continuing. In the water, he noticed an unfamiliar white man, possibly in his sixties, standing waist-deep, talking with two Kenyans.

Once he reached the fence, Brett stopped and stared through it to the forbidden area and wondered what lay beyond the rocky headlands jutting out into the darkening sweep of the sea. The dogs beside the Ridge-Taylors' cage, N-1, were barking at him constantly while he stood there. He could not see the barrier restraining the dogs, but he imagined they were fenced off to prevent them getting onto the beach. He reasoned that there must be a fence running parallel to the wall, otherwise the dogs would escape into the forested reserve zone.

Turning around to head home, Brett noticed that the European was wading towards the shore. Their paths intersected, so they nodded to each other. The man was stocky, well built, and tough-looking. He was perhaps 5' 8" tall, with short-cropped hair. "Hello stranger. I'm Peter Lancaster, how do you do?"

Brett extended his hand saying, "Pleased to meet you at last, Peter. I'm Brett James." As they shook hands, Brett sensed that Peter was applying pressure with his thumb to his right hand, but he ignored it. He thought he might be one of Miles' brotherhood friends. He continued, "Miles mentioned that you had returned. Welcome home."

"Thank you, it's good to be back and taking my first dip in the old briny. I missed that in England. I'm feeling a bit tired from all the travelling; let's sit in the shade for a few minutes. Pull up a palm tree," he said, indicating a log lying parallel to the high-tide mark. "How long have you been at the Zoo?"

"I arrived in the middle of August," said Brett.

"So, I just missed you before I returned to my personal Battle of Britain. Sorry, that won't mean much to you; it's just my intolerable family…crowded hospitals…harried doctors…" mumbled Peter.

"Sorry. Several people have told me about you, and the amazing contributions you have made to the developments of the Zoo. We are neighbours; I'm down at cage N-12. I am loving it here, especially the people, and my work at the polytechnic."

As Peter responded to those comments, Brett noticed several old scars on different parts of his body. Although he was fairly tanned, white lines and ridges indicated that he had received some major surgeries, and perhaps some wounds. He had a gold chain around his neck from which hung a pendant. At first, Brett thought it was a cross, but it had an additional loop at the top. Peter referred to Brett's cage number. "N-12, that was Jed Walker's old place. An unfortunate affair…wish we could have handled it differently…" Peter stared out at the waves, seeming to be talking to himself. Brett wasn't sure how to respond to this surprising comment, so he said nothing. They chatted for some time, each enjoying the shade and the gentle onshore breeze.

Eventually, Brett stood up, brushing the sand off the back of his shorts. Peter said, "I'd better drag this old carcass of mine up off the beach, while it still moves. Nice to have met you, old chap. Look forward to seeing you again, maybe over a drink one evening." They shook hands. There it was again: the uneasy grasp. As he turned, Brett noticed an ugly scar across Peter's neck and several smaller lines running down to his waist. He wondered if Peter had also received an injury to his right hand which might explain his awkward grip.

On Saturday afternoon, Brett joined Len for a long session on the windsurfer. Brett was impressed by the board, and also by Len's skill. Although the north wind was not yet fully established, the level of the breeze was ideal as they were both a bit rusty. As they washed the sail with fresh water afterwards, Len told Brett that he would leave the rig set up so he could use it at any time.

Brett appreciated Len's kindness, knowing he would need the stress relief. The police visits and Sita's arrest were troubling. He was feeling some anxiety over the increasing background tension in this, otherwise perfect, tropical paradise.

4

"Always remember, we are the outsiders here. You have to learn to think like an outsider."

Peter Lancaster

On the Sunday after he met Peter, Brett joined his friends in church. Following the service, the main topic of conversation was the arrest of Hamud Sita. The lack of any definite news was counterbalanced by the large number of opinions expressed. "You'd think Boniface Chengo would be able to do something, with the influence he has in these parts. After all, he's the Executive Officer, Senior Administrator, and Chief Everything Else around here." This came from Matthew Fletcher, the sincere but sceptical retired sheep farmer.

"I wouldn't expect too much from him, Matthew. I mean-to-say, he's probably keeping his head down as it's a financial issue they are investigating," pointed out Brigadier Thomas, glaring down at everyone beneath him. The discussion swirled into smaller, animated eddies as the couples continued expressing their opinions and their concerns. Thomas cornered Brett and asked, "What's your full name, young fellow?"

"Bretton Morris James."

"Hmm…BMJ. Well now, BMJ, very nice to have you with us, old chap. Look forward to getting to know you better," smiled Thomas as he shook Brett's hand vigorously.

Brett started to walk back home with Matthew. The brigadier's Range Rover pulled up alongside them and Violet wound down the window. "Do join us for lunch one Sunday, Brett dear, won't you?" And they drove away. As they approached his cage, N-16, Matthew said, "Rum deal over Sita, isn't it? I hope someone can bail him out; maybe old Emerson. He's still got a few tricks up his sleeve, I bet. Well, goodbye young fellow."

Brett continued with his lesson plans and then went into the kitchen to make a cup of tea. He noticed Tony Colburn's letter from England on the side, so while the kettle was boiling, he opened it and read it again. Tony gave him an update on some of the activities he knew Brett would be familiar with. He ended by saying he and Jane were well, but he had another appointment with the specialist, planned for mid December, and Brett's prayers would be appreciated. He finished his tea, quickly did the washing up, and put his papers in his briefcase, just in time for the 6 o'clock news on the shortwave from the BBC in London.

He heard a gentle knock on the front door and *"Hodi?* Can I come in?" When he opened it, he saw Tili standing there. He was surprised because she didn't work on Sundays, and, in any case, she would not be knocking at the door as she had a key. She explained that her son had still not recovered from his fever, and she asked if she could take some time on Monday to visit her brother in Kilifi who had some special medicine that she knew was very effective. Brett half-wondered why it was necessary to go so far, but his instinct warned him not to question it. He invited her to step inside, and he went to his bedroom to collect two Kenyan-pound notes.

"Please use this towards the matatu fare."

She took the money and said, as she left, "Thank you Mr. Brett. I will travel with a bus on the journey to that place." He sat down in front of the fan again, took out his Bible, and added 'Tili's trip' to his prayer list, below her son's name, Tony and Jane, and Hamud Sita.

Monday was busy for Brett, with several lessons and two staff meetings. He went to the canteen for lunch and saw Boniface Chengo in the hallway afterwards. Chengo was a large, rotund man of impressive stature and dignity. He made a good leader, due to his affable personality and obvious experience. He was bringing the letters from the post office in town. Brett asked if there was any news about Sita. Chengo shook his head and said in his gruff voice, with his curious pronunciation which always fascinated

Brett, "No, Mister Brett, it is looking like, somehow, a little bit of a difficult situation for him. I have to get means, or there will be no otherwise to be helping him." Brett took from his remarks that things were still unresolved. In the evening, Tili's mother visited Brett to ask if he had seen Tili, as she had not returned from her trip to Kilifi. She told him that the boy was feeling better with the medicine that Memsaab Emerson had given him the previous week.

At mid-morning on the Tuesday, Brett was surprised when the office boy brought the guesthouse manageress, Khadijah, into his office. He had enjoyed a comfortable relationship with her since his first week when she had taken care of him so well in the guest house. He had found out later that she was Tili's older sister. Apparently, the family was getting quite worried, and wondered if Brett could do anything. She had heard a secondhand rumour, originating from a person who had recognized Tili on the bus, indicating that she may have been arrested.

Brett was unsure what to do. At lunchtime, he visited Steve and Coreene. Steve thought Peter Lancaster might have some contacts with the local police force. That evening, Steve took Brett over to Peter's cage. Peter told them that his Land Rover's registration had expired, but said he was willing to go down to Kilifi if he could get transport. Brett offered to drive Peter. By late Wednesday, there was still no word of Tili, and her sister told him there had been no information from the inquiries she had made in the Muslim quarter. She pleaded with Brett to go with Peter to see if he could help. She felt that having two white men acting on her behalf would be helpful. Peter and Brett arranged to drive down to Kilifi, as Mr. Katana had agreed to organize substitute teachers for Brett's Thursday classes.

At 8am, Brett drove his pickup along to Peter's cage and collected him. Peter was carrying a brown leather briefcase and wearing slacks and a smart dress shirt, "My, you're looking pretty spiffing, Peter," Brett commented.

"I need to impress whoever I can today." As they looped around in front of the main buildings, Peter joked, "Look, there's Miles walking across, and Len is with him. See if you can hit them."

As they passed the pair, Miles waved to them to slow down. "We just heard that Hamud Sita has been found guilty and sentenced to three years in jail."

"My goodness! That's bad," said Brett. As they passed through the main gate, he told Peter, "Three years seems pretty severe, just for a clerical misdemeanour."

"No, it was more than that. He had set up a duplicate receipt-book system, making it look legitimate on the surface, but keeping some cash for himself and issuing fake receipts to anyone who he thought would not be sophisticated enough to question it."

"That might include me," said Brett.

"He fooled a lot of people – including Chengo, it seems. He's going to be smarting for a while, as it reflects poorly on his oversight. Also, he needs to find a good replacement for Sita quickly because the accounting setup at the Zoo is pretty complicated."

"Why would anyone with a good, steady job like Sita had, risk it all and ruin his life that way?" wondered Brett aloud.

"Why? Yes, it makes you wonder, doesn't it? Some individuals will exploit opportunities and take risks like that. Often, they don't look to the future or consider the consequences. Of course, you never know what sort of pressures he was facing, or what demands were being made on him. Often the family has urgent needs and anyone with a job is under an obligation to help."

As they drove through Malindi, Peter said, "Let's just call into the police station here and see if they have any information on Tili. You never know, it might save us going all the way down to Kilifi." Emerging half an hour later from the police station, Peter seemed irritable. "No help there. They have no record of her name anywhere. Let's head on." Brett kept quiet for a while, letting Peter cool down. Brett had watched him walking as he left the offices and made his way back towards the pickup. His steps were slow and determined. His stance resembled a person who had been told to stand in a narrow corridor and not let anyone or anything pass. There was a muted belligerence, and an aura of mild defiance in his posture. He thought, *One does not mess around with Peter.*

As they continued their journey along the steamy highway, they encountered two police check-points where they were required to stop while the officers looked at the tax disc on the window. As Brett drove, they chatted about various things – the Zoo, sailing, travels, adventures, and life's little disasters. Brett was looking for an opportunity to probe

Peter about his faith and his possible connection with Freemasonry. The odd handshake still intrigued him. He raised the topics obliquely. On Freemasonry, Peter revealed nothing, and Brett did not mention Miles Jolly. Peter expressed scepticism of faith, describing himself as a 'fallen Catholic' who had been drifting for a long time.

"And searching?" prodded Brett.

"We're all searching I suppose. Who knows the answers? I'm not even sure of the *questions* any more. I sometimes say, 'don't continue to fight battles you have already lost'." With that abstruse comment Peter seemed to indicate that the subject was closed, but then he appeared to think again and added, "Of course, I respect those who do have a faith, and I have admired all the good work I have seen the churches do here over the years." After a further interlude of reflection, he added, "I suppose I'd better sort things out with the old fellow up in the sky soon. I have another birthday coming up next month. I think I've seen too many of those."

Peter Lancaster's inquiries with the police in Kilifi likewise turned up nothing. There was no record of Tili's name in their books, and the officer questioned why they were inquiring in Kilifi, simply because the bus passed through there. Peter had to admit that he wasn't even sure if she had taken the bus, but Brett confirmed that it was her intention to visit her brother in Kilifi. The officer at the front desk spoke respectfully to Peter, and suggested that he fill in a missing-person report.

They left, both feeling discouraged, tired, and hungry. Peter sighed, "Let's get some lunch. I know a nice restaurant here. Come on, I'll pay. You forked out for the petrol on this fruitless search." They enjoyed a tasty lunch, with coffee afterwards. Watching Brett tucking into a creamy dessert, Peter said, "I have to watch my weight a bit. But I don't think it's overeating that's slowing me down these days, just wear and tear on the old body. Still, I've led a long and adventurous life, I suppose. Of course, it's been difficult since my wife died." Brett wondered if this was an attempt to open up, because he was finding Peter difficult to talk with. He seemed guarded when he was first asked a question. He always thought before replying – not like Miles who was immediately open and chatty when any new topic came up in conversation. Gently, Brett asked Peter when he had lost his wife.

Peter seemed willing to talk about it, explaining that his wife had been killed in a bizarre traffic accident in England. Near Gatwick Airport, a tourist from continental Europe who was new to the British road system, had mistakenly driven anticlockwise around a roundabout and collided head-on with her car. He and the two children were devastated, and his daughter never recovered from it. For some strange reason, Peter felt she blamed him, but he was not with his wife at the time. "Perhaps that is what she holds against me," said Peter. "I'd love to restore that relationship."

Peter asked about Brett's parents and his life in England before he came to Kenya. He was very interested in details of Brett's time in Nyeri and, like Louise Emerson, his questions indicated an intimate knowledge of the Central Province, but he offered no details of his life or work there. Instead, he abruptly changed the subject by saying, "I wonder why Tili felt it necessary to travel all this way for medicine in the first place."

"She told me her brother here has some special medicine." As he said it, Brett suddenly wondered about witchcraft. When he suggested that, Peter said the same thought had crossed his mind too. They were both enjoying the comfort of the air-conditioned restaurant, so they lingered over their coffee, neither of them feeling enthusiastic about the return journey.

As they were walking back to the pickup, a small plane flew low overhead. For some reason this seemed to startle Peter and he glanced up at it quickly. "Cessna 150," he said, "5Y-..." he mumbled, as he read its number.

As they drove north out of Kilifi, Brett said, "You mentioned the name of the person who used to be in my cage–"

"Jed Walker."

"Yes, what happened with him? A couple of people have mentioned him, in a vague way." Peter was silent and then said, "I tell you what, old chap, if I fill you in on a few details, promise to keep it under your hat, won't you? I'm not sure how much is generally known. I wouldn't want to be accused of spilling the beans." Brett nodded, so Peter continued, "It all came to a head about 18 months ago. Jed Walker came down from upcountry, somewhere, and settled in the Zoo – in the cage you now have. He was some sort of a writer and a bit of an artist too, I think. Anyway, he hired a full-time maid from this region. They got on very well together, if you know what I mean. A bit too well for her family's liking. Anyway, there was an informal liaison which attracted some mild reproof, and snickering interest from the local kids who, half-jokingly, called her 'Mrs. Jed'. But that wasn't the real problem because, as you know, folks here are fairly relaxed about these things, as long as people are discreet. In fact, there's a fair bit of promiscuity around – that's why they have such a serious problem with certain diseases.

"Anyway, he was an opinionated fellow, and too loud – especially when he got into the suds. He became quite mouthy, initially about the way the Zoo was run, but then he started to voice his political observations. That didn't go down too well with some of the local bigwigs, I can tell you. He started to ask a lot of questions, related to the Emersons and finances, so he also angered our leaders. Several of us tried to warn him, but that didn't seem to help. Then he said something at a party about the senior politicians in the country and someone reported him. It wasn't long before he had a visit from a couple of officials. He claimed he was only repeating what he'd heard other people say, which may well have been the case, but it didn't help him.

"The Elders at the Zoo were informed that he was going to be deported. There was nothing we could do, even if we had felt inclined to help him – which we weren't, particularly. Three days later, he was hustled on a plane to Europe and that's the last we heard of him. Of course, we had to clean up the mess here – paperwork, documents, his possessions, etc – and pacify his girlfriend. Someone eventually arranged a job for her at a hotel in Malindi. The whole Walker affair wasn't handled as well as it could have been, although others in the leadership here didn't want to be bothered to try to bail him out. There is a bit of a warning, though: we have to be careful what we say, especially with political comments. We should be aware of who's listening. Basically, I suppose we aren't here to criticize, but help out where we can."

Peter looked out at the ocean, with the deep-turquoise water spread beneath a cobalt-blue sky. He pointed to the distant specks of cloud floating above the sharp horizon. "We need rain. We usually get some each month, but we should expect a bit more soon. I've been told the short rains have been pretty good so far up in the highlands. They deserve it after, what I hear was, the worst drought in living memory and officially the driest period for a hundred years."

Brett continued driving; as they passed along a narrow road through a small coastal town, ahead of them they saw a man on a bicycle with several long planks of wood strapped to his rear carrier. They were sticking out at right angles from the bicycle on both sides, and he was wobbling uncertainly. To their horror, they watched a matatu overtaking them and careening down the road. As it roared past the cyclist, it struck the wood which was projecting on the right side of the bicycle, spinning him around several times. Then it roared off in a cloud of white dust. The man flew off his bicycle and crashed into a roadside stall ahead of him and lay in a tangled mess amongst the wood, twisted bicycle frame, and the partly demolished stall. Plastic jugs, bowls, and lids were rolling about on the ground. It all happened within a few seconds.

Brett immediately slowed down and was about to pull over to see if he could help the man, when Peter shouted, "Don't stop! Drive on."

Brett said, "But–"

"Just drive on!" commanded Peter. Brett instantly obeyed. He drove out through the town, and said, "Maybe we could have helped him. We should have stopped."

"Yes, and soon have a crowd gathering around, accusing us of hitting him. Trust me. I know these situations, and how they can develop. You get yourself in a position like that, with an angry mob – most of whom would not have seen what happened – and you can get into big trouble. I know it seems callous, but we did the right thing. Always remember, we are the outsiders here. You have to learn to *think* like an outsider."

Brett was taken aback, but he understood what Peter was saying. He said, "I'd like to pray for him, and trust that he was not badly injured."

Peter responded, "You can pray for him if you think it will help, but it was clear to me that he was killed." They drove in silence for a while, Peter's lined face set blankly in thought. Brett felt subdued and disheartened, but he knew Peter was not a person to be disobeyed in a crisis.

After dropping him at the central building, Brett drove back to the polytechnic. Most of the staff had gone, but he was able to look at the notes describing the work that had been covered by the students during the day. Several people noticed his pickup outside and came in to ask him for the news of Tili. It was disappointing for him to say there was none.

Friday was a worrying day, but he was busy all day at the college until about 6pm. On his way over to the cafeteria, he saw Khadijah running towards him from the guest house. It was an unusual sight, because adults do not run in Kenyan culture, especially with the heat. Excitedly, she told him that Tili had returned. He was very pleased, and asked where she had been all week. She explained that Tili had been travelling on the bus to Kilifi to see her brother. She was standing up on the bus when it swayed and lurched to one side. She was thrown against a man who hit his head on the window, and cracked the glass. The bus driver thought that they had been fighting, so, at the next stop, he called the police and they were both arrested and thrown in jail. She stayed there for days without being able to communicate with anyone. Eventually, the police had believed her, and one kind policeman gave her the bus fare home. The first question her mother asked her was, "Did they beat you?" They had not, but they did beat up the man who was arrested with her. She added, with resignation, "It can happen."

He continued on to the cafeteria and ordered his supper. Many people were discussing Tili's return, and several were expressing thanks for answered prayers. Afterwards, Brett told Louise about the day with Peter. They agreed that Tili's return was a huge relief, but shared their disappointment over Sita's imprisonment. "It's been a stressful time, the last month," said Brett. "It seems we've had a crisis every week."

"Many years ago, I remember Heinrick saying that, at the Zoo, we were facing a crisis every day, so I suppose things have improved!" joked Louise, as they went their separate ways.

Climbing into his pickup, Brett thought, *Heinrick? Who's Heinrick? Was she referring to Henry?* Surrounded by the warmth of the darkening evening, in the heavy and humid air beneath the whispering palms, he felt the familiar ripple of disquiet, and an inexplicable chill of uncertainty.

5

Louise Emerson and Brett James in conversation:
"As you know, access is restricted beyond the wall.
And there are dangerous creatures."
"Like what, snakes?"
"Yes, and the monkeys are vicious. People are afraid to go through there."

It was a Saturday morning when Brett and Len climbed the hill across the road to the west, to look at the spring. This was the Zoo's fresh water source. From that vantage point, they were able to see a lot more of the peninsula, projecting eastwards into the Indian Ocean, and the area to the north of the Northern Bay. Len mentioned that the isolated, swampy area farther up the coast contained many wild animals, and he had once seen elephants and cape buffalos down by the beaches. Friends had reported seeing topis, a form of antelope, and bushbuck beside the tidal creeks and among the mangrove swamps.

Climbing back down the hill, Brett asked Len about the history of the Zoo. Len told him that, in the early years, the Emersons and Peter Lancaster had seen the potential of the area, and had worked with the local authorities during the initial stages of the Zoo's development. Their proposals matched the official mandate for the area, providing infrastructure for housing, and opportunities for employment in the section of the coastal strip south of Mwakindini.

One afternoon, Brett saw Steve talking with an elderly woman that he recognized, but could not recall where he had seen her. Steve introduced her as Miles Jolly's maid, Muzhere. Brett greeted her as *Mama Mzee*, the respectful term for an old woman, which seemed to please her. She was very affable, and spoke some English. She was walking towards the Muslim area, and invited Brett to see her home. He glanced at Steve, who gave an imperceptible nod. Brett and the elderly woman walked to the south along a wide path, almost a road, between some cages, into the crowded plaza, and along a winding street towards the central section. She told him, "I have my family here. In cage S-17. You will meet them."

Her small cage was just off a side road, leading towards the sea. There was a tiny reception area for guests, with two stone seats in a cool nook. When two female members of Muzhere's family saw the guest, they disappeared, but soon a man appeared with a cup of tea in a cracked china mug. As it was very hot, Brett sipped it slowly while being greeted by a variety of children and a few young men. No women were visible, apart from Muzhere herself. Conversation was limited due to language difficulties, which he knew was acceptable. He felt comfortable with that, until an older boy of about fifteen arrived. He spoke good English, and was happy to chat away, asking many questions. He said he was a nephew of Mama Muzhere. Once Brett had finished his tea, the lad offered to show him around their area.

On the way, Brett saw the southern portion of the eastern wall, as barren and sterile-looking as the northern section. It had a double-door opening in it, but it was shuttered by a heavy grill. A dog was barking at them from the other side of the compound: there may have been a couple, Brett could not tell. Faded lettering indicated *Hatari…danger*.

He noticed a two-storey building to the north, built up to the west side of the wall, and asked about it. The boy told him that Bwana Emerson and Memsaab lived there. An African man was watching them from the doorway. Brett pointed over the wall to the nature reserve, "I thought Mr. Emerson lived over there."

"He comes here sometimes," said the boy nodding to his left.

"Have you seen him?" asked Brett.

"He comes here, but not much now," was the only response. As they looked at the wall, several people were staring at them. "What is through that gate?" asked Brett. The barking continued.

"Very dangerous dogs. Bwana Emerson has his animals there. He studies them. There are big monkeys. They can scratch you. And they do bite." The lad was obviously becoming uncomfortable.

"Can we go to the sea?" asked Brett. They walked down a narrow pathway between the walls of the cages, and were soon on the beach. They strolled past the mosque, along the pathway above the high-tide mark towards an open sandy area. Then Brett said goodbye, shaking hands with the boy. He headed north to the main square, feeling honoured to have seen inside the Muslim quarters.

One morning in late October, between classes, he needed to return from the college to his cage to pick up his T-square. He saw Tili on a mat, praying, facing north to Mecca. She had a white scarf over her head. He waited outside for a few moments, and then went in. He thought it would be a good opportunity to tell her that the church members had been praying for her during her mysterious absence.

"That's nice, thank you," she said.

Brett asked, "Why do you pray?"

She replied, "We pray five times a day."

"What do you pray about?"

"I say what the Imam taught us. I don't know what it says."

Brett explained to her, "When we Christians pray, it is to our God, telling what is in our hearts. We can say anything, in our own words. We thank God, or ask for things – like your safety. Many of our group met together to ask God for your safe return when we did not know where you were."

"You said that for me? Oh, that's nice. We follow in the path we are told," said Tili.

"We are obeying our God too when we pray because that is what He taught us to do," responded Brett.

"Thank you to take care for me like that," whispered Tili with her head slightly bowed.

As he left the polytechnic that afternoon, Brett talked with Coreene who was also heading to the central building. She told him, "Yesterday, Steve visited Hamud Sita in prison, south of Mombasa. Did you know?"

"No, I did not know he was planning to visit him. I wasn't even sure if it was permitted."

"As a clergyman, he is sometimes allowed to, but he never knows until he actually tries. Sita says he is innocent. Apparently he was the scapegoat – trying to cover over several irregularities. He told Steve that others are involved. Steve is going to try to contact the lawyer who dealt with the case." With that information, Coreene left Brett.

Reaching the main building, he walked in with Louise. They were met by several others. Matthew Fletcher called out, "Oh, here's Louise. Welcome to the old boys' club, Louise. Sit down. What would you like to drink?"

"Thank you. I'll have a soda please, but I can't stay long. I'm in the middle of a project."

Len said, "We are always happy to see the charming wife of our big chief in the old boys' club. In fact, I think we should make you an honorary Old Boy."

"I'm not sure if I should be flattered or offended by that suggestion," laughed Louise, taking her drink from Miles.

"I'd go with flattered – and be grateful for the attention," advised Marie-Anne Moore.

"Actually, I'm looking for a strong, young man," Louise said.

"Aren't we all, dear? I suggest you try him," said Marie-Anne, nodding towards Brett who shrank down in his chair.

"Well, I'm a bit busy enjoying my drink right now. Steve is coming here soon; ask him," joked Brett.

Matthew noticed Peter in the hallway and said, "Oh, here comes trouble."

Peter came in, looking hot and frustrated. Louise rose, "Sorry, got to go. Will you be able to come along later, Brett, and help me unload some supplies please? They may be messy."

"Yes, give me 15 minutes to change my clothes."

As she left, Brett saw Louise place her hand on Peter's arm and pat it. She left it there slightly longer than Brett would have expected. She said softly, "Sorry I can't hear about your stressful day, Peter."

Miles asked, "Had a battle with a crooked insurance agent, did you?"

Brett said, "So, what happened, Peter?"

"As I was leaving Malindi, I got stuck behind an incredibly slow and smelly old lorry crawling along and blocking the road. I saw it was safe to overtake, but immediately ahead there were two traffic police. The cop said I was driving dangerously and should not have overtaken at that point…"

Just as Steve appeared at the door, Brett said, "I have to go. My youthful strength is required next door. I'll hear the rest of the story later, Peter."

As he started to leave, Coreene walked in. "Here comes the boss. Look busy everybody," said Matthew.

Coreene smiled and told Steve, "Supper in half an hour."

"Okay, thanks. That will seem peaceful compared to all the comings and goings here."

The group gradually dispersed, and soon Steve and Peter were alone. Steve spoke in a low voice, "I visited Sita the other day."

"They let you see him?" questioned Peter.

"Yes. He says he's innocent."

"They all say that, don't they?" Peter picked up his empty glass and swirled it around as though there was still liquid in it, then mindlessly attempted to drink the nonexistent dregs.

Steve continued, "I'm inclined to believe him, but I'm not sure. He says there are other irregularities in our accounting system. And other areas. I wonder if I should follow up with the legal counsel."

Peter shifted uneasily in his chair, and turned towards Steve. "Best not to. It's all settled now. I wouldn't interfere if I were you, Padre. Boniface Chengo has things under control. Everything seems to be working smoothly."

"It's just that…one likes to feel that justice is done. I don't like to see an innocent person suffer."

"You must do what you feel is best, of course, but I wouldn't hold out much hope. It all went through the regular channels, with legal procedures and everything. Might be best to let that sleeping dog lie."

"Maybe you're right. I'd rather not get involved. I must pray about it"

"Why? I've already given you my advice!" joked Peter. Steve laughed. Peter said, "On another subject, Father, I see a lot of activities around here that you would probably describe as sinful – dishonesty, corruption, sexual promiscuity and perversion, and so on. What's the church's view on those? What's your feeling?"

Steve seemed taken aback. He thought in silence, looking out of the window at the moving casuarina pines with the swaying palm branches beyond. Peter sat thoughtfully as further questions formed in his mind. Steve responded, "The church's teaching and my feeling? Those are two separate questions. First, the church's position is, of course, based on the Bible which clearly describes many sins. But, when I view the behaviour of other people, I need to remind myself that I too am a hopeless sinner in need of repentance and forgiveness myself. I cannot look at any fellow human beings without seeing them as precious objects of God's love, struggling in a fallen world. I cannot judge or condemn, but only view them through Christ's eyes for what they can become – if they would allow Him to restore them to the true image of God."

"You speak of forgiveness. But can we be forgiven everything?"

"God will not reject a truly repentant heart. I plan to preach on forgiveness in a few weeks so you should come along and listen!"

"Oh come on, don't make me wait."

"Okay, my professional integrity prevents me from withholding instruction from you, Peter, so I will give you a homework assignment. Do you have a Bible in your cage?"

"I think I've got one somewhere."

Steve took out a pen and picked up a paper serviette from the table. He wrote down three New Testament references and handed them to Peter, saying, "Find your Bible, and look up these verses. See what they say to you." Peter took the napkin, looked at it, and slipped it in his shirt pocket, thanking him. Steve added, "I think you'll find those references helpful."

Peter thought for an instant and added, "I have my own creed. The golden rule: treat others the way you'd like them to treat you. But, I go even further. I do not hurt even those who harm me. Otherwise I would have throttled Miles Jolly years ago!" Steve laughed, then noticed that Peter wasn't smiling.

Seeing Steve's disquiet, Peter added, "I try to get on well with most people, but I'm pretty unforgiving in some areas – particularly towards that louse Jolly."

"I had sensed that there was some tension between you two."

"Nicely put Padre. Nicely put! Some tension, yes. Too much history there. Too much history. Sorry, I didn't mean to involve you in any of that nonsense." Peter stood up. "Well, I appreciate the chat, Father. Thanks. I'd better send you on your way home or you'll be late for supper. And I'll probably be blamed!"

As Steve was walking out, he saw Brett on his way to the Muslim section. "Louise wants me to help lift some things," he said. "I am hoping she can arrange for me to meet Mr. Emerson sometime. I have some questions for him."

"It's good of you to help her, but I'd be a bit careful about asking too much related to Henry. It all seems to be rather sensitive, reading between the lines," said Steve.

"I'm just curious."

"Remember that curiosity was not conducive to the cat's survival."

"Oh, I thought Curiosity was the Mother of Invention," said Brett.

"No. That was Necessity," replied Steve, smiling.

As he walked to the south of the central building, Brett came to the Emersons' cage, S-33, built into the wall to the north of the Muslim section. Their white Peugeot 504 was parked outside. Beside one of the doors, he noticed the man he had seen previously. A battered pickup stood outside which he thought he recognized as the one used by the Central Stores. Louise explained that they needed to unload some bags of dog food that the driver had brought in from Mwakindini. "Mjuhgiuna has hurt his back. I wonder if you'd be able to help please," she said. "We'll put them in our store and Onesimus Njuguna, the brigadier's helper, will take some over to their cage in a wheelbarrow tomorrow. Sorry to pressure you, but Mr. Butt needs the pickup returned soon."

Brett said he was pleased to help, and started struggling with the heavy bags in the heat. He dodged the miserable-looking black Alsatian that was straining at its chain and trying to take a nip at him every time he passed. "That's an efficient guard dog I'm sure," he said, nodding towards the growling animal.

"Oh, Kali? She's a sweetie, once she gets to know you. As long as I'm nearby."

"I'm glad she's chained."

"She's fine when she gets used to you."

"And she's chained up," added Brett. "There seem to be several dogs around. I heard some along by the Ridge-Taylors' place when I reached the fence by their beach."

"Yes, they have always had extra space there to accommodate the security dogs. Njuguna cares for them."

"What do the locals think about them?"

"They hate them. That's why Kali is so effective as our guard dog. They know that *Kali* means 'fierce'."

"Yes, *mbwa kali*, fierce dog," he said looking at Kali as she glared at him.

"She's effective protection for us," Louise stated.

"There, just a few more bags, then I'm finished," said Brett.

Louise said, "Just as I left, I heard Miles make reference to his crooked insurance agent. He is very bitter about a bad experience he had a long time ago. We have advised him to forget about it, but he insists on hanging on to his anger. It can't be healthy for him." As he completed the unloading, Brett was listening. "Many years ago, he had a small house to the west of Nairobi. It was destroyed in a fire, and he discovered that he was severely under insured. He did not receive any sympathy from the insurance company, and he was awarded only a tiny settlement. He claims that he was misled by the original agent who sold him the insurance. Who knows? Anyway, that is why he is so resentful."

"That's a shame. It's understandable that he is upset, but it does seem a bit silly to keep dwelling on it after all this time."

"He actually does more than brood on it. Every few months, he sends a card to the agent in Nairobi, reminding him how he ruined his life. He once showed me a greetings card before he posted it, which he had modified to read 'I was doing fine until I met you', or something similar. He seems to draw some satisfaction from keeping the resentment alive. Maybe it feeds a need in him, but he's hurting no one but himself. I doubt if the agent takes the slightest notice of it."

"It's good to be aware that it's a sensitive topic for him. He's such a nice chap, that I can't see him carrying that burden of resentment. He's become a good friend to me."

Louise did not respond: she had started to walk over to speak with Mjuhgiuna. Her dog reacted immediately and started barking furiously. "Kali! Be quiet, you stupid dog!" she said, slapping her across the nose. Brett knew he wouldn't dare do that, thinking that he'd probably lose a couple of fingers. "Have you met Mzee Mjuhgiuna?" Louise asked Brett, as the old man limped towards him. Brett extended his hand, and they exchanged the lingering handshake of respect, while both smiling.

"No, but we have seen each other from a distance," Brett said. Mjuhgiuna nodded his thanks for Brett's help with the unloading, and Brett gave a sympathetic comment on his bad back.

As he walked back to his area, Louise told Brett, "He likes you, and he appreciates what you and Peter did to try to find his niece, Tili. I was so relieved that she was okay."

"She's so sweet and kind. It's interesting, having a Muslim working with me."

"Yes. Imagine, if we had been born just the other side of those walls, in the southern quarter, we would almost certainly be Muslims."

"I suppose that's why Steve wants everyone to hear the Good News. At least they would then have a chance to make an informed choice," added Brett.

"And what of us who have heard the 'good news', as you call it? We have had that choice most of our lives, and what have we done with it?" pondered Louise.

"Steve hopes to see the transformation of lives in the Zoo, even a renewing of the whole society. But first, he and Coreene know they need to establish relationships with people as friends, and show love through service and kindness."

"Do they really foresee a transformed society?" asked Louise skeptically.

"I think they simply wish to share the good news of freedom with anyone who will listen, leaving the outcomes to a higher authority."

The bags were all stacked in the small store between the Emersons' front entrance and the doorway to Mjuhgiuna's quarters. "There, the pickup is ready to be collected anytime," said Brett as he raised the tailgate.

Louise motioned for him to sit down in one of the outside chairs, "Cool off a bit. Mjuhgiuna is bringing us sodas."

"Thank you, but I won't stay long. I have a pile of marking to get through tonight." He noticed an interesting plant in a pot beside him. It had ugly-looking stems but beautiful pink flowers.

Just then, Kaleem Butt arrived. "Will you join us for a cold drink?" invited Louise.

"Thank you, but not now. Lots on the go at present. I'll just collect the pickup if that's alright with you."

"Certainly, thank you for arranging the delivery," said Louise.

"Happy to help. How is Mr. Henry?"

"About the same."

"We miss seeing him around these days," said Mr. Butt.

"Thank you. Things are…a bit difficult," said Louise.

As the vehicle drove away in a cloud of fumes, Brett told Louise, "I'd like to visit the headland."

"It's inaccessible," Louise stated flatly.

"There must be some way through…to be able to explore the area a bit."

"As you know, access is restricted. And there are dangerous creatures."

"Like what, snakes?"

"Yes, and the monkeys are vicious. People are afraid to go through there."

"I'm not. Sorry, I don't mean to be pushy, but with proper precautions, surely you or Mr. Emerson could show me around. It can't be that unsafe, as some people do venture that side of the wall," argued Brett.

"I agree that some fears are probably exaggerated in people's minds, but things are quite complicated."

"Yes, that's what I was beginning to conclude," said Brett, finishing his drink.

"Some areas are a bit sensitive."

"Everyone keeps telling me that. I would like to meet Mr. Emerson and suggest some ideas that I have."

Part 1: Mysteries

"Sorry, it is not possible. There are too many complications that I cannot explain. A lot goes on behind these walls," Louise said, waving her hand above her head in a wide horizontal circle.

Brett realized he may have appeared rude, so he politely mentioned another area that intrigued him: "If you don't mind my asking…what I can't figure out…are the finances of the Zoo. I mean, there is no income from external sources, and there can't be much generated from within. How is the whole place financed? Are any foundations or companies supporting it? Surely the Kenyan government and local municipality can't be contributing. In fact, we probably pay them monies from our rates and taxes."

Louise listened to Brett's questions and then said, "Several businessmen live here, and staff from many companies. A few of our cages house wealthy residents. Some of us have means: we were not exactly destitute when we came here, you know! Many of the original settlers had sold farms and property up country before they moved here and made their contributions to the running of the Zoo."

"But that was a long time ago. Those folks are not going to be able to continue to finance the operation forever are they? Many are getting old, and what about their health?"

"I know what you're thinking. I don't know details of many, although, as a nurse, I can guess a lot by looking at the external symptoms. Actually, Peter's health is not good. He got pretty beaten-up during the war, and has had several surgeries since then. Miles…his heart is weak, and he's looking a bit wobbly these days."

"I thought he always walked like that!"

"You're unkind! He lives one heartbeat at a time. As we all do, I suppose. But his are more tenuous, I suspect."

"I know Mr. Emerson is unwell, but how is your health, if I may ask?"

"Oh, fine thanks. 1941 proved that I am indestructible. These days, I live a day at a time, taking all sensible precautions – mainly, by not asking too many questions! Now, off you go, have your supper, and then get on with your marking. Thanks very much for your help."

As he walked through the compound, Brett looked at the Zoo through slightly different eyes. He saw the variety of people of all races and religions eating and talking in the central buildings; he noticed the pathways and the gardens and the cages, and had to admit that the original concept of the place seemed to be working well.

In a tumble of thoughts, he reflected on his discussion with Louise. *She has an expressive face, with an impressive repertoire of fascinating expressions, all intensified by her bright, grey-green eyes. But her warnings and evasive answers?…and what mysteries is she hiding?*

He abruptly dismissed the thoughts, telling himself, "Too many complexities. And Kali is the ugliest dog I've ever seen!"

6

Brett asked Kinyanjui if he knew Maina…
"We are age mates. We shared the same circumcision knife."
"That means you are like brothers."
"Even closer than brothers."

Brett woke unusually early for a Sunday. It was still dark. He put on the kettle, made a large mug of tea, and carried it to the sea's edge. As he stood looking out across the silvery, still water, gentle waves rippled along the sand as they washed in along the beach in a sweeping curve. It felt good to be alive. He sat on a sandy log, supremely happy to be in Kenya. He felt gratitude for all the blessings he had been receiving: a job he enjoyed and the chance to meet new people. A flock of terns swooped low across the shimmering water.

He noticed it was getting light. He could not see the sun rising behind the headland as it was far to the southeast at that time of year. A soft pink hue reflected on the delicate clouds behind the palms. He studied the bay, as he felt the first touch of a soft breeze. Behind him, the spiky palms were silhouettes against the lightening sky, and they began to move very slightly. The beauty of the morning was being revealed. "Welcome to another day in paradise," he whispered. "Thank you Lord for the wonders of your creation, and the opportunities ahead." He asked for guidance in the weeks to come as he sensed there may be challenges.

The Zoo

Walking up the beach, he disturbed three sooty gulls that were feeding along the shoreline. As he returned to his cage, planning a shower and a leisurely breakfast, he smelled the distinctive aroma of coffee brewing and heard the sound of a neighbour's maid scraping burnt toast. He knew that was what he needed: caffeine and a slice of carbonated bread to help prepare him for the day ahead.

A group of his friends gathered as they left church, and they discussed the sermon. Brett and several other neighbours asked Coreene to elaborate on what Steve had said about forgiveness. Brett said, "As I recall, all sins can be forgiven if a person is truly repentant."

Coreene clarified, "Yes, but willfully persisting in sin prevents a person having access to divine forgiveness."

Violet Ridge-Taylor came up and, in a breathless torrent of random thoughts, bombarded Brett with a shower of rapid questions: Did he follow the sermon? Had he lost a little weight? How were things at the university? Had he seen her Bible? Isn't it awful about Hamud Sita? Is he remembering to take his antimalarials? Where were her keys? And when was he going join them for lunch? Then she drifted away in a delightful flutter of confusion, waving to everyone as she tripped towards the waiting Range Rover.

Steve was standing beside Brett who looked at him and muttered, "I assume she wasn't expecting answers to all those questions!" He added, "A person could die of starvation, waiting for her to issue a formal invitation to lunch."

Steve laughed, "No chance of you starving, my well-fed friend."

After church, Brett hurried back to his cage to eat, followed by some test preparation and marking. He also took time to write to his parents, and Tony and Jane. He knew Tony's critical appointment with the specialist was coming up soon so he hoped the letter would reach him in time to assure them both of his prayers.

Part 1: Mysteries

On the following Tuesday, Brett wanted to have an early, light supper and then borrow Len's windsurfer or, if the wind did not pick up, try some snorkelling. With that plan in mind, he approached the cafe. Miles was standing to the right of the entrance, in the shade beside the patch of open ground. He was watching some supplies being unloaded from a lorry parked at the rear of the kitchens. He had placed his crooked stick, probably picked up on the beach, against the wall. After brief greetings, they turned towards the feeding centre, and were surprised to see a blue police car pull up in front of the building. Two officers emerged and Miles whispered, "It's your friend Ochieng and his sidekick Kinyanjui."

"Good afternoon Mr. Bretton," said Ochieng. He and Kinyanjui shook his hand and Brett asked if they knew Mr. Jolly. Noncommittal smiles revealed nothing as they all shook hands in a perfunctory manner. Brett wondered where Ochieng got his full name, Bretton. *Has he been looking at some official documents?*

Ochieng told them he had an appointment with the Executive Officer. Miles directed him inside and Ochieng walked determinedly along the corridor and entered the office of Boniface Chengo. Miles continued down the hallway, leaving Brett with Kinyanjui. He still felt uncomfortable about their earlier interview and saw an opportunity to reduce the tension. "I'm going to have a snack, would like to join me?" offered Brett, waving towards the cafe.

"It is so kind, thank you. I have to be waiting for Mr. Ochieng." They entered the cafe and sat near the window.

Brett poured a mug of tea while Kinyanjui enjoyed a cold drink. Brett said, "So, Bwana, you are visiting us again."

"Yes, Senior Sergeant Ochieng has some matters for Mr. Chengo. Questions, it is."

"How does he know my full name? I never use that. Everyone calls me Brett or Mr. James."

Kinyanjui hesitated before stating: "On the immigration forms. Plus your map application."

"How did he see that?" There was a short silence.

"Did you meet Mr. Maina at Resource Data Imaging?"

"I saw him briefly but did not speak with him for long. How is he connected to the map office? Why is he interested in my details?" Brett asked those questions with surprise.

"You know, I would be a very bad person if I answered that. Mine is to ask questions."

"I see. But I cannot understand why there is so much fuss about my asking for a simple map, and I don't see what Maina has to do with this."

"Mr. Ochieng thinks you are a reliable person. We like the way you are working with our youth."

Brett tilted his head slightly to the side in a diffident matter, saying, "Always happy to help. I enjoy working with the staff and students at the polytechnic."

They watched several other people enter the cafe and seat themselves, with polite nods to Brett and Kinyanjui. The late afternoon sun had moved around to shine in the cafe windows. "Let's move to the air-conditioned section," Brett suggested. They carried their drinks farther inside. Brett asked Kinyanjui if he knew Maina.

"Yes, he is from my home area."

"Really, where are you from?"

"Murang'a. We are age mates. We shared the same circumcision knife."

"That means you are like brothers."

"Even closer than brothers. As you know, the circumcision ceremony produces a strong bond. Tell me, Bwana James, I hear that Mr. Emerson is the big man here."

Brett realized that he should be careful not to disclose too much as Kinyanjui could be fishing for information – not that he knew much. "I have not met him, but everyone says he is the main force behind the operation of the Zoo," acknowledged Brett, adding, "That is a long meeting Mr. Ochieng is having in there with Mr. Chengo."

Ignoring his comment, Kinyanjui said, "You met Hamud Sita I think?"

"Yes, a couple of times before he–"

"Before he was arrested," Kinyanjui completed Brett's sentence. "We are still…there are some matters…but I cannot speak of this."

Brett probed to find out what the meeting with Chengo was all about but Kinyanjui revealed nothing. Then he spoke of the area of the coast where the Zoo was located. Brett asked, "Do you know why access is so restricted on the headland?"

"No, that is a mystery to us."

"Is it because of the animals, or maybe some other resources?" Brett enquired.

"There are some sensitive areas along the coast. We need to protect the marine environment," was all Kinyanjui was prepared to say. It seemed with some relief that he noticed Ochieng in the corridor outside the cafe. He stood. "Thank you Mr. Brett. I am very pleased for the refreshment. When you visit Murang'a, I will show you our place. But you know of our excellent Kikuyu hospitality already, yes?" He rejoined Ochieng, they got into the police car and drove around the back of the kitchen block.

After they left, Brett returned to the cafe to sign the chit for the snacks when the ubiquitous Miles Jolly appeared. "They are over in the southeastern area now. What are they up to? I noticed Ochieng called you Mr. Bretton."

"Yes, I was surprised by that as I only ever use it on official documents. Kinyanjui thought he got it from my map application or the immigration form."

"Well he obviously has access to those. It's an unusual name," proffered Miles.

"Yes, I think it refers to a person from Brittany. But my father was an economist and he chose it because he admired the 1944 Bretton Woods agreement."

"Oh yes, I remember that. So, what did you two chat about?"

"Things at the Zoo, his home in Murang'a, a fellow in Dr. Phillips' office. He said they appreciate what I am doing in the polytechnic, and my work with the students."

"Beware of police giving compliments! Do you think he was pumping you for information?"

"Hard to tell. He may have been. I don't have much to tell that will be of interest to them. I don't know anything that goes on here!"

"Be grateful, and try to keep it that way. That would be my advice," chirped Miles. Brett shrugged. He noticed he had been shrugging quite a lot recently.

"Actually, I saw his kind words more as an apology for the aggressive grilling they gave me at the interview."

"Maybe you're right. Or perhaps you should also beware of police bearing *apologies!*" He thought for a while, and added, "I get uneasy when those two are creeping about asking questions."

"Why?"

"Oh – no reason in particular. It's just that they often seem to be harbingers of trouble." His face was smiling but his dark eyes revealed a deeper concern. As Miles waddled off towards the guest-housing block, Brett wondered if it was even a flash of fear he saw in his eyes. He could not tell. He was too late for windsurfing, but he still intended to go swimming.

A quarter of an hour later, Miles was sitting on the bench outside the church, chatting with Coreene and teasing the children, when the police car drove past and parked in front of the church. Ochieng got out and went into the church office. Miles and Coreene speculated on what was happening. After about ten minutes Ochieng came out and the car drove away. Miles wandered over to Steve's office and popped his head around the door. "So, you had a visit from Ochieng too did you?" Steve nodded. "What did he want?" asked Miles.

"I can't reveal any details other than that he was asking about Hamud Sita."

"What did you tell him?"

"Come on, I trust you Miles, but you know I can't tell you any details. Anyway, I revealed very little to Ochieng. I have learnt to be extremely circumspect in these situations."

"Very wise. Does he know you visited Sita in prison?"

"A leading question. He didn't mention that specifically, but he must know, and he was clearly trying to find out if I thought Sita was innocent."

"And?" Miles raised his bushy eyebrows. Steve thought he looked rather comical.

"I indicated what I have mentioned to a couple of other people, that I sometimes wonder about his guilt. Now, off you go, Miles, and stop squeezing me for confidential information." Steve took Miles' arm and ushered him towards the door. "Go on, otherwise I'll find a job for you in the church that requires you to sit and listen to my sermons every Sunday."

As he left, Miles turned and said, "You know I'm always happy to listen to what you have to say Steve – even when you are unwilling to actually tell me anything!"

The next evening, Brett's post contained a letter from Tony, expressing his confidence over the pending appointment, and trust that, with the Lord's strength, he and Jane would be able cope with whatever came up. Leaving the building, Brett noticed Miles walking with Marie-Anne and Len, who was whistling as usual. Brett joined them as he wanted to ask Len about using the windsurfer, but Miles dominated the conversation. "I must say, Len, that your whistle is pretty irritating at times."

"A cheerful whistle helps the work along," responded Len.

"But it sure annoys the neighbours," shot back Miles.

"Only the annoying ones."

"I was wondering, can we come to a compromise?" suggested Miles.

"What, I whistle half the time and you complain the other half?"

"No. I was thinking that you stop whistling and I'll end my complaining!"

Marie-Anne was enjoying this exchange, and said, "You're not going to win this one, Len!" All the while, Brett was waiting to speak.

As they reached the Moores' cage, Brett noticed Muzhere walking down to the beach, carrying a rolled-up mat. "Where's she going?" he asked.

"She goes down there to pray five times a day, in the shade beside that bush. She has a little shelter set up there – an enclosure of some kind – facing north," Miles told him. Len and Marie-Anne went inside. "She even goes out to the beach with her mat at night to pray. Probably to get away from my cassette tapes of Italian opera. Puccini usually drives her out of the place for at least half an hour. I tell her it's my revenge for the smell of her cooking fish at 3am during Ramadan! We have our little jokes, and get on quite well. She's worked with me for over 12 years. We have no illusions about each other."

"That's interesting," said Brett.

In a serious tone, Miles continued, "Actually, she seems quite worried about my health, and keeps suggesting strange brews and potions. I humour her by trying them but I don't have her faith in their curative properties."

The following Sunday, after the church service, Brigadier and Violet Ridge-Taylor followed up on their lunch invitation, and directed Brett towards their Range Rover. He sat at the back, enjoying the view from the high seat, as they drove into Mwakindini. In the restaurant, the brigadier took the menu and examined it enthusiastically. "Right, BMJ, let's have a look at the agenda – develop a battle plan for the meal, so to speak." After they ordered, and Brett was delicately spreading his serviette on his lap, the brigadier glared at him, "So, tell me young man, are you 'Military' at all?"

"Pardon?"

"Well, mean-to-say, BMJ, do you have a *military* background?"

"No, sorry I don't."

"Well then, were you in the cadets?"

"No. Sorry."

"Oh." He paused. "Scouts?"

"Yes, I was a scout for several years," Brett replied, with some relief.

"Wonderful! Jolly fine organization. Jolly fine. Mean-to-say, you do have a military bent in you then?"

"Well, not really. But I have a great-uncle who was a Commodore in the Navy."

"Well well! Amazing. Splendid. I could tell you had a military heritage. Obvious to me," Thomas said, turning to Violet, nudging her with his elbow, and grinning jubilantly.

During the meal, with excellent food and attentive service, the Ridge-Taylors spoke of their lives in the Central Province, and many aspects of the Zoo. Brett found their perspectives on events and people fascinating, although they acknowledged that they were getting a bit out of touch. Both Violet and Thomas were interested to hear of Brett's work in Nyeri as they knew the area. They discovered they had a few mutual acquaintances, mainly through the Anglican church. They chatted for a long time, as other patrons gradually left the restaurant.

"It's December already. I must get a new diary," Thomas stated.

Violet gave a weak smile, "You know Brett, he is stubbornly insisting on buying himself a five-year diary. I told him it was a waste as he wouldn't get the use out of it."

"The old diary is finished, so I need to get a new one."

"Yes, but maybe a one-year diary would do?"

"Ha, I like to put positive thinking into action. You won't get rid of me within a year – unless you're planning something sinister. Are you Vi?"

"I'm just joking, my dear. You can have a five-year diary if you like. What do you think Brett, dear?"

"Oh, none of my business…"

"You must have an opinion though," prompted Thomas.

"Well, it probably isn't an insurmountable expense, so why not?"

Thomas beamed triumphantly, "Good! That shows positive thinking. Demonstrates the finely tuned military mind at work: think strategically, evaluate the cost, plan ahead, get your equipment in order. A five-year diary makes perfect sense at my age."

As they had finished the main course, Brett began to look around hopefully for the dessert menu. Violet disappointed him by saying, "Whew, that's enough food."

But Thomas said, "You'll want a sweet I expect, then we'll have coffee. They have a fine stock here, and they brew it fresh. I hate stewed coffee. Some places boil the living daylights out it."

Brett thought it might be a good moment to gently ask a few questions about the wall and the headland beyond. He tried to sound casual as he said, "You have a lovely location at the end in N-1. Do you ever experience much of the headland to the east of your cage?"

Violet looked intently at her table serviette, but battle-hardened Thomas simply replied, "No. It's out of bounds. Off limits. A necessary barrier."

"I imagine it's really wild and beautiful out there. It's a shame there is not at least some controlled access."

"It's a nature preserve. Mean-to-say, we don't want every Tom, Dick and Harry trampling through there, do we? It's important to keep it unspoilt. Keep the troops this side of the battle line, eh? There's lots of beauty in the Zoo without going outside the camp, you know, BMJ."

"I wonder if Mr. Emerson would allow me to visit that side sometime. I'd respect all the rules of course."

"No! It was established near the beginning of the Zoo that we should not breach that wall, so that's the way it is. We all accept that. It's never caused a problem."

"I suppose the dogs patrolling the other side of the wall are a pretty effective deterrent?"

"Yes, although they kick up a heck of a row sometimes."

Violet frowned, "Don't say 'heck' dear." Turning to Brett, she added brightly, "They are our security. And we do have the extra space in N-1 to house them along that side. As you know, ours is a double-sized cage."

"Njuguna does a marvellous job at keeping them well fed and under control."

"If you are anxious to see how the promontory looks, you could go out with Miles on one of his fishing trips. He sometimes gets the local chaps to take him out beyond the headland," suggested Violet.

"Yes, he likes to do deep-sea fishing. For pelagic fish, such as sailfish and marlin, I believe. Not that his health is up to it. He has to be careful," noted Thomas.

"Also, he can't be very good at it because he never comes back with any actual fish!" laughed Violet.

The conversation about the wall slumped towards an inconclusive end with a few more benign comments and noncommittal replies to Brett's further enquiries. They watched in admiration as he consumed his large pie, while he concluded that their minds were closed and they would countenance no further discussion. If they knew anything else, they were not going to tell him. They seemed to communicate a naive acceptance of the boundary. But Brett had a definite itch to know more.

After the meal, they had coffee which was carefully analyzed by the connoisseurs. It generated reminiscences from them about their coffee-farming experiences. Thomas explained, "Kenya's Arabica coffee is among the finest in the world. We are fortunate to have it readily available in its pure form. It's often purchased internationally to be blended with other inferior coffees. The Kenyan flavour is deep with a rich aroma. That's due, in part, to our fecund volcanic soils." They described their farm, noting that the quality and yields were generally good, although they had been located near the southern range of the productive coffee-farming region in Kenya.

Part 1: Mysteries

They drove back to the Zoo. The Ridge-Taylors dropped Brett outside his cage. Thomas struggled to get out of the car. He shook Brett's hand vigorously and, looking down at him, said, "Well, goodbye BMJ old chap. Nice to discuss tactics with a military-minded man. Mean-to-say, Violet doesn't get some of the strategic stuff, you know." He winked as he climbed back into the Range Rover, adding, "You should have a chat with my neighbour Peter. He's 'Military', you know. Got a fine strategic mind – and a few stories to relate, I can tell you. Yes, have a chat with Major Lancaster. Jolly fine fellow. Well, must be off. Goodbye."

December arrived, and Brett knew his annual report to his supporters was due. Also, another idea was forming in his mind. He had asked several people if he could meet Henry Emerson, but it was looking unlikely that Henry would agree, so Brett was planning to write him a letter with some suggestions. He felt it would be more effective if it could be typed, so he intended to ask the college secretary if he could use her typewriter for both projects.

Late one afternoon Brett met the boy who had shown him around the Muslim quarter. "I have a baby goat. You want to see him?" he beamed. Brett was glad of an excuse to look at the wall and gate again. They walked along the main pathway and were soon accompanied into a secluded area by Faiz, the Imam. They found the goat sitting on straw in a boarded-off corner. It was tiny and pure white. The lad pushed it towards Brett and it butted him gently with its rounded head. Brett made appreciative comments, knowing that goats were prized creatures. Faiz strolled back with Brett, stepping around a couple of donkeys tethered to a fence. Faiz was wearing his white flowing tunic, the *kanzu*, and the traditional round white cloth cap, a *kofia*. Rounding a corner as they entered the square just south of the Emersons' cage, two ladies almost bumped into them. They were each wearing the black full head and body covering worn on the coast. Brett looked at the wall and noticed two security cameras, one directed at the heavy gate in the wall.

He asked Faiz, "This gate…is it used?"

"People come through."

"The Emersons?"

"Yes, and their helpers."

"Staff?"

"Yes, their helpers. Some of our community," said Faiz. *I suppose they would need some staff over in their place*, thought Brett. He asked, "Through this gate? It doesn't seem to be used."

Faiz was casual as he answered. "It is sometimes used. But I heard there may be another way."

They walked along the wall towards the shore. They reached the end of the wall at the high-tide line. The fence began there and extended out into the deep water, just as it did on the northern beach. "Is it possible to go that way, towards the east, over to the headland?"

"No. Impossible. It cannot be done." Faiz was emphatic.

"Around the end of the fence out there at very low tide?" suggested Brett.

"No, that is difficult. It is dangerous." He squinted out towards the open sea and added, "Some fishermen take their canoes there, but only at high tide because of the rocks. When the tide is low there are small channels out past the reef. The local fisherman know them well."

An old man with a long grey beard had been peering at them over a low wall. Suddenly he shouted, "*Mzungu*, whiteman! *Mzungu, Mzungu!*" He shouted some more, but Faiz ignored him. The man's imprecations unsettled Brett as they walked along the shore.

Faiz reassured him, "Give no attention to him. That mzee, he is harmless." Brett looked closely at the obviously neglected mosque. It reminded him of some ruins he had seen farther south. The small dome had a hole in it where the stone roof had fallen in. It seemed to have been temporarily repaired. Several walls had collapsed, but most of the main building seemed usable. Faiz stopped on the stepped platform outside but he did not invite Brett to enter.

As Brett left Faiz, and headed back towards the central building complex, he noticed a large grey rain cloud forming in the blue sky above. He returned to the cafe to continue with his planned supper.

After his meal, Brett left the central building at the same time as Peter. They stopped in the entrance just as the welcome rain began to fall. They appreciated its refreshment. "Any plans for Christmas?" asked Brett.

"No. Just the usual…alone, thinking of some things that used to be – and other things that might have been. Ghosts of Christmases past, you might say."

"That's a shame. I'm sure you won't be alone."

"Probably not. I'll be busy too."

Brett was surprised and asked, "Busy? I thought you were well-and-truly retired."

Peter gave him a sidelong glance, "I still have contacts, do small favours here and there, discreetly deliver confidential messages, letters etc. You know, helping friends, now and then."

After the rain had eased off, Peter started to stroll towards the eastern path. Brett took the opportunity to walk with him along the western side of the wall, stepping around the rapidly draining puddles in the damp murram surface. He asked about the security cameras. Peter smiled and said, "They don't work, but they may still fool a few people."

"They don't work?"

"Pardon?"

"I am surprised they don't work." Brett noticed Peter was not hearing him well.

"Only one of them was real and that broke years ago. Len fabricated a few dummy cameras from odd tubes and plastic boxes and we painted and mounted them. There's one up there," Peter said, pointing to a dusty, cobweb-enveloped assembly under the eaves.

"That's funny," Brett said.

"There is no risk that anyone is going to come over the wall from the east, and that barbed wire is enough of a deterrent to anyone attempting to cross from this side. In any case, why would they even want to?" Peter stood looking at the faded lettering and then stared at the top the wall, observing, "Some of that security wire is sagging and seems broken in places. Probably rusted away."

Brett looked more closely at the high wall to the south and saw part of a heavy stone construction built into it. It linked across to the Emersons' cage. He saw what looked like buttresses and battlements, giving it an imposing, fortress-like appearance. "That's pretty solid construction," observed Brett.

"Yes. You know, we used to call it 'Kismet Kantara'. That was Henry's and Louise's poetic name for the edifice – the bridge of fate – or something like that!" He laughed, shielding his eyes against the southern sun. "Some of those wall structures date back to the Portuguese era I think – maybe even earlier. There used to be a walkway along the parapet at the top. I haven't been up there for years. I doubt if it's ever used now." A small plane flew low across the headland, over the Zoo and banked towards the west. Peter followed its path. "Five seater," he said, continuing to watch as it receded to a tiny dot in the sky. Then, looking at Brett as though he had just noticed him, he added, "Never quite sure what they are up to these days."

As they walked, Brett recounted Miles Jolly's complaining of Len's whistling. Peter said, "Miles is a clown. He likes to portray himself as a peripatetic purveyor of mirth."

"Yes, he's fun. And he has helped me with a lot of useful information," said Brett.

Suddenly, Peter added a strange comment, "Seeing you chatting with Miles made me think. You know, he's a one-way valve. He takes in information and absorbs it like – like a sea sponge. But he rarely supplies it – at least, not gratuitously, and always in accordance with his calculated purposes."

Brett was taken aback by this, "I thought you two were friends."

"What's that? Umm – well, not really. We've known each other a long time, true, but I find it hard to trust him. Enough said!" Brett did not reply, but he wondered why Peter had said that.

They continued walking the short distance along the wall until they came to the Ridge-Taylors' cage. As they approached, the dogs started howling. Brett and Peter stood beside a storage shed built against the wall. Njuguna's voice was heard inside quietening the animals, and then the door slowly opened and his head appeared. He smiled when he saw them and stood in the doorway, grinning. "Is that shed used to keep the dog food?" Brett asked Peter.

"Yes, and tools – rakes, shovels, and brooms. Njuguna keeps the bare section along the wall clear of debris." A pile of palm fronds was stacked alongside the wall. "The women use those fronds for weaving their coconut thatching."

Part 1: Mysteries

Peter's man Mwangi appeared at the side door, smiling at Brett. They waved and Brett call out a Kikuyu greeting. "You're a budding linguist, aren't you?" said Peter. "Bye for now."

As Brett strolled along the firm sand to his cage, he tried to process some of Peter's comments. Those, along with Louise's evasive replies, heightened his curiosity. They were additional clues in the complex Zoo crossword puzzle that his mind was struggling to understand and – perhaps soon – solve.

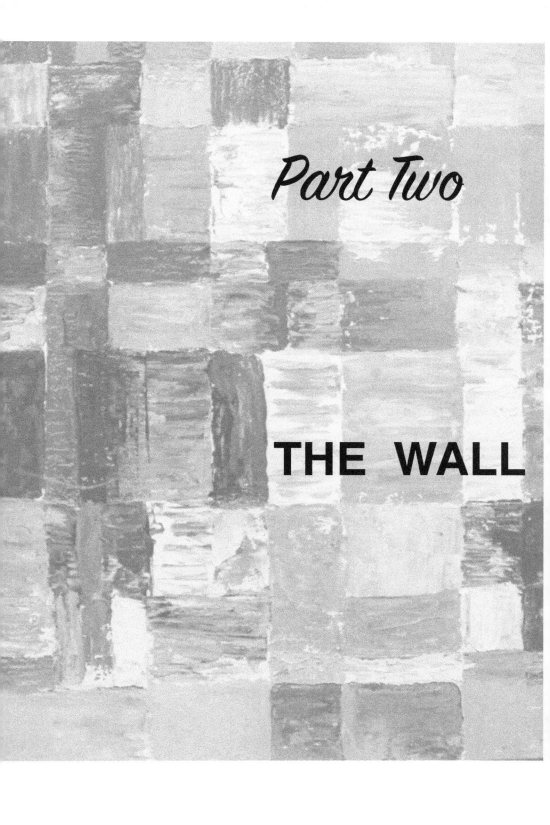

The fictional characters introduced in Part Two

Richard Beaton, Henry's friend, upcountry farm manager
Taran Sembhi, antiques shop operator, Mombasa
Mechanic in Malindi
Tej Singh, owner of Excel Auto garage in Mwakindini
Alan Emerson, Louise's son in Australia, with wife and three children
Geoffrey Matherton, the father in Matherton & Son, lawyers

7

*"I wonder why the police are showing
such a keen interest in your area?"*
John Phillips

It was the first week of December 1984 when Louise spoke to Brett about driving to Mombasa together. He had mentioned a planned lunch meeting with John Phillips who was in Mombasa for a conference. She realized it was the same day as a Kenyan Women's Society event. "Let's go together. We can share the driving."

"I also have to get some supplies, and I'd like to enquire about having a safari suit made," said Brett.

"That's fine, we'll have time for those things. But you won't be able to come to the Kenyan Women's Society meeting; you don't qualify!"

"Because I'm not a Kenyan?"

A few days later, as Louise drove across to collect Brett, she spoke with Miles which delayed her a few minutes. She explained to Brett as they left the Zoo compound, "Miles was right there as I left."

Brett smiled, "Miles is always 'right there' – wherever that is! He's constantly hanging around and asking questions! He is very curious about what the police are investigating." Driving past the shop at the entrance, they saw the owner standing outside, dressed in a formal grey suit with tails. He was wearing his black top hat. When he recognized the car he gave a princely wave and bowed very formally. "Is he okay?" enquired Brett.

Part 2: The Wall

"Oh yes, he's completely rational. He's just eccentric, that's all. He sees himself as a member of the British aristocracy. Why not? I like to think the Zoo community is broad enough to accommodate a few unconventional characters. Even Miles! In spite of his many faults, the one thing I admire about Miles is his alertness and attention to detail. I'm sure it has aided his survival in a hostile world."

"A hostile world?"

"Yes, haven't you noticed? It's a hostile world." Brett thought about that as he sat back enjoying the comfort of the soft suspension and efficient air-conditioning of the Peugeot 504. He was grateful that the world didn't feel at all hostile to him at that moment, although he had some general unease about suspicious things at the Zoo.

Louise had to stop in Malindi to drop something off at a photographic supply shop. Brett remained in the car, partly to continue appreciating the air-conditioning, but also as a guard. "I'll bark at anyone who comes close," he assured her. She returned, carrying a package that she silently placed in her bag at the back of the car. She covered it with a *kanga*, a patterned local cloth. He noticed she was dressed smartly for her meeting. She had a white handbag and was wearing white shoes and a turquoise and blue paisley-patterned dress. She looked elegant with her metallic-grey hair.

As they continued south, with Louise driving, Brett asked her to continue the story of how she and Henry first met. She described when they were introduced. "Mutual friends were performing in a concert so we went as part of a foursome. We admired and liked each other a lot, which, as Henry remarked at the time, was a pretty good basis for a long-term friendship! We were married after the war, in 1946 in Nairobi. Later, we did some travelling, including some memorable times in England. Things were picking up there – in the 1950s – as they recovered after the war. We even visited the new developments where my parents' house used to be." She was silent for a while, and then continued, "Once the rebuilding programme was underway, there was a tremendous feeling of hope. People were anxious to put behind them the oppressive memories of the war, and look ahead to a bright future."

"I was born in 1954. So, of course, everyone was optimistic!"

Louise smiled. "1954? Umm…1954. 1949 was…" as the words faded, her thoughts seemed to drift.

Brett watched her and ventured to ask. "And your family?"

"No family to speak of. My family is of no significance, really." Her curt reply surprised him and he felt that, the more she told him about herself, the less he knew her.

Louise perked up, "In the mid 1950s we travelled a lot in Europe and North Africa. Algeria was special to us, as was Morocco. So many recollections for me, and significant memories for Henry too. Those were good years." They travelled in silence for a while, both thinking. Louise seemed to remember something. "We almost became farmers, you know. Before we got interested in the Zoo concept, Henry and I invested in a coffee farm. He received a substantial gratuity and I had some savings, so we went into partnership with Richard Beaton. He had experience managing a coffee farm so, together, we purchased one in Nyeri district. Once the Zoo idea took off, we left our investment in the farm and Richard managed the whole affair. Imagine, I could now be the wealthy wife of a retired coffee-farm owner!"

"Things must be difficult now, with Henry's limitations."

"Everything is about the same as it has been the last couple of years." Again, she paused for a long while. "We all carry on as best we can. We adjust to the onslaught of increasing years. Of course, it's not the way it was in the early days of the Zoo, with the heady excitement at the possibilities – some of which came true."

"When was it set up?"

"In the early 1960s. The construction, and all the negotiations, and legal paperwork and so on, took a long time."

"Who was the inspiration behind the concept, Henry?"

"Yes, Heinrick had the vision of a mixed community village with different parts for Africans, Whites, and Muslims. There are some Hindus and other Asians too. As you know, the concept was separation…individual retreats to go back to, and community mixing for social events. You have seen how it works, right?"

"Oh yes, I have seen the good community spirit and intermixing, including the different religions."

"The intention was not to separate people, but it's just set up that way to help people feel comfortable with their neighbours. They live with their particular group, in their own cages. Look, we're nearing the German-run

Part 2: The Wall

Seaside Lodge. Let's stop for coffee. I enjoy the atmosphere there, and I like hearing German spoken again." Brett wondered if her interest in German related to her using the name Heinrick, but he was reluctant to ask another personal question.

After the brief break, Louise asked Brett to drive. As they passed through the town where the cyclist had been killed, he showed Louise the exact place. She shuddered slightly. He saw that the wrecked stall had been rebuilt. As Brett continued driving carefully along the coast road, past a police check, Louise seemed relaxed so he felt bold enough to raise the matter of the wall and the number of regulations in force in the Zoo.

Louise replied, "The rules are a legacy of the initial set-up by Heinrick, but they still serve us well, I think." *There it is again*, Brett thought, *she's calling him Heinrick*. Louise continued. "He was very definite about the regulations in the early months of the Zoo. He wanted no noise so there is a ban on church bells and the muezzin call. Still, he strove to safeguard various minorities, but within limits because he knew from history that sometimes a very small tail has wagged an extremely large dog. He wanted to avoid minorities having too much influence or taking over. Heinrick was acutely aware of the dangers of militant minorities, and their incremental ratchet effect, if they became too influential."

"Was he thinking of the war?"

"Partly, yes, the war. He saw the leverage that a slight minority can exert. It definitely coloured his thinking."

They drove to Biashara Street in Mombasa because Louise needed some fabric and Brett hoped to order a tailor-made safari suit. Louise knew her way around and directed him first to a small bespoke tailor where he chose the traditional khaki weave. Louise left Brett to be measured, and explained where she would be. After the quick measuring process, he gave the minimum deposit required and followed the tailor's assistant to find Louise.

Entering the haberdasher's shop was like stepping into another world. The heady aroma of the smoking joss-sticks, the substantial bustling ladies in their saris, and the mounds of brightly coloured cloths made his head spin. Every table was laden with mounds of multicoloured materials, stacked in wobbly piles as high as gravity would allow. The walls were lined with vast shelving racks, again stuffed to the ceiling with every imaginable hue and texture of material. Louise was choosing cloth to repair some seats and make cushion covers. After deciding on two rolls of fabric, the search began for sewing notions, elastic, and lacing. Louise gleefully scanned the lace edging, coils of piping, stiff facing, and frilly bands of trim. Brett was becoming anxious about their lunch arrangements. Then the slow wrapping process began, so Louise said they'd return that afternoon. They dashed along the steamy streets to their respective noon appointments. They agreed to meet by the car in two hours.

On the second-floor Palm Tree restaurant, Brett was pleased to see John Phillips sitting at a table near the window. Dr. Phillips looked at him and asked, "Are you alright? You look like a piece of chewed sugar cane. What happened to you?"

"Shopping for sewing supplies with a woman. Choosing fabric and wadding for cushions. It can take all the stuffing out of you! Plus hurtling over here in the midday heat. How are you? Nice to see you again, John."

"Fine thanks. Here, let me order you a drink," he said glancing towards the nearby waiter. John sympathized over the shopping, "I understand. I sometimes get dragged into helping my wife in these places." Once the drinks had been ordered, Brett went to wash his hands and face while John did a preliminary investigation of the menu.

Returning to the table, Brett suggested, "Let's each pay for our own. Last time, questions were raised!"

"Oh?"

"I had a visit from the police who asked who paid for our first meal together."

"Ah yes, you had visitors. I heard – in a blue car."

"How did you know?"

"One of my staff mentioned it. You remember Maina?"

"Yes. The government official in your office. Kinyanjui told me they shared the circumcision blade."

"That makes a strong bond between them. So, Kinyanjui interviewed you? Those fellows…they are digging into everything."

"I wondered if I should warn you, but I wasn't sure how," Brett said.

"No, not necessary. Thanks, but everything is above board. It's just that—" The waiter brought their drinks.

Brett asked John, "How did the detective, Ochieng, know about us meeting on the plane? And us sitting together?"

"Maina, again, almost certainly. When you came to our office I explained to him how we had met. But why would they bother to follow up…"

"Just because I requested a map?"

"No, it doesn't make sense. I wonder why they are showing such a keen interest in your area. I know security is tight farther north near the Somali border, with the recent bandit attacks, but south of the Tana River, down around Malindi and Mombasa…it should be just a matter of keeping the tourists safe – and behaving themselves."

"There are no obvious peculiar activities at the Zoo, just ambiguous warnings and a few baffling restrictions, such as no access to the headland beyond the wall," added Brett.

John stared out of the window at the glaring, azure, cloudless sky. "I wonder if something's going on there? Could there be precious minerals? Perhaps gold? In years past there were rumours of gold found down towards the south, but nothing came of it. There is even speculation that this area was the basis of the King Solomon's Mines legends."

"Well, they are concerned about something. There's been an arrest, and they have interviewed our Executive Officer," Brett informed him.

"Maybe it's an internal matter within the Zoo." John thought for a while and added, "Of course, there are pirates off the coast but that's all a long way out to sea and wouldn't affect the mainland coastal region. Now you've got me curious. This conference I'm attending covers some new computer-enhanced imaging techniques. Tell you what, if we get the software, I'll try to run through the satellite data on your peninsula. It might sharpen up the detail a bit – maybe reveal if there is evidence of digging, an old quarry, or any resource exploration. On another subject, did Kinyanjui come to interview you a second time? Maina hinted as much."

"Not officially. I saw him outside the office and invited him for an afternoon snack. It was quite pleasant. He may have been listening for information, but it was an informal discussion."

"Umm. I'll see what sort of interest Maina is showing in that area – maybe ask him a few innocent questions and see if he reveals anything."

"Is he likely to tell you much?" queried Brett.

"He's actually very open with information, at least when he knows it's safe to reveal it. It's what he *doesn't* tell me that makes me anxious!"

After they had ordered dessert and coffee, Brett expressed his thanks for any insights John could give, but assured him it was only curiosity that motivated him to find out why people were being questioned by the police, "…as though we were criminals or something."

"I'll see what I can pry from Maina. He's got connections with several folks who may have some idea. I can probably trade it for some harmless, but ostensibly confidential, information he has been pestering me about!"

"Thank you. Only if it can be done without causing difficulty for you."

"No problem. I hate all this intrigue but we have to protect our clients' confidential information. I'd like to visit this Zoo of yours sometime. Maybe we'll arrange it when I'm at the coast again."

"Certainly. You can even stay at the guest house if you don't mind our basic accommodation."

Brett returned to Louise's car and waited nearby in the shade. It was just after two when Louise joined him. They returned to the haberdasher's shop and collected the huge package of purchases. Brett struggled to carry it back to the car through the crowds on the narrow pavement. "Now we should head over to the textbook shop as I need some supplies," Brett told Louise.

"First, I need to see Mr. Sembhi, just along here," Louise replied. "You'll find his place fascinating."

They dove down a narrow alley and entered a half-concealed door in a recess. It led to a flight of steep stairs. On the dark landing, Brett saw a grilled window and a door. Inside he was introduced to the owner, Mr. Taran Sembhi. He was imposing, and as slender as a bamboo pole. He had a distinctive profile, high sloping forehead, and aquiline nose. His skin was very brown, setting off his striking grey hair. Brett sensed that he was somewhat cool towards him, almost as though he regarded customers as an intrusion into his private domain. Looking around, Brett saw the place was a mass of ancient objects and a jumble of dusty artifacts, with every inch of wall space covered in paintings and prints. "This may interest you,"

Part 2: The Wall

Sembhi said, casually pointing to a frame containing a faded map of a coastal peninsula.

"That's the Zoo," said Louise. Brett was intrigued, as he had been wanting to get an overview of the area. He studied the print, trying to absorb as many details as possible of rocky outcrops and projections of coral out into the waters.

"How old is this? When was it made?"

Sembhi replied, "Late nineteenth century. A pre-colonial cartographer drew it. See the name: *'Kisiwa wa Kima'*, Monkey Island. I doubt if it was ever a true island as the connection here – the narrow section – was probably never covered in water."

"It might as well be an island for all the access we have to it these days!" blurted out Brett. He immediately realized that he had committed a *faux pas* and apologized to them both. There was an awkward silence, so Brett politely asked what it might be worth.

"Priceless," declared Sembhi in a peremptory tone.

"I imagine that it would be worth a lot to a collector."

"I am a collector," came the curt reply.

Things seemed to be getting tense, so Louise intervened, "Brett dear, I'm not sure if I locked my side door on the car. Would you mind checking please." She handed him the keys. "I'll be down in a minute or two." Brett left the upper shop and returned to the car. When Louise returned, she was holding a bulky envelope. As she climbed in the passenger seat, she placed it in the basket on the floor behind her, next to the large package of materials, carefully covering it with the kanga, her sarong.

"What's in there?" Brett asked.

"Documents. We don't have much time, but let's see if we can park easily at the textbook place. What is it you need?" she asked irritably. Brett drove through the Mombasa traffic, describing the books Katana had asked him to check, and the art materials he wanted. She didn't seem to be listening.

"Whose idea was it to take me to that unpleasant fellow, Sembhi?"

Louise hesitated and replied, "Miles Jolly suggested it."

"Why?"

"You know that *Biashara* means buying and selling?"

"Yes, what of it?"

"It's a good place for those things."

"There was plenty to buy, I could see that."

"Mr. Sembhi is a collector." "Yes, he told me."

"He collects things."

"I imagine he would. That's what collectors do. His shop sort of reinforces that impression too!"

"He has permits and certificates."

"I suppose he would have."

"Yes, but he's an expert in his field."

"We all are," said Brett, wondering what she was getting at.

"I may have some things to take to him. I mean, we have some antiques that he might be able to sell for us. Would you be able to remember his shop if I need something delivered there – at some time, in the future?" A car swung out in front of them.

"If I don't die first." Brett yelled as he braked suddenly.

"You are driving so slowly that he probably thought you were looking for a place to park."

"I was driving slowly to avoid that hand cart being wheeled at us from the right side of the road, over there," countered Brett.

Louise apologized, "Sorry I didn't see that. You just concentrate on your driving."

Through Brett's mind flashed: *And you just concentrate on your scheming. How is Miles connected to all of this?*

They were pleased to see an empty parking place near the large stationers, so they swung in there. As Brett entered the shop, Louise said, "I'll stay near the door and watch. That package can't be seen through the dark windows, but I want to keep an eye on things. You go ahead."

Brett found his way to the book section and quickly saw three of the textbooks he needed, but he was told that two others on Katana's list were unavailable. Then he looked at the art supplies, and selected some colours as he hoped to do some painting during the Christmas holiday. After paying cash for the books and paints, he returned to the car. Louise met him, "That was quick. Get what you wanted?" He told her he would have liked to have stayed longer, but he would have to return in a few weeks to pick up his safari suit, and he would have more time then.

He added, "I think we should start home if we are going to make it before dark." Easing his way through the afternoon traffic, he told her about the oil paints he had chosen. "I bought more cobalt blue and ultramarine blue." Louise silently watched the traffic ahead as he drove past the huge imitation elephant tusks arching across the road. "I rarely use pure green. I prefer to mix it from blue and some of the yellows."

As the traffic thinned, Louise listened in a more relaxed way, and said, "I like wearing green as it brings out the colour in my eyes. But it's a hard colour to match."

"Chameleons have the same trouble!" joked Brett.

"That's the first time I've been compared to a chameleon! That reminds me of something I haven't thought about for a long time. I used to describe Henry as a chameleon when he was on some of his – er – assignments."

"During the war?"

"And afterwards, but I cannot speak of those things now." Louise's tone was firm. They drove in silence for a while. Then she said, "I can take over the driving any time. We are well clear of the Mombasa traffic now."

"I'm fine at the moment thanks. Maybe we'll stop for a cold drink sometime. I expect you know a suitable place."

Looking past Brett through the window at the occasional glimpses of the ocean, Louise nodded and then asked, "Why are you so fascinated by what is the other side of the wall at our place?"

"I don't know, it may be just curiosity or perhaps I see it as kind of challenge. I was thinking the other day that the mysterious and inaccessible headland matches something I read in a Thomas Hardy novel. Are you familiar with Hardy's work?"

"Yes, I have read a couple of his novels."

"Have you read 'Jude the Obscure'?"

"No, I haven't."

"It's one of the most oppressive and utterly depressing novels ever written, I believe! But he describes so well the lure of the universities and their complete remoteness and total inaccessibility to the poor man, Jude. It seemed to Jude that the universities, which he so desired to enter, were protected behind an impenetrable physical barrier. But they also presented social barriers based on his impoverishment and low social standing. It may not be a complete parallel with the Zoo, but the similarities intrigued me – especially my strange attraction to what lies beyond an impregnable barricade."

Louise listened carefully and was about to say something, but seemed to decide against it. Instead, she gave a bland response, "Well, whatever attraction it holds for you, you will have to be content with life on this side of the wall. There are plenty of interesting and attractive activities to occupy your curiosity, I'm sure." Brett nodded his agreement. He was about to mention his idea of writing a letter to Henry but decided to say nothing as he planned to send it formally through the Zoo office. Instead, he spoke of the euphorbia and the spiky aloe plants along the wall. "Were they planted as a deterrent? The euphorbia has a sap which can burn the skin, right?"

"Yes. That one is struggling as it normally flourishes in the higher plains but Henry brought the plant down and nursed it along. There are some Spanish Bayonets and sisal plants there too. Stay clear of their thorny edges."

Later, when Louise was driving again, they spoke of the leadership in the Zoo, security, and Peter's role as the *de facto* security officer. Brett said, "I imagine you and Henry must have known Peter for a long time."

Louise glanced at Brett and responded briefly. "Yes. There is a bit of history there. All water under the bridge." She thought further and sighed, "Many bridges. I don't think Peter is well. He smokes too much and he seems to be losing his hearing. But he's too stubborn to admit it and get hearing aids."

As they drove through Malindi, Louise noticed the car dealership. "Steve and Coreene need a more reliable car so I am going to talk to the Peugeot dealer and see if they have a smaller car for me, so the Brandons can have this one."

"That would be great. They would appreciate the extra space."

"Yes, this is too large for my needs now, and Heinrick–"

"Henry?" Brett interrupted.

"Yes. This car would suit them well."

Brett felt uncomfortable challenging her on her husband's name, so he changed the subject, "It's getting dark. In Nyeri they'd say this is the time the thieves come out because their movements are not so easily detected among the crowds rushing to get home before nightfall."

She said, "Peter carries a gun when travelling. Of course it's hidden in his Land Rover but he has it with him, especially on safari."

"For wild animals?"

"For anything. Any emergency. We don't hunt animals now of course. Don't tell him I mentioned it. He keeps it in a concealed compartment just behind the battery. He built a small enclosure there. He has another box on the other side welded to the lower inside engine compartment. He stores ammunition in there. A few people know about it – including his trusted mechanic in Malindi, no doubt."

"Let's hope he could retrieve the weapon in time if he encounters some threat on the road. How does he get it past the police checks?"

"I've no idea. It's well hidden I suppose. Things may be getting tense in the country. It partly depends on the seasonal rains and how good the food supplies are."

After some thought, Brett said, "I suppose our only real security is in God as our protector."

After a brief pause, Louise replied, "As you know, I'm pretty lukewarm on religion." There was a long silence as Louise watched the matatu in front of them, swerving and wobbling with its heavy load of passengers stuffed inside, and three carefree youths standing on the rear bumper and waving wildly. "That one looks like a demented windmill!" she said. They looked at the massive load of vegetables and housewares piled precariously on the roof. Brett was silent. She said. "Coreene and I have had some good discussions. Henry and I were always a bit sceptical about organized religion. It's alright for individuals, of course, and I see their religions satisfy some deeper need. That's fine as long as they keep it to themselves."

"But that's not what Jesus told us to do! He said we should tell others His teaching. In any case, isn't it normal to share good news? That's what we do in every other sphere of life."

"I suppose so…now you express it that way."

"But we should only do it in love. Jesus even said we should love our enemies."

Louise exhaled, "Love! I don't see much love among some of my neighbours."

"Christians still need to show them love. It's a command for us. You see, the false ideologies are the problem, not the people. They are victims."

"Try telling that to Faiz, the part-time Imam over there."

"Part time?"

"He does other work too, teaching and some carpentry I believe."

"Jesus was a carpenter. Perhaps I will talk to Faiz on some deeper issues if I get a chance."

"Good luck. You know, I've lived close to that community for a long time. I hear things. I see things. I'm a nurse. The women talk to me about their lives."

"It's got dark very quickly," said Brett.

"Yes. It has. Darkness. I see it."

Brett told her that, since arriving at the Zoo, he was making a conscious effort to use Steve's sermons as a foundation to study many aspects of the Christian faith. He was determined to master the basic concepts and terminology in order to clarify his own thinking, and be ready to give a clear answer to anyone who asked him questions. Louise supplied such a question: "Aren't all religions just different expressions of a basic human desire for meaning and a faith of some kind to cling to – to help us all cope with the challenges and hardships of life?" She paused. "Maybe I should have a serious chat with Coreene sometime."

"Me too, as there is so much I don't know, and I have lots of questions."

"I'm sure you do!"

"Steve told me Christianity represents love and truth."

"I'm not interested in heavy theology, but Henry and I appreciated the lovely Muslim staff who have worked for us over many years. We have relied on them a lot and developed wonderful relationships with them – even now with all the domestic tasks and practical duties in our cage and around the compound."

"I met your manservant, Mjuhgiuna, and I have seen two young women working with you."

"Yes, they are gaining practical experience and developing marketable skills as I train them in the household activities. I help them learn more about sewing and cooking too, plus improving their English. Perhaps, one day, that will lift them out of their circumstances. They have taught me a lot about their culture and customs, and even advise me on how to deal with certain intercultural situations that crop up."

Louise thought for a few moments and then said, "Sorry, I don't mean to criticize your beliefs. They are good for you I know. As I say, fine, as long as everyone keeps it to themselves. We need have no fear of foreign teachings influencing the well-established values and lifestyles of western democracies. Our freedoms are so well entrenched. Your Christian principles and practices are deeply embedded in our culture. They are safe."

Brett nodded, then noted, "We are near the Zoo."

Louise said, "Can you help me unload my things and then I'll drop you off at your cage?"

He helped her carry out the shopping and her basket with the mysterious envelopes she had collected, which he pretended not to notice. Then she looped back around the road and dropped him off at his cage. As he retrieved his supplies from the back, he noticed a beige card wedged behind the passenger seat. He pulled it out and read 'CPZ 2pm 28th'. He handed it to Louise who looked at it and said, "Oh, where did that come from? It's old. Thanks very much for your help today. Interesting discussions too. Goodnight."

8

"The place is called Kisiwa wa Kima, Monkey Island.
Henry researched the monkeys — to his cost.
One could spend a long time there — in isolation."
After that cryptic introspection, Peter Lancaster was silent.

Brett's days following his tiring trip to Mombasa were filled with routine teaching and paperwork. He had used the Jamhuri Day Independence celebration on the 12th of December to draft an outline for both his annual report and his letter to Henry Emerson. He felt well prepared for those typing tasks when he could arrange to do them. Also, he had set aside time to pray for Tony's medical appointment in England, and he asked Steve to remember that in prayer too.

The northeast winds were well established on the coast. As they approached the third week of December, Brett saw the sun was almost at its farthest point south. Over the Christmas holiday, he took advantage of his free schedule and the steady winds to windsurf, gradually exploring within the reef farther along the headland as he gained confidence.

A group was meeting in the cafe. Once the meal was started, Matthew mused, "So, 1984 is almost over. George Orwell was wrong in his ideas of a totalitarian society."

"Wrong only in the date, I think. He gave an accurate description of what was going to happen," said Len. "The control of thought and speech by powerful groups is coming, I fear."

Marie-Anne added, "The dystopian novel was written in 1948 and Orwell simply reversed the numbers in the date to get his title: 'Nineteen Eighty Four'. His predictions projected the action into the distant future. Who knows when that will be?"

Len suggested, "Perhaps he should have dated the book about 50 years later. His ideas were valid. Mass control is coming. When you dominate the use of words you control thought. That was Orwell's point."

On the Friday afternoon after Christmas, Brett arranged with the secretary to have access to her office to do his typing on the Saturday. He knew the annual report would be relatively straightforward to type, but he wanted to try to make three carbon copies. The top original would go to his UK funding agency, The African Educational Foundation; one copy for Tony and Jane's Alliance Community Fellowship; and the third one to be sent to the NCCK. He would show Simion Katana his last faint copy. He was anxious to avoid the inconvenience of trying to find a working photocopier in Mwakindini.

Having completed the report, he turned his attention to the letter to Henry Emerson. When he had finished the typing, he re-read it:

Dear Mr. Emerson,

Please excuse me writing this letter, but I have been hoping to meet you since I arrived at the Zoo at the end of August. I understand that you are slightly uncomfortable at meeting people, so I am taking the liberty of writing down some of my thoughts for you to consider, please. I have spoken with Mrs. Emerson on several occasions, and have appreciated her knowledge of the history of the Zoo.

The Zoo

    I have been very impressed with the Zoo and its organization, and I wish to congratulate you on the initial concept and all of the hard work you have put in over the years. However, in the last few months I have noticed a few things which might be improved, if you agree, so I will note those here for your consideration:

1. There are some areas where the aesthetics could be upgraded, particularly the signboard at the front entrance and other signs and notices around the place. I would be willing to assist with this repainting.
2. The dustbins outside the cages are becoming quite unsightly as some are badly rusted and in need of repair or replacement. Might it be possible to construct some enclosures for the dustbins? A simple wooden or concrete box with a lid would help the appearance, and possibly the sanitary aspects.
3. During my time in Kenya, I have become extremely sensitive to fire hazards. May I suggest there should be a second water tank available for emergency firefighting in the areas around the kitchens and dining hall, to supplement the main water tank near the front entrance.
4. Also, related to fire safety, we are totally dependent on the single entrance road for emergency egress or evacuation of the Zoo in the case of fire. Would it be possible to construct another roadway, even with a temporary murram surface, along the southern shore, as a second means of escape?

    Thank you for allowing me to make these suggestions. I hope we have an opportunity to discuss them in the near future. I would be happy to visit your place if you would kindly arrange for an escort over there. Thank you.

Yours sincerely,
Brett James, N-12.

He was going to write about the electrical wiring, but decided to leave that for another time. He had noticed an odd mixture of 5-A and 15-A outlets in the older buildings, and the modern 13-A ring-mains circuits in the newer structures. He felt the older systems probably should be upgraded. He decided to ask Len before commenting on it to Mr. Emerson. Also, he was concerned about some of the electrical equipment he had seen in the kitchen and food-preparation areas, particularly the way staff were using it in bare feet with water sloshing around on the floors. *I'll mention that to Len too, and not bother Henry with it*, he thought.

When he read the letter again, he re-typed the first page, changing, '…you are slightly uncomfortable at meeting people', to '…you have not been able to meet with people recently.' He thought it seemed less personally intrusive. Feeling satisfied with his efforts, he dated and signed the letter and the copies of the report, found some envelopes, and completed his morning's work. It was time for lunch. He wrote a brief thank-you note to the secretary and left it on the typewriter, placed all of the documents, including his drafts and rejected copies, in his brief case, locked the office, and headed across to the central buildings. He thought he would treat himself to a meal in the restaurant, depending on who was there to sit with.

As he approached the building, Brett noticed an unfamiliar car. It was a large black Mercedes. Two heavyset men were positioned in the shade. He greeted them, but they ignored him which he found very unusual. As Brett walked to the front entrance, another stranger pushed past him. He was wearing a white *kofia* hat worn at the coast, a long white *kanzu* robe, and a formal black jacket. He was smoking a cigarette. He quickly got in the back of the luxurious car and, immediately, the driver and his hefty companion climbed in and drove away.

Boniface Chengo was leaving the complex when he saw Brett. He appeared agitated as he said, "Come, I want to show you something." Clutching Brett's hand, the likeable giant walked him outside, along a sandy path, and across the open plaza by the southern beach. "Look," said Chengo, pointing to a deep hole in the centre of the playing area. "It is a hole. Someone has taken a lot of sand." They joined several other people standing mournfully around the rim, and staring into the hole. "I tell you Bwana, it is wrong to take sand like that," Chengo proclaimed. Everyone agreed and several people looked directly at Brett. He wasn't sure whether they were silently accusing him of excavating the sand, or if they expected him to offer an explanation. He shook his head in an appropriately sympathetic way.

Chengo asked a bystander if he knew anything. "No, I just met this hole here," he replied. A man pointed out some indistinct tracks leading to the shore. Several people offered suggestions as they confidently pointed in opposite directions along the beach.

Walking back, they discussed the distressing theft. Brett said he couldn't understand how anyone could remove that much material without being seen. Chengo said, "It happened last night."

"Yes, but, even in the dark, someone must have been watching."

"Not at night. Nobody comes out at night. The person had a cart and an animal. I think, a donkey."

"Even more reason they would be detected. Donkeys make noise," said Brett.

Chengo shook his head and remained mystified. Then he said, "We need to bury that hole. More sand, it is needed."

"Maybe it will fill in naturally, as people kick sand from around the edges."

Chengo would not be comforted, "It is not allowed to take sand like this – that way. We have to fill in that very hole. Make it more firmer."

Brett had done his best to sympathize but he was thinking that, on a large coastal beach, surely there wasn't exactly a shortage of sand. He thought, *The wind, rain, and natural movements will take care of it. I'm getting hungry.* He realized it would not be a good time to give Henry Emerson's letter to Chengo, so he parted with, "I have something to give you. Maybe I can meet with you next week."

Chengo agreed, saying, "Yes. Anytime. You come anytime."

In the restaurant, Brett saw several people he knew. Len and Marie-Anne offered him a seat at their table. Miles Jolly and Matthew and Esther Fletcher came in and sat at an adjacent table. They spoke of the mysterious disappearance of the sand. Then Brett asked about the three strangers who visited. From the ambiguous replies, he got the impression they came occasionally to visit the Executive Officer but never spoke to anyone else.

Part 2: The Wall

Miles said he had met the man – the smoker – who was visiting Chengo. "A strange fellow. A man of mystery," said Miles.

Len laughed, "There are no mysteries around here for you Miles. You seem omniscient."

"Whereas you, Len, are a specialist of Things in General. But I'm serious about that mystifying stranger."

"Does he collect sand? Maybe that's his hobby," offered Matthew.

"In which case, Chengo would be interested to interview *him*," said Brett.

Suddenly, Miles went very quiet. He explained that he was not feeling well. "Is it the old ticker again?" wondered Esther with genuine concern.

"Either that or a touch of malaria perhaps," said Miles.

"Several people are down with it. It must be a bad season," said Marie-Anne.

"I could have got attacked by one of the Little Five…" said Miles, "…mosquitoes, bacteria, lice, ticks, or an arachnid."

"Don't make light of such things," Marie-Anne admonished him.

"No, okay. Anyway, I think the placebos I'm taking are really having an effect."

"They don't fool us," said Brett.

"Me neither!" declared Miles.

Marie-Anne was more sympathetic, asking, "What tablets are you taking?"

"Just give us a capsule summary!" said Matthew.

During this exchange Len had been trying to say something. He kept opening his mouth and then closing it again. Brett watched him and thought he looked like a moray eel feeding outside its hollow in a coral pool. Marie-Anne suggested to Miles, "Perhaps you should get a blood test."

"Good idea. I believe in the right to bare arms," Miles replied.

"I hope they won't be searching in vein," Len teased, patting Miles on the back.

On New Year's Eve, walking past the central block after lunch, Brett noticed Peter and a small group meeting in one of the back rooms beside the cafe. Later that afternoon he saw Peter sitting outside in the shade drinking a cup of tea. Len was standing chatting with him. Peter beckoned Brett over to join them. "They have discovered who took the sand."

"Really, who?" asked Brett.

"There's a crazy old man who lives near the boundary at the east end of the beach. Apparently, he spread a wide mound of sand along the fence. Faiz noticed it."

"Why would he do that?"

"He planned to form a high sand bank against the fence to keep out witches. He's a bit unstable and fears that the spirits are crawling through the fence from the headland to enter his cage. He instructed his two sons to collect the sand and pile it across the beach. Of course, it is gradually being dispersed now. The elders are not taking any action against him, although they did speak sharply to his sons."

"Well, Mrs. Emerson does feel we have space here for a few idiosyncratic personalities, so she shouldn't be too upset."

"Chengo is furious they got away with just a reprimand. He thinks the sons should be made to return the sand. But there's not much left of it now."

"Let the punishment fit the crime," offered Brett.

Peter continued, "I told Faiz to stress to the family that taking sand like that is not the done thing. Sand belongs to everyone." Len told them he had to go, and wandered off, whistling. The waiter brought a tray of tea and some fried donuts. As Brett started to enjoy them, Peter yawned and said, "I hear Miles has been unwell. I think his heart is a bit dodgy."

"We were wondering if it was malaria," replied Brett.

"Could be I suppose. Let's hope he makes it to 1985," Peter replied in an apathetic voice. "You had a successful trip to Mombasa? Who did you meet?"

"Several people. Did Louise describe our day?"

"Yes. Who did you have lunch with?"

"I saw John Phillips from Nairobi."

"Oh yes. He's in resource development isn't he?"

"Sort of. He's a geologist, involved in satellite imaging. I met him on the plane and he offered to look at some aerial shots of the region around the Zoo and give me a bit of a description."

"Did he? Now you've got me stumped. Why do you need that?"

"I was curious to see the layout of the Zoo, and the beaches and the reef on the headland. As it happened, he is not able to provide a map or sketches due to some government restrictions. I have ordered an official survey map from the ministry. He is fascinated by our community, though, and may try to visit sometime. Apparently the geography along the coastal strip is unique, and the whole area has a rich history."

"Oh, it's fascinating all right. Louise said you saw an old map of the area."

"Yes, a collector's piece."

"Did it show any details?"

"An outline of the coast, and some contours of the rocky sections. It was named *Kisiwa wa Kima*."

"Monkey Island. Henry researched the monkeys – to his cost. It's not an island, but it resembles one due to the separation and the isolation there." He drew on his cigarette, and mused, "One could spend a long time there – in isolation."

After that cryptic comment, Peter was silent. Brett changed the subject. "Did you have a meeting?" he asked, nodding towards the back room. Peter flicked the ash from his cigarette with his thumb and took another drag. Squinting at Brett through half-closed eyes, he replied. "The Security Committee. Our regular meeting."

"How many committees are there? I've not been able to grasp how the Zoo administration is structured."

Peter described in detail the work of the public committees, and added, "That's at the operational level. There is also our committee of Elders. We are sometimes called 'The Keepers'! That open group is made up of the chairmen, or women, from the committees. Sorry, I forgot to mention the three zone representatives – like area wardens. Each of the three main sectors – White, African, and Muslim – have a coordinating group to deal with issues within their own jurisdiction. Matthew handles White, Katana coordinates the African, and Faiz leads the Muslim. He wears two hats as he's also involved on the Facilities committee with Len. Did I mention that?"

"I don't think so."

"Pardon? You'll need to speak up. There's a bit of background noise out here."

Brett shook his head, "No, you had not mentioned that."

"Stop me if I repeat myself. Anyway, all those committee reps are coordinated on the Elder's Committee. Officially, that's chaired by Henry Emerson but recently he hasn't been there so Louise has stepped in as Chair of the Elders."

"Louise?" asked Brett. Peter located a shred of tobacco on his lips with his tongue. He absentmindedly placed his forefinger on his tongue to remove the fragment, flicking it away.

"Yes. She's very good. With her background in…in everything…she steers us along efficiently. She acts more like an MC than a chairperson actually. She coordinates the conversation, relying heavily on the specialists in their particular fields for detailed input into our discussions."

"Are those meetings open too?"

"Theoretically, yes, but in reality no one joins us unless a particularly contentious issue crops up. Can't remember when that last happened. Around the time of Jed Walker's expulsion I think. I told you about him?"

"Yes. So that's it? That's how it's all run?"

"Well, not quite." Peter hesitated as he waved to a couple who walked by. Brett smiled at them. "From the Elders, three of us form the Executive to deal with the day-to-day things. You see, the main committee meets only once a month. So Chengo, one of the Emersons, and I form the Executive Council. We call ourselves the Big Five!"

"Ha. Are your meetings public?"

"Not on your life! What I mean is, they are far too detailed and sensitive for that, I can tell you. No, we just get on with the running of the show."

"That's very interesting. Thanks for explaining it all."

Peter stood up stiffly and said, "Happy to oblige old chap. At least you're now a bit more *au fait* with our *modus operandi*."

"My goodness, another polyglot."

Peter smiled, "Well, I must be off to my *adobe hacienda*. Have a brief siesta."

"Wrong language."

"But," said Peter, "right idea! Happy new year, old chap."

"Thank you. You too, my friend."

That evening, Brett read through his letter to Henry Emerson, sealed the envelope, and addressed it. He wondered again if he should send it via Mrs. Emerson but his instinct directed him away from that idea. When he mentioned Henry, her response was usually vague and she was obviously protecting him.

Two days after the New Year, Brett went to see Boniface Chengo. As he entered the accounts office, he saw Grace sitting at her desk. After a brief conversation, he asked if Mr. Chengo was in. "Not unless I check," replied Grace. Brett knew she meant they should wait for Mr. Chengo to call him in. She added, "He likes you. He said you shake our hands and, when you ask how we are, you listen for what we tell you." Brett smiled. On the desk was an opened stapler, lying on its side. He asked Grace if it was working and she said, "Yes, but there are no staples."

"How do you fix pieces of paper together?"

"We use pins. There is no otherwise."

"Do you get scratched?"

"Honestly, I tell you. Yes, all the time!"

Brett said, "An accounts office without a stapler is like…" He waited to see if Grace would suggest anything. She didn't. He continued, "…like a teacher without a box of chalks! Do you have the code number for the staples? I can get some for you when I am at the stationers." He made a note of the code. He was trying to think of a joke about a hiker stranded on Mount Kenya without his tide tables, when Grace told him Mr. Chengo was ready to see him.

Brett entered the office, greeted him, and handed him the letter with his right hand. Mr. Chengo received it with his right hand and noticed that it was addressed to 'Mr. H. Emerson'. "Please, you sit down Mister Brett," he said, waving a large hand towards a chair. He gently placed the envelope in front of him on the desk and looked at it for a moment. Then he picked it up and held it towards the window as though he expected it to become transparent and reveal its contents. He then set it down vertically on the desk in front of him holding the edges with both hands and tapping it up and down as though he were aligning a pack of cards after shuffling them. He glanced up at Brett and then continued to stare at the letter. He laid it horizontally on the desk again and patted it with both his chubby hands. Finally, he looked up at Brett, with his hands resting on the letter as though he was preventing it from escaping. Brett watched this routine with interest, but said nothing.

Chengo took a deep breath and said, "So, it is a letter. A letter for Mr. Emerson."

"That's right, just a letter," said Brett.

The Executive Officer looked directly at Brett, "Please, what it is about, this letter?" Brett explained the reason for writing and making some practical suggestions. "Well, it is a bit difficult, you know. Because…" He hesitated and then explained that Mr. Emerson does not receive letters, as he leaves the running of the Zoo to the other officers and the committees.

"That's okay, I understand that. Perhaps you could just hand him the letter please," said Brett, standing to leave. As he did, Mr. Chengo explained it would be easier for him to follow up on the letter if he had a better idea of its contents. "Please may I ask you and inquire about the nature and purpose of this letter of communication?"

"Well, I've told you basically but, I have a carbon copy I would be happy to give you if you like. I'm sorry I didn't think of doing that before. I'll bring it over later this afternoon, so you will have a chance to read it," said Brett as he shook Mr. Chengo's large hand.

They parted amicably with the usual farewells. As Brett left, he saw Chengo continuing to stare at the letter on his desk. *I like Boniface Chengo,* he thought. *He's carrying a lot of responsibility here. He has the stature and presence to match his authority. He'll probably be the person Emerson will get to follow up on my suggestions.* He felt confident the letter was in good hands.

9

"Questions! That's all I get from you, questions. Louise said you were getting pretty inquisitive with all of your questions. Back off! That's my advice," shot back Miles.

The post from overseas typically arrived once a week. At the end of the week after New Year, Brett checked and saw two letters from England: one from his parents and another from Tony. He opened Tony's letter with some apprehension. At the appointment, Tony had been warned of the possibility of thyroid cancer. A biopsy would be required, and monitoring as his symptoms may be caused by something else. If necessary, a tumour marker test may be performed. Otherwise, he was feeling positive, and trusting. He was determined, with Jane, to continue their ministry work and enjoy life as much as possible. They appreciated Brett's continuing prayers.

By the middle of January 1985, Brett was surprised, and slightly irritated, that he had received no response from Henry Emerson. In the meantime, he had been thinking what gift he might take to Henry when he met him. He wondered if his letter may have been interpreted as critical, or even impertinent, with the practical suggestions he had made. He felt an appropriate gift might be in order. The difficulty was deciding what to take him.

Brett was speaking with Louise one afternoon, trying to probe into Henry's interests, when Len joined them, asking if he would be willing to serve on the Facilities Committee. Brett agreed, and he and Louise thanked him. Brett mentioned that he intended to drive to Mombasa in a couple of days to collect his safari suit, more art supplies, and books. Louise asked if, while he was on Biashara Street, he would take something to Taran Sembhi for her, and possibly bring back a package for Miles. He agreed to do that, wanting to help and seeing nothing wrong with it.

Two days later, Brett drove to Mombasa and parked in the same guarded compound that Louise had used. He stopped briefly at a small coffee shop for a break. Suitably fortified, he made his way to Sembhi's store. Entering the alley, he was disturbed to see three scruffy youths lurking farther along the passageway. As he entered the door to climb the stairs, two of them called out and whistled softly. At the top, he was, once again, impressed by the shambles that confronted him inside. Taran Sembhi greeted him with a friendly outstretched hand. Brett handed over the envelope from Louise, which Sembhi opened. He examined the enclosed photographs of a chess set and commented, almost to himself, "Interesting. Ivory. Definitely pre-ban."

Brett asked, "I wonder if I could have another look at your map of the Kima Island please? I would like to sketch some of the features of the headland, if it's all right with you."

"Certainly, go ahead Mr. James. Very happy to oblige." He seemed uncharacteristically pleasant which troubled Brett a little. Brett took out his sketch pad and stood in front of the print on the wall, with Mr. Sembhi watching closely. Brett smelt the heavy bouquet of garlic on his breath. He was uncomfortable with his ingratiating manner because it was in such contrast to their first meeting.

Having completed his sketching, Brett said that Miles had asked him to collect something. That seemed to be the cue Sembhi was waiting for, as he immediately moved over to a crowded desk, unlocked a lower drawer, and removed a fat package. "Could you give this to Mr. Jolly?"

"What is it?" Brett asked.

"Just something to take to Mr. Jolly."

"Can you tell me what it is?"

Sembhi's noble brow furrowed as he hesitated, but then whispered, "Some cash."

"Cash? How much?"

Sembhi was clearly irritated. "Why does that matter?"

"Well, if I'm carrying cash I'd like to have some idea how much it is."

After a short pause, Sembhi's reply was acerbic: "It's a lot."

Brett weighed the envelope in his hand and then handed it back to Sembhi, saying, "Sorry I can't risk–"

"What's the risk? Just take it."

"It's too risky."

"Stuff it in your underwear. Be careful, that's all."

"You know it's not safe walking around with large amounts of–"

"Okay forget it," Sembhi snapped, grabbing the package. "Jolly said you could be trusted."

"Did he?" Brett picked up his sketch pad, and turned towards the door. "It's not whether I can be trusted or not. It's those three young men I saw at the end of your alley, sneering at me as I came in."

"All right. As I said, forget it. Goodbye Mr. James."

Stepping back into the alley, Brett heard a jeering call, "*Ayye, Mzungu…*" and the snapping of fingers. He ignored it and was relieved to soon be back among the crowds on Biashara Street. He hurried to the tailor to try on his safari suit. He was thrilled with the quality and fit. He returned to his pickup clutching the brown-paper wrapped package under his arm.

In an adjacent tourist shop he noticed some tee shirts with the word 'Mombasa' and the iconic elephant tusks printed on the front. He bought two, along with three pairs of casual shorts which would double as swimming trunks. He entered another shop because he saw a mosquito net hanging in their window. He bought a rectangular-shaped net to replace his old one.

Then he drove to the textbook supply store. He treated himself to a leisurely visit this time, looking at the tempting canvases, brushes, painting knives, and other art materials. He bought two boxes of staples for Grace in the office, and some other stationery supplies for himself, along with two publications for Simion Katana. He searched for a book on monkeys for Henry, but they contained little information on the coastal region, mainly describing the species in the interior of Africa, so he selected a beautifully illustrated book on coastal birds instead.

As he arrived back at the Zoo, darkness was falling. He stopped at the main building to check his pigeonhole for letters. Miles appeared. "Did Taran Sembhi give you anything to bring to me?"

"He tried to," Brett replied.

"What do you mean?" His eyes narrowed. Brett thought, *He has dark black eyes like Kali, Louise's horrible dog.*

"He wanted me to bring back something, but I refused." For a brief moment Miles' ebony eyes flashed his anger, but he quickly hid it with a faint smile.

"That's okay. It's just that I can't travel about as much as I used to with my heart problem. It would have been helpful if you could have brought it."

"Sembhi reluctantly admitted it was a large amount of cash. I can't risk walking about Mombasa with that on me."

"I thought you had some precautions that you took in Kenyan towns."

"I do, but they don't make me invincible. They just reduce the risk, that's all. Three louts were hiding in the passageway outside Sembhi's place. Also, you know how we can run into police roadblocks on that coast road."

"They are not likely to search an *mzungu*."

"No, maybe not; but it's too risky to put myself into those situations. Cash is always a dodgy commodity."

Miles gave him a look which signalled, 'Don't lecture me on safety precautions, boy', but he simply said, "I didn't think it would be such a big issue for you, sorry."

Brett was annoyed. "It was a bit sneaky of you to set that up with Sembhi, so I was put on the spot in his shop. You've been a good friend to me, Miles, but I'm sorry, I can't take risks like that."

"You should be honoured that I trust you!"

"Oh I am! Deeply honoured. Don't ask a rabbit to carry lettuce, right?"

"You've been vetted by Ochieng and pronounced clean," Miles said.

"That's quite the endorsement, I suppose! But I am curious, how much money was it, and in what form?"

"It was a lot. A lot of US dollars, the only currency that counts these days. That's all I can tell you. He sold something for me. Let's forget about it shall we?"

"What did he sell? Why so much money? Why involve me in this?"

"Questions! Louise said you were getting pretty inquisitive with all of your questions. Back off. That's my advice," shot back Miles.

"Great! Now you're giving me fatherly advice, thanks!"

Miles stepped closer and emphasized, as he looked up at Brett, "One more piece of advice: just be careful. Be careful, Brett. Things may not be as they seem to you – and certainly not as simple," said Miles, and immediately his face softened and he patted Brett on the shoulder. "Anyway, let's just forget it. Okay?" His expression brightened and his frown eased. His anger had faded, so Brett relaxed too, and nodded with the best attempt at a grin as he could muster. They parted, smiling, but Brett felt uneasy. The ground beneath him seemed to have shifted slightly.

That evening, he installed his new mosquito net, with attachments across to four corner anchor points. He decided to keep the old, slightly torn, net for camping. He was still troubled by the confrontation with Miles, thinking that mosquitos were not the only creatures to be concerned about at the Zoo.

At the next meeting of the facilities committee, everyone admired Brett's new Mombasa shirt. Then Len and Imam Faiz presented a list of jobs to be tackled. Brett was surprised to see two of his suggestions on the sheet: the upgrading of the front entrance sign and the proposal to repair and enclose the dustbins. After lengthy discussion, it was agreed that two of the members would come up with a couple of possible designs for bin enclosures. Brett and Faiz, who Len said was a good carpenter, agreed to look at what needed to be done to refresh the appearance of the main entrance sign.

A mechanic had inspected Steve's old Toyota, and looked carefully at Louise's Peugeot. He pronounced her long 504 estate car to be in excellent condition, which prompted Steve and Coreene to negotiate with her to purchase it. Within a week, Louise had taken Steve with her to the Peugeot dealer in Malindi and purchased a newer 504 car. She was delighted with her smaller vehicle as it was easier to park. At the same time, the Brandons were thrilled to have her larger and more reliable vehicle.

The Zoo

The hot, dry season was well established and Brett was finding the heat oppressive, although the air was clear. In order to relieve the stresses of his work, Brett used Len's windsurfer whenever he had a chance when the tides were suitable.

The more he looked at the broad sweep of the northern beach, the more he yearned to explore that forbidden region. Rugged piles of coral rocks blocked the view beyond the headland. One evening, out on the board, the fragment of a thought entered his consciousness. It receded, and then reappeared. He suppressed it as being out of the question. As he came to shore, he realized that he was fearful of its implications. He returned the sail and board to Len's store and decided that his notion was totally impractical and ill-advised.

He walked up Len's alleyway on his way home and he encountered their neighbour Miles Jolly, who mentioned the improvements that the facilities committee were working on and spoke of some of Brett's suggestions. Brett was surprised, and wondered if Miles had seen his letter to Mr. Emerson. Jolly professed innocence, but said, "Good for you. We need a few fresh ideas around here – not that I get involved in any of the administrative details."

"Really? It seems to me you get into *all* of the administrative details!"

On the Saturday morning at nine, as arranged, Brett drove to the Muslim quarter to collect Faiz. They planned to look at the main entrance sign. With the well-dressed eccentric shop owner watching them, they assessed what would be required to spruce it up. There were traces of the original lettering and symbols in the faded and peeling plywood. They saw that the supporting posts and braces would need replacing. It had been suggested at the committee meeting that they update the name to better reflect the current community, and avoid confusion over the possibility of animals being on display there.

It did not take long for them to become hot and thirsty, so they headed over to the small stall in search of some cold sodas. The quasi-Englishman sat them down in the shade on the bench seat in front of his wooden store, and treated them to drinks. He offered some thoughts on the front entrance, and assured them of his full support in dressing up the image presented to visitors. Brett and Faiz got on well, and sketched out some ideas, along with a materials list.

Brett suggested that the sign could be painted black, two intermediate tones of grey, and white, to provide a varied, three-dimensional background for the brightly-painted main letters across the front. "Let's have them reading 'Community Resort'," suggested Faiz. The shop operator nodded so vigorously that he almost lost his top hat. They drove into Mwakindini to look at a hardware shop that Faiz knew, and obtained prices for the material that they would require for their project. "We'll need to check with the committee and get some cash," said Faiz.

"And let's start work earlier next time, before the sun gets too hot," suggested Brett.

The following week, the facilities committee met to approve the sign-restoration project, the funding, and the preferred title: 'Community Village'.

After two months of silence from the enigmatic Henry Emerson, and no indication that he had even received the letter, the idea that had begun to form in Brett's mind resurfaced. His hope that he might be invited to visit Henry at his research facility, or even in their cage, was looking unlikely. He wondered if it was possible to go over and see Henry without an invitation. He told himself, *That's completely impractical! And intrusive.* However, his recognition that he would be breaking the rules was offset by his increasing frustration at not being able to communicate with the Zoo leader. At the outset, it was clear to Brett that his plan must be kept secret. He had received enough warnings that breaching the wall was forbidden to realize he had to avoid anyone suspecting his intentions.

His initial plan was to wade around the fence out in the south bay beside the Muslim section. He looked at the tide tables to see if an upcoming spring tide would cause the extreme low water level to coincide with dawn because he would have to get around in darkness to avoid detection. He wandered along there during the next extremely low tide but quickly realized that it would be impossible to cross to the east that way. Even with the exceptionally low water, the fence was high and constructed far out into the bay. On his return, he toyed with the idea of attempting to go through the large gate that Faiz and the boy had shown him but it would be impossible without involving someone who had a key.

He thought about the possibility of windsurfing along the southern beach and making a landing in front of Henry Emerson's hut. After careful consideration, he realized it was impractical on several counts. He would be seen, he was unfamiliar with the rocks and channels there, and he intended to take some gifts to Henry…no, it would not work. Recalling what Faiz had mentioned about another way through, he looked carefully at the wall to the north of the Emersons' cage to see if there was any other opening that way. There was nothing. From what he had seen in the area to the north, around Ridge-Taylors' cage, there would be no access through there either. In any case, the dogs would alert them to his presence. Another difficulty remained: the dogs patrolling the far side of the wall. He had heard vague descriptions of a narrow raceway with a parallel fence to allow a path for the dogs to patrol the boundary. These difficulties seemed insurmountable so he set aside his plan, hoping for further inspiration later.

Brett and Faiz's joint effort on the sign was going well. They had started at dawn to avoid the midday heat and they rebuilt the whole supporting structure and completed the lettering. They were pleased with their efforts. There was considerable interest from all who passed by. Brett appreciated working with Faiz, and he felt they were becoming good friends.

At the March meeting of the facilities committee, the members praised them for the fine work they had done on the sign. Several residents had said they were grateful for the improvement. Recognizing that many people would continue to use the old name, they asked for a small plate to be added, saying, 'Formerly known as The Zoo'. They then asked Brett if he would be willing to repaint the warning notices along the eastern wall. He agreed to allow some time for that during the Easter holiday at the start of April. The next afternoon, he walked along the wall and examined the condition of the plastering, and the painted letters so he could order the materials he needed. He looked carefully at the rusting barbed wire that Peter had pointed out, and decided to suggest to the committee he renew that at the same time.

Part 2: The Wall

Then a dramatic idea struck him: if he was going to be working along there with ladders, maybe he could remove some of the barbed wire, hop over the wall, and dash along to Henry's place! He became quite excited about this possibility and spent many hours thinking through its implications. The thought of the dogs roaming along the other side troubled him greatly, but other aspects of the plan gradually fell into place.

Getting over the wall without being seen was the main priority because, once he had met Henry, he reasoned that returning openly through the gate would not be a problem. He had no idea how he was going to keep his scheme from Tili and his neighbours, so he devoted considerable time and attention to the details and the timing. The element of deception that it would require troubled him, but he resolved not to tell any direct lies. He could use the local strategy of vague replies to any questions that were raised. He had a compelling urge to meet Henry and an increasing obsession to explore the forbidden headland. That driving motivation overcame any hesitation that surfaced in his mind. He told himself: "When you make a major decision you have to accept the minor consequences that follow in its wake."

Once the college term was over, and the Easter holiday had started, Brett was able to prepare his wall repainting project. Faiz had shown little interest in this second job and, in any case, he was due to go away for further training, so Brett knew he would be on his own. He kept his materials in the small storeroom adjacent to the Ridge-Taylors' cage. Njuguna unlocked it when Brett needed access. He noticed that an inner door provided a way through to Njuguna's quarters, and presumably the dog compound. He saw the bags of dog food were stacked up on pallets. Brett kept paints and dry materials inside, along with brushes, trowels, floats, and other tools. The repairs to the plaster took a while, and then he started to renew the warning lettering. He saw it was going to take some time, but he knew the long rains could begin any day, so he pushed himself to get that phase completed before the downpours started. He wasn't surprised to see Miles hanging around the store, sometimes chatting with Njuguna or Violet. He seemed to be everywhere. On several occasions, the Emersons' manservant, Mzee Mjuhgiuna, wandered by to look at his work. Once, Brett thought he saw Mjuhgiuna taking a photograph of the progress, as he walked on his way to see Njuguna, Thomas' helper.

Brett intermixed the work with teaching Ruth, Andrew, and Graham how to windsurf with more confidence. It was fun to explore a little of the southern beach area. He was surprised at how many small boats were out in the southern bay, compared to the few to the north of the Zoo peninsula. He observed outboard-motor boats, and larger inboard-engine craft in deep waters. Farther out at sea, large dhows drifted by with their billowing lateen sails, and massive tankers were visible out towards the horizon.

Once the tide went out, and the sail boards were put away, the group explored the reef or worked on their sketching and painting together. Brett enjoyed being part of their family. He was content to stay around the Zoo for the Easter holiday as it helped him save money and, besides, his thoughts were constantly coming back to his secret plan. He decided to string out the wall project for as long as he could. He did not feel guilty, as he was volunteering for the work and no one else was involved. He completed the painting before the rains came, but deliberately delayed tackling the barbed-wire repair. He left the borrowed ladders and some equipment padlocked together and covered, at the base of the wall. He had resolved to climb over the wall late one night, wait on the other side and go along to Henry Emerson's remote hut the next morning. The only question was, when to do this? He had to choose a time when he would not be detected.

One important consideration was what gifts to take to Henry, in addition to the bird book. The dilemma that he had earlier remained: he simply did not know enough about Henry to prepare anything suitable. But over a period of days, looking around in his cupboards, he became quite creative. He still had the special treats Mary Gossard had given him which he had been saving for a special occasion. *This might well be that occasion,* he mused. Clearing space on a high shelf in his kitchen, Brent made a small pile of cans. They seemed insignificant, but they were unique. He assembled Canadian pink salmon, some Dutch cheese, and a can of German sausages. Alongside these, he placed a packet of Belgian biscuits, and a miniature French liqueur someone had given him. He thought, *Well, that should satisfy most members of the United Nations. I wonder what condition the biscuits are in after all this time in the humidity and heat? Never mind, it's the thought that counts. Even if he doesn't want them, his staff will enjoy them.*

In the days following, he added the book on coastal birds he had purchased, and a union-jack keyring he had bought himself at the airport in London. He assumed Henry had electricity or a generator so he included a cassette tape of Brahms' Double Concerto.

As his plan became more real, he tried to imagine the night. It would be best without a moon so he checked his calendar and suddenly an idea struck him. He knew the end of Ramadan was later in June. That meant a new moon would be quickly setting so the sky would be completely black. The best dark moon would be on Tuesday 18th of June. Then he saw that the end-of-Ramadan holiday, Eid-ul-Fitr, was on Thursday the 20th of June. There would be a small waxing crescent moon which would present no problem. Further, he imagined that Tili would be away on holiday then, which would be perfect during his final preparations and the night he would be away. He would have to discreetly check with others if they normally gave their Muslim staff time off during the festival of Eid. *That's it then,* he thought, *the night of 20th June. Time to make all the plans and develop a story to cover what I am doing.* He felt pleased at his groundwork so far. He reasoned that unusual activities take place in the community over a holiday, which could also provide something of a cover.

He was a planner by nature: he could already see in his mind what would happen, step by step. He was, in a sense, creating reality ahead of time, anticipating problems in advance as best he could. In the weeks following, he felt energized and focused by the plan, quickly squelching any intrusive thoughts that he might be about to do a dangerous thing. He prayed for guidance and protection, not feeling totally comfortable with asking God's blessing on a scheme like his, but sensing that a higher purpose might be in view. *You can't make an omelette without breaking eggs,* he told himself. He was unsure of the theological validity to that, or even if the analogy was fitting.

During the third week of March, the sun had crossed the equator, and completed its zenith pass overhead to the north, bringing stronger winds and torrential rains. The heavier rains during April were appreciated in the Zoo. Brett loved hearing the rain pounding on the broad banana leaves, and enjoyed the birds sounds. They seemed to be more active during the rainy season.

After the Easter holiday, the college routine continued smoothly. Sailing was more challenging due to the variable and unpredictable winds. After a particularly strong storm, he went to see how Len was doing, intending to gauge how he felt about him using the windsurfer in the strong wind. Len was sitting dejectedly on his patio looking at the wreckage from the storm around him. Miles was standing unhelpfully beside him. A strong gust had hit their area badly. The tea tray was on the ground and a cup lay smashed alongside. "No problem," said Len, "it's just a teacup in a storm."

"But look at that mess," said Miles pointing to the tangle of wires and broken poles from the energy project in the water in front of Len's cage. "I told you it was unsafe, and it all needed to be secured more."

"So, you were right. Are you satisfied?" Len growled.

Brett recalled Miles' dislike of the experimental installation on aesthetic grounds. He glanced at Miles who was looking rather smug and saying, "In addition to this mud, I am sloshing around in justified self-righteousness. It's a wonderful feeling. You should try it sometime, Len." In spite of his misery, Len managed a gracious smile.

Brett asked Miles if he still went fishing in the deeper waters, hinting that he would like to go along too. Miles was vague, saying, "I never know when the chaps will invite me. It isn't arranged in a way that would suit you." Brett mentioned to them that his pickup seemed to be stalling intermittently as he drove to Mwakindini. Their noncommittal reaction suited him. Later, in response to his casual enquiry, Miles confirmed that people normally gave their Muslim staff time off at the end of Ramadan. "Muzhere usually spends the time with her family over in the Muslim section."

"Is it that time again?" asked Len.

"Ramadan starts on the 20th of May," Miles assured him. Brett thought, *Then I'll have just one month left until my daring incursion into the restricted zone.* He felt a shudder of apprehension. It was definitely excitement at the challenge, but partly fear too.

10

Suddenly, he heard a distant cry that sent a flush of heat up his back and across his face. It was a piercing scream that sounded as though someone was being murdered.

Brett continued with his hectic routine, in addition to thinking through the details of his plan to climb over the wall. He decided to give the impression that he was away at the Safari Club Hotel in Malindi for the Eid holiday. But he intended to park his pickup close by in Mwakindini to the north, and walk back late at night. It would be less noticeable outside Excel Auto among similar vehicles. The garage was on the southern edge of town so the walk would not be too demanding, although he would have to carry all his supplies for the night's adventure, including Henry's gifts. He could not risk being seen near his own cage, so he planned to walk along the shoreline in the dark. If asked, the fiction that he was intending to promulgate was his pickup had started to stall again on his way down to the hotel so he drove it back to Mr. Tej Singh's garage for servicing and took a bus to Malindi.

Brett spent several evenings in mid-May ambling around the area to check out the route he would take. Twice, he walked towards the main gate late at night. On both occasions the watchman was alert, and greeted him.

He strolled to the southern beach and out onto one of the jetties. He watched the thin crescent moon – seeming to be laying on its back – as it set beyond the coastal hills. The sky was dark, with stars visible beyond the waving palm branches. It was an idyllic scene, but his thoughts were on intensely practical matters. He drew some comfort from the sand-removal episode which taught him that few people were about at night, even in a densely populated region like the Muslim section.

The main wrinkle in his plan was the dogs. He told himself, "If I'm attacked, I'll just give them a slap across the nose like Louise does!" He had not heard the dogs recently, even though he had been working along the wall for some time. Over the course of a few weeks, he casually asked Thomas, Louise, and Matthew about the number of dogs and their freedom to roam along the corridor on the outside. Louise was thrilled that he showed some interest in dogs. She spoke enthusiastically about her beloved Kali, but communicated no helpful information about the dogs kept at the Ridge-Taylors' cage. On the basis of his helping to unload the dog food, Brett chatted with Brigadier Thomas about the dogs in his area. At the end of the conversation, he had the distinct impression that there were just two and they were kept enclosed beside the wall near cage N-1. Brett enquired no further. "Well, BMJ, nice to chat. Thank you for your help with our pets," huffed Thomas as the two of them walked, perhaps too quickly for Thomas, past Peter's cage to look at the sea.

It was Matthew Fletcher who, unwittingly, was the most informative. He innocently revealed that the dogs were all confined. "What about them running along the fenced pathway the other side of the wall?" asked Brett.

"A convenient myth," confided Matthew with a sidelong glance that almost amounted to a wink. He added, "We used to have a system like that in Molo around our house at the sheep farm until a thief got himself trapped in the raceway and the dogs had a go at him. I wasn't pleased about it, but we had to get the fellow treated, at our expense, as they were our dogs. Also, the blessed things kept escaping, so we did away with the whole idea. Saved upkeep on the outer fence too."

On the following Saturday, when he was standing on a ladder and working on the barbed-wire repairs, Brett took some time to reconnoitre the other side of the wall. The trees and bushes had been cleared for about three metres, but a few shrubs had grown back and actually touched the wall. As he leaned over, he saw a winding path along the eastern side of the wall, which could have been made by animals. Unfortunately, as he was peering over, his arm knocked a hacksaw he had been using. It fell and became caught on a branch far below, and out of his reach. He tied a piece of rope on one of the upright supports and let it dangle over the back of the wall so he would be able to locate it when he was over there.

All the while, he was considering which would be the best point to place the ladder just before his night-time adventure. He decided to leave a 12-ft ladder up against the wall, as it would cause too much noise moving it at night. Later, he reasoned that he would leave a second ladder on the other side when he had climbed over, and retrieve it the next morning.

From then on he worked with two ladders side by side, ostensibly for stability, occasionally leaving both up against the wall. He was trying to establish the pattern he intended to use closer to the night of Eid-ul-Fitr. He would have liked to practise swinging the second 12-ft ladder over the wall but he could not risk being seen doing that.

Ramadan started during the third week of May, so Tili began her daily fast. This gave Brett an opportunity to let her know she could take some days off around the Eid festival. She said she would like to visit her family in Malindi for the celebration.

As the details of his plan developed, he walked his two-kilometre route from Mwakindini. Knowing it would be during a holiday, he expected people would be out of their normal routines, so unusual movements would be more likely. He hoped that his would be less obvious. Checking the tides, he thought that he could walk along the foreshore, even though the high tide around the dark moon would cover much of the beach. He would wait until about 10pm, climb the wall, drag one ladder over with him, and leave it on the far side. At the chosen location, he spent some time working on the barbed wire there. He fashioned four small hooks at the ends of the wire strands so he could quickly separate them from the upright stanchion post, and then loop them back again once he was over. He trusted that no one would notice the small hooks.

He left a large jug of water under the tarpaulin covering the ladders and other equipment. He knew he would need water overnight but did not want to lug it all the way from where he would park his pickup. He also risked placing a fire extinguisher, two cans of insect spray, and an old camping sponge mat rolled up tightly. The fire extinguisher would be his only defence if an animal attacked him. He tucked a thin tarpaulin under the large one. That would act as a groundsheet for his sleeping mat.

He wanted to take a stout stick in case of an animal attack, so he placed alongside the ladder a thick pole he often used when walking across the corals to the reef. He also stored away one of his large kitchen knives.

He observed that no one took any notice of what he was doing, or the equipment he used. Even Mjuhgiuna was nowhere to be seen after the first few days. However, he dared not leave other supplies, so he would have to carry those. That thought prompted him to review the list of items to take with him. It was quite long. He couldn't assemble a pile of things, as some of the items might appear odd to Tili. His list included: an extra shirt in case it got chilly in the night, a snack for breakfast, his old mosquito net, several ropes of various lengths and thicknesses, his torch, a peaked hat, sunglasses, a small pillow, and mosquito-repellant cream. He put a few medicines in a bag including aspirin, anti-itch ointment, a tube of antibiotic cream, and two tablets to help him sleep. With his list, he kept the copy of his letter to Henry, as he wanted to discuss those points with him.

As he was finalizing his equipment and elaborate plans, he acknowledged to himself that there was more to his plan than meeting Henry. Beyond that, he wanted to explore the forbidden region and try to uncover some of the mystery that the place held. Based on the hints he had received – and the information that was obviously being withheld – he sensed that more was going on than Henry's research into a protected species of monkey.

When he looked at his list, and saw the pile of gifts for Henry up on the shelf, and imagined those in his rucksack, he realized it would be quite a heavy pack. Once Tili had left he would do a trial pack and take a second bag if necessary. Later he added an old towel and some handkerchiefs to the list. "This is getting exciting," he mused, "Just over a week to go."

He began to drop vague, but true, comments about a possible trip to Malindi. He managed to do all of that without actually lying. *Refined deception*, he thought. He was comforted when no one appeared to show much interest in his plans. He felt guilty, but had already accepted the deceptive component of his intentions, and had become reconciled to that. Once the new moon had been sighted on the Wednesday, he gave Tili some cash for her matatu fare and she left. He was then able to pack his kit, and get as much rest as possible in preparation for his adventure on the Thursday, the significant night of Eid-ul-Fitr.

During the day on Thursday, Brett did the final packing, and immediately realized he would need to carry a second bag. He prepared the clothes he would wear, acknowledging that one outfit was not suitable for the range of activities he was planning, so he compromised with his Mombasa tee-shirt and a pair of light slacks, with hiking boots. He told himself, "Not a suitable combination for my evening meal at the hotel restaurant, but ideal for sleeping on the sand and exploring the unknown pathway through to Henry's hut."

He hard-boiled a couple of eggs for his breakfast and packed some cheese and bread spread with margarine. He ladled peanut butter and his favourite pineapple jam thickly on other pieces of bread. He knew he would have to sacrifice his early morning tea or coffee, trusting – perhaps too optimistically – that Henry would offer him some later the following morning. "Maybe he'll just throw me out," the thought came to him. He decided to take no cash with him other than sufficient money for his supper at the hotel. He ran through the whole planned event in his mind and then went for lunch at the cafe. There were very few people around – certainly none of his close friends – for which he was grateful.

He rested during the afternoon, and was pleased to sleep for a couple of hours. At the last minute he decided to put a note on the kitchen table explaining where he was, just in case things went wrong and he didn't make it back. "At least my friends will know where to look for my body!" he told himself cheerfully. He wanted to drive to Malindi while it was light, so, at about 5pm, he applied insect repellant, collected his breakfast package from the fridge, placed it in his bag, checked his final list, closed up the cage, put a bottle of water and his two bags in the pickup, climbed in, and drove away.

As he passed the watchman at the main gate Brett truthfully told him he was going to Malindi. After an hour's drive, he arrived at the Safari Club Hotel. He was surprised at the crowds there, and soon learned that the restaurant was fully booked. He found a quieter cafe beside the pool area and established himself there for a few hours. Several of the staff recognized him and they chatted about the excitement over the end of Ramadan. He did not get the substantial meal he had looked forward to, but managed to eat sufficient food for his night adventure. Later he found a seat in a secluded corner of the pool deck where there was a slight breeze from the ocean. He felt calm, and grateful that everything had gone so well so far. At about 8:30pm, he left the hotel, meeting the manager on the way out and speaking with him about how crowded things were. The manager said it would be a busy weekend and everyone was very excited.

As Brett drove slowly back to Mwakindini, he noticed more traffic on the road than normal, including many vehicles without lights – as was often the case. He drove past the Zoo entrance, hoping no one would recognize his pickup in the dark, and made his way to Excel Auto. The area was deserted, apart from two watchmen chatting in the entrance to the pharmacy adjacent to the car mechanic's workshop. They ignored him as he parked alongside another Datsun pickup. He quickly switched off his lights and sat quietly processing the situation.

Over the next hour, two cars drove past and a group of young people walked along the side of the road. Nobody noticed him sitting in the dark. The two watchmen separated and sat in front of their respective buildings, both facing away from the darkened parking area. He relaxed and thought about the next steps in his escapade.

Brett checked his watch. It was a quarter to ten. Time to go. Quietly, he attached the steering-wheel clamp, climbed out, and put on his heavy backpack. He silently pushed the door closed, grasped the small bag, and crept along the dark lane towards the main road. He crossed to the seaward side and started along the footpath. There were no other pedestrians, but occasionally a vehicle drove by. When he heard one coming, he stood still beside a tree or rock until it passed. The road to the Zoo was longer than he remembered, particularly in the dark. He was feeling the weight of his load when he heard voices on the path ahead of him. He stopped. A group was heading towards him. He quickly slipped over to some bushes, and froze against a palm trunk. Three men and two girls walked past him chatting

Part 2: The Wall

loudly. They had not seen him. He continued quickly and soon turned to his left along the trail towards the northern beach. He had walked that way in the light but found it more challenging in the pitch-black night. His route took him through some mangroves and to the north of the Central Stores and the informal workshops.

Soon he was on the beach heading towards the residential area. He walked slowly, all the while watching and listening carefully. There was no movement, apart from the gentle rustling of the palm leaves, as he came in front of Miles' and the Moores' cages. He thought he heard Len whistling to his right, and hoped his silhouetted form would not be visible against the dark water on his left. He stood still for a while, listening. Gentle music and occasional voices drifted across the northern bay, possibly coming from the bar next to the sailing club. There was virtually no artificial light shining down to the beach, so he confidently moved eastwards along the shoreline.

He plodded past his cage and cautiously made his way towards the end of the beach. He had decided to slip up the last pathway, beside Peter's cage, as that was less distance in the open area. Walking slowly along the path, he saw dim lights in the homes. "Normal people, doing normal things," he muttered, "and here am I, creeping around like a criminal. Snap out of it Brett, you decided to do this!" It was an easy distance, as he strode over to the wall and stood by the ladders. They were both as he had left them. He had decided that, if anyone spoke to him, he would pretend he was checking the equipment. There was no one, but he heard muted voices, faint music, and the sound of a radio broadcasting in Arabic.

He climbed one of the ladders, carrying his bag, with the rucksack still on his back. He had not thought through the manoeuvre and he found it extremely challenging to unhook the four barbed wires, get his bag up onto the wall, and remove his backpack. He struggled to balance the small bag on top of the narrow wall in the almost complete dark. *Darn it! I should have practised this,* he thought. *I imagined there would be a bit of light.* As he wrenched the backpack off his back, the small bag fell over the wall, and then the larger pack became caught on the wire.

At any moment he expected to hear a voice from behind challenging him, as he stood on the ladder. After a struggle, he freed the rucksack and laid it to the right on top of the wall. He stood up, balanced on the top of the wall and hauled up one of the ladders as quietly as he could. He laid it like a seesaw across the top of the wall, repositioned himself, and then slid it down the other side. He knelt on the wall to do this, and quickly realized how rough and sharp the coral stones were. A piece of barbed wire hooked itself around his ankle and cut him. It tore his trouser leg as he tried to unwrap it. *Brilliant! What a mess this is,* he thought. *Great planning, you twit.*

He slid the backpack down the wobbly ladder and dumped it beside the small bag. Everything was so dark. He climbed back over and unwrapped the heavy items he had stored under the tarpaulin. He removed them one by one and carried them up the remaining ladder. He laid the knife, the fire extinguisher, and his large water jug on the wall. The fire extinguisher rolled back down with a crash. Immediately, the dogs started barking and continued for several minutes. He stood frozen on the ladder and waited. Nothing happened. He retrieved the fire extinguisher and eventually carried all of the extra items down the ladder on the far side. He climbed back over again to the Zoo side and confirmed that it all looked as normal.

He made his final scramble over the wall and down the other side. It had been more of a hassle than he expected, but he was over! He struggled to untangle the foot of the ladder from the bushes and was about to pull it down when he realized he had forgotten to reconnect the hooks for the barbed wires. Wearily, he placed the ladder back against the wall and climbed up to re-hook the wires. Once completed, he stood on the ladder for a few seconds and permitted himself the indulgence of looking back at the dark and deserted Zoo from the other side of the wall, before climbing back down into the unfamiliar darkness.

He was sweating. He paused, breathing deeply, and suddenly thought about where he was. The enveloping dark and silence were frightening. He realized he would have to use his torch in order to set up his mosquito net and arrange the bedding. There was scant chance of the light being seen as long as he kept it covered and did not shine it upwards. He cautiously shone it around, partially covering the lens with his hand to reduce the glow.

He was surprised at the amount of vegetation pressing in upon him. A slight pathway was visible in both directions so he went looking for an open area to hang up his mosquito net. He found a suitable patch and carried his equipment to that area. He smoothed the sand with a branch, spread out the tarpaulin, unrolled his sponge mat, and placed his bags on it. Unraveling the mosquito net, he located three anchor points on branches and tied the fourth string around a projecting piece of coral in the wall. He felt his setup might offer minimal protection against ants, beetles, and spiders, although he was less confident about snakes, lizards, or rodents. *Maybe they sleep at night*, he told himself, without conviction.

He confirmed that he had brought along everything except the ladder which he had already laid at the foot of the wall. He placed the torch on the ground and suddenly saw two eyes staring at him. They were down near the ground and close together so obviously it was a small animal, possibly a bush baby or a genet cat. *Do they attack tourists?* he wondered. Then he comforted himself with, *Maybe, but not tax-paying residents!* A moment later, it had gone. He listened carefully and the only sound was the chirping crickets. He felt thirsty and exceedingly tired.

He scrambled under his net and found his pillow. He sat quietly in the dark thinking about the last few hours. Then his scratches, bruises, and mosquito bites started to hurt and he looked at the scratch on his leg. He located his medicines and applied some antibiotic ointment and anaesthetic cream to his bites. He wished he had brought a few more first-aid supplies. He found his sleeping tablets and immediately realized that he had forgotten to pack a cup or glass. Tilting the large water jug, he managed to swallow the sleeping pill. He wrapped his food in the small bag and placed it inside the rucksack, in case the smell attracted animals. He rubbed the mosquito-repellent on his exposed skin, and made sure that the heavy stick, sprays, and fire extinguisher were handy in case an animal approached. Then, he lay down to sleep.

Instantly, he felt alone and isolated. He thought about the community sleeping just the other side of the wall and felt they were a thousand miles away. He had chosen to separate himself from the group. He was now the outsider, the vulnerable one. Then a thought struck him: *Henry is just down the path. I wonder if he feels lonely and cut off? How does he cope with the solitude? Perhaps some staff stay with him. Too many questions. Stop Brett! Tomorrow will bring answers.*

He remembered a sermon when Steve had told them that Christians are never alone, as Jesus is always with them. All they had to do was pray for protection and comfort and a lack of fear. "Trust in Jesus, your ever-present friend and comforter," Steve had urged them. Brett drew considerable solace from that thought, and he began to pray for the people who came to mind.

Suddenly, he heard a distant cry that sent a flush of heat up his back and across his face. It was a piercing scream that sounded as though someone was being murdered. He lay absolutely still, terrified. He heard it again, and it sounded vaguely familiar. Then he remembered the nighttime screech of a tree hyrax which had been known to send campers diving into their tents in terror. He had not realized they existed at the coast. *Or perhaps it is some form of amphibian, closer than I imagined at first. It's difficult to judge distances of unfamiliar sounds at night – especially when I am tense like this.* Then, reasoning calmly, he thought perhaps it was some other harmless animal, or possibly a bird. They can all make strange sounds at times. It did not continue, but Brett's prayers did – even more earnestly.

His final thoughts were of his friends, just metres away. As the swirling images filled his brain, his thoughts became confused in a jumble of interwoven patterns, and soon sleep overcame him.

The light woke him. He sat up and at looked at his watch. It was 6:25am. He felt stiff, uncomfortable, and thirsty, but he had survived the night. He lay down again and looked up through the mesh to the trees above. Birds were chirping and narrow horizontal rays of light penetrated the dense foliage from the east. It felt good to be alive. He saw clouds of early-morning mosquitos, so decided to remain inside his net for a while. There was no hurry. He imagined not arriving at Henry's place until at least nine. He felt grateful for the food he had prepared. He washed his face and hands using a corner of the towel he had brought and began to eat his breakfast. Halfway through he was startled by a loud crashing sound nearby. Quickly he realized that it was a dead palm frond falling to the ground.

He ate all his food, drank a lot of water, and then wiped his skin all over with insect repellent. He wondered about wearing his second shirt as it had long sleeves. He had not needed it during the night so it probably looked bit fresher than the one he had worn the previous day. As he changed, he became aware of many aches in his arms and back due to the strenuous and unfamiliar activities the day before. *Still, I'm here and soon I will achieve my goal. Then I can return to my cage to get comfortable.* Then he intended to get a lift or take a matatu to Excel Auto to retrieve his pickup.

He lay back and waited, listening to the sounds. The wind had not picked up, so the heavy aroma of the tropical plants was overpowering, and the bird songs were rich and penetrating. A group of large birds flew over. He could not identify them through the dense trees, but he saw they had an unfamiliar flight pattern. *Oh, I wonder if they are fruit bats? Those are supposed to be dangerous. But only if they bite you, I think,* he said to himself. *Or they could be vultures. Now I'm talking to myself,* he thought. *Not surprising as there is no one else around!*

He needed to get out and stretch, so he reluctantly left the limited protection of his net. He was tempted to explore to the north but did not want to risk setting off the Ridge-Taylors' dogs. *That can be done later, once I get Henry Emerson's permission to explore around the area.* He then realized that this was a huge assumption, considering he would be trespassing in a place where he had not been invited. *Where,* he acknowledged, *I was specifically not invited. Forbidden, in fact!* He looked at the wall. It was much rougher and more unfinished than on the other side. It had similar angled indentations, but the base was wide and buttressed. Apart from the small footpath, the vegetation had taken over. It all looked like a natural and undisturbed region which he thought would be perfect for scientific research.

Brett took down the mosquito net, rolled up his sponge and tarpaulin, put on his hat, and carried everything back to the ladder. He angled the ladder against the wall so it could not be seen, but could be reached from the other side when he needed to retrieve his belongings later. He wondered about hiding everything, in case someone climbed the far ladder and looked over the wall, but he felt it was extremely unlikely in the next few hours. He decided to take the fire extinguisher and sprays with him, in case he encountered some animals, but he left his water bottle and the bedding rolled tightly in the tarpaulin and tied to the base of the ladder. He didn't want any animals to drag those things away. He had heard some strange rustling and grunting from the dense bush, and was uncertain what he might meet on his walk to the far shore.

Imagining his approach to Henry's place, he thought he would most likely encounter a member of staff first. As that person would not be expecting him, he would have to be careful how he presented himself. As he got closer to the dwelling, he felt it would be good to make some noise or even whistle or sing. Thinking of his appearance made him wish he had brought along a small mirror, and then he suddenly realized he had forgotten to pack his shaver. *I'm going to look an unshaven mess. Not the ideal house guest. Never mind, Henry will understand*, he thought. *Or maybe he won't. He will probably be extremely upset with me. I must approach his area with great caution and respect.*

His introspection was interrupted by a crashing in the trees above and a cacophony of sharp barking sounds. Looking up, he was astonished to see a family of monkeys shrieking down at him. Thinking they might attract attention, he decided to move away from that area towards the south. He quickly packed into the rucksack everything he was taking with him, include the gifts for Henry and the copy of his letter. He placed the long knife in the side pouch of the backpack, handy to grab if needed.

He grasped his stout stick in his left hand, held the fire-extinguisher in the other hand, and trekked off, following the narrow winding path along the east side of the wall. He was on his way to meet Henry. *Well, I wonder what's going to happen today*, he thought to himself. *The moment has come.*

11

*He was still very much on his own, an outsider, and a trespasser.
It was imperative that no one spotted him.*

The walk towards the southern shore was less than half a kilometre. He took it slowly, waving his stick along the ground in front of him in wide arcs as a blind person might use their white stick. He wanted to check for snakes. He knew there were deadly mambas, but he particularly dreaded the puff adder as its defence was to remain absolutely still, coiled up and ready to strike if a person came too close. Most other snakes would dart away at the first sign of danger.

Studying the wall on his right side, and the opposing vegetation on his left, Brett kept his ears and eyes open for threatening sounds or movements. He was slightly fearful as he recalled the tales of wild animals and the multitude of other unspecified dangers. But, at the same time, this was offset by a feeling of elation to be where he was, having yearned for months to explore that side. The barely discernible path followed a predictable route and, as he walked, he imagined the corresponding sections of the wall on the other side that he was familiar with. In several places the path ran close to the base of the wall so he could see the wire and stanchions he had worked on.

Gradually, the trees thinned and it became lighter and hotter. He passed by a large wrought-iron grill set in the wall. It appeared to be an old gate in front of a wooden door. Obviously it had not been used for a while judging by the growth of grass and short vegetation in front of it. A little farther on he noticed some construction above the wall so he knew he was beside the Emersons' cage with its crenelated stone parapets and formal arch built above the wall. He tried to recall what Peter had said they called it, Kismet Kat-something?

Suddenly Kali started barking furiously. "Good for you, you wretched dog," he whispered, with an element of admiration of how alert she was. After he passed by, thankfully she quietened down. Glancing ahead through the glistening sun's rays, he thought he spotted some movement on the upper wall but he concluded that it was the palm fronds waving in the sunlight. The intricate stonework continued along the wall, and evolved into another built-in quasi-arched feature above the large door he had seen from the other side. The pathway from it joined his trail and became more clearly defined as it swung towards the east. So far, things had appeared as he expected, apart from the first small door he had seen, and the extent of the elaborate stone constructions over that section of the wall. He guessed that some of the edifice was old and had existed long before the Zoo had been built.

He heard some distant voices across the wall as he passed along the edge of the Muslim sector, so he quickly moved away, turning to his left and following the path just above the shoreline. This was the area where he thought he might meet someone as, through gaps in the bushes, he occasionally saw dugout canoes and larger craft farther out. He was careful not to be seen from the ocean. The path gradually wound along the forest edge, sometimes turning inland to avoid large outcrops of coral, other times passing just above the debris of the high storm tides. Clearly, the path had been trodden in recent times, but the overgrowth of vegetation indicated that it was not frequently used.

Moving carefully along the trail, Brett remained alert and continued waving the heavy stick ahead of him. Looking out for the slightest signs of life or movement, he was prepared to call out greetings if he saw someone. Based on what John Phillips had described, Brett expected to see some structures within about two or three hundred metres. Ahead of him he noticed a small hut and called out as he approached it, but it was deserted, with the roof partially collapsed and the old door hanging on one hinge. He passed by the decrepit dwelling on his left, and continued towards an open clearing. There he received a tremendous shock.

He expected to see signs of life, but he was astonished at what he encountered. Instead of inhabited dwellings, he saw two partially collapsed buildings on the edge of a rubbish-strewn compound. Another building stood in the far corner. The place was deserted. He called out several times before walking cautiously towards the first structure. As he went, a green mamba suddenly darted across the open area, swerving in rapid gliding movements as it escaped. The first empty building had no door, so he peered inside and several bats swooped past his head and up into the trees, causing him to jump. The structure contained large damaged boxes and some broken animal cages. Walking across the compound to the second building, he disturbed a large gecko that was sunning itself on a rock. To the left of the rear building Brett saw some ancient foundations. The only remaining feature was a floor slab and a heavy steel door laying horizontally, with much fallen detritus on top.

Turning his attention to the solid-looking building on the right at the back, partly nestled in the trees, he saw that its windows and door were intact although some glass panes had been broken. Approaching slowly, he called out again and tried to look through the windows. All he could see were some cabinets, shelving, and a desk. At the back of the ramshackled structure was an open door leading to an Asian-style toilet set in the floor, and another section with torn papers and files and wooden boxes scattered around. Looking closer, he saw where animals had chewed the materials and made nests.

Brett was shocked at what he was discovering. Obviously this abandoned site had not been used for a long time. He scouted around the area and up a few paths, but they all petered out into the dense undergrowth, except one, which wound up over a ridge towards the east. He wanted to explore that, as it appeared to be the only accessible footpath, but he was becoming thirsty. He knew he would have to return for his drinking water. It was hot and only a minimal breeze had begun from the south.

He found a wooden crate in a shady corner, brushed off the twigs and leaves and sat down to survey the wreckage around him. He pondered the reality of what he had discovered. Obviously, Henry did not live here. He wondered if there was more to be seen farther on but, based on what John had told him, this was the only evidence of any development. He stood and walked back to the main building and tried the door handle. The door was locked. He stepped around the back of the building and noticed other windows, but no doors. He felt deflated, but he had no alternative but to get a drink and reconsider his situation.

Returning to the place where he had left the ladder, he maintained his cautious procedure of sweeping the stick ahead of him. He was careful as he passed alongside the residential quarters, past the two doors, and back into the shaded forest. Kali did not react this time. Realistically, he knew he would have to wait until darkness before climbing back over the wall, so he resolved to explore as much as he could while he was there. He looked at his remaining water supply and immediately regretted using it for washing. He estimated that he had less than two litres, which would get him through if he was careful. He realized he had no food apart from the biscuits, so he ate half and held the rest back for a snack later. Ruefully, he turned over the cans of meat and cheese he had intended to give to Henry. The pictures on the labels look extraordinarily appealing.

Once he had adjusted his thinking to accept his new circumstances, Brett saw it was a wonderful opportunity to explore what he had been dreaming of. He decided to risk walking quietly towards the north to see what happened to the pathway along that side of the wall. He managed to get close enough to cage N-1 to see the ocean in the northern bay. He was surprised to see a door in the wall on his left. It was similar to the one at the other end. He thought it led into the brigadier's cage, or at least the servant's quarters or dog compound. He quietly crept away without disturbing the dogs and walked back, past the ladder, along to the southern shore, and over to Henry's abandoned buildings. This time he carried water instead of gifts. He would have loved to have walked down to the beach to swim, but he did not want to risk being seen.

Cautiously, he started to climb the trail which led inland and up over a series of ridges. He remembered John's description of some cliffs which led across the top of the peninsula and dropped down into the ocean at the far end of the headland. He doubted if he would get far, but he wanted to explore wherever he could – once again being careful not to expose his movements towards the seaward direction. The path wandered side to side and became difficult to follow in places but there was definitely an upward movement as he travelled inland. Suddenly, Brett was startled by the unexpected movement of two animals rushing away from him. They were pigs of some kind, possibly bush pigs. Sometime later, another troop of monkeys spotted him and shrieked at him for invading their territory. They looked like omnivorous Sykes monkeys but Brett did not see them clearly enough to be certain. He saw many butterflies, several brightly-coloured lizards, and a chameleon. It was a utopia for wildlife which was obviously rarely disturbed.

After about half an hour of strenuous climbing Brett reached a plateau and a series of steep rocks blocked his path ahead. The trail separated, with one path heading inland to his left, and the other, to the right, leading towards the shore. He rested at the junction in a shady spot and appreciated the southeast wind that was blowing steadily by then. He wondered if there was any water supply, because the animals would require that, but perhaps there were sufficient puddles from the rain. Then he wondered if animals like the pigs could get enough moisture from the vegetation. John had mentioned that there were informal paths crisscrossing the headland. Probably the pigs had made these trails through the forest.

He wandered a short distance down a couple of other small trails but they did not seem very definite. He was becoming tired and hot, so he made his way back down the path to the buildings and sat for a long time on the wooden crate in the shade, looking around, thinking, and imagining.

Before he left, he made one more careful circuit of the compound and discovered a small shed at the back that he had missed previously. Again, there was no door, and the roof was partially collapsed. He looked inside and noticed that, on the floor, there was another slab of rusty metal. It had an ancient padlock on it. With his stick he brushed aside the dust and debris to reveal some large hinges. Looking at the padlock, he poked and wiggled it with his stick but it seemed firmly attached and tightly locked. He noticed some stains of oil on the metal hinges and padlock, so he wondered if they may have been used recently.

With some regret, he left the compound. In one sense he felt like an intruder, but at the same time there was a feeling of satisfaction in resolving one small part of the puzzle. Walking back slowly and cautiously so as not to disturb Kali, he tried to absorb the atmosphere and mood of the area. It seemed so different from the other side of the wall. True, there were no people, but it was more than that. There was a sense of serenity but, at the same time, he sensed an undercurrent of disquiet. In spite of his disappointment at not seeing Henry, Brett had a sense of fulfilment.

The euphoria did not last long. As soon as he arrived back at the ladder, the reality of his vulnerability struck him. He could no longer look forward to any protection or sense of justification from having met Henry, and returning home legitimately. No, he was still very much on his own, an outsider, and a trespasser. It was imperative that no one spotted him. That meant another late-night foray over the wall and another circumvention of the Zoo under the cloak of darkness. This was going to be a long day and he was getting thirsty and hungry. The remaining delicious Belgian biscuits were tempting but he kept them. He also felt tired, so he went to the trouble of re-erecting his mosquito net and setting out the mat so he could get several hours of relaxation, and possibly some sleep.

Before that, he wanted to try splitting open a coconut. He had seen several of the large green shells on the ground, but he had never opened one himself. Taking his large knife he stabbed and hacked away at it for a long time, eventually levering apart the two outer halves. He found inside the brown fibrous core and gouged out the hard, smooth nut. It had taken a lot of effort. All the time, a group of crows was flapping in the trees above him squawking and scolding him while he struggled. He remembered that one of the germination pores at the top was soft, so he prodded the three eyes with the knife blade until he was able to bore a hole. The nut eventually yielded its milk, drop by drop. He tried hurling the empty coconut at a rock to crack it open but it made a loud noise, so he managed to wedge it between two rocks and crush it with a larger stone after getting it into position. He was able to split it open and dig out the soft white flesh. He enjoyed it, but it was a lot of work for just a few bites.

He sat down to rest after his battle with the coconut. Brett's frustration increased as he looked at the pile of cans. *If only I had included a tin opener...* he thought, but then realized there would have been no purpose in that according to his original plan. "Is there any way of splitting them open with rocks or sharp stones?" he wondered. He tried it and succeeded only in denting the cans and scraping his fingers. Then he attempted to open them by jabbing the tops with the large knife. That did puncture them so he was able to suck the salty water. "This may not be a good idea with your water supply running low," he warned himself.

He began to fantasize about climbing the wall, looking over, waiting until there was nobody around, and making a dash for his cage. He could retrieve his belongings later when he was ostensibly working on the project again. He quickly dismissed the idea, as he was bound to be seen, either by Joram Mwangi or another neighbour who would be certain to ask some awkward questions. No, he would have to wait, and preserve his story about being in Malindi for two nights. He lay back and surrendered to his drifting thoughts, before slipping off to sleep.

Nearly two hours later, he awoke, refreshed. With the vivid clarity that often arrives upon waking, a remarkable thought struck him. The hacksaw! He had completely forgotten about the hacksaw. *I wonder if it's possible to open a can with that? It's worth a try. But can I find where it fell?* He crawled out from under the mosquito net and stumbled along the wall looking for the piece of rope that he had left dangling. It was getting towards sunset so he knew there was not much light left.

He found the rope and was surprised that he had not noticed it when he had walked past, but the path moved away from the wall slightly at that point. He felt heartened when he saw the rope and scratched his way through the bushes, searching for the tool. He remembered it had caught on a branch but he could not locate it. In frustration he returned to collect his torch and long knife. It took a lot of cutting and scraping in the gloom, but eventually he spotted the elusive hacksaw which had become wedged between a tree trunk and the wall. He managed to retrieve it and gleefully returned to the three cans which seemed to be glaring at him defiantly in the twilight.

In the rapidly advancing darkness, he found several suitable rocks and carefully wedged a can between them. By the light of the torch, with a gentle cutting action along the side of the can next to the rim, while making as little noise as possible, he managed to open enough of the top to push in the knife and prise apart the metal edges. This allowed him to dig out the delicious pieces of salmon. He did the same thing with the other two cans but restrained himself from eating their contents, knowing he had a long evening and night ahead of him. He set the precious sharp-edged cans between two rocks beside his net and covered them with a large slab. He enjoyed the long-awaited treat of opening the small Cointreau bottle and taking a few sips. Again he crawled under the mosquito net, flapped it across the cans so he could protect his valuable food supply, and lay back enjoying the rich and varied sounds of the African dusk. *This is back to basics: food and water*, he thought. *How quickly these things can become vital. And how often we take them for granted.*

Before switching off his light to preserve the battery, he applied more cream to his cuts and bruises, and the additional bites he had acquired during the day's explorations. Then, in the darkness, he thought carefully about his next steps. Everything had changed, so he was forced to adapt, whilst maintaining the basic fiction that he had been away at the Safari Club Hotel. It took a while, but he figured out a workable plan. He was not looking forward to it, and it had its risks, but it was the best he could come up with. Another gulp of the rich liqueur offered a minuscule measure of pyrrhic comfort, accompanied by the remaining long-resisted biscuits.

Once his plan was settled in his mind, he allowed his thoughts to turn to the question of where Henry was. He was obviously not living in the beach hut, so he must be staying upstairs at their house above the wall. Brett had briefly glimpsed some stairs leading up there, and Louise had the staff and capability to care for Henry, so he need never be seen in public. That was the most likely answer, unless he was living somewhere else, perhaps in a care home. Brett evaluated that possibility for a while but felt it was unlikely as there surely would have been some clue, from someone, if that were the case. And why keep it so secret anyway? It was clear to everyone with eyes, and a nose for details, that Henry was no longer in charge and Louise had moved into his role with help from others around her. Was she maintaining an illusion? Was the ongoing fantasy of Henry still being the boss helping the stability of the Zoo? He doubted it; so the mystery remained.

He tried to see some stars, but the foliage was too dense. He did not intend to go wandering around to find an open clearing. He just waited, listening to the strange sounds of the night, and thinking about the new revelations. His musings were interrupted by a scurrying and scratching sound just outside his net. He shone the torch to reveal a group of tiny creatures. *Probably elephant shrews*, he thought. *Harmless company. This*

Part 2: The Wall

must be a rich, diverse, and protected habitat for many animals. His thoughts reverted to the central problem: how long would he be able to maintain the deception he had fabricated – assuming he got back to his cage the next day unnoticed? It would be interesting to see. Maybe people are not as observant as he thought. Or possibly folks are simply not interested in the odd antics of a recalcitrant bachelor resident – particularly when they are not affected directly. The evening dragged on, but he mellowed into the unfamiliar luxury of several empty hours all to himself. He began to think of his next safari, and the possibility of driving back to Nyeri to see some old friends and take a camping trip to a few places that he had enjoyed previously. He wondered if he should go alone or if there was someone compatible with whom he could share it. No one obvious came to mind, so he resolved to plan it by himself.

Around 9:30pm, he excavated his remaining two cans. He ate the sausages and cheese, drank his final drops of water, drained the miniature liqueur bottle and set it aside. He started to work by the light of the torch. He needed to prepare his things to get them back across to the other side. The rucksack contained only the essentials for the final phase of his venture. The rest of the items, including the empty cans and the water bottle, were bundled together and attached by ropes so he could loop them around the upright pipe in the wall and retrieve them the next day. He knew he would not be able to climb back over the wall to collect anything, so it all had to be accessible from the top of the ladder on the Zoo side. He dare not take time that evening, once he was over, to pack up any items at the base of the wall. He had to get away from the area as quickly as possible.

When everything was ready, he set up the ladder and slowly climbed up to look over. Everything seemed peaceful, so he quietly unhooked the four barbed wires and began suspending the prepared bundles from the stanchions. He left the small bag hanging with some items inside, including the remaining inedible gifts. Finally, he lugged up his rucksack and balanced it on top of the wall. It was the reverse process to the one he had employed the previous night. Wrestling the ladder up and over went more smoothly and he was able to quietly slide it down the wall. He knew he was vulnerable during the next few minutes while lowering the rucksack and climbing back up to fasten the four wire hooks. He checked to confirm that the loops of rope around the upright post were not too obvious, climbed down, and looked around. Lifting the rucksack, and grasping his strong pole, he quickly walked down beside Peter's cage onto the beach.

The journey along the beach in the dark was uneventful, although he followed the same precautions as before. This was no time for carelessness. The trip along the road went similarly, but this time he encountered two groups of pedestrians whom he avoided by using his proven hide-and-freeze tactic. A few vehicles drove by, which he saw coming, and remained still as they passed him. He was grateful to see his pickup in its place and waited for a long time in the shadows before approaching it. He was concerned that he did not see a watchman, so he held off going over to his pickup until he felt certain that a guard was not patrolling around or likely to see him from another position. He walked calmly to his vehicle, quietly unlocked the door, and slipped in. He was extremely grateful for the small bottle of water he had left there, but he took only sips as he had many hours until morning.

Then the long period of waiting began. He lay across the bench seat to sleep. His legs ached after so much walking. He wished he had brought along his pillow, but he had left that with the other bedding. *Bad decision, Brett*, he chastised himself. While laying down, he was confident he could not be seen unless a person came right up and stared in.

He attempted to sort out the kaleidoscope of confused thoughts in his mind, but the more he tried to reason things out, the more stressed he became. Why had he put himself through all of that? There was an inexplicable draw towards the enigmatic Henry Emerson, certainly; but why? Perhaps meeting him would offer the chance of access to the forbidden zone, and the satisfaction of exploring its pristine remoteness. Might he be willing to discuss the ideas Brett had for improvements in the Zoo? He forced himself to think of other things. He went through a long mental list of friends and situations to pray about, including all of his Kenyan friends, others in the community, and his students. He took time to pray for everyone at length, including thanks for his safety while over the wall and on the clandestine journeys. He prayed for individuals in the Zoo, especially Louise and Henry, whatever their situation was. He knew few details, except that things were difficult for them. He remembered, in prayer, the small church community, and Tony and Jane in England.

Part 2: The Wall

Soon he was feeling sleepy. It was just after midnight. He reasoned that he should stay there until at least 5am or whenever he heard the muezzin's call to morning prayer, as that would be when people started moving about. He used his rucksack as a pillow. Unfortunately, he was only able to doze in short and fitful intervals due to his confined and cramped position on the narrow seat. He used the wakeful periods to remember some of the many happy times he had enjoyed in Kenya during his first five years, and the people he knew who he might see again soon.

Eventually, he got through the long and difficult night and was grateful when he heard the loud calls from the nearby minaret. He waited until vehicles were moving along the lane, and several men had passed by on their way to the mosque. Then he started the engine, and slowly made his way down to the main road, turned right, and drove past the Zoo towards Malindi and, he hoped, a substantial breakfast with lots of hot, fresh, Kenyan coffee.

As he walked into the hotel lobby, he suddenly became conscious of his scruffy appearance, so he slid into the gent's room and glanced in the mirror. His unshaven face was a mess, as was his hair. He looked at his torn slacks and knew he could not repair the tear, but at least he could wash out the blood stains and try to clean off some of the dust and grime. Feeling slightly more presentable, he counted his remaining cash. The main buffet breakfast was 55/- but he had only 47/- left. He had often thought about hiding a small reserve of cash in the pickup but had not found a safe storage place. So, he would have to see what the little snack bar outside could offer him for breakfast within his budget.

He managed to order his long-awaited coffee and a bacon-and-egg sandwich. He felt slightly guilty about the 'forbidden' bacon, but accepted that it was in a tourist hotel so it would not be an issue with the staff. Generally, he avoided pork, in deference to his Muslim housekeeper. *It's like walking through a social minefield here sometimes,* he thought. *You never know what innocent action or casual comment might suddenly blow up in your face.* On the counter, some mangos had been sliced in half, cut in a diamond pattern, and turned inside out. They resembled porcupines. He loved the delicious fruit so he ordered two along with some sticky pastries. With a 6/- tip, his money was gone. It felt quite freeing.

A review of the last two days occupied his mind, but his aching body and cut ankle would not be relieved. He looked longingly at the pool, knowing a swim would help but he had no swimming trunks, and no money to pay the entrance fee. He was starting to feel like an outsider. He could not even buy himself another cup of coffee. Maybe penury was not so freeing after all. No doubt he could persuade the waiter to bring him more coffee, or ask the manager for some concessions, but his pride made him reluctant.

Suddenly, he felt exhausted. He wandered into the airy hotel foyer. He caught a glimpse of a family from Mwakindini. He knew them casually, having seen them in the bank from time to time. *They would lend me some cash, I'm sure*, he thought, but he quickly rejected the idea and avoided them. He found a comfortable chair in a secluded section just at the end of the reception hall. Everything seemed quiet, so he stretched out with his bag on his lap and arms folded across it.

He felt lonely in that crowed place, separated, and lacking legitimacy; weakened by lack of money, or failing to possess the right things, or not wearing appropriate clothing. He had placed himself in that situation by his choice to go where he shouldn't, and he was now experiencing the consequences.

He timed his return to the Zoo to match one's expected arrival after an overnight hotel stay. He was anxious to quickly clear up the things he had left hanging over the back of the wall, so he drove straight there. The area was deserted, and he immediately climbed the ladder and pulled up his bags, placing them in the pickup before anyone came along. He left both ladders upright as usual. He allowed himself a few seconds to glance along the wall. But he was looking with fresh eyes now. He knew what lay the other side. He had crossed the forbidden barrier.

Suddenly, he remembered that he had left the hacksaw beside the rocks, where he had used it to cut open the cans.

12

"Be careful," warned Miles. *"Things are often not as they appear."*

By Tuesday, most of the students had returned from their break, and full classes had resumed. Tili was back in the Zoo too. Brett sat one evening listening to the Brahms cassette that was intended for Henry, looking through the bird book, and admiring the union-jack keyring laying on the table. He smiled to himself. "Gifts not yet given. Soon perhaps." His smile did not remain for long because of the main concern that was constantly on his mind: had anyone seen him, and if so, when would he hear about it? And what would the consequences be?

He continued to say nothing to anyone. He gave no hint that he knew what was over the other side. No one had asked him about his time away, or put him in a defensive mode where he had to reply vaguely to enquiries. Later that week, he completed the wall painting, having removed the hooks and finished the barbed-wire repairs. He returned the ladders to the Central Store and transferred the remaining paints, tools, and other materials from Njuguna's store to the appropriate sections of the maintenance team.

For Brett, life in the Zoo continued as normal…until about three weeks later when, at 4pm, the office messenger at the polytechnic, delivered a note to Brett in his office. It summoned him immediately to a meeting of the Executive Council in the main office. "What, *now?*" he thought.

He grabbed his briefcase, and drove across to the central buildings, wondering what it was about, although he feared that it was related to his foray over the wall.

The secretary, Grace, met him at the entrance. "Mr. Chengo needs to see you. Upstairs."

"Where's that?" Brett asked.

"Here, I will show you." She guided him along the corridor, stepping across a large puddle on the floor by the toilets, and around three harried-looking plumbers struggling with their tools. They walked out into a hallway beside the Emersons' cage. Turning to the left, Grace pointed him towards the stairs. "You go there. They are in the room at the top," she said. "It's there up. On the left," she said, pointing upwards with her chin.

Brett climbed the stairs onto a narrow landing. Turning to the door on the left, he knocked. "Come in," a man's voice called from within. He entered a large room and saw three people sitting at a table. He was directed towards a chair in front of the group and he looked across at the Executive Officer, Boniface Chengo, in the centre, with Peter Lancaster on his right, and Louise Emerson sitting to Chengo's left. *So, the Executive Council. This is where they meet: Peter's 'Big Five'*, he thought as he quickly looked around the sparsely furnished room, which was in semidarkness with all of the curtains half closed.

Chengo spoke first, "We thank you to be…joining us…Mister Brett. It seems that you are causing us a bit of a difficulty…"

"What Mr. Chengo is saying is you have become a darn nuisance," snapped Peter.

"Yes, it seems that you are giving us more than we can be able to cope up with," continued Chengo, obviously uncomfortable.

"You climbed over the wall three weeks ago, correct?" said Peter.

Brett paused, surprised. "Yes," he admitted.

"You positioned the ladders to make it appear that you were working on the barbed wire."

"Yes."

"That little ruse fooled nobody."

Brett shrugged, "I doubt if anyone else knows."

"Why did you do it?"

"I very much wanted to meet Mr. Emerson. I'm sorry. I had written a letter which was ignored–"

"Not ignored," interjected Chengo.

"Well, let me rephrase that: I didn't receive a reply or any response–"

This time Peter interrupted him, "Some of your suggestions have been implemented."

"Yes, thank you for that; but I wanted to discuss other ideas with Mr. Emerson, so I thought a visit might be in order."

"Definitely out of order!" This retort also came from Peter. "Plus, you were particularly curious about what is over the other side of the wall, were you not?"

"Yes."

"Even though you knew it was out of bounds? I told you myself."

"I am sorry for the inconvenience. I did no damage. I simply wanted to see the other side and meet Mr. Emerson."

"Illegally breaching the wall was not the appropriate way to do that," explained Peter with fake patience.

For the first time, Louise spoke, "Look, Brett, we have rules that you agreed to. And certain expectations. One of them is we respect the wall and do not go over that side. There are dangers."

"I knew of the dangers and I accepted the risk."

The three looked at one another silently. Behind the trio, the curtains were almost closed. To his right Brett noticed a large shelving unit, curiously positioned beside the door. *To use a natural alcove, I suppose*, he thought. Chengo was speaking, "Have you spoken…told another person you did it? About this bad thing you did?"

"No. I've told no one. I will not say anything."

They seemed relieved. "Good. Please do not mention it to anyone. We should do nothing to jeopardize the security and stability of the Zoo. Besides, we don't want a parade of people leaping over there," said Louise to faint smiles from the others. The tense mood had eased slightly.

Peter said, "Of course, we do have a certain admiration for your pluck and ingenuity." Brett was surprised by this. *Goodness, they are going to congratulate me next*, he thought. *But how did they find out? I wonder if they'll tell me.*

He decided to be bold. "May I ask how you found out?"

"The security photos."

"The photos? I thought the security cameras—" Brett started to say.

"As you know – or have recently found out –" Louise said, glancing across at Peter, "the security cameras are fake. But that does not mean we do not have a security record."

Peter continued, "Every day, usually in the afternoons, the Emersons' man, Mzee Mjuhgiuna, takes photos of the wall from several locations. If he is not available, one of us does it." Brett remembered seeing Mjuhgiuna walking along there sometimes. *So that's what he does,* he thought. *He was there when I was working on the painting.* Chengo sat glumly in the centre while Peter continued, "Naturally, it would be too expensive – and unnecessary – to make prints when nothing happens, so we have the rolls of black-and-white film processed about every two or three weeks and we examine the negatives. Usually they show nothing unusual so we just store them by date. Occasionally, if something interesting or unusual appears in the images, we will order a set of prints."

At that moment, as though they had rehearsed it, Boniface Chengo lifted his briefcase from beneath his chair and placed it on the table in front of him. He removed a package and opened it to reveal a set of 3" x 5" prints. Chengo took the photos and bunched then together vertically between his thick hands. Brett remembered seeing that gesture before. Chengo selected several prints and placed them in front of Brett. He was surprised, and quite impressed. Peter and Louise watched Brett's reaction with barely concealed amusement. Louise glanced, almost imperceptibly, over to Peter behind Chengo's back.

"We ordered these prints from the photographic shop in Malindi because the negatives showed, through a magnifying glass, that one of the ladders against the wall disappeared." Lifting one of the photographs, Chengo read the date on the back. "This was on the morning of – er – the 21st of June. That was during the Eid-ul-Fitr festival, you may remember." Brett nodded in silence, wondering to himself where this was leading. He confirmed the date on the back where Chengo laid it upside down on the table: 21-6-85. Chengo lined up the three prints again and said, "The series of photos here shows the disappearance of the ladder, and its return the next day."

Part 2: The Wall

Peter spoke, "On its own, that image would not raise any concern because you may have moved the ladder and laid it flat earlier, so it may not have necessarily have shown in the photo." Brett looked puzzled, and may have communicated, with a slight shrug, that he saw nothing significant in the photos.

Peter continued, "These photos meant nothing to us on their own. But you were seen walking along the north beach late at night on Eid which, when we connected the dates, made us suspicious."

That was a shock. "Oh, who saw me?" Brett remembered hearing Len whistling. "Was it Len?"

There was a brief silence. Chengo turned and glanced at Peter who told Brett, "Mama Muzhere saw you when she was on the beach praying. She told us."

"So late? I would have expected her to be with her family during the celebration," said Brett.

"No, she was alone on the shore. Even her seeing you would probably not have alerted us to anything unusual…except that Mrs. Emerson, here…" he turned, leant across in front of Chengo, and directed an upturned hand towards Louise, "…later recalled Mzee Mjuhgiuna telling her that one of his relatives looked over the roof parapets to the east on the Friday and saw a man moving."

"From the top of Kismet Katna – or something like that?" asked Brett.

Louise looked surprised, "He knows about that?" she whispered across to Peter.

"Yes."

"You told him?"

"I mentioned the name of the structure, yes," admitted Peter. Louise glowered towards Peter. On previous occasions, Brett had seen her direct her withering glare at someone that way. She glanced across at Brett. "What doesn't he know? He seems to know everything." Clearly, she was annoyed.

"'Kismet Kantara' is the correct name," continued Peter unperturbed. "Seeing a person on that side was very unusual, so she told her uncle and he mentioned it to Mrs. Emerson. At the time, she did not take it seriously, until these other revelations came to light." He tapped the photos on the desk in front of Chengo. "And then we realized someone – probably you – had been over the wall."

"Correct. It was me. I thought I saw someone moving up there."

"Sometimes the women go there to pray…or for a break away from… family responsibilities," explained Louise.

"Well…so, when we were confronted by three coincidences…each on its own insignificant perhaps, but together…" said Peter.

"…we came to the conclusion that it was you," stated Louise.

There was an awkward silence, during which Peter and Louise leant forward in front of Chengo and began to whisper to each other. Chengo moved his chair back slightly and looked across the two heads towards Brett. Brett felt sorry for him, as he liked Boniface Chengo. Brett continued to study the odd-looking shelving behind them. It made a fitting sombre backdrop to the triad before him. It seemed that Chengo was getting impatient. Brett thought, *Okay, they know I did a bad thing, but what now? Will I be punished?* So far, he had not revealed what he saw of the Emersons' former buildings. They had asked nothing about that. He sensed it was prudent to not fully disclose his explorations unless asked.

He caught snatches of their conversation as they talked quietly between themselves. He heard them expressing appreciation for his contribution at the polytechnic and support of the Facilities Committee. Then Jed Walker's name was mentioned. Brett recalled what Peter had told him about the outspoken Englishman who had been expelled. Peter said, "Some of us will be speaking with you individually later. We need to explain some things. Our instruction to you now is to continue to say nothing about what you did or anything you saw. Do we have your assurance of that?"

"Yes, certainly. And I do apologize, once again, for the trouble I have caused you."

He left, feeling bad about the difficult meeting. After all, he respected all of them and considered each one of them as a friend. However, he was troubled by the reference to Jed Walker.

The following afternoon, Miles met him in the corridor. They walked out of the building together. In a low voice Jolly said, "I hear you got a grilling from the Executive."

Part 2: The Wall

Brett was surprised. "I thought it was a private meeting. You're not supposed to know."

"The walls have ears my friend. But I didn't hear any details. So, how did it go – from your point of view?"

"It was a good discussion," was all Brett was willing to reveal.

"I'm just being my silly-old curious self. Nothing better to do, really," confessed Miles.

"They want me to stay mum."

"Be careful," warned Miles. "Things are often not as they appear."

Brett grinned, "Charming. Your cryptic comments are not very helpful."

"Nevertheless, be careful my friend. Just a timely warning, that's all." Once again, Brett felt the familiar flutter of tension. He watched Miles plodding back along the corridor, carrying his worn satchel and leaning on his piece of driftwood.

Two days after the Executive meeting, Louise saw Brett. "Would you be able to join me for tea after your classes one day please?" she asked.

"Yes, thank you. Maybe tomorrow?" he replied. They arranged for him to call at her cage just after 4pm. He wondered whether he would be meeting Henry at last. He decided to take along the three remaining gifts. The next afternoon, Mjuhgiuna met him by the door. Brett was expecting to be shown into their downstairs reception area, so he was surprised to be directed to the base of the same stairs he had climbed for the Executive meeting. He climbed up and called out "*Hodi*, may I come in?" and the door on the right opened. Louise ushered him into the upper apartment.

Immediately, he sensed a different atmosphere from the rest of the Zoo. The space radiated class and elegance. He took it all in with several discrete glances. The furniture was solid and ornate. The pictures on the walls were tasteful, with detail and dramatic colour, but were not kitsch. The shuttered windows afforded a cooling breeze, yet created a subdued lighting effect to enhance the aesthetic mood. He felt apprehensive as he was directed to a chair beside a small table. The only irritant was the dog Kali sniffing around his ankles. "She'll settle soon. I think she likes you," Louise said, trying to reassure him.

"Yes, yes, good dog," he muttered unconvincingly in Kali's direction. He thought, *This place makes my cage look like a …a cage!* He told Louise, "Your home is lovely – so elegant and relaxing."

"Thank you. We have been able to get it the way we wanted over the years…our style of furniture…some special things, acquired in many places."

"The paintings are very striking, I see already."

"I'm glad you noticed them. Some people don't, you know. Mjuhgiuna will be bringing us tea soon. I expect you'll have some scones and cake too, won't you?"

"Well, yes, thank you. It is very kind of you."

She was quiet briefly, then said, "You know, I am sorry about that awful meeting. We had to go through all that because you had, well, breached the regulations."

"Oh, I felt you were all very restrained, considering what I did."

"There will be some follow-up, which is partly why I asked you here. Peter will be speaking with you too. You can ameliorate the effect of your misdemeanour by keeping absolutely silent about it. Ah, here's Mjuhgiuna," she said.

Mjuhgiuna entered respectfully while struggling with a large tea tray. He delicately set the tray on the table and then left. Within a minute he returned carrying another tray with several plates of cakes, butter, jam, and cutlery. Brett thought, *Is she expecting anyone else? Will Henry be joining us?*

Louise sat in the comfortable chair next to Brett as they manoeuvred their way through the age-old ceremony of serving and delicately consuming tea and the baking. Brett was enjoying every minute of it, and Louise seemed relaxed and comfortable, skillfully making Brett feel at ease. They chatted for about twenty minutes, covering trivial matters, current happenings, his teaching at the polytechnic, malaria, gas shortages, and people in the Zoo.

After a while, Louise sat down in a hard chair across the table from Brett. He sensed the true purpose of her invitation was about to be revealed. She cleared her throat and glanced over at Brett as she sat upright in a prim posture. She pulled her skirt tightly over her knees and absentmindedly brushed away a crumb of cake. Then she placed her hands together in her lap, the left hand clasped above the right. She looked through the partially shuttered window, beyond the waving palm branches across to the horizon and, seemingly, far beyond it. "Brett, there is something very important I

Part 2: The Wall

need to tell you. This won't be easy, so please do not interrupt me." She paused and looked down at her hands. "I have not been entirely honest with you. Or, I should say, I have not been able to tell you the full truth – not until now, that is." Brett waited. He was confused and apprehensive. She seemed so frail and pathetic that he wanted to stop her, but her demeanour restrained him. He shifted slightly to a more comfortable position and waited. "There is so much to tell," she sighed, shaking her head slightly, "but I don't know where to begin." There was a silent pause. She seemed to be remote, as though in another place, or at least in a different time. "In the 1940s, during the war, I served in North Africa – that much you already know. You have heard about that–"

"And the award."

"Yes, but I asked you not to interrupt."

"Sorry," he said, settling slightly lower in his comfortable chair and stretching out his legs, with one foot resting across the other. His eyes focused intently on the cup and saucer in front of him as though they were positioned at infinity. Kali settled lower and sighed as if she had heard the story before.

"After the war, Heinrick and I met and got married. We worked in several places, but mostly here in Kenya." Louise lowered her head. She inhaled slowly, held her breath, and breathed out slowly with a long sigh. She continued, "We all live under constraints, and limitations…much of the time we have no control…Circumstances force their own responses, don't they? To some degree we are all victims of previous choices – ours and those of others." She seemed to be intoning a soliloquy. Brett dared not interrupt.

Then, suddenly, she appeared to have made a decision. Her green eyes swung towards Brett and she stated, quite flatly, "Heinrick is dead."

The news hit Brett like a splash of cold water. "Henry? Dead?"

"Yes, Henry is dead."

"When? How?" He did not know what say.

"Yes, you need to know. When, how, and why have we kept it a secret?" Louise nodded. Brett's thoughts were racing as many things slowly began to fall into place. "He was killed in a car accident just over three years ago… in June, before the military coup…in Laikipia, west of Mount Kenya. It was a tragic loss for me and the Zoo. He was so pivotal. He held everything together and gave it all…meaning. More than that, he brought credibility and stability. We had to keep it a secret. Without him – or his aura – things could collapse. Would have collapsed! People respected him. Without that solid…charisma…without his presence, so much would've been lost, and… don't you see? It had to be kept under wraps. No one could know. That's what we decided. No one knows, only Peter…and…very few. Now you know…" Her words trailed off.

"I won't tell anyone," Brett assured her. It was all he could think of to say.

"No, you must not. Don't. Thank you. This is just for you to know. We need to have continuity – and the stability – that Heinrick brought to us. He still provides that. People's respect for him lives on. We must keep that." She was thrusting out rapid thoughts as they came to her. "Henry's power and influence are still felt now. And needed, in a way. He was such a strong personality. A creative force in his lifetime." She paused. "You had so many questions I could not answer. I tried not to lie but you had so many questions…that I couldn't answer. I'm sorry." She dropped her head and placed her hands over her eyes.

Brett said, "I'm sorry too. Sorry for your loss, but also for being a nuisance with all my questions."

"Thank you. Let's have some more tea shall we? I feel quite exhausted, but relieved that you know. You are on our side; part of the team now. The Executive knew you could be trusted and will keep quiet."

"Thank you. I'm sorry I forced that on you by my actions over the wall. I had assumed Henry was being looked after over there, here, or somewhere. I never considered he was…" Louise started to pour more tea but realized it was cold so she stood up and walked to the wall and pressed one of two buttons.

"What's that for?" asked Brett.

"These operate some little bells on springs in the kitchen. They let the staff know I need them. That one's for Mjuhgiuna. If I press the other button, one of the girls will come up. Heinrick had them installed to avoid a lot of shouting and banging on the floor!" They both laughed.

In a moment, Mjuhgiuna appeared at the door with a fresh pot of tea and more milk. "He is very efficient," commented Brett.

"He's marvellous," agreed Louise.

Before drinking more tea, Brett needed to use the toilet as it had all taken longer than he imagined. He started to leave with Mjuhgiuna to head downstairs to the cafe toilets but Mjuhgiuna told him they were still closed for repairs. "Here, use my bathroom," Louise said, pointing to a door just down the hallway.

As he was washing his hands, in the mirror he saw a map of Australia on the wall behind him. He turned and saw two photos of young children set in the centre. 'Happy Christmas Grandma. We love you. We miss you,' read the message.

Returning to continue his tea, Brett decided to be blunt and asked, "You have grandchildren?"

Louise seemed surprised. "Oh, you saw the large card…Yes, I have two grandchildren in Perth, Western Australia. They're my son's children. I keep that Christmas card as it's special. I don't have much contact with them. That's part of the story I have not told you. Yet."

"Do you have other children, or grandchildren?" Brett inquired gently.

"Before I answer, there is something I need to stress. Although I can give you some information, there is a lot I cannot reveal to you. There are other forces at work…we all live under restraints. What I do tell you will be true, but there are some things I am unable to discuss."

"That's interesting. Miles has hinted at that too."

"He will not reveal much either. But I believe what he does say will be the truth. He's wise enough to know that lies can backfire and entangle a person when the deception is discovered. But there are things that slippery Miles keeps to himself. The other thing is, I cannot protect you – particularly against the outcome of any more stupid things that you might choose to do! You must be very circumspect. As I said, we are all subject to larger forces swirling around us."

"It sounds very mysterious."

"Umm. Anyway, continue to keep your lip buttoned. You must not discuss your escapade climbing over the wall, or anything you saw. Certainly not with Miles, or Steve, or Coreene. Nobody. That is a strict stipulation of the Executive if you are to be allowed to continue here." Brett caught the sombre tone in her words, and it troubled him.

Louise saw Mjuhgiuna at the door, and went over to speak to him. That left Brett some time to rapidly process what he had heard. What did she mean by her reference to bigger influences? He recalled the reaction of the crazy old man and his attempt to construct a sand barrier against witches. *She can't be referring to witchcraft. Surely she doesn't believe in that!* He had heard of its influence on many people in some parts of the country, but here, at the Zoo? His thoughts were swirling. As Louise returned, Brett remembered he still had a question from his interview with the Executive, so he asked boldly. "I can't understand how Mama Muzhere saw me on the beach. Wasn't she with her family for Eid?"

Louise smiled, "Miles gave her the time off for the celebration, but she is getting old and found all the excitement too much. I heard quite a lot of noise and loud voices myself from there." She lifted her chin towards the window facing to the south. "She told Chengo she had retreated to her favourite spot on the beach to pray, facing north to Mecca. That is where she saw you walking along the sand at an unusual hour." Brett felt rather subdued, acknowledging that, even after all his careful planning, he had been caught. He was further downcast when she added, "We three discussed expelling you from the Zoo. Peter was inclined to do so – as Security Officer. I was against it, so Chengo had the deciding vote. He particularly values your good relations with the Kenyans here and your contribution to the college. So, you can stay." Brett absorbed that new information.

Louise changed the subject: "You asked about our children. Heinrick and I were married in 1946 in Nairobi and our first son, Alan, was born there the following year. In 1949, our second son was born, but it was an extremely difficult pregnancy and birth, and he died after three days. In a different place, at another time, perhaps he could have been saved. It was a terrible blow for both of us. There were no more children. Heinrick was devoted to Alan and put double love and attention into him. Double expectations too. Everything was focused on Alan, and giving him the best opportunities possible. He was the centre of Heinrick's life. He always imagined Alan to be everything that he was not – or could not be, with all of the restrictions he had grown up with, the war, and everything. So Alan was raised under a lot of pressure and with high demands.

Part 2: The Wall

"Things were difficult during the teen years, as he became rebellious, and was bothered by some of the business contacts Henry was developing. Alan believed there was an illegal element involved. In his early twenties, he left the family and wanted nothing to do with Henry. Of course, that affected me too. He became estranged from us both. He moved to Australia and we heard nothing from him for several years. It was as though he too had died. For us, he ceased to exist." While she was talking, Brett remembered her mentioning 1949 when their second boy was born *I wonder if she sees me as a replacement son in some way?* he thought. *Probably not. He would be about five years older than I am.*

Louise continued, "Then, one day, we received a letter from Alan, saying he was getting married. His wife had insisted that he contact us. She is a Christian and he bonded with her, as he had developed an interest in religion. That may be partly why he rejected both of us – over the question of religion – knowing our atheistic views. So he married a lovely Australian lady. She already had a girl from her previous marriage, and they have since had their own children, a boy and a girl. I hear news occasionally – too rarely for my liking. You have seen photos of the grandchildren. They write at Christmas and once or twice a year. Oh, on my birthday too. I send cards, letters, and small gifts from time to time. I hope relationships will improve. Actually, when Alan heard of Heinrick's death, he sent several long letters, explaining a lot from his perspective, and I sensed the possibility of some reconciliation. After all, his main antagonism was with Henry, not me. He even said that."

"Do you think you would ever visit them, or they come here?"

Louise shook her head. "It's too far. And a complicated journey. I couldn't cope with a trip like that, and they have their own lives in Perth. Kenya means little to Alan now, and nothing to the rest of his family."

After a thoughtful pause, Brett said, "You use 'Heinrick' and 'Henry' interchangeably."

"Do I? I hadn't realized."

"You often do, actually," Brett responded. Louise smiled – at least her mouth moved in a smile but her eyes didn't. Sometimes her facial expression showed she was processing a private inner thought. He often found he had no idea what lay behind her countenance.

"I can't believe you have been able to keep Henry's death a secret for – how long? – three years. How did you manage that? I can't even keep an innocent overnight wall-hop secret around here for a few weeks!"

"Not so *innocent*, my boy! But to explain, I'll have to tell you the details of what happened. It was only because Henry was away in a remote location at the time that the idea of suppressing his death even occurred to us."

Louise moved back to the comfortable chair and began to speak. Brett and Kali sat and listened. "I mentioned before that Heinrick and I went into partnership with Richard Beaton. He was a friend of Peter. Or at least they had some association through a club of theirs. It was a limited investment because, later, our savings went into developing the Zoo. Richard managed our coffee farm west of Nyeri but the area wasn't really suitable for effective coffee production as it was a bit too high. Coffee does well up to about 6,000 feet but the bushes become a bit scraggly higher than that and, of course, a rare frost will destroy them. That's normally the elevation when tea production becomes viable, due to the greater rainfall. There is a transition zone where people attempt to grow both crops, neither of which does famously. That's the region where our property was located, so it was a bit of struggle to run the operation. Credit is due to Richard for what he did accomplish. Thomas Ridge-Taylor has often reminded me that we were too high for large-scale quality coffee production.

"Richard removed some of the coffee bushes – they make great firewood by the way – and switched over to more tea production. We struggled on for a number of years, but eventually Richard decided to sell the farm and buy a cattle ranch up north in Laikipia district, over to the west of Nanyuki. He offered to buy us out, but Heinrick and I decided to leave our capital invested with the new venture as it seemed very promising. And it did do well.

"But about three and a half years ago, we ran into some financial difficulties here at the Zoo which forced us to consider cashing out our share in the farm. The difficulty was, Richard Beaton had everything invested in the ranch, so there was very little available in cash. There was a lot of communication back and forth, and then Richard started to demand more for his management efforts over the years than the share we had agreed. It began to get a bit nasty. Things dragged on until Peter advised Henry to go up and meet face to face to challenge Richard, and push for a resolution.

Part 2: The Wall

Henry was sanguine about it, saying he wasn't worried about the outcome, because we had gone into the investment knowing there were risks. He also added something that still puzzles me: 'If it falls through, we've still got our hidden nest-egg to fall back on.' He did not reveal what he meant by that, so I assume it was one of his separate accounts that he kept.

"Henry and I drove up to Nairobi together, and I stayed at the Norwich Hotel in town to visit some of our friends, while Heinrick rented a car to drive up to confront Richard. The whole visit was complicated by the hotel telephones being out of order. Peter Lancaster happened to be in Nairobi too because he needed some medical tests and had several other meetings. One morning, after Henry had been gone three days, the hotel reception sent a messenger to my room with an envelope. When I opened the note, I read, 'Z. Must talk. CPZ. Blue Posts. Tka. Noon. P'. I knew exactly what it meant. Peter was telling me to meet him at the New Blue Posts hotel in Thika at 12 noon that day. The fact that he was using our codes indicated to me something was serious, so I drove up to Thika right away."

Brett was confused. "Did you say Z and P? What did they mean? Oh, I suppose the P was for Peter."

"Actually, no. P represented Phoenix and Z stood for Zephyr. Let me explain about our secret codes. During the war, Peter and Heinrick had worked together on several undercover projects, so they developed a coded communication system between them. Henry was Cipher because that suited his strategy of staying low key and invisible. A nothing. He loved that image during his career. However, when he retired and managed the Zoo, he allowed his charisma to shine forth. Peter's code was Phoenix. He chose…he chose that…because he felt he had risen from death in…an earlier situation. Maybe one day I will tell you the details. Later, Heinrick brought me into their confidence and I was given the code name Zephyr.

"I parked at the Blue Posts hotel. I found Peter sitting in the outdoor restaurant area, smoking. He had a pile of papers on the white wooden table in front of him. When he saw me, he stood up and placed a heavy wooden chair for me to join him. The chair wobbled, as they usual do! The waiter was hovering, so I ordered white coffee with some extra hot water as it was usually too strong." Brett sat still, letting her recount the story in her own way. The memory was clearly vivid for her, and the details were still significant.

"Peter got straight to the point. 'Sorry, I have some terrible news. There is no easy way to tell you this. Henry has been killed.' I was incredulous and said nothing, so he continued. 'He was in a dreadful car accident up near the ranch. It was late at night. Henry had just left Richard's place. He was driving alone. The police in Nanyuki found one of our publications in his case which had my contact address in Nairobi, so they tried to telephone me. They couldn't get through, so one of our chaps here in Thika knew enough to get a message through to me in Nairobi. He called me up here to convey the news. A friend drove me here and then delivered my message to you in Nairobi. I wanted to tell you in person. I think we should drive there together, if you are up to that.'

"I wasn't prepared for the 150-kilometre journey but I wanted to go there and see the situation for myself. My coffee arrived and I ordered a simple lunch for us both while Peter went to try to contact the police in Nanyuki. This gave me some time alone to deal with the devastating news.

"After I'd finished lunch, Peter was still on the phone and then needed to eat his cold food, so I walked down alone to see the Chania Falls. Looking at the brown, muddy water rushing over the distant falls, I remembered Heinrick saying, 'One man's silt is another man's topsoil'. I needed those moments alone, watching the falls, appreciating the river which represented life, flowing life, continuing…life. That water flows into the massive Tana River which winds its way across the northeast, and eventually discharges into the ocean just north of here.

"Once he'd finished his lunch, Peter found me and we drove up to Nanyuki, just north of the Equator. It's quite a good road, as you know. We immediately went to the police station and heard a few of the terrible details. The officer kindly suggested one of his men go with us to show us the accident site. Peter phoned Richard before we left but he hung up immediately. The police sergeant said he was refusing to speak to anyone about what had happened. Peter suggested we look at the place while it was still light, if I felt okay doing that.

"We found the crash site, on a remote rural road, and saw a wrecked lorry with a car smashed to pieces in front of it. It looked as though the small vehicle had exploded, with pieces of wreckage scattered everywhere, and a pool of oil soaking into the murram ground. The wreckage was unbelievable – a terrible mess. The front section was totally crumpled, with shattered glass and pieces of metal all around. Even one of the wheels had been hurled over into a nearby field. They must have hit at an incredible speed. Henry would have been killed instantly.

"We noticed that the accident had occurred on the boundary of private land, across a fire-break road which was formed as a barrier to stop the spread of fire across the huge ranches. The policeman told us that in the morning, when the accident was discovered, Heinrick's body had been taken to the local hospital.

"We drove back to the police unit. On the way, we learnt from the officer that the lorry driver had run away, and had not been found. The lorry was uninsured and unregistered. Although he thought it belonged to a local farmer, there was no proof. Subsequently, a mechanical inspection showed it had no lights and there were many defects. The police sergeant at the main desk gave us the few personal items they had found in the car, including Henry's briefcase and the document where they had located Peter's phone number. The officer then sent us to visit the hospital morgue for identification.

"Peter was marvellous. He went in to see what was left of Heinrick. I simply couldn't face doing that. Afterwards, Peter was obviously distraught but he told me nothing of what he had seen. It was almost sunset by then, but we decided to risk the dangerous drive in the dark back to Nairobi, knowing it would take a few days to sort out the mess. Peter said we should contact Geoffrey Matherton. I remembered him as an irritating fellow, but an excellent lawyer. We knew we were going to need help."

Brett spoke for the first time: "But what was the cause of the accident? Did you ever find out?"

"No. It's still a mystery, and of course Richard Beaton did not know what happened after Heinrick left him. However..." she took a deep breath, "...later interviews with Richard's house staff revealed a few details. They heard a terrible row between the two men and then, later in the evening, they reported that they heard shouts and a car door being slammed. The final words that Richard shouted were 'stinking nasty'. I think I know what he really said, as the staff would not know the word Nazi."

"What do you mean? Stinking Nazi? Why would Mr. Beaton call Henry that?" Louise ignored the question and continued, "The other strange thing is they said the two men were drunk. Now, Richard does like his booze, I know, but Heinrick rarely touched alcohol. I couldn't imagine him getting drunk to the extent it would affect his driving. He may have had a sip to be sociable at first, knowing it was important to Richard – he'd sometimes do that – but that would be all. Much later, it was clear to the lawyers, Matherton and Son, that Richard knew nothing of what happened after Heinrick left him, although he did admit to them that they had argued about the continued financing of the ranch.

"The next day, we began our dreadful round of meetings, including contacting the insurance people and the bank. We got his life insurance settlement eventually, and completed all of the banking details. I was surprised at..." She paused.

"What?"

"Oh, nothing. Never mind. And then we began to deal with the car-rental company. They were understandably upset, and that started an enormous hassle because the insurance company baulked at paying up."

"Why?"

"Two reasons, as I recall. First, no one could decide if the accident had occurred on public or private land as it was right on the boundary. That affected liability apparently, although don't ask me why. Also, they discovered a discrepancy between the name on the insurance documents and Heinrick's driving licence. He would use Heinrick and Henry interchangeably – as I do, apparently – and had written 'Henry' on the rental forms. They used that as an excuse to wriggle out of meeting the insurance claim.

"We decided not to tell Miles, as we knew we'd never hear the end of it! In fact, that was when Peter and I developed the idea of trying to cover up the whole affair. Geoffrey Matherton reluctantly went along with it, thinking we might get away with the deception down here as it had happened a long way from the Zoo, and only a few local people in Laikipia district knew. We arranged a cremation and small private internment. Unfortunately, it meant Henry never received the recognition he deserved from his community for all he had contributed over the years. And I never got to fully grieve and process what had happened, as everything had to be suppressed."

"It must have been tough for Peter too – losing his friend that way."

Louise thought, staring vacantly past him at the wall beside the entrance door, and eventually replied, "Yes. I suppose it was. He was a real brick through it all. I fear I didn't give him enough credit, or thanks, for how he helped me during those awful days."

"Well, I'm amazed you have got away with the cover-up for so long."

"So am I! We arranged to arrive back here late at night, telling people the next day Henry was ill and confined to bed. It's interesting, you know, people believe what they want to believe, and that's often the story that suits them best. But, to be honest, I wonder if the staff we had working for us were convinced. They were quite close to us so they must have suspected something odd had happened. But they are very circumspect and by nature do not enquire openly. On one occasion, Imam Faiz appeared to indicate that he did not believe the narrative that Henry was alive, implying that Muslims cannot trust what infidels say; but he did not openly challenge us, and he has never mentioned it since.

"The other point is, we came up with a pretty convincing – obviously convincing – narrative to explain why Heinrick was never seen again."

"Having been bitten by a monkey?"

"Yes. And being disfigured so he could not appear in public. But it was not entirely fiction. He had been badly bitten by one of the monkeys he was researching."

"So that wasn't just a myth?"

"No, it really happened, but we embellished it and fabricated the story about his severe disfigurement. A large male monkey was injured and he had a go at Henry when he was trying to treat it. It bit his hands and face which became infected and took ages to heal. He had a permanent scar across his cheek."

"Why was he so interested in the monkeys?"

"He noticed a similarity between the troop here and a species found only in the interior, towards the border and over into Uganda. He speculated that some monkeys had been brought to the coast in earlier centuries, possibly by the slave and ivory traders, and had established themselves on this isolated headland. That's why it's important we keep the area free from human incursion." Brett was then the recipient of one of her disapproving glances. "You probably saw some of the monkeys over there."

He said, "Yes, I met some. But we weren't formally introduced."

Louise smiled, which softened the atmosphere, and she continued, "It is vital we maintain the story, even though it means some verbal gymnastics at times. Peter and Chengo are in on the deception. Oh, Matherton too, of course. We will keep it going it as long as it helps to hold things together within the Zoo." Brett thought that Louise's plausible explanation for maintaining the isolation of the headland may be only part of the story but he had no basis to question her further.

He said, "I shan't say anything, but surely you can't keep this facade going for ever. Someone must find out sometime. What about the official, paperwork side of it all – income tax and so on?"

"We deal with it. Geoffrey Matherton is very discreet and capable. He handles official details."

"What about staff and the people who used to help you over there?" he said, nodding towards the east.

"They believe he is confined up here and I take care of his needs. They know I am a nurse. Anyway, I told you, people believe what suits them. And so far, this plot either suits them or, in most cases, doesn't affect them, so they don't care."

"I should be going," said Brett finally. He stood to leave and Kali immediately jumped up. Louise rose too, saying, "I get a chuckle sometimes. Heinrick would have loved the idea of his nebulous self continuing to exert influence after his departure. He would be tickled pink to know we managed to maintain the fiction for so long!"

"That is amazing. Thank you for the tea and cakes, and explaining so much. I appreciate your trusting me with all of this. And I am so sorry to learn the news of Henry. I was very much looking forward to meeting him. In fact I bought some gifts I had carried over there to give him. Here, you may like to look at them. I ate the others, I'm afraid." He grinned sheepishly as he handed her the package from his briefcase.

"Thank you. That's sweet of you." She turned them over respectfully. "A British keyring. I'd love to look through the bird book and listen to the Brahms if I may. It's actually quite therapeutic for me to explain some of the history. There's a lot more to tell. Have you walked along the shore past South Beach? I think the path down there would interest you. I'd enjoy walking down there again. I don't go along the shoreline much, since Henry died. Maybe we could meet early Saturday morning, before it gets too hot?"

"Thank you. However, I have arranged to spend this Saturday morning with the Brandon family, helping with some homework and windsurfing when the tide comes in. Could we make it the following week please? Saturday mornings are usually good." Louise agreed.

As he walked to the door, he noticed a large shelving unit behind the door, made of dark, heavy wood. It seemed strangely familiar. Louise followed Brett down the stairs. "Perhaps Richard Beaton was not a total shyster because, when he sold the property last year and returned to England to retire, he voluntarily gave me half of the profits realized from the sale. It was a lot. But he did not want to see me, so he arranged all the details of the transfer through the lawyers. Sorry, too much detail for you. But at least that part of the story has a happy ending, I suppose."

As he left, Brett remembered that the shelving unit was exactly the same style as the oddly positioned shelf cabinet in the meeting room where the Executive Council had interviewed him two days previously.

Part Three

THE ATTACK

The fictional characters introduced in Part Three

Patrick Lancaster, Peter's son in England
Julie Lancaster, Peter's daughter in England
Wejiha, nurse in the Zoo clinic
Sister Maria, Mwakindini clinic
Dr. Patel, doctor in Mwakindini
Mr. Badr, assistant bank manager, Mwakindini
Moshi, the mysterious stranger
Kelsey McNeil, American anthropologist
Mzee Kamau, injured Kikuyu man in Nairobi
Mrs. Katana, Simion's wife, teacher.

13

> *"Heinrick learned to think like a cipher. He loved to be seen as the person of no significance – a non-entity."*
> Louise Emerson

Very early on the agreed Saturday in July, the sun sent its bright rays across the tips of the taller trees on the headland, down the bare rock faces, through the gaps between the palms, and into the Zoo. A new day was beginning. As arranged, Brett went over to Louise's cage for their hike beside the south bay. She had advised him to bring a backpack, hat, his walking stick, and sunscreen, along with several bottles of water. She was wearing a broad-brimmed straw hat and had set a basket on the table outside, beside her potted desert rose. She transferred some cool packages of snacks for him to carry in his backpack, picked up her basket, and they set off.

Making their way around the bay, they passed the sewage treatment plant and the smelly lagoon near the entrance. "That is going to need to be upgraded sometime," said Louise, "probably at the same time as we plan an alternative escape route along here. I think you mentioned that in your letter."

"You read my letter to Henry?" asked Brett.

There was an awkward pause and Louise appeared slightly nonplussed, "Yes, Boniface Chengo brought his copy to the Executive. We were able to act on some suggestions, as you know, but others had to be tabled for later consideration, depending on finances."

Part 3: The Attack

"I wonder what happened to my original letter?"

"Chengo still has it, unopened in his desk."

"I suppose it doesn't matter now," said Brett.

"It does, and we too are concerned about safety issues. But funds are very low at present." They made their way through a dense group of mangroves and came out of the thicket into an open area which afforded a pleasant view of the bay. Finding a log in the shade, they sat and drank some water. Several fisherman were out in their dugout canoes. Louise said, "I envy them their simple lives, governed by the seasons and the tides, and their religious traditions. Those fishermen instinctively know the tides, the complex currents, the varying weather patterns, and the motions of the sea. It seems that the tides synchronize naturally with their personal circadian rhythms!"

They noticed the unmistakable swaying flight of a lilac-breasted roller. Louise seemed to be in a reflective mood, so Brett chanced asking about the secret code she had mentioned previously. "You were called Zephyr, is that right?"

"Correct. Heinrick and Peter had their codes, and they were running low on inspiration when they got around to naming me! So I got the tame code name Zephyr. What does that word mean to you?"

Brett thought, and responded, "It's the model of a Ford car in England."

"Yes. A Ford Zephyr won the safari rally in 1955," said Louise proudly.

"And I think it's a kind of wind isn't it?"

"Yes, a gentle zephyr breeze, such as we are experiencing now from the ocean. Heinrick also discovered another, older, meaning. It used to describe a fine, light gingham cloth. So, the term was sufficiently nebulous for Heinrick to apply it to me. Either I was a gentle breeze, a successful car, or I could be thought as an old rag! Henry said the name was so simple and obvious that no code-breaker would spot it."

"And Peter was Phoenix," recalled Brett.

"Phoenix, the mythological bird that rises from the ashes. The survivor. The one that offers hope, perhaps. Peter liked the image of himself as rising from the ashes of war's destruction. Heinrick, named Cipher, learned to think like a cipher. He loved to be seen as the person of no significance – a non-entity. The word also relates to writing in code. He enjoyed that connotation too."

"It's interesting, I feel I know Henry in some ways, but he still remains a deep mystery," confessed Brett.

"Exactly! Wonderful! That is precisely how he wanted to be seen. He'd thank you for saying that. He was hard to define – a chameleon. We spoke about that before, didn't we? It applies perfectly to Heinrick. He'd do all he could to blend in and not be noticed. That was why he was so good at his undercover intelligence work."

"Espionage?"

"He disliked that term. He thought it sounded too sinister. He said it was simply a matter of keeping your eyes open and your mouth shut. But, yes, he got into many secret missions for the military and the government – always inconspicuously. For example, if he was offered tea or coffee he'd say he liked it exactly the way the host was having it – white or black, with or without sugar, never mind. He'd adapt."

"He must have had some preferences, though."

"Well yes, but he'd suppress his personal wishes to match the situation. You know how the Kenyans serve their tea – strong, milky, with loads of sugar – 'kitchen tea' they call it? They boil it for ages. Well, Henry didn't like his tea that way, so he'd just think of it as a different drink. Not tea; simply a rich, sweet drink. That way, he'd appreciate it."

"Fascinating. It makes me seem a bit picky."

"No, that was just his method of remaining low key. It was the same with clothing. He'd try to dress in a similar way to those around him, whatever his own desires. If they wore a hat, he would. If they dressed formally or casually, he'd try to do the same. If practical, he'd follow them."

"He'd follow suit!"

"Ha ha, very good. He'd even feign an interest in alcohol, or he'd smoke, if the situation warranted it: anything so he did not stand out or draw attention."

"So, how did you use your codes? Were they seriously helpful or just a fun bonding thing with the three of you?"

"We used them for serious exigencies. With Peter also being involved in some pretty sensitive stuff, there was a possibility one of us might get caught up in…in some tricky situation where we wanted to communicate secretly. Or we used the codes as a disguise."

"Why?"

"If we were under coercion or something was wrong, we would use the codes in a special way so the other person was alerted."

"Did you have to use them often?"

"No, but occasionally it was useful. For example, if we were in danger or in a critical situation and could not speak openly, such as being kidnapped, or we wanted to keep things between ourselves, or signal something else. Say, we were forced to write a message, we'd either deliberately spell our name wrongly and build our code name into the message so the others would reverse what we wrote, or they knew something was wrong. Yes, we used the codes a few times. We never employed them to convey anything other than a serious situation."

"Hmm. That's interesting."

"Actually, we'd routinely use the system as a check on the phone. It was simply a confirmation that it was one of us. One would say their code name and the reply would have the other's name imbedded. It's not used much now."

"So it's safe to tell me about it as it doesn't mean much these days?"

"It's not that. In fact, it still means a lot to me – and Peter I imagine – so be honoured I am letting you in on the secret!"

"Yes, I feel honoured. Thank you. As I said, it's fascinating, and all a bit mysterious."

"One more thing, then we'd better walk on. For some purposes, we'd combine all our codes into CPZ, Cypher-Phoenix-Zephyr, representing all three of us. For example, we'd close phone calls with CPZ as a confirmation that the call was authentic. Simple but effective. Heinrick would say, 'Keep it simple, out in the open. That way it will be missed by the enemy'. CPZ was our significant link, between the three of us."

Brett immediately thought back to the card he'd found in Louise's car. He remembered it said 'CPZ 2pm' and a date that he had forgotten. He started to say, "So that's what…" but his instinct restrained him so he finished with, "…you did. So many codes, including CPZ."

"Yes…well, that's one you don't need to remember. Let's go."

They left the shade of the mangroves and doum palms and followed a well-worn path along the shore down the coast to the south. Louise said, "It's nice to have company on this walk. Henry and I used to come here with

Kali." The path widened as they approached a small village. A group of small children spotted them and ran up asking for sweets. "Sorry. No, they are bad for your teeth," Louise explained to them in several different ways, including gestures. They ran off giggling. "They have no idea what I told them. And, in any case, how would they understand that anything to eat could be bad?" Turning towards the sea, they looked across to the headland of the Zoo projecting into the ocean. Brett was pleased that he had brought his binoculars. "We won't stop here," said Louise. "Let's move on a bit past this village where it's more private." She pointed to a small path winding towards the sea and over to a distant headland. "We can have our snack in the shade of those whistling pines, beside that huge baobab in the distance."

After a long walk in the increasing heat, they found a suitable place. They noticed that all the vegetation was bent over by the prevailing southeast monsoon winds. The trees were clearly dying back on the windward side, but growing with refreshing green growth, on the leeward side. In this sublime setting, they opened the food she had prepared. As they ate, they looked out at the sparkling sea, and appreciated the gentle breeze. Brett kept scanning the distant headland, and saw several interesting features. After a while, he sensed it might be an appropriate moment to probe more into Henry's background. Louise was willing to talk, and started to speak of his military responsibilities in East Africa during the war.

"Explaining Heinrick's work is a bit like describing a vivid dream. Some of the details are sharp and the actions clear in themselves, but, overall, very little connects logically or makes any sense. I did not follow much of what he was involved with." She stared out towards the thin white line of waves gently rolling across the far reef as the tide receded. "He, of course, did not offer much to aid my understanding, probably to protect me. Although I knew enough to be vulnerable – or dangerous – in the wrong circumstances."

She clumsily tilted the drinking bottle back, spilling water down her neck. The wind caught her steely grey hair, but she seemed to be at ease. While talking, they had been enjoying the amusing antics of some greenbelts and golden palm-weaver birds. She then thought for a while in silence, looked over at Brett, and seemed to have decided something.

"Perhaps I should start at the beginning, otherwise some of the later story will not make much sense." Brett nodded and stretched out with his hands behind his head. "Heinrick Emmerich was born in Germany in 1908. His father was German, his mother English. Not a convenient combination during the early and middle parts of this century. Somehow, the family got through the first war and managed to survive the inter-war years when Heinrick was in his teens.

"His mother maintained close connections with her family in England. Heinrick's father was inclined to support the moves towards greater German influence, although his parents had no strong political convictions. Very few of their friends were true Nazis, but some favoured the return of German pride and authority in Europe. In the late 1920s, his mother returned to England with Heinrick for an extended holiday. While they were away, his father was killed in an industrial accident. I think he worked in a steel-making factory, I can't be sure."

While she was talking, Brett was trying to match this new information with what he already knew of Henry. It was now clear why Richard Beaton, their rancher friend, had called him a Nazi. But he wondered to himself: *How strong were Henry's convictions, and how could someone with his background be doing British intelligence work in East Africa?*

Louise continued, "His mother wisely changed their surname from Emmerich to Emerson and did her best to hide her German connections. She persuaded Heinrick to call himself Henry, and not speak German. Oh, I forgot to mention he spoke fluent English and German along with a good understanding of several other languages. He picked them up very easily. He had a brilliant mind, no doubt of that. He could analyze and process information in unique ways. It's hard to describe.

"He went to a local college in England to study linguistics and international relations – something like that. Later, he moved into intelligence work…small things…doing private investigations and documenting trends, analyzing published works, and so on. I never knew the details. At any rate, that gave him a good background so, in 1938 when he was 30, he applied to the foreign office in London to work in investigation activities with them."

"That's surprising with his German heritage, so close to the start of the war," said Brett.

"In a way, but just think of the situation: everyone hoped there would not be a war and many believed that, but information-gathering on German activities and communications was becoming vital. With his knowledge of the country, German culture, and his skill in the language, they found Henry a risk worth taking." The tide had gone out and the sun was burning intensely onto the exposed coral in the open area, so they were glad to be relaxing in the shade. "Let's have some more water and then we'll start back," suggested Louise.

"Yes, we've still got lots. I'm sensitive to running out of water after my experience over the wall," admitted Brett. He thought for a moment, and then asked, "How sympathetic was Henry to Germany? Was he ever a security risk?"

"Now you're getting ahead of the story, but to answer your question, no, he was totally supportive of the British cause when he saw all that was happening in Germany and Hitler's madness. But he had respected his father – they had got on very well, and he was a fine man from what I understand – so he did not totally reject his German roots. He had to vigorously suppress any indication of his background – although his supervisors knew, of course. He and his mum ignored their history and, if forced to disclose information, they gave the story of extended holidays in Germany, with solid English connections.

"Anyway, when war broke out, Henry joined the British army and was assigned to the intelligence corps. It wasn't long before concerns grew over German activities in their former territory of Tanganyika – present-day Tanzania. After the first war, in 1919, Britain formally took over control of the country as a Trust Territory under the League of Nations, but German influence remained in some areas, particularly in local administrative structures. By the second war in 1939, most Germans in Tanganyika – and there were a lot – had been rounded up in camps, but the Nairobi section of British intelligence in Kenya kept a close eye on activities beyond the border." Louise nodded towards the south.

Putting on their hats, they began their return journey, with Louise continuing the story. "Henry was well established in his role with the forces in Nairobi when, suddenly, Peter Lancaster, an Intelligence Officer, arrived from London. As I understand it, they disliked each other intensely. I think Henry resented Peter, who was about eight years his junior, barging in and taking over. But it was wartime and there was no room for personal animosities, so they developed a reasonable working relationship. I gather they had a grudging respect for the other's skills. Oh, the other fly in the ointment was Henry was uncomfortable with Freemasonry, and Peter was a senior Mason.

"By the way, please don't mention any of this to Peter, or ask questions which might indicate that you have some knowledge of this history. He's intending to meet with you, so, whatever he decides to tell you, that's his affair. I wouldn't want him to think I've been speaking behind his back – which I have, of course, but only as it affected me and Heinrick. I don't ever want to imply any criticism of Peter, as he's one of the finest men I've ever known."

"Maybe I'll tell him that," joked Brett.

"No, don't! He'll know I told you more!" said Louise, laughing.

They walked back along the track towards the Zoo. Their path intersected a trail from the beach which the fishermen used. Louise recognized one of the men walking from his dugout canoe which had been grounded in the bay by the receding tide. It was anchored to large rocks to secure it when the tide returned. He carried a long pole and the wrapped sail. As he approached them, his face was expressionless, but once he recognized Louise, he smiled warmly. After chatting for a while, the fisherman turned to head inland. Louise asked him to bring her some fish or a lobster the next day, if possible. She would pay him well, and it would give her an opportunity to send some nutritious items back with him as a gift for his family.

As they walked, Louise suddenly saw the distinctive swoop and red flash of a carmine bee-eater, telling Brett that it was unusual to see one at that time of year. She continued her recollections: "A lot of the action in the East African campaign occurred in the north and, to some extent, along this coast. Henry's work was focused mostly to the south, where there were incursions and skirmishes. He worked primarily on intelligence-gathering. Henry maintained connections with some of the Germans living in Tanganyikan detention centres. He was inordinately cautious and strategic in all his activities, particularly as it involved some clandestine liaisons with a few Germans. Henry was always planning, anticipating, and triple-thinking everything. He was the only person I knew who refilled his stapler before the staples ran out! He was a *details* person – a belt-and-braces man. He took every possible precaution. To you, this must all seem furtive and elaborate, but to Henry it was simply a survival strategy.

"Unfortunately, these activities brought him under some suspicion and, when details of his early life became known, a few elements in his organisation suspected him of pro-German sympathies. At one point, Henry needed to make a clandestine rendezvous with a contact from the south. I never knew who it was, or why they needed to meet, but this required a safari down to the Tanganyika border where the Masai Mara Park meets the Serengeti Plains. The plans aroused suspicion in his senior officers. By the way, I know only parts of this story, having gleaned fragments of information from Henry and Peter; but they never spoke to me together about what happened. I think both of them preferred not to discuss the details. So, I'm a little hazy on some aspects, although I do know the main facts about what took place. In later years, Henry often referred to specific details too. Let's stop here for a while. It's getting hotter and I'd appreciate a break.

"A few days before Henry's planned journey, Peter was summoned by his seniors and briefed on their concerns over Henry's intentions. As I understand it, Peter's commanding officer made it clear he was not instructing him to kill Henry, but if Henry happened to meet with some inexplicable fatal accident in a remote area, no questions would be asked – and, in fact, there may be rejoicing in some quarters. It may sound brutal, but it was wartime and a tough period, and there were few opportunities for niceties. This was an extremely serious situation, but Peter knew it was the closest thing to an order he was going to receive. In essence, he was commanded to get rid of Henry and make it appear to be an accident.

"However, the secretary in their office was sweet on Henry and she overheard enough of the conversation – and saw some cryptic notes relating to the discussion – for her to realize the danger Henry was in. She warned him, taking a huge risk herself. Henry knew he could not indicate to anyone that he knew of the plan. He set off to Narok without speaking to anyone about it. From there, he arranged a local driver to guide him down into the Mara Park in an army Jeep."

"A Jeep? Not a Land Rover?" asked Brett.

Part 3: The Attack

"No, the Army used Willys Jeeps during the war. The Land Rover wasn't developed until the 1950s. The two of them set off towards the southern end of the park beside the Sand River. This winds its way near the Kenya-Tanzania boundary. As they approached the area where they would be camping, they stopped on a ridge and looked back to see another Jeep following them. Henry assumed it was Peter with his driver. Naturally, he wanted to give no indication that he knew he was being followed, so they drove down to the edge of the Sand River. On the way, they noticed a large and belligerent-looking buffalo beside the road. They avoided him and set up camp for the night. The planned meeting with the person from the south was to be the following morning. They saw nothing more of the others, so Henry assumed they had camped some way back. He was relieved as he did not want a confrontation with Peter, knowing his intentions.

"Just after their breakfast the following morning, before they broke camp, Heinrick and his guide heard a loud rifle shot, immediately followed by a second one. The shots appeared to have come from close by. Henry had no idea what they meant. They could either have been a signal of some kind, or they might have meant trouble. He decided to walk back up the road to investigate, leaving his driver with the vehicle, and instructions to tidy up the camp and remain there. Henry walked along the road so he could approach quietly, rather than driving up and attracting attention. As he moved towards where he thought the sound came from, he wished he had a larger weapon than his Enfield rifle and the Webly revolver. He often told me he wished he had been carrying a double-barrelled .470 rifle, as that would have protected him against most large African game."

Louise stood to stretch and watched a row of sandpipers as they ran along the shore. "I can continue the story another time if you need to get back."

"I'm fine. Don't stop now!" urged Brett.

"After about ten minutes, Henry spotted the Jeep beside the road. He stopped, waited, and listened. He wondered if the rifle shots were a signal to attract him and it may have been been a trap. After a few moments, he noticed some hooded vultures circling overhead. Moving in a wide circle – as he had watched lionesses do when hunting – he carefully made his way towards Peter's camp from the north. Everything was quiet and still as he approached. What he saw astounded him." Louise continued, "The Maasai driver was lying beside the wreckage of their tent, and Peter was slumped in the back of the Jeep. Approaching cautiously with his rifle in hand, Henry first passed by the African. He was covered in blood and looked as though he had been gored or trampled. He was obviously dead. Making his way cautiously towards the vehicle, he checked Peter and saw he was unconscious, but still breathing. Looking around at the devastation, and footprints, it seemed clear that the buffalo had attacked them.

"Weeks later, Peter confirmed that the old buffalo had charged their camp, ripped apart the tent, and then turned on them. The guide was badly gored and then the animal turned on Peter who was attempting to get his rifle. Before he could fire, Peter was attacked as he ran towards the Jeep for shelter. The wild bull returned to the driver, who was lying on the ground. He continued goring him until Peter managed to fire two shots at his head, driving him off. Then Peter slumped across the back seat as he lost consciousness.

"Checking the Maasai again, Henry confirmed he was dead. He gathered some canvas from the shredded tent and made a temporary shade to protect Peter from the direct sun. He then took the remaining pieces of the tent and laid them across the driver. Henry took a few moments to consider the situation. As he studied the tragic scene before him, he knew he had two options. He could try to rush Peter to medical help, or he could walk back to his camp and meet up with his counterparts from Tanganyika, pretending he had not seen anything until they drove back later. If he chose the latter approach, he immediately realized two things: he would have to remove the canvas pieces he had just placed in position, in case anyone discovered the disaster before he drove back. He wouldn't want anyone to know he'd been there and left. The second dreadful thought was he would be abandoning a fellow soldier to an almost certain death. If Peter did not die from loss of blood then the wild animals in the area would soon be moving in on the destroyed camp.

"After a few minutes, Heinrick had made his decision. Grasping his rifle he walked over to the Jeep, watching all around in case of further animal attack. He checked to see that Peter was positioned so he could drive slowly down to his camp for help from his waiting driver. Then he tried to start the Jeep. It would not start. He began cranking the starting handle, being

Part 3: The Attack

careful of the kickback, but after exhausting himself, he realized the vehicle wasn't going to start. He found Peter's drinking water and refreshed himself while sitting in the shade, re-evaluating the new crisis he was in. Henry never rushed important decisions. He often infuriated colleagues by taking all the time available to ponder his options – even in dramatic situations. One of his favourite expressions was, 'Important decisions should be made as late as possible'.

"Sorry, where was I? He wondered about firing a shot to see if it attracted his driver but it depended on how he interpreted the signal and whether he decided to drive up. If he walked up, as he had seen Henry do, then they would both have to walk back for the Jeep. So he had no choice but to abandon Peter and dash as quickly as he could to tell his companion what had happened. He trusted the tent coverings would deter the vultures for a while. In view of Peter's precarious condition, he resolved to drive him back to Narok as quickly as possible and forget about his arranged meeting. I've no idea if the person or persons ever turned up, or what happened about that arrangement.

"Henry was hot and tired by the time he got back to his camp, so he was pleased to see that everything was ready to move. They both got in the vehicle and, as they drove back, Henry tried to prepare the driver for what he was going to see. It was bad because the two drivers were from the same tribe and knew each other well. They made several attempts to jump-start the broken-down vehicle, but to no avail. Between them, they managed to load the dead man into the back, with Peter, barely alive, beside him. They did not waste time dealing with the wreckage of the camp but drove carefully back to their Narok base camp. They were both filthy and covered in blood. On the way, they saw the old buffalo with blood oozing from one of his eyes. They thought it might be one that attacked the camp. 'We must warn our chaps when they come down,' Henry said. His companion did not reply.

"Immediately the medics saw Peter, they gave him some temporary stabilizing treatment and quickly drove him to the main hospital in Nairobi. Peter remembers regaining consciousness at one point on that journey, and then everything went blank until he woke up in hospital a couple of days later. He was very badly injured but he did recover. The commanding officer listened to Henry's explanation of what had happened and told his sergeant to deal with the dead man while he arranged to send a group down to the accident site. His fellow driver stood beside his mangled friend. Henry briefed his fellow soldiers on the situation they would have to deal with when they reached the wrecked camp, and then he travelled back to Nairobi."

"Then what? Apart from the official story, did he and Peter ever discuss what actually happened?" asked Brett.

"Not until after the war. It was essential that Henry conceal the fact that he knew Peter's intentions, in order to protect the secretary. She was soon transferred back to the UK anyway, but both Henry and Peter had to maintain secrecy. Henry was led to believe Peter had been sent to follow him to provide backup if the mission went wrong. As I said, they had a tacit agreement to forget the whole affair. However, it's interesting how things happen, as they became fairly close after that. I suppose Peter realized that he owed his life to Henry."

"Did they develop a friendship?"

"Not so much a friendship, more of a truce! They associated with each other, as required, but operated in different branches. Peter continued in special operations and Henry maintained his contacts with the intelligence agencies. Their lives intersected a bit during the rest of the war, but more so afterwards, as they both moved into police work and government administration once the war was over. That was when I came on the scene and met both of them."

"Hence CPZ was formed," said Brett.

"Hence CPZ was formed. The deadly triangle! Let's go, it's been a long morning," said Louise, smiling.

"But lots of amazing information, thank you for explaining all of that," Brett said.

"Thanks for listening. There's more to the story, but that's for another day."

As they walked around the shore, Brett asked if there had been any further suspicion or persecution of Henry in the Army. Louise replied, "I don't think so, other than a few nasty comments from individuals occasionally. Henry's considerable contribution and other achievements soon dispelled any doubt over his loyalty to Britain."

As they came within sight of the Zoo, several people were shouting and they saw a nurse from the clinic running towards Louise. A patient had been brought in. He was a young man with an awful leg wound. They learned that he was cultivating the vegetable garden and swung a sharp hoe, hitting his lower leg. Louise said to Brett, "You take my things over and give them to Mjuhgiuna, please, while I deal with this. Thanks for an interesting outing."

14

"They used to call themselves 'freedom fighters'.
Others may have had different terms."
"Sorry, I didn't mean—" said Brett.
"I know. I know. It was all a long time ago," Peter reassured him.

After church the next morning, while Brett was walking home, Peter drove up, and stopped. They chatted for a while beside the road. Peter told him he would like to show him the beach past the fence beside the brigadier's cage. Brett was surprised, but he assumed Peter felt a new openness in their relationship since the executive meeting. Peter assured him that, as security officer, he had access to the east side of the wall. He needed to check the area occasionally, so Brett could accompany him if he wished. They figured out what time a low tide would occur during the early morning when the beach would still be in shadow. On the Tuesday, Brett's students were doing their final trade exams, so he was free to meet Peter in front of his cage after breakfast.

"Bring along some water and a snack, and wear strong boots as we'll be hiking across some corals," Peter told him. He added, "We'll keep this jaunt to ourselves, okay?" Brett agreed.

Two days later, as they met, Brett asked, "How are we going to get over there? It's still too deep around the end of the fence."

"There are two ways actually. There is a locked gate in the fence on the beach side of the Ridge-Taylors' cage, but it's too visible. I'll show you another way." They walked over to the store where Brett had kept his painting supplies, and Peter unlocked the door. He said, "Let's try to do this without disturbing Njuguna or setting off the dogs." They entered the store and Peter grasped the edge of an almost-empty shelving unit. Brett was surprised to see it was hinged, so Peter was able to swing it away from the eastern wall. This revealed the other side of the metal gate Brett had seen during his brief exploration of that section. Unlocking it with another key, Peter carefully opened it and they went through, pulling the shelf unit back in place and closing the grilled door. They crept as quietly as they could along the pathway to the northern beach, but the dogs detected their presence and started howling.

"Never mind, let's keep going," whispered Peter as they made their way through the bushes to the open beach.

They walked along the shore towards a massive pile of rocks. These forced them to step towards the sea, out onto the coral, in order to continue their journey along the northern edge of the headland. Brent was delighted to be walking through this unexplored area as his previous visit was mainly on the south.

"Follow where I walk," said Peter as he stepped ahead. "Be very careful of crevices or overhanging projections in the brittle coral under your feet. This all looks solid on the surface but there are deep pools and fragile edges on some of these overhangs." The pair continued walking, making their way across a stretch of squishy seaweed and back onto a secluded beach. Peter headed towards a palm log, up on the bank. They sat down and drank some water. Behind them, the vegetation was very dense, with low bushes and swaying palm trees.

Brett noticed many birds and wondered about animals. He asked Peter about it, "What wildlife are we likely to see?"

"Possibly some bush pigs near the shoreline. They use the many trails through the forest and down to the beach. I expect we will hear some monkeys complaining about us disturbing their peace. Mostly there will be birds. See the African fish eagle up in that tall tree?" Brett looked and immediately wished he had brought his binoculars.

Peter opened his bag and brought out a pair, saying, "Here, these should bring it in closer. I think I saw an osprey earlier but I wasn't sure as they are usually winter visitors." Brett was enjoying the close-up view of the eagle, and the details of the distant reef that the binoculars afforded him. Brett mentioned how loud the breakers sounded on the reef, but Peter could not hear them. After a moment, Peter asked, "What animals did you see when you were over this side?" As he listed the creatures he had encountered, Brett was thinking, *I wondered how long it would be before that topic was bought up.* He looked closely at Peter and noticed he was breathing heavily and seemed a little uneasy. *He's probably needing a cigarette soon,* he thought.

As though he read his mind, Peter said, "I need a smoke, but I'm trying to hold out as long as I can. All my medical advisors keep telling me to stop smoking." Brett thought Peter looked quite pale, so he ventured to ask, "How *is* your health? How are you?"

"I'm between diseases at present! If one of my many doctors examined me right now, he'd probably conclude that I am still technically alive. But that's a temporary condition!"

Brett laughed, "Oh, you poor old moribund fellow. You are determined to be cheerful on this beautiful day aren't you!"

Peter said, "What you see before you is a mere shell of my former self. I'm a dried-up husk, empty inside."

"Too many battles?" asked Brett sympathetically.

"Too many birthdays!" retorted Peter.

"But, generally, are you okay?" Brett asked, thinking, *Please don't die here.*

"I'm not unwell," replied Peter, standing up. "Let's move on. This coast curves a long way down there towards the east."

As they walked along the shore, the sun shot its rays between the branches of the trees, directing its sparkling shafts of light across the water, and scattering highlights of brightness over selected patches of sand. Peter pointed inland to a trail that led over the bank and up between the vegetation. "An animal path," he said. Rounding another tumble of large rocks, they came upon a beautiful, deserted beach from which they looked out towards the waves breaking across the distant reef.

"I believe there are reef sharks beyond those waves," said Brett.

"Yes, even in the bays and inlets along the edge before it drops off deeply."

"Are they dangerous?" asked Brett.

Part 3: The Attack

"The larger sharks down in Kilindini Harbour can be. They follow the vessels in. There are so many hazards around, it's a wonder any of us survive for long." They found a dry patch of smooth rock in the shade, in front of a cave. Peter set his bag behind a rock and said, "Let's rest for a while." He began fumbling for his cigarettes. With obvious relief, Peter began to enjoy his smoke. Brett drank some water and was grateful he had brought along some food for later. Peter seemed to be content to watch the terns and sooty gulls as he relaxed. Brett thought, *He talks a lot less than Louise.*

Peter was wearing an open-necked tee shirt which occasionally revealed his gold chain and the top of the pendant Brett had noticed before. He was waiting for a natural opportunity to ask Peter about its significance. Just then, a plane flew across the bay, over the line of the reef. Immediately, Peter looked up and said, almost to himself, "Cessna 195. Four passengers, plus pilot. He'll turn north soon I expect."

Brett said, "How do you know that? You are very interested in planes aren't you?"

Peter seemed startled by the question and quickly glanced across at Brett. "No, not particularly," he muttered as he turned his gaze back towards the small plane and stared at it intently as it disappeared into the distant clouds. "Knew he was heading north. Probably to Lamu," he commented, while he enjoyed his cigarette, flicking the ash with his finger, and squinting as he drew on the smoke.

Peter looked at Brett and said, "Are you hungry? I've brought along quite a bit of food." He started to unstrap his bag. "Mwangi always packs far too much for me. Let's have a snack now, shall we?" He pulled out a flat, plastic container and opened it to reveal an appetizing array of sandwiches with tomatoes, cooked sausages, and pieces of cheese. They shared the spread, and then Brett brought out his amateurish-looking provisions to share with Peter. A group of raucous crows joined them, swooping down onto the sand from their perches in the tall palm trees. Later, they enjoyed a variety of assorted fruit. "Were you hungry when you were over there searching for Henry?" asked Peter, nodding towards the south. "You were gone longer than you planned, I imagine." Brett was relieved to talk about it. Peter listened carefully to Brett's description of the whole adventure. He seemed to reveal, perhaps unintentionally, a degree of admiration, as he said

The Zoo

"You were pretty ingenious, I must admit." Brett said nothing. Peter said, "It seems you have not spoken to anyone about it."

"Only Mrs. Emerson," said Brett.

"Good. The Executive Council is concerned that you might say something, or speak out of order. Be careful! You'd better keep it all to yourself – the information about Henry, everything."

"Yes, I will. That's what I told the Council I'd do."

Peter looked out to sea, then along the beach, over to the caves, and finally at Brett. He said, "I need to apologize for being a bit abrupt at that meeting."

"Oh, no. That's fine. I know I broke the rules, so you were all justified in being angry."

"It's simply that we have to protect what we have at the Zoo. It's all very vulnerable, you see. Quite delicate – and vulnerable."

"And keeping Henry's death a secret is important – in that respect?"

"Pardon?" Brett repeated what he'd said and Peter responded: "Yes. But I don't know how long we can keep up the deception. You had a couple of long chats with Louise, I hear."

Brett nodded, saying, "But she has not yet told me much about the start of the Zoo."

"She probably will. She will reveal what she feels comfortable talking about. Just accept there will be some topics she cannot discuss. She is an intelligent and sensitive woman."

There was silence while Brett ran through, in his mind, about ten questions that he wanted to ask, but he said nothing. His instinct told him to wait for Peter to speak. What he said, surprised him: "Henry's death was a great shock to us both."

"Yes, it must have been terrible. Were you badly affected by it? You three were very close, I believe," said Brett.

"We were a trio. We had special codes to link us together. There were serious reasons for our code names." Peter stopped speaking, deep in thought. He added, "It was an interesting grouping. Henry and Louise were obviously the couple in love, I was the outsider, with an odd relationship with Henry. I've heard the term 'creative tension' which I think fits. But Louise and I…" Brett waited, pretending to study the sharp horizon. "Louise and

Part 3: The Attack

I – how shall I put it?– were at opposite poles. We were friends, but often in disagreement; close, but also distant."

Brett took a huge chance when he asked, "And since Henry's passing?"

Peter, the old warrior, simply smiled. After half a minute, he said quietly, almost to himself, "More close. Yes, more close, naturally. And, at the same time, more distant!" Then he laughed and looked at Brett, "Now, enough of your personal questions my boy! Let me show you the cave and I'll tell you a story."

They walked into the deep cave behind them. The partially drained sand sloped gently upwards towards the back. It was a pristine surface until they stepped on it. Above them, the roof dripped and dark green plants drooped down. Many tiny striped crabs and several black-bodied crabs with their bright-red legs scurried along the rock faces ahead of them, dashing for cover. "This is washed out completely by the high tides twice a day, except at the slack mid-tides. Any activity here is routinely disguised. It was used by smugglers in the past, as were many of the caves along here. There are lots, some much deeper than this one. There are several dry caves higher up in the inland rocky region." They looked out at the bright scene on the beach, framed by the dark arch of the cave mouth, with the glaring, exposed reef beyond the still partially shaded sand bars.

Brett said, "This reminds me of the Mau-Mau caves I visited north of Nyeri. Apparently, the freedom fighters would hide there. Even the smoke from their fires was dispersed along the steeply sloping cave roofs, and up into the dense trees, so they could not be spotted from the air."

"I know," said Peter, narrowing his eyes against the brightness of the scene outside. "I know." Brett immediately realized he had said something wrong, so he remained silent. Peter added, "They used to call themselves 'freedom fighters'. Others may have had different terms."

"Sorry, I didn't mean–"

"I know. I know. It was all a long time ago," Peter reassured him. "Look, I'm feeling a bit tired, but if you'd like to explore farther along the beach, beyond that group of coral rocks, I'll stay here and maybe have another smoke and take a short nap. Don't be more than an hour, though, as we have to get back past those large rocks before the incoming tide cuts us off."

Brett was thrilled by this suggestion, and prepared to head along the beach, carrying his stick and water bottle.

"Here, take this whistle in case you have trouble," said Peter. He pulled out an old towel and spread it on a dry sandy patch to lay on. "Oh, here are the binoculars. Just watch out for snakes if you go up into the bushes. There may be some large lizards but they'll avoid you. And don't tease the monkeys. They are not accustomed to it!"

Enthusiastically, Brett set off along the beach towards the distant rocks which jutted out into the coral bay. He felt elation and freedom as he trod new ground alone, along the northern flank of the protected region. The far promontory had always been appealing to explore as it looked so dramatic and beautiful. *Is that true?* he thought, *or is it tempting just because it is forbidden?* He savoured the sight of every rock, salty puddle, hidden channel, clump of seaweed, and tapering gap between huge lumps of fallen coral. He appreciated the views of the swaying trees and narrow paths, leading inland. He dared not venture up those, but he was pleased to be able to make his way around the massive rocks which, after a surprisingly long distance, revealed another large glistening-white sandy beach and more rocks blocking the view beyond that. He noticed a movement which he saw was a large monitor lizard darting back into the dense green cover.

The whole area was more extensive than he had envisioned from the description John Phillips had given him. Looking to the seaward side, he noticed rows of birds: great-white egrets, a single green-backed heron, and an orderly parade of terns. It was all so pristine and pure, with an almost sacred quality. He marvelled at the intricacy and incredible beauty of God's creation. He offered a prayer of thanks for the beauty, and he prayed for Peter and Louise who both seemed to be wrestling with many issues. Then he knew it was time to return to Peter.

He found him, fast asleep on the sand. He sat beside Peter for a while and wondered about him and his life. *An adventurous and interesting man,* he thought, *What tales he might have to tell, if only he would.* He shuffled the sand noisily with his feet and succeeded in waking Peter who appeared startled at first until he realized where he was. As he stood and prepared to leave, Brett handed back the whistle and binoculars. Peter asked about his trip along the beach, which Brett eagerly described.

Part 3: The Attack

On their long return journey, Brett described what he had seen. Peter added, "Henry and I explored as much of this place as we could. We even drew up a map, showing the salient features like footpaths, major caves, bays, channels, and deep pools out within the reef. We could not get right to the far end as that promontory is totally wild and inaccessible, even by boat from the seaward side." They continued walking in silence along the sand and around the rocks. The water was rapidly encroaching onto the sandy strip. Peter plodded along, thinking. Then he spoke: "You asked whether I was affected by Henry's death. I was, and it forced to the surface a lot of memories that had been suppressed. Henry and I did a lot of exploring together. We did a lot together actually. I expect Louise has related some of it. Don't tell me what she's told you. That's her affair." Brett simply smiled.

Peter took a deep breath, stared at Brett, and said, "You know, once, I considered killing Henry. Maybe one day I'll tell you the details. I felt terrible about the memory of it in later years. The fact that he then saved my life, added salt to the wound." He looked at Brett as he spoke, gauging his reaction. Brett tried to convey nothing but, from his expressionless features, Peter could tell that he knew. "Louise told you. That's okay. She has her own understanding of what happened, and I'm sure it was healthy for her to share the story – in confidence – with a friend she could trust. Did she tell you about Henry's fatal accident?" Brett nodded. "She has suffered much more than I have. In fact, I feel she has not yet fully dealt with Henry's passing and the pretence that he's still alive. I have full sympathy for her. And deep respect." Peter continued stepping on the small rocks embedded in the soft sand. "We've known each other for a long time." Brett desperately wanted to ask, 'Do you love her?' but what business was it of his? He was not involved in their lives. Or was he?

Peter seemed lost in thought. Slowly, he turned to Brett and confided, "You cannot imagine how bad Henry looked at that morgue in Nanyuki – you know – when I had to identify his body. Unbelievable. Thank goodness Louise didn't see him. But what hit me then – and still haunts me – was the sudden realization that, years before, I was sent to kill him. It was dreadful, standing there looking at him…dead. So much later…knowing he had saved my life…and I was the one to be with him at the…" His voice trailed away. They walked on, side by side, in silence, each looking down at the sand.

The Zoo

After they rounded the large rocks, they knew they had plenty of time before the tide threatened them, so they slowed down. Peter spoke briefly about his two children in England. He revealed that he had some infrequent contact with his son, Patrick; but his daughter, Julie, had virtually cut him out of her life. "She did write a brief letter a few years ago, saying she was praying for me, but I never replied. I didn't know what to say."

Brett asked, "She was praying for you? Is she a Christian?"

"I've no idea. I wasn't sure what she meant by 'praying for me'. I still have the letter. Perhaps I'll take another look at it. It would be nice to know how she is doing. I miss the contact with my family."

Brett said, "You know, in his sermon on Sunday, Steve spoke about reconciliation through Christ."

"What did Father Steve say about that? I spoke to him once about my family."

"Our relationships can be renewed through Jesus' love. If we build our relationship with Christ, then He is able to work through us to strengthen our bonds with our friends and families. Steve explains this much better than I can; but I know that, if we are yielded to Jesus, then He will bring deep peace in our lives."

"You know, Steve gave me some Bible references. I looked them up. They mentioned love and forgiveness. Apparently, our sins can be forgiven if we truly repent and ask for forgiveness. So many complicated words, I don't really understand it all."

"No, I don't fully understand it either. But Steve stressed that if we reject God, we are prevented from receiving forgiveness of our sins because we would be blocking the very channel through which forgiveness flows."

Peter wondered out loud, in a lugubrious tone, "So, to restore my relationship with Julie…we would both need to show forgiveness and love. Maybe that's what she's praying for. I don't think I have enough faith for that. I don't have a belief in God, other than the Masterful Architect, I suppose."

"Yes, but He's much more than that. He's the creator, sustainer, and provider for all of life. It's important to understand the true nature of God. He is King and His kingdom and rule have been established for ever."

"Well, I don't grasp all the fancy words and complex teachings."

Part 3: The Attack

Brett replied, "It's not complicated, in spite of all the special terminology we use. Words are important because they convey specific meanings. You know, Peter, it's simply a matter of asking God, in faith, to forgive our sins and fill us with His righteousness. That's the basis of reconciliation in all our relationships."

"Well, lots to think about," sighed Peter, wearily. "I'll talk to the Padre again sometime. On another subject…" he said as they rounded a projection of rock, getting their boots splashed by the rising water, and coming in sight of the Zoo, "…up until quite recently, as I said, those caves and footpaths were used by smugglers."

Brett thought, *How recently, I wonder?* But he said, "Really? What were they smuggling?"

"Contraband, weapons, booze, drugs, documents, even the occasional person — whatever needed to come into, or go out of, the country under cover — beyond the eyes of the authorities. Apparently, it was quite lucrative, even if a bit naughty."

"What kinds of drugs?"

"You name it…*bhang, miraa, khat,* cannabis, plus stronger stuff — cocaine, heroine. Anything valuable and portable."

"How was it paid for? What currency?" He was thinking of Sembhi, and Miles' mention of US dollars.

"Cash of various forms, mostly American dollars. Also gold, silver…I even heard mention of diamonds once, but I've never seen any!"

"But where did it all connect to, how did they get stuff in and out?" said Brett.

"Some of the local fisherman know the channels, the rocks, the pools, the caves, and the tides, so they find ways to glide in and out pretty efficiently, even at night. Others provide the land connections." Peter glanced sideways at Brett, "Don't tell anyone I mentioned it. Keep it under your hat, old chap, won't you?"

As they reached the fence, and the dogs started to bark furiously, Brett replied, "I won't say anything."

Afterwards, Brett collected some items from his pigeonhole. He saw a letter from Tony and Jane Colburn. He decided to wait until he reached his cage before opening it. Feeling sweaty from his hike, he washed his face in cold water and sat in his small living room. Eagerly opening the letter from Tony, he found that the news of his thyroid illness was not as bad as he had feared. It described Tony's adjustments to his work and life routines, in order to cope with his reduced capabilities. Generally, Tony and Jane seem positive, and were relying increasingly on God for strength.

Brett thought about his time with Peter. He looked at the sketch he had drawn from Sembhi's map and was surprised at the close match with the details of the coastal features he had seen that day. It was clear, though, he had walked only about a third of the way around the northern edge of the reserve towards the far eastern point. *Lots more still to explore*, he thought.

Walking to the polytechnic the next morning, Brett noticed an attractive young Kenyan lady waiting for a matatu. He greeted her formally, and was surprised at her slightly saucy response. He shook her hand and she clung to him and even started to sidle closer as he asked her where she was going. Just then, Coreene passed by, carrying a newspaper. She smiled politely at the girl and continued on, so Brett gratefully attached himself to her as they walked towards the college together.

"Be careful of her," Coreene whispered. As discreetly as possible, she confided that the girl often came up from Malindi to stay overnight in the guest house. Her visits always coincided with the monthly inspection of the bookkeeper from a Mombasa accounting firm – the company the Zoo used to validate their accounts. "The man who checks our books and audits the statements each month is also regularly accommodated in the guest house. We don't like it, or the implications, but when Steve has mentioned it to Chengo he has been brushed off with vague explanations."

Brett said, "Now I know what Tili meant. She told me that her mother had been angry with the girl who stayed in the guest house with the accountant. She said, 'Mama told her she should not do that. She should get a good job. Girls, they can get pregnant and there are bad diseases that you can end up with'."

Part 3: The Attack

Later, Brett found himself sitting next to Miles at lunch. They chatted about recent trivial incidents and then Miles surprised Brett with, "Louise Emerson doesn't like me."

"Oh, why do you say that?" asked Brett.

"Are you surprised? Hasn't she indicated that to you?" Miles paused and asked, "What has she told you about me?"

Brett was taken aback by the question. "She hasn't said much about you at all." He thought for a moment and added, "She said I could trust anything you told me."

"She said that? I'm surprised. I imagine she also warned you that there is a lot that I will *not* tell you."

Brett could not conceal his amazement as he said, "Yes, that's exactly what she said. I'm not sure what was behind the remark, though."

"She's just being her usual evasive self and trying to put a mysterious gloss on things."

"I've noticed that when I inquire about certain things."

"What does she tell you about Henry?"

Brett glanced at Miles cautiously. "She has often been vague."

"She's protecting..." Miles hesitated.

"Protecting what?"

Miles breathed deeply and got up to leave, saying casually, "She may be protecting that area of her life."

"You must know Louise very well," said Brett

Miles turned back and said, "We've shared a few things together but I wouldn't say I know her well."

As Miles left, Brett thought to himself, *I wonder what their relationship is? Are they closer than it appears? I sometimes see them in serious discussion together. Surely it's not a deep relationship. They seem to dislike each other. What about Peter, how does he fit into all of this? ...Ah, too many questions – and none of them any of my business!*

15

Brett savoured, once again, the sweet fragrance of the frangipani tree beside the road in front of his cage.

The following Friday was an uneventful day at the polytechnic as all the students had left. It was about 5:30pm and Brett still had some end-of-term papers to mark, so he stuffed them in his briefcase to complete that evening. He went to the restaurant and had supper with several of his friends. He briefly greeted Miles outside the office, and walked home to his cage.

It was a pleasant evening, with a gentle, warm breeze. It was his favourite time of day, with the mellow light softening behind the palm trees. He particularly enjoyed the laughter of children playing, while their parents worked in the small gardens. Even the squawking of the raucous crows did not seem as harsh as usual. Strolling amid his friendly, smiling neighbours, he did not hurry as he simply absorbed the serene mood and the familiar environment, feeling at peace in the community. He savoured, once again, the sweet fragrance of the frangipani tree beside the road in front of his cage.

As he reached his front entrance, and put the key in the lock, he was surprised to find the door was unlocked. *That's strange, Tili can't be here this late*, he thought. *Would she have left it unlocked? Very unlikely.* As he pushed open the door and entered, he called out, "Tili, are you…"

The first blow hit him across his left cheek. It came so unexpectedly that it made him gasp. The second punch struck him hard on the right side of his head and caught him off balance. He spun to his left, catching his

Part 3: The Attack

leg against the sharp edge of the umbrella stand. He dropped his briefcase and it flew open, scattering papers everywhere. In a blur of pain he cried out as he slipped down on the side of the stand, the jagged metal edge ripping a gash through his thigh. He let out a second shriek of pain as he fell awkwardly across the top of the low coffee table, sending several items smashing onto the floor. Brett looked up through a mist of pain to see two men leaning over him. They stared down at him for a moment while he looked at them in astonishment.

One man grasped his shoulder and said, distantly, "This is a message from someone you know. Be careful and keep your mouth shut. And cooperate." Then the man slapped him hard again across his face. Immediately, the two intruders slid out through the front door in silence. As they fled, Brett saw that they were both wearing light grey running shoes. In spite of his confusion and agony he noticed that the taller, rougher one who had hit him and spoken to him, was unshaven. As they slipped out, they left the front door open.

In a surge of pain, Brett slid across the floor to the door and pushed it closed. He struggled up on his right knee. With great effort, he reached up and bolted the door. *What was that all about?* he wondered as he slowly stood up, and limped into the bathroom. He removed his shoes. He saw blood streaming down his left leg, soaking through his torn slacks, and running down to his ankle. Painfully, he tried to roll up the trouser leg to see the injury. It wasn't possible, so he quickly removed his slacks to reveal a deep gash about five inches long in his lower thigh. "Oh no! This is serious," he muttered to himself. He grabbed a towel and tried to wrap it around his leg to pull the cut closed and stop the bleeding. "I need to get to the clinic quickly," he said to himself. Then he looked in the mirror and was shocked to see the blood and bruises on his forehead and cheeks. Balancing his left leg awkwardly on the counter, in an attempt to relieve the pain and reduce the bleeding, he ran some water in the basin and splashed his face, drying it with a face flannel.

The blood was oozing through the towel on his leg. He unthreaded the belt from the crumpled slacks on the floor and tried to tighten it across the towel above the wound. The belt holes didn't quite align so he quickly wound it around again and forced it into the last hole. *Got to wrap it some more*, he thought. *But what can I use?* He hopped into the bedroom and grabbed a clean tee shirt which he stretched across the wound and wrapped it tightly around his leg. He reached across and pulled the white cloth belt from his light dressing gown. He sat down on the bed. He wound the cotton belt around the tee shirt below the cut. He adjusted the top belt, thinking, *That should hold for a while. Now, think Brett, what are you going to do? Think! Let's hope the clinic is still open. Should I check around to see what they stole? No, I need help first. I can drive.* He removed his dirty and torn shirt and thought about what to wear. He knew he could not get ordinary shorts over the bulky temporary dressing so he found his new loose-fitting swimming shorts and put them on. *This will have to do. It's more decent than going out in my underwear*, he thought. He grabbed another shirt and pulled that over his throbbing head.

He stumbled across to get the pickup keys, collect his small briefcase with important documents and cash, and hobbled out into the warm early-evening air. He was sweating, and feeling weak from shock and pain. Operating the clutch caused a dart of pain to stab up his leg. As he drove slowly in second gear over to the clinic in a daze of pain and befuddlement, he quickly fabricated a story. He sensed that he should not tell the staff about the attackers. He would say he stumbled on the stupid umbrella stand, cut himself on the sharp edge, and banged his head on the table. He told himself, *Essentially that was what happened. They won't be interested in details. I'll work out the rest later.*

Driving was extremely awkward, but he reached the clinic and was pleased to see the door open. The nurse took one look at him, gasped at the blood-soaked lump of cloth tied around his leg, and asked, "What happened?"

"I fell and cut myself badly. It's about this long and quite deep," he said spreading apart the fingers on his hand to indicate the length of the cut. "I think it will need stitches," he added.

"You must go into Mwakindini. Go to see the Sisters. Can you drive there?"

"Yes, I think so," said Brett.

"I will send Wejiha with you," she said beckoning, with her hand pointed downwards, towards a young nurse. Brett had seen the girl in the clinic before, and agreed it would be good to have someone along with him. He did not want to delay and try to find anyone else to accompany him.

Part 3: The Attack

"Could you send a message to Reverend Brandon please? I may need help later. Thank you."

He limped back to the pickup and slid in with difficulty. He reached across and opened the door for Wejiha. As he drove into town, the pain was throbbing up his leg in waves. Wejiha was silent for a while, and then she asked, "How is it now? The Sisters will help you. You can get sutures and some pain killers." After Brett nodded, she said quietly. "It seems it is bad. The clinic is on the right, past the bank."

As he pulled up in front of the small building, Wejiha climbed out and went ahead into the Catholic Sisters' clinic. When Brett entered, he noticed a few people sitting on functional wooden chairs, but the place did not seem too busy. Three sisters were inside, bustling silently in their comforting, crisp uniforms. Looking at Brett's bloody face and leg, one of them spoke in Swahili with Wejiha. Then she called Brett into a small room. With a noticeable southern European accent, she introduced herself as Sister Maria. She sat him down and told him to raise his leg on a chair, asking what had happened. He was vague. *I can't lie to a nun*, he thought. *It doesn't seem right*. As they together unwrapped his messy, improvised bandages, he twitched at the stabs of pain.

When Sister Maria looked at the cut she immediately said, "This will need sutures. I will see if Dr. Patel can come. His office is close by." Gently, she placed a sterile cloth over the wound and wrapped white tape around it to close the gap and hold back the oozing blood. "Please, you wait here." Brett was feeling nauseous with the pain, and delayed shock from the attack. "I hope Dr. Patel brings some anaesthetic," he mumbled as he sat stoically with his foot up to ease the pressure.

"So, there you are. What happened? How are you?" he heard Coreene say from the door. She walked in and stood in front of him. "Steve is at a church meeting so I thought I'd come and see if you need any help."

"Thank you. I had an accident. There is a pretty ugly cut on my leg."

"I see it. A bit of a mess. You poor thing. And your head too. What happened?" Brett went through his attenuated description and asked Coreene to see if Wejiha needed to be driven back. He assured her that he would be fine to drive. "No. I'll wait until they have treated you, then we'll see what condition you are in to drive. The children are okay on their own for a while. Steve is just next door at the church."

Dr. Patel entered. He shook hands with them both and said, "Let me see what we have here."

"I'll leave you to it," said Coreene as Sister Maria came in. "I'll wait outside with Nurse Wejiha. And I'll be praying for you Brett."

Dr. Patel removed the temporary dressing and said, "This doesn't look good. It will need suturing I'm afraid. It's an unusually long cut. Most are up to about five centimetres but this is over twice that. I expect it will need about ten stitches. You must be feeling some pain Mr. James. I will give you a local anaesthetic. We'll get you comfortable very soon. This stuff is pretty potent and fast-acting. How did you do this?" The first injection felt like a red-hot needle burning into his leg, boring deeper and deeper and shooting stabs of pain into his flesh. Brett gripped the base of his chair and clenched his teeth. "Sorry. Just relax. The first injection stings a little. The second one will be less painful as we'll use some borrowed numbness from the first shot!" Brett managed a wan smile.

Then relief came, as the soothing anodyne took effect. *How wonderful. Now I can relax*, Brett thought as he looked up at the wall behind the doctor. There was some dull pulling in his leg but otherwise Brett felt nothing as Dr. Patel worked. He tried not to imagine the stitches being inserted. Then his head and the bruising on his face began to hurt. He tried to focus his attention on a calendar on the wall. In its tattered condition, it still proudly displayed December 1984. Even in his dreadful state, he managed a grin. He knew it was August 1985. Clearly, the staff were reluctant to relinquish the last calendar they had received.

After ten minutes, the doctor said, "There, nearly done. Twelve sutures. That should hold you together." The Sister helped the doctor by finishing the bandaging. Dr. Patel looked at Brett's forehead. "Some bruising here, and on your face. You were rather careless Mr. James. Sister will give you some antibiotic ointment with a local anaesthetic to make that comfortable." He glanced at the notes that Sister Maria had made. He wrote a few lines on the chart and then shook Brett's hand and started to leave the room.

"How do I pay for all your wonderful treatment?" Brett asked.

Part 3: The Attack

"Oh, the Sisters will let you know before you leave. If not, come back in a few days for us to check you and we'll settle everything then. After about ten days, we'll remove the sutures. No, wait, you are at the Zoo aren't you? They can deal with it. Does Mrs. Emerson still help there? She is excellent. A wonderful lady. A truly wonderful lady. Also her husband, a real visionary. Please pass my greetings to them if you get the opportunity."

"Thank you very much for your help. I do appreciate it," said Brett as Dr. Patel left.

Sister Maria gave him a tetanus injection and looked at his face and head. She wiped them with an antiseptic swab, and applied an antibiotic ointment. She handed him some tubes and tablets, with instructions, and helped him as he stood unsteadily. The nurse picked up his belts and soiled wraps and stuffed them in a plastic bag. He thanked her as he tucked them under his arm, and put the medications in his small case.

"This feels great," he said as he walked out into the waiting room.

"That's an impressive bandage. It makes a statement," commented Coreene. Wejiha looked awed too.

"Yes, a statement about my carelessness."

"Do you feel okay to drive? I can take you two back and return with Steve for your vehicle later," Coreene said.

"No, thank you. I'll be fine."

"Well then, I'll take Wejiha and then come to see you at your cage. I'm concerned you may get a delayed reaction." As they stepped out into the dark, humid air, Brett thanked them both for their help. Driving home, he thought, *I need to find out what it was all about, and what those two yobs were up to. It's bad. How long can I continue to pretend it was an accident? What's the point? Too much to think about now.* It was completely dark outside as Brett drove home safely, parked, and hobbled stiffly to his front door, feeling for the first time an ache in his ribs and chest.

The scene that greeted him was a shambles. Papers were scattered everywhere and a trail of smudged blood patches on the painted concrete floor traced his movements after the attack. He flopped the bag of soiled items in the bath, picked up the bloodied slacks and dumped them in, and ran some cold water. *Let them soak. I'll see if the slacks are salvageable. If not I'll cut them off as shorts.* He slowly shuffled around his cage, checking the valuables and his little stashes of cash. There was no sign of theft, or anything being disturbed. *They were not here to steal, obviously. Otherwise why would they have waited for me? Clearly, they were sent to give me a message. What was it...from someone I know? Surely not in the Zoo. In town? Why the warning?*

He heard a loud knock at the door. "*Hodi?*" called Steve, walking in. "Coreene told me what happened. How are you feeling?"

"Not bad, at least until the anaesthetic wears off. Thanks for checking. I appreciated Coreene's help."

"She sends her best wishes, but she's dealing with the kids now. My meeting finished early so I came over. Is there anything I can do to help? Are you hungry?"

"No, I had supper but I'd love a cup of tea," said Brett sinking wearily into a kitchen chair and maneuvering his left leg up onto another chair. "It helps to elevate it," he explained. "I'll direct you where the tea things are."

As Steve boiled the water, and located the things he needed, he said, "Coreene told me the time at the clinic was a blessing. Apparently, Wejiha was very moved when she saw Coreene praying for you in the waiting room. They spoke about it on the way home. Wejiha hadn't experienced that kind of spontaneous prayer before."

Brett replied, "That's wonderful. They were both so sympathetic."

"So, what happened exactly?" asked Steve. Brett described his falling down and the actions he took afterwards. "Here's your tea, you clumsy oaf," joked Steve as he brought the tray across. "You look as though you've been in a fight."

"I feel like it. I'm worn out. I can't wait to get to bed. I've got enough tablets to sedate a rhino if I need them. Oh, could you find Simion Katana in the morning and tell him what happened please? I'll try to get over in the afternoon."

Steve prayed with Brett, and then tidied up the mess of papers and broken items on the floor. "Do you have any old rags or paper towels?" Brett directed him to look under the sink and Steve wetted the cloths and washed the blood off the floors.

Part 3: The Attack

As Steve started to leave. Brett said, "Also, can you put that wretched umbrella stand outside please, just by the store door. I'll deal with it another day. Be careful, its edges are sharp."

"Are you speaking from experience?" said Steve. "I'll come over later in the morning. If you need anything before that, send Tili over with a message."

"That's a good point, can you write a simple note for her please, explaining what happened, in case I'm not up when she comes tomorrow? Leave it on the table here. I'm off to bed. Thanks for your help, mate." Steve left and Brett took his antibiotic tablet and half a sleeping tablet and crawled, just as he was, under the mosquito net and collapsed in bed, with his left leg supported on a cushion. He fell asleep immediately.

The stabbing pain woke him hours later. It was still dark. It took a while for him to become fully conscious, but eventually he surfaced to a full awareness of his pain and condition. He lay still, trying to analyze his agony. There was a general low-level burning glow of pain – a buzzing sensation. Overlaying that, throbbing stabs which matched his heartbeat. In addition, he occasionally felt a sharp surge of stabbing pain which then, thankfully, subsided. *It's no use, I'll need a painkiller,* he told himself as he struggled up and into the bathroom. It was 3:15am. He took one of the prescribed tablets and limped back into bed, falling asleep after about ten minutes.

In the days that followed, his modified description of the incident became briefer and less specific each time he told it. He decided to maintain the fiction until more information surfaced. He did not want to worry people, or prompt any revelations about his adventure over the wall. He planned to wait to see if anyone reported similar incidents, or sightings of two strangers within the Zoo. He tried to recall their appearance. Placing himself back in the situation, he tried to visualize them. Both seemed poorly dressed. Everything else in his memory was a blur, except that his attacker spoke in clear English. He reasoned they must have been waiting for a while as they would not have known he would be delayed after his supper. Nothing had been disturbed, so he reckoned they had sat on the floor in the corner of the living room so they could listen for his approach.

He tried not to think about who had sent them, but the underlying question kept niggling him. The attack, and the warning it conveyed, was obviously a direct consequence of his misdemeanour over the wall, and only three people knew of that. They had all urged him to say nothing, but they may still not trust him, and may have felt he needed a further indication of their seriousness. *Yes, that's probably it. So which of them arranged it? Maybe all three conspired?* he thought. *But Louise seems an unlikely candidate as her whole demeanour militates against such an action. Chengo? Maybe, as he is the one with easy access to my cage key. He's a bit of a mystery, and I really don't know him. Does he have a ruthless streak? What was his involvement with the Sita affair?...and what about those visits from the police, and that strange, smoking character with his two goons in the Mercedes...? Chengo would have easy contact with local ruffians. But Peter is the most likely to be involved, as he's operated in violent situations and probably understands the need for strategic offensive action at times, when justified.* He wanted to have me expelled from the Zoo but he was overruled by the others. But that does not match with our open and friendly conversations just a few days ago. His thoughts swirled around, but yielded no conclusion.

He wondered if it would be wise to tell Steve the truth about what happened. After careful thought, his intuition told him not to. He reasoned: *He'd almost certainly advise me to tell the police or, worse still, forgive the two men! I cannot see myself doing that. In any case, it wouldn't be fair to bother him. He has enough difficult situations to deal with as it is.* He thought about telling Louise, possibly to test if she already knew, but thought, *There again, what could she do? No, it would only worry her.* He processed all of his options and the likely outcomes. By a round turn, he was back at his initial resolve to say nothing about what had taken place.

During the week after the attack, he was grateful it was the August holiday so he did not have to force himself to teach, although he still had exams to mark. He limped around painfully, and used the full allocation of analgesics during the first few days. To avoid walking, he drove around the Zoo whenever he could. People were sympathetic when they saw him. Nurse Wejiha changed the dressing every three days, and Louise looked at his injury when she was in the clinic. "We need to watch out for infection, that's the main concern. Also keep it dry and clean and elevated whenever possible." She also recommended a first-aid kit that he should keep in his cage.

As Brett limped to the post boxes one evening, Coreene walked beside him. She said, "I'm expecting a letter from America. An anthropologist read about the Zoo and wants to visit sometime. She found Steve's contact information and wrote to him. He asked me to follow up with this lady, so I sent her more information. We are waiting for her response."

"She's coming all the way here, just to visit the Zoo?" asked Brett.

"Yes, she's working on her Masters degree and wants to include us as an example of…well, I'm not sure exactly!"

After about ten days, Brett returned to the Catholic clinic in Mwakindini and paid his bill. Simion Katana drove him there. He was surprised that the charges were so reasonable, and he settled it in cash, including an extra amount as a donation. While they were in Mwakindini, they saw Mr. Badr, the Assistant Manager in the bank. Katana said he had known him for several years as a competent and honest man. The outing left Brett drained of energy, and his leg was still quite painful.

16

"You kept blundering around in your stubborn way, asking questions and poking your nose into things that don't concern you. I warned you it could be dangerous."
Miles Jolly

Brett was in his cage late one afternoon nearly two weeks after the attack. He was just settling down to write a letter when he heard a faint knock at the front door. When he opened it, he was surprised to see Miles Jolly standing there.

"Is Tili here?" Miles said.

"No. Why?"

"Can I come in?"

Miles entered and Brett waved him towards a chair, thinking it was unusual for Miles to visit. In fact, this was the first time. "It's good to see you, Miles. Would you like a drink?"

"No thanks." Miles shook his head.

Brett said, "Well, sit down. How are you?"

"Fine. Thanks. How are you?" Miles glanced towards Brett's bandage above his knee.

"It's healing, thank you. I had the stitches removed a couple of days ago. They were getting tight and uncomfortable. I just have to let it heal completely now. Wearing shorts is more comfortable than trousers."

Miles nodded and stared at the back of his hands which lay flat on his knees. Brett saw a tiny glint of light reflected from the gold ring on Miles' right hand. Addressing his hands, Miles said, "You remember I was asking what Louise thought of me?"

"Yes, it seemed a bit strange," said Brett as he sat down.

Miles looked up, saying, "I suppose it did. Of course, I know exactly what she thinks of me. I was simply trying to find out what you knew, and what you did with that information…how honest and discreet you were. It's a delicate balance: information and discretion." Brett was puzzled, but he did not interrupt, as Miles continued, "You are circumspect, but my only concern was how much more inquisitive you would become. I tried to warn you, and Louise also gave you some strong indications of areas which are off limits, but you persisted."

"What are you getting at Miles?" Brett asked. Miles gazed down in silence. Brett thought he looked small and fragile. Miles turned towards the window and spoke quietly to the trees outside: "Have you told anyone about the two men who came here?"

"No, I haven't…" Brett started to say when suddenly a grim thought hit him: *I haven't mentioned them to a soul. How did Miles find out?* "Have they spoken to you?" asked Brett. Miles shook his head and turned to face Brett, with eyes that appeared black in his round, brown face. Very deliberately, Brett asked, "How do you know about the men?"

Miles leaned forward slightly and again peered intently at his hands. After a few moments he said, "I sent them."

Brett was stunned, "What?"

"I sent them."

"*You* sent them?"

"Yes."

Brett was incredulous. "I don't believe it!"

Miles looked across at Brett, nodded, and said, "I let them in, and gave them instructions."

Brett breathed out slowly and asked, "You? What on earth for?"

"I was trying to protect you. I felt a strong warning was necessary."

Brett jumped up, painfully. "Oh, great! Great! You thought I needed a strong warning to protect me? It was unnecessarily vicious, though, wasn't it?"

"It was not meant to be so extreme. It went wrong and you got hurt more seriously than I expected. I could not have foreseen that."

Brett was speechless for a moment. Then he shouted, "You should have! You set two thugs on me, and now seem surprised that I got hurt." Miles was silent. Brett added, "You're pathetic. Pathetic. Or simply naive."

Miles stared back, and then explained, "They were supposed to slap you to get your attention, and then he was to tell you he had a message from someone you knew, and you should be careful, cooperate, and keep your mouth shut. I rehearsed him carefully in what to say."

"Oh, he did that alright. And a lot more besides." Brett felt confused and deflated. "Were you really thinking you would protect me?" He sat down again and added a further thought, "Or were you guarding some interest of your own?"

"What do you mean? Look, I misjudged the situation. I made a mistake. I tried to warn you but you wouldn't listen. You kept blundering around in your stubborn way, asking questions and poking your nose into things that don't concern you. I warned you it could be dangerous."

"Huh! It *was* dangerous! It seems that I am being punished for…for something."

There was an uneasy silence as they both stared at the papers on Brett's coffee table. Then Miles asked, "Did you get a good look at them?"

"No, not really."

There was a pause. Miles asked, "Would you recognize either of them again?"

"I hope not! I don't want to see them again. I don't know, maybe I would recognize them. I have an impression of what they were wearing. I remember that one was taller than the other. He was unshaven."

They sat in silence for a full minute. Brett was trying to recall something that had been troubling him. Suddenly, he asked Miles, "How were you able to let them in? There was no damage to the lock."

"I have access to the central key cabinet. But please don't tell anyone that."

Brett was outraged, "Great! You use an official key to break in, get me beaten up, and then ask me to keep quiet about it. Brilliant!"

Miles nodded. "Getting the key was easy. Chengo is careless with his keys sometimes." He tried to defuse the situation with, "I am impressed that you have not said anything about what happened. That means you can keep counsel and not blabber around."

"I saw no point in upsetting others. I just kept quiet until I heard some more information from another source. Now I have. From you!"

"I'm sorry. I know you'll never forgive me, but I'll make it up to you. It may take a while, but I'll find some way to compensate you."

"Thanks! I don't know how you'll get rid of this injury, and the limitations in what I can do now, and the permanent scar that I'll probably have."

"I know, sorry. How is it healing, is it painful??"

"Huh. Now you ask. As though you care! Thanks for your sympathy!"

Miles was nonplussed. "I can see you are still upset."

"Upset? Of course I'm upset! And pretty disillusioned with you too. I thought we were friends. Now I see you differently, Miles. I can't trust you."

"Can't we still be friends?" whispered Miles.

Brett thought, *He's talking like a little girl. He doesn't seem able to face the consequence of his actions. Maybe he's not as bright as I thought.* He was about to ask Miles how much he had paid the two men, but, looking at him slumped in a diminished heap, he decided against it. But he felt his anger rising and blurted out, "You say I've been poking my nose into everything, but you are the one always snooping around, asking questions."

"I know. It's my investigative nature. Part of my past. Call it instinct," said Miles.

He looked so forlorn and pitiful that Brett suddenly felt sorry for him, and his anger faded. "Can we just forget this whole episode. Please?"

Miles immediately brightened, "Yes, and you won't mention this to anyone else will you?" He reached into his pocket and pulled out a bulky envelope. He laid it on the table in front of Brett and attempted to press it flat with both hands. "I want you to have this, towards the medical treatments and the inconveniences you have suffered."

Brett leaned forward and picked up the bulky envelope. He peeked inside and saw a bundle of cash. "I can't accept this. It's not necessary, thank you. You are not exactly wealthy."

He pushed the envelope back across the table towards Miles, who replied, "I'm alright. I have a small – er – contingency fund. Please keep it – as a sign of good faith." As Miles stood to leave, he said, "I will not forget my promise to compensate you further." Brett followed him to the door. Miles half turned, as though he was going to say something else, then nodded slightly and left. Brett watched him shuffle away, and he locked the door. He thought, *Louise said I can trust what he tells me. Let's see if she's right in this case.*

He lifted the packet of cash from the table. The dirty, worn notes were aligned in groups of nine with the tenth folded around the set. He had observed this was the way banks handled money in order to facilitate counting. Quickly he counted the folded bundles. Three hundred Kenyan pounds! He stared at them.

Then he walked into his bedroom, found the key in its hidden location, came out to the safe, and locked the envelope inside, thinking, *I'll deal with that later when I've had a chance to think about all this.* He strode into the bathroom and washed his hands to erase the rank smell of the dirty notes. As he dried his hands, he thought: *How come Miles Jolly can get his hands on the cage keys? I thought only Boniface Chengo, as Executive Officer, had access to that cabinet. Surely he's not so careless as to leave his keys lying around. Was Miles telling the truth?*

Brett felt weary. He entered the kitchen. Sitting on the edge of a chair, he wondered why Miles had resorted to such severe means to warn him. He reasoned aloud, "Of course, he didn't intend it to be so bad, and he didn't know I'd fall and cut myself so badly…but still…was he truly trying to protect me? Does he genuinely have my interests at heart – or his?"

Returning to the bathroom to switch off the light, he noticed the first-aid box with the additional bandages. He told himself: "I'm prepared, next time, if Miles decides to send any more of his roughneck friends over to visit me." He entered the living room and sat down at his small desk. He stared for a long time at the locked front door. Then he turned his attention to the correspondence on his desk.

After his tense meeting with Miles, Brett felt depressed. He thought he knew him but now the whole relationship had changed. Even though Brett had found Miles odd, he would never have thought Miles would deliberately hurt him.

He opened the safe and removed the envelope of money from Miles. He took the exact amount the medical treatment had cost him, and replaced the remainder. He thought, *I'm sure some worthwhile need will crop up, where I can use the balance.* Another irritant was his leg injury meant he would not be able to make the long drive upcountry during the remaining August holiday as he had planned. However, he still needed to go to Nairobi to sort out his income tax, collect the map that he had ordered so long ago, and meet up with some friends. There was no alternative, he would have to fly, and accept the expense and the lack of a vehicle when he was in Nairobi. He resolved to visit the travel agent in Malindi as soon as he could. Once he saw the high cost of the flights, he decided to take a third of the cash Miles had given him to offset some of the extra expense.

The next day, he saw Louise in the clinic when he was having his leg inspected. She felt he had taken care of it well and it appeared to be healing. He mentioned his plans, and she offered to drive him to Malindi, as she had a hairdressing appointment the following day. They arranged to go down together.

"Let's leave early. My appointment is at ten," said Louise. Apart from the convenience of having someone drive him, Brett welcomed the opportunity for further discussion with Louise, because he had thought of several more questions for her.

As he drove across the Zoo, parked, and limped stiffly to the cafe, a large black Mercedes drove up alongside and parked in front of the main complex. The smoke-enshrouded stranger whom he had seen previously, got out, holding a cigarette. Their paths intersected. This time, the man could not avoid eye contact, so Brett introduced himself. The stranger simply nodded reluctantly, limply shook Brett's outstretched hand, and scurried into the building. Brett followed him, meeting Grace in the corridor. He asked her the visitor's name, once he was out of earshot.

She frowned and said, "They call him Mr. Moshi."

"Moshi? That means smoke doesn't it?"

"Smoke, yes, like that," giggled Grace, adding, "He comes to see Mr. Chengo."

Miles appeared and overheard their conversation, butting in with, "Moshi? A man of mystery. Shrouded in smoke and veiled fog. Don't worry, he won't try to engage you in social affability! There's no point in trying to be friendly with his two bodyguards either." Grace left them, and they entered the cafe together.

During their meal, Brett suppressed his continuing anger with Miles and listened as he told Brett that he was thinking of selling his car. Brett expressed some surprise – mainly that anyone would want to buy it. Miles retorted, "Yes, believe it or not, my ancient Volvo is attracting some interest from a collector in Europe. Apparently, that model had a limited production run, and they are in demand from those who like such things. The Kenyan climate is good for cars, even at the coast, evidently."

"Do collectors feel it's worth paying the cost of transporting the cars back to Europe, with all of the export hassles and so on?"

"Well, yes. It's in good condition you know!"

"I didn't know. Appearances can be deceptive!" confessed Brett.

"Well, whatever you think, I will be driving it up to Nairobi soon to meet this eager collector, and see if we can agree on an outrageously high price for my desirable old jalopy."

Brett privately doubted if the car would make it up to Nairobi, and he felt glad he was not relying on it for transport.

On the way to Malindi, Louise answered Brett's inquiries about her early years with Henry, and the establishment of the Zoo. She described more of Henry's philosophy on life, and his approach to his secretive work. "He used the German expression 'Spiegel-im-Spiegel' to illustrate how his life seemed at times. It describes the optical effect of two mirrors on opposite walls. If you look in one you see the image reflected in the other and the ever-diminishing reflections seem to continue forever. The curious thing is, though, you can never see the mirror-in-mirror effect completely because you always have to stand slightly to the side otherwise all you see is the reflection of your face in one mirror! Does that help to explain Heinrick's way of operating?"

"To some extent, yes. Did you learn German?"

"We travelled a lot in Germany and Switzerland, so I became reasonably competent in understanding and speaking German. He took me along with him in Europe, and we presented ourselves as a carefree married couple on holiday. In a way, it was all part of his disguise."

"Like the hat, drinking alcohol, and smoking?"

"Yes. I suppose I was just another theatrical accessory! I can't describe the details of Heinrick's work because they were never revealed. But I knew enough to feel confined. I was held captive by my knowledge. Trapped. Oh, to fly free like those seagulls there." They watched the flock swooping across the road in front of them.

Brett pondered her phrase, 'Held captive by my knowledge' but he felt uncomfortable asking her about it. Instead, he enquired, "Did you enjoy the excitement of espionage?"

"No. Well, I never thought of it as espionage; more like mundane observation, routine information-gathering, maintaining contacts – that sort of thing. There were dangers, I suppose, chiefly because Heinrick could not be sure who he could trust. He said he never knew whether he was dealing with a genius or an idiot as the symptoms were often the same!" Then Louise added something that surprised Brett. "Accept everyone for what they are, but you never know who you can trust – even in the community at the Zoo."

They were nearing the town, and Louise said, "We have time to pop into the photographer's shop. I have the usual security film to deliver, and collect last month's negatives. Then I'll drop you at the travel agent. Will you be able to walk across to the hairdressers in about an hour and a half? There is a coffee shop two doors down where you can wait." Brett agreed. Louise said, "I've remembered something else that Heinrick used to say, which relates to the novel by Hardy that you mentioned – Someone Obscure…?"

"Jude the Obscure."

"Yes. Heinrick compared his life to a character from a Franz Kafka book, *Das Schloss*, The Castle. Have you read it?"

"No."

"The story describes the protagonist called K, a land-surveyor, who is intent on gaining access to the remote Castle on the hill, but the whole novel depicts his futile struggle as his goal becomes increasingly unattainable. Perhaps all of the barriers he faced mirror your impression of the wall at the Zoo. Heinrick felt those impediments, and may have established the wall as his protection, in a sense: you know, his domain in isolation from the crowd, on the other side of the wall. Maybe he saw it as his Castle. I don't know, it's just a thought I had."

Brett picked up on her comment, saying, "I'd be interested to hear more details of the initial building of the Zoo."

"Okay, I can tell you some of it later. Here we are at the photographer's shop now. Please wait with the car. I won't be long."

Louise dropped Brett at the travel agent's office before her hair appointment, and he made arrangements for his flight to Nairobi. Afterwards, walking across the town on the uneven pavements, his leg was quite painful. The coffee shop service was indifferent, but he was grateful to establish himself at a window table, take a pain killer, and enjoy his coffee while reading a newspaper. Later, as they met outside the hairdresser, Louise said, "Let's have lunch at the Silver Sailfish, shall we? Then we can head home, unless you have anything else to do here."

"No, I just needed to arrange my flights, that's all."

"Did you get what you wanted?" asked Louise as they reached her car.

"Yes, thank you. I leave next week and will be in Nairobi for two weeks. I hope the Gossards will be able to collect me and put me up at their place. I'll phone them when I get back."

Over the course of a leisurely meal, Louise gave details of her work in the 1950s at two of Nairobi's hospitals while Henry was continuing his confidential government work. She trained nurses, in addition to her on-call hospital duties. She described the challenges of juggling her work, home duties, Henry's responsibilities, and raising their son, Alan. "As Henry approached retirement, we investigated various possibilities at the coast here. Peter Lancaster and his wife were at about the same stage when the four of us stumbled upon the property south of Mwakindini, and the idea of building an inter-cultural community evolved. When we started out we were pretty naive, given all that happened later."

"Were there problems?"

"There were challenges right from the outset. Mainly related to water supply, permits, and permission to install infrastructure and start building. We bent over backwards to reassure the few residents and the officials in Mwakindini that all of their interests would be accommodated, and they would benefit from this unique community. Generally speaking, we received enthusiastic support from the local people. But there were pockets of resistance."

"You both brought your families down to the Zoo?"

"Well, the older kids were at boarding school and later Peter's children transferred to England. That is where his wife was killed – in late 1966 – so she never experienced much of the Zoo community. It upset their children: the daughter, Julie, particularly."

"Miles Jolly wasn't part of the initial group, was he?"

"No, Peter brought him in later, in the early 1970s I think."

"Miles told me that Peter suggested that he came down, and he helped settle him in."

"Yes. It's interesting…they appeared to be friends, but later it became obvious it was an uneasy relationship. There does not seem to be much love lost between those two, although they must have a lot in common with their service in the colonial government. Plus I know they have some joint involvements with their little-boys' club."

"Now you mention it, they don't seem to be together often, or have the easy-going friendship that others have."

"No, they avoid each other if they can. But, if anything other than muted antagonism is going on between them, they hide it effectively." There was a pause as Brett ordered dessert and they both asked for coffee. They chatted about the spectacular view of the coast, the yellow weaver birds flitting busily in the tree outside, and the desultory service in the restaurant.

Louise said, "After Henry died, there was a battle between Peter and Miles as they struggled for dominance. They were like two old buffaloes fighting it out to maintain control of their territory. Mind you, neither was in a position for a battle as they both had health problems."

"What happened?"

"What you see now: a standoff. But we all operate within a compromise of sorts. Peter is very influential, while Miles drifts around in a friendly way, poking his nose into everything!" The waiter brought the bill which Louise grasped. "I'll pay," she insisted.

"I can contribute too," said Brett.

"No, please let me pay. I'll be honest Brett, I can afford it. I didn't tell you before, but Heinrick's estate yielded a lot. I was surprised at how much he had in reserve. Henry kept separate accounts for all of his lucrative work-related matters. Also there was the life insurance settlement. So, at least I don't have financial worries to deal with, on top of everything else."

Brett had several more questions, so he broached the subject of the arched structure on the wall. "I hope you don't mind me asking, but what was the point about the Kismet arch?"

"Oh, that. I was surprised Peter had told you about it. Kismet Kantara, Bridge of Destiny. That was the affectionate name Heinrick gave to that arched structure over the door in the old Portuguese wall. 'Kismet' means fate or destiny, and Kantara is the name of a lovely arched bridge that we admired in Algeria. I can show you the walkway from the inside when you next come to my cage. There is a lot of interesting construction as we built on one of the existing structures, although many were in disrepair."

"I also wanted to ask, who is Moshi? I met him the other day."

Louise frowned. "Moshi. Man of smoke. Have nothing to do with him. He's not nice. He has dealings with Chengo. I don't like it. You don't want to have anything to do with Bwana Moshi!"

Arriving back at the Zoo, Louise dropped Brett off at the Brandons' cage so he could try phoning Jim Gossard. After several attempts, he managed to get through and tell him his arrival details. He was grateful to hear that he could stay with them. Then the phone line was cut off. While trying to phone back, Coreene told Brett about the American researcher, called Miss McNeil, who was arriving soon in Nairobi for a month's visit. She wondered if Brett might be able to change his return flight from Nairobi so he could meet her and travel with her back to the Zoo.

"Can't she catch the train?" asked Brett, as Steve joined them. Brett gave up trying to redial.

"We can't subject her to the train. It's quite intimidating for a new person – and slow," said Coreene.

Steve added, "Did you know that the Mombasa train is mentioned in the Bible?" Brett looked confused until Steve clarified, "Yes, in Genesis it says God created all crawling things!"

They laughed, and Coreene said, "It's an interesting experience, but maybe another time."

"Okay, I can meet her," said Brett.

"Thank you. She'd appreciate that as it's her first visit outside of the USA and she's a bit nervous. Steve or I will meet you both this end."

They phoned the travel agent in Malindi, and Brett was able to change his return flight to a couple of days earlier. He felt sure that he would still have time to do what he needed in Nairobi.

17

Brett did not sense any caution from John, so he felt emboldened to ask Maina, "Do you know why the police are making inquiries at the Zoo?"

The following days were taken up with paperwork, social activities, and meetings. Brett prepared the documents and his bags for the Nairobi trip. He was pleased to have enough time to spend a few hours working on the oil painting he had started some weeks previously. Tili was impressed as she watched him use the 24" x 12" canvas with a beach scene and palm trees against a dramatically-heavy sky and rich blue sea. She was planning to spend a few days with her family while Brett was away, so Steve drove them both to Malindi.

The flight to Nairobi gave Brett an opportunity to see the dry and barren landscape which was in stark contrast to the green coastal strip. Jim Gossard met him at the airport and they drove back in time for the meal Mary had prepared. They were sympathetic over his leg wound, and the brief fictional story of how it had happened.

After an early lunch on the following Monday, Jim dropped Brett at the government office for him to collect his map. He presented his receipt at the front desk, apologizing that it had taken so long to collect it. The official disappeared, clutching the form. After a long wait, he returned saying the map was no longer available. Brett questioned this and was told simply, "No. It is not possible. It is not still available, that map. Your money, you will get it back" Brett saw it was pointless to argue, so he went to another wicket to claim his refund.

Feeling dejected, he made his way to John Phillips' office where he was hoping to see the more detailed aerial images of the Zoo. As John was showing them to Brett, Maina joined them. John appeared unruffled and he encouraged Brett to describe different aspects of the Zoo's layout. They were sitting in Dr. Phillips' office in a relaxed manner around a table strewn with maps. Avoiding any mention of features beyond the wall, Brett outlined the other areas and described some details of the northern and south bays. "Sorry I cannot give you copies of this material: but it seems you now have a good overview of the Zoo region," said John.

"Yes, I am getting an impression of the whole area. I saw an old map in Mombasa and was able to make a sketch of it."

Maina frowned and said, "A map? I thought those were restricted."

"Current maps are," interjected John.

Brett continued, "Yes, evidently they are, because I was not able to purchase one from the government office. The old map in a collector's shop was made by an ancient cartographer." Maina seemed satisfied with that explanation.

Maina said, "I hear you met my good friend Kinyanjui. He likes you. He tells me you have mastered Kikuyu."

"Well, I know a few greetings, yes! We have met twice. He said you and he are age-mates."

"Yes, we are both men from the Slopes – the slopes of Mount Kenya. We shared the blade."

"You are like brothers."

"Without doubt. You know, Mr. Brett, we appreciate your work in our schools. I have a nephew who went to your school in Nyeri when you taught there. You may remember him, Joseph Gichuki."

"Oh yes, Joseph," Brett bluffed, as he often did in similar situations, as he did not recall many individual students years later, "How is he getting on?" They chatted for a while about schools, exams, fees, and the high cost of student uniforms. Brett did not sense any caution from John, so he felt emboldened to ask Maina, "Do you know why the police are making inquiries at the Zoo?"

Maina seemed surprised by the question, but quickly responded, "No, but there may be some small things, here and there, that need to be investigated. Maybe, let's say, it could have a bit to do with something like accounting, and things like that."

John joked, "Well, I'm glad it does not involve satellite images or resource exploration!"

All three laughed and then Maina became serious, "I don't know if you are aware, Bwana Brett…I think I heard a rumour… something to do with your leader. Mr. Ellison, is it?"

"Emerson. Henry Emerson. You heard a rumour?" asked Brett hesitatingly.

"It seems someone in the Muslim area is thinking that Mr. Emerson is not still there. That maybe he is, somehow, not still alive, let's say. Maybe dead. Probably not, but I don't know."

Brett tried unsuccessfully to hide his surprise so John quickly intervened. "No point in taking rumours too seriously, is there?"

"It is more than just a rumour, Sir. Kinyanjui says they checked with their staff in many offices. The Nanyuki police station has records showing that Mr. Emerson was killed there three years ago." Brett tried to maintain a neutral expression, until Maina asked directly, "Have you seen him?"

"No, never," admitted Brett.

"How long have you been there?"

"About a year."

John sensed Brett's discomfort, and again spoke up, "Well, gentlemen I have work to do, so let's call it a day. I am still hoping to visit your intriguing community sometime, Brett."

As he left the office, Brett shook hands with Maina who said, "Please greet Kinyanjui if you see him again."

Brett waited outside for Jim to pick him up. As always, he appreciated the cool Nairobi air, although the traffic fumes were distressing. When they were driving back, Jim told him of a curious thing he had heard that afternoon. Their house-helper was friendly with the maid next door whose cousin lived in a unique community at the coast. Their maid had been telling Mary about the previous week when she had met up with her cousin who was visiting Nairobi. Apparently, some of the local women down there were saying their leader had died, but it was a secret. Jim explained, "I normally don't listen to those conversations, but my ears pricked up because it sounded a lot like your Zoo. Is there a problem with the leader?"

Brett breathed deeply. "Yes. That means the cat is out of the bag."

"What do you mean?" asked Jim.

"I heard the same information from a fellow in John's office. Old man Emerson was killed a few years ago, but they tried to suppress the information because he was a major stabilizing force in the community. The leaders felt that news of his passing would be disruptive, so they have concealed the fact."

"But you knew?"

"Yes, but I only found out recently. I agreed to keep quiet about it, which I have. But now it's an open secret, it seems. I hope it doesn't cause trouble."

Brett wanted to repay Mary and Jim for their kindness, so he suggested he take them for lunch the next day. He had arranged to start the process of filing his income-tax forms in the morning, so they agreed to meet at the Lobster Haven at noon for a special meal. Once Jim and Mary arrived, they ordered a chowder soup and a king fish curry. After the meal, Brett excused himself to pay the bill at the cash register beside a window overlooking an inner courtyard. Casually, he looked down into a small parking area between the buildings and watched a large white Mercedes pull in. Then Brett was amazed to see, parked beside the wall, an old green Volvo like the one Miles drove. *I thought that model was very rare*, he said to himself. Suddenly it struck him: *That is Miles' car!* He saw a man open the Volvo door and pass a package through the window of the Mercedes. The driver took it. They spoke for a while, shook hands, and then the Mercedes reversed and drove away. *Has this got anything do with the sale of his car?* he wondered as he waited for the clerk to process his payment.

He turned to see an old Kenyan man limping across in front of him, moving slowly from the gents' room to a corner table. As Brett completed paying, the old man sat down. Next to him, Brett saw the unmistakable outline of Miles Jolly, with his back towards him. He was deep in conversation with two other men: one white, an Asian, and the old Kenyan man who had just joined them. As he returned to Jim and Mary, Brett looked carefully at the white man facing towards him. The others were not clearly visible. He decided not to disturb them.

While he was in Nairobi, Brett celebrated his 31st birthday with a small, low-key party. He met several other friends afterwards and caught up with news of the Nyeri community. Soon it was time to welcome the visitor from America, and return to the coast. Jim and Mary drove Brett to the airport with his bags. They arrived early to meet the plane from Amsterdam. Mary stayed with their car to watch Brett's bags while he and Jim entered the large arrivals hall.

"How will we recognise this visitor we are meeting? What's she like, this American?" asked Jim.

"I've no idea. Just a typical-looking female American anthropologist, I suppose."

"Whatever that looks like," added Jim. "How old is she?"

"I don't think Coreene was told. Old, I suppose," ventured Brett.

"Oh, bound to be old I should think, being an anthropologist," said Jim.

"You're not thinking of an archeologist are you?" They both laughed.

Waiting in the bustle of the crowds, as the passengers appeared through the arrivals door, they held up a cardboard sign with 'McNeil' written on it. They each watched for who they imagined the passenger to look like. Neither of them was ready for the person who suddenly appeared in front of them, pointing to the sign and saying, "That's me." They were astonished. "Hi, I'm Kelsey McNeil. I guess you guys are here to meet me. That's cool." They both looked at a smiling, plump, young lady wearing very casual, if skimpy, clothes and hauling two large suitcases. She had a winsome, smiling face, surrounded by a tumble of blond hair.

"Well, hello, pleased to meet you," said Brett shaking her hand.

"Yes, nice to see you Miss McNeil. Welcome to Kenya," said Jim, extending his hand to her. Steering her through the crowd of drivers offering taxis, they each pulled one of her cases, and directed her towards the car to meet Mary.

"How was your flight?"

Part 3: The Attack

"Man, don't ask. What a hassle! I've been in the air for days it seems. It's crazy. I've lost count of the number of flights I had to take. And those plane seats are so small. But back in there, through your customs and immigration, man! I'm, like, what's going on in this place? No one tells you anything. And I couldn't understand what people were saying till this English guy came up and helped guide me through the whole shebang. It's, like, chaos back there."

"Well, you're here now, and we'll take care of you. Won't we Brett?" said Jim, winking at Brett.

"Yes, I'll accompany you to Malindi, and then Steve will meet us and drive up to the Zoo," Brett assured her.

"Awesome. Thanks." She paused, "Zoo! Ha. When I read that I was, like, holy cow, zoo? That's the weirdest thing I've ever heard."

"Yes, and we live in cages," said Brett, enjoying himself.

"Cages! People living in cages. I read that too. I was like, man, I've gotta go check this out this special place for myself. It can't be for real. Cages! Is that so uncool, or what?"

"Do come and see my wife, Mary. She's been looking forward to meeting you," chuckled Jim as suavely as he could manage, putting on his ever-so-British accent for good measure.

After the introductions, they all made their way to the domestic departures area and, with some relief it seemed, Jim and Mary left Brett and Kelsey to wait for their flight to the coast. "We must stay together, and watch our belongings the whole time," said Brett. "What are your immediate needs, are you hungry or thirsty?"

"No, I'm fine thanks. But I need a cigarette. It sure is hot here. Why is this place so crowded?"

"People heard that you were arriving!" teased Brett.

"Ha, that's funny. So, how old are you Brett? I'm 26 but I look younger, right?"

"I'm just 31."

"So, we are almost the same age. That's cool. But you're taller than me. And thinner too."

"Do you have your plane ticket? We'd better confirm we're on the same flight."

They checked the documents, and found they were sitting in different sections of the plane. He saw that her passport had been stamped with a 3-month visitor's visa. He was already feeling that it was too long.

"Let's see if we can sit together," said Brett looking around for the airline desk.

"Your call," she said.

As they checked in their bags, they managed to change Brett's seat into the smoking area, which he was not pleased about. He hid his disappointment over the move and suggested, "Let's have coffee, shall we?" They found a place, as they had about 90 minutes to wait.

Once they were settled, Kelsey jumped in, "So, tell me about this zoo. I couldn't believe what that article said about the place. I thought, 'Man! I have to go there.' So here I am."

"So here you are, indeed. Well, it's just called The Zoo. That's the name, and we all get used to the little cottages being called cages. I found it strange at first – everyone does. Don't worry, you won't be in a cage. Coreene said you'll be housed in the guest wing. And you'll have most of your meals in the cafe or restaurant so you'll have a chance to meet lots of interesting folks. We call it the feeding centre. Like a zoo, eh?"

"Yeah. Cool. Coreene? Oh, she's the lady who wrote me. She sounds real nice."

"She is. And her husband, Steve. How did you find their address? You contacted the Reverend Brandon through a church office somewhere?"

"No. The article I read in this magazine gave his name as the pastor, vicar, priest, whatever."

"Are you connected to a church?"

"Man, no! The opposite, I'm an atheist."

He said, "I see. We have a few who believe the same in the Zoo! We have honest and respectful discussions. You'll like them."

"Sure I will."

"There are many religions represented within our community. Tell me what you have read about it, and why you were interested enough to come all this way." She explained about her studies into unique cross-cultural communities, and the appeal that the Zoo had, based on the article she read and the information Coreene had supplied. Brett was impressed by how much she already knew, and the clear direction of her questions.

Part 3: The Attack

They chatted for a long time, and eventually, Kelsey said, "Well, I feel like I'm getting a handle on it all. Thanks for getting me up to speed. It sounds cool. I'm looking forward to seeing the place. And I need to work on my suntan while I'm here. Catch a few rays. I'm so pale."

"Where are you from? What part of America?" Brett asked.

"Savannah, Georgia."

"Is that, like, in the south?" Suddenly he thought, *Oh no. she's got me saying 'like' now!*

"Yes, the south-eastern U.S.. It's cool. Well, warm actually." She laughed in her natural and endearing way.

"Did you bring a camera?" Brett asked.

"I sure did, and loads of film. I hope the camera was okay through those x-ray machine thingies. I kept the unexposed film in my hand luggage. Anyway, yeah, I plan to take lots of photographs."

"Just a warning on that. Don't take photos of any government buildings, military or police personnel or vehicles, or prisoners working outside. They wear white uniforms."

"Okay. Got it. Thanks for the heads up."

"Also, it's best to ask people before taking their photo. The person you are with will guide you. Kids are okay, but don't pat them on the head. The adults believe it implies you are trying to limit their growth. Anyway, as an anthropologist, I expect you know all of these cultural rules."

"No, but they are fascinating, thanks. Each society has its own norms and they are all different! I don't want to be caught out in left field on this one."

Brett nodded. "Yes, it's confusing at first. Generally, the Kenyans are used to tourists so they tolerate us."

"Good. I wanna get these cultural things straight, right from the get-go, you know, straight out of the gate. Thanks. Tell me about your teaching," said Kelsey, lighting another cigarette. He described the programmes at the polytechnic. He spoke of the importance of interpersonal relationships. Then he mentioned that they should always use the right hand for giving and receiving gifts, food, or money, never the left hand as that is considered unclean. "Also, never point at a person." Then he thought of something else. "The sun is very intense here on the equator. Always wear a hat and use sunscreen. Even wearing a hat and staying in the shade, you'll get brown from the glaring reflection off the white coral ground."

"Right. Got it. You've got me curious, how do I point out a person if I need to?"

"That's your first week's assignment. Observe, and find out how the Kenyans do that!"

"Ha ha. I see you're definitely a teacher."

Getting on the plane with Kelsey was a hoot. She charmed and blustered her way through the whole process, finally locating her place next to the window. "Let me see if I can wedge myself into this narrow seat. I don't know why they make them so small" Once settled, she turned to Brett and confessed, "After this trip I'm gonna lose weight." He smiled and nodded in silence. "Yeah, right. Sure you are, Kelsey," she said to herself. "I'm not skinny, I know. I can say that, but I don't appreciate anyone else telling me," she stated, glaring at Brett.

"No. No, of course not," agreed Brett quickly. He suddenly felt small, and quiet – and very English. He thought, *How are the ladies going to react to her? More to the point, what will the chaps think? I can just imagine Peter's reaction. And Miles! Oh my, Miles! This is going to be interesting. How is she going to go down in the old boys' club? Len will have a field day.*

After the take-off, Kelsey lit a cigarette and turned to Brett, interrupting his thoughts. "So, how long is this flight going to be? I've had it up to here with flying." She waved her hand near her neck through the smoke.

"I'm not sure exactly, about–"

"Just a ballpark figure. Hey, look at that mountain. Is it Kilimanjaro? How high is it?"

Brett had learnt the height, "19,340 feet. The peak is in Tanzania, although the body of the mountain straddles the border. When the colonialists carved up the territory, they arranged the boundary lines so that Tanzania had a snow-capped peak, as Kenya had its peak at Mt. Kenya. Amazing that they are snow-covered all year, even though they sit on the equator."

She looked at the smooth, rounded peak of the mountain. "That's cool. Wow, 19,340 feet. That's almost as tall as Mt. McKinley in Alaska. That's the highest mountain in the States, you know. 20,310 feet. We learned that in school." Kelsey rummaged in her bag and took out a notebook. "So, tell me about the structure of the Zoo, the organization, funding, leadership – that sort of stuff."

"You're well organized and keen," said Brett, admiringly. He was appreciating her ebullient personality and sparkling eyes.

"Hey man, I might look like a tourist, but I'm here to work. I need to hit the ground running. I want facts, and a thorough understanding of how the unique setup works." After giving her a brief outline, similar to the explanation Peter had given him, Brett was impressed at her follow-up questions, and the detailed notes she took. When he described the three zone representatives, she called them the 'Block Parents'. He thought, *She's intelligent, and she analyzes things well.*

"You pick things up quickly." he said admiringly.

"Thanks. Like I say, I wanna study how this all works. My dad ponied up the cash for this trip, so I feel an obligation to make the most of y'all as a case study."

"We're a case study?"

"Yes, kind of – but in a low-key sort of way, you know. I'm gonna incorporate into my Masters thesis a real illustration of a viable community which was based on an original cultural group, with a different social structure grafted on."

"In essence, I suppose that's what happened."

"So, who is the head honcho?"

"What, the leader?"

"Yes, where is the source of power and control? Is it democratic?"

"To a degree, yes. Henry Emerson was the inspiration behind it all. Others will tell you details. Don't forget, I'm fairly new myself, so I'm still trying to sort out some things."

"Are there strong religious authority figures? In many societies, religion and culture are intertwined."

"That's certainly true of the Muslim group. Less so among the *mzungus*."

"The what?"

"Oh, sorry, that means the white people. *Mzungu* is the singular from and *Wazungu* is the correct plural word. The Europeans. That's what they'll call you."

"Me? A European? That's so cool. But, back to religions, which ones are represented at the Zoo? Mostly Muslim, I guess. Unpack that for me, would you."

"The coastal region is 99% Islamic. Many Muslims live in the community. But there are Hindus and Sikhs in the Zoo, along with the Christians. Plus many who don't profess a formal faith."

"Any Buddhists?"

"None, as far as I know. Very few in Kenya actually. Kenya is mostly a Christian country. The number of Muslims at the coast is not typical of the rest of the country. I imagine it's because of the history of Islamic invasions along the coast over the centuries. But you said you were not interested in religion."

"I'm, like, so totally not into religion myself, but I'm interested in the belief systems of different ethnic communities. I've studied all the religions – at least their basic tenets." She paused. "None impressed me."

Brett looked past her out of the window. He was feeling tired, and his lungs stung from the unfamiliar tobacco smoke. She continued, "There are many branches in Anthropology. I'm mostly interested in social anthropology, including how religion affects people, and bonds communities. All religion is developed within a cultural context. Actually, all morality is culturally based too."

Brett's head was spinning so he said, "I expect you are feeling a bit jet-lagged?"

"Yes, I'm so disoriented. Maybe I'll try to sleep for a few minutes. Okay?" She put away her pen and notebook.

"A good idea," said Brett. As he closed his eyes, he thought about the complex person sitting beside him: one minute, frivolous, outspoken, and insensitive; the next moment, serious, inquisitive, and intellectual. *An impressive young lady. This is going to be an interesting month. How will she be received at the Zoo? Will she be able to find out the things she has come to learn? I'm glad the new polytechnic term is starting soon and I'll be busy, so I can hand her over to someone else in the Zoo! I will have done my bit, just getting her down there.*

18

Peter Lancaster suddenly frowned. "This is not good. It looks like Moshi."

For over a week after Brett's return, Miles did not speak of his Nairobi trip, but unexpectedly raised the topic when they were alone in the cafe.

Miles said, "I have a bone to pick with you."

"Oh, what?"

"Why did you ignore me in the Lobster Haven?"

"Oh, you saw me. So I might ask you the same question," replied Brett.

"I asked first," countered Miles.

"I didn't see you until we were leaving and you seemed to be deeply engrossed in discussion with three other men. It didn't seem appropriate to disturb you."

"That's okay."

"Why have you waited for a week to raise it?" asked Brett.

"It was a test to see if you would mention it to me."

"I didn't see any point," Brett stated.

Miles nodded, "Did you happen to notice the Kenyan I was with?"

"Yes, I saw him as he returned to your table."

"How would you describe him?"

"He was an old man, with a noticeable limp. Other than that, he looked like a typical, smartly-dressed Kenyan in a jacket and slacks, perhaps feeling slightly out of place. I don't know....who was he?"

"I've known him for a long time and he has an interesting background. He is Mzee Kamau. He was injured during the Mau-Mau uprising. I'm afraid I can't tell you any more details."

"That's all I ever get from you – half a story!" said Brett.

"Be grateful you get that much! Most of us have to blunder along with far less. Who was the couple you were with?"

"The Gossards. Jim and Mary – you know, my friends that I stay with in Nairobi."

"Ah, the dear lady who makes such delicious picnic lunches! You should have introduced me and I could have thanked her," smiled Miles.

"Sorry. Maybe next time. As I said, you seemed very involved in your discussion."

That was all Brett said about the restaurant. He asked if Miles had sold his car to the overseas buyer and was informed that indeed he had – for such a good price, he could easily afford the airfare to return to the Zoo, with lots of spare change in his pocket. Then Miles asked about Kelsey McNeil, "Who is this creature you collected in Nairobi? She seems to be having quite an impact here."

"Oh, yes. I can't wait for you to meet her," chuckled Brett. "If I had known you were going to be flying down from Nairobi, I would have got *you* to accompany her. It would have been good for you."

"What's that supposed to mean?"

"You'll see." Then Brett asked, "What will you do about transport now?"

"I'll get a nice pickup."

"I thought you didn't have much money."

"I have to be careful with the old moolah, but I said I would compensate you for your leg injury, and I will somehow. I think I can afford to help out an old friend, don't you?"

Two days later, Simion Katana mentioned to Brett and Coreene that some students had commented on Kelsey McNeil's clothing and her smoking. Coreene offered to explain to her that she might want to modify her dress while staying next to a conservative Muslim area. Leaving Katana, Coreene walked with Brett to the central buildings. "Kelsey wants to get a tan. I suppose she does dress rather casually. Anyway, she's getting some interesting cultural experiences. Yesterday she had a trip to the market with our maid."

Brett said, "Sorry, Coreene, I can't stop. I received a note from the Executive Council saying they want to see me again at 4pm."

As he left her, he talked himself through some rapid ideas: "What now? Maybe they've heard the news about Henry's death being discussed by some people. I hope the Big Three don't think I blabbed about it." He went over to the meeting room after his classes, and once more, painfully climbed the stairs and knocked on the door. Entering, he saw the same group as before.

Boniface Chengo pointed to the chair where Brett had sat previously. He got straight to the point. "Mister Brett, we hear that some people in Nairobi know the news about Bwana Emerson."

Peter snapped, "I hope you didn't spill the beans. Were you yapping around in Nairobi?"

"Yapping, no. Flapping, yes. My ears were flapping and I heard the rumour from two separate sources. I had said nothing about what I knew. Then I heard it from two others."

"Who did you hear it from?" asked Louise.

"First Maina, the government liaison specialist in Dr. Phillips' office. He's a good friend of Kinyanjui who likes to visit us here." He paused for laughter but there was none. "Then Jim Gossard, a retired optician, related a story from their next-door maid who has a cousin here in the southern sector. It seems that some of the women over there don't believe that Henry is still alive." He nodded towards the south.

Chengo said, "That man, Ochieng, the detective person, he came to see me. He said there are rumours about Bwana Emerson, that he is nowhere. The Muslim girls, they used to see him, here and there, but no more. Not now."

Peter added, "Apparently, Ochieng checked the records at their stations across the Central Province and here in the Coast Province."

Chengo said, "It was the Nanyuki attachment which confirmed his death."

"Detachment – the Nanyuki *detachment*," said Peter, correcting him.

"Yes. Those people there. They say it is true."

"So, we do not need to pretend any longer. That will be a relief," sighed Louise.

"I just hope the loss of Henry's prestige won't affect things operationally," said Peter.

Chengo relaxed and said, "As for me, myself, I think we can just carry on. We have the green light to be honest now."

"Well, that's good," said Brett, standing. His leg was throbbing.

"Wait, we must still keep quiet about your climbing over the wall. No one must know what's over there," warned Peter.

"Why the secrecy, may I ask, now it's known that Henry's not there?"

The trio looked at one another. Peter answered: "Things go on – er – there are activities…related to the – er – animals that need protection from interference." He looked as though he was not convinced himself. He quickly continued, "So, secrecy has to be maintained and you must stay quiet."

"Otherwise, it will not be good for you," added Chengo.

"That sounds like a threat," said Brett.

"Not a threat. That's too strong a word. Let's say, a warning," said Peter.

"Oh, I've had plenty of those," quipped Brett. Not one of them smiled, so he added, "Yes, of course, I will keep silent. I am sorry for the inconvenience I caused."

As he left the group, Brett wondered how long it would be before Miles heard about it all.

The meeting with the Executive unsettled Brett. He was ready for a cup of tea and a change of company, so he wandered into the cafe to see who was there. An amusing scene presented itself: the old boys' club was in session. Several of the men and a few women were sitting in a semicircle with Kelsey McNeil slumped in a comfortable chair in front of the group. He heard laughter as he entered.

Len was speaking, "…anthropo-logical, psycho-logical, physio-logical… as long as it's *logical* we're fine with that, right Brett?"

"Keep me out of this, I just need a cuppa. Hello Kelsey. How are you settling in?"

"Great. But things sure are strange here. Like, the light switches are all upside down, and what about those weird electric plugs with their three fat pins. And I don't like seeing ants in the sugar bowls. In the States, sugar never moves about! And you guys eat with a knife and fork. That's so cool. I'm going to try that. You know what, I even saw Louise use a knife and fork to eat a pineapple the other day!" Everyone laughed, as she continued her entertaining monologue: "But it sure freaks me out when you guys drive on the left. So scary around those traffic circles. Man, I can hardly watch. I went to the Mwakindini market yesterday. It was real interesting. But, boy, what an eye-opener! We travelled in one of those mata- thingies. So crowded and dangerous. Men pushing in, getting closer than I liked. I've never been overseas before and I thought everywhere was, like, the way it is in the States. You know, clean and efficient. Everything is different – even the oranges. Oranges here are not orange like they should be, they're green! They should be called 'greens'," she joked, in her deep southern drawl.

"You can call them 'greens' if you like, but you may be given the wrong kind of produce." This warning came from Matthew who added, "You may be interested to know that a roundabout is called a *Keepilefti* in Swahili."

"Keep-i-lefti. Oh, I get it: That's so cool."

"It's very logical, and makes as much sense as our term 'roundabout', I think," said Marie-Anne.

Kelsey smiled. "That's, like, a traffic circle, right? By the way, you guys, I love your accents. I wish I had an accent."

The four men almost collapsed onto the floor, laughing, "You *do* have an accent!" Kelsey joined in the laughter.

"And it's very nice," added Marie-Anne, trying to salvage the situation. Louise joined them, ordered a tea, and sat down, glancing at Brett.

Once the hilarity had died down, Matthew said, "Len, you should explain to Miss McNeil about your energy-conservation projects. That should go into her report." Len modestly outlined his ideas. Kelsey made notes as he spoke. "…aiming for a fully-independent integrated energy system," she said, looking up from her notepad. "Wow. That's neat. We've only just met but I've got you figured out already, Len: you are a taciturn genius who loves humour. Am I close?"

Len hesitated, "Oh, this is weird, are you a psychologist or what?"

"No, an anthropologist," said Kelsey, smiling.

"Any kind of -ologist is unsettling around here," interjected Miles. "We don't like to be studied and analyzed."

The Zoo

"Pity, that's just why I'm here! But don't worry. I won't embarrass anyone."

"Sorry I can't promise the same," snapped Miles, obviously irritated.

"Boy, this is a tough league! Talking of names, I saw that the front sign does not call this place the Zoo. It's Community Village, now, right?"

"You are observant, Miss McNeil," said Len.

"Thanks. Well, must go. See y'all later. These clothes are getting so tight." said Kelsey, standing.

Marie-Anne said, "Cloth shrinks over time. We all find that, dear."

Brett followed Kelsey out, feeling the need to be gallant. "Are you alright? How's it going?" he asked.

"Fine, thanks. But who is that cute little guy with the round face and tufts of hair over his ears? Man! I don't think he likes me. What's your take on that?"

"That's Miles Jolly. He's a bit strange, but he'll be fine when he gets to know you."

"I may have come on a bit strong, you know, with the oranges and all."

"It's just that they are not used to your style. That's all. By the way, never make any remarks about political stuff or the organization of things in the country — the government and things like that. You could be reported."

"Wow, okay. Thanks for the heads up. Bye."

Returning to the cafe, Brett sensed a tense atmosphere. He said, "She feels she may have come on a bit strong with some of her remarks."

"Oh, no. No more than the average steam-roller in a delicate flower garden," said Miles sarcastically. "She makes me uneasy, that stout wench."

Marie-Anne tried to pacify him, "Don't be unkind Miles. She has observant eyes set in her pretty face. She's young."

"But, seriously," said Len, "someone should talk to her about her modesty…she doesn't realize how she is viewed by the local men."

"Speak to her about it then, Len," suggested Matthew.

"No, I can't see myself as custodian of her modesty, or an interlocutor in the matter. I'm hardly a female-fashion maven."

"It sounds like a job for Coreene. I know she is aware," said Brett.

Part 3: The Attack

"Coreene. Good idea. I'll mention it to her," said Louise. "Also, I may get a chance to speak with Kelsey myself. She's such a sweet, intelligent girl, I'd hate there to be any misunderstanding."

"That's a relief. Now that we've appointed Coreene and Louise as Kelsey's sartorial advisors we can relax," said Len.

"Well, I'm glad you're all enamoured by that anthropomorphic-apologist, whatever she calls herself," scoffed Miles. "I'm not so keen on that girl, with her loud American accent, going around behaving like a tourist."

"We can afford to be a little generous and lenient, Miles," said Brett.

"Ha, you brought that ample anthropologist down here."

Louise glared at Miles, "I'm not sure that I am comfortable with the way this conversation is going..."

"It's simply that I don't like being studied and analyzed as part of her research, and having to listen to her criticisms," Miles mumbled.

"You have a nerve complaining about her comments, just when you are all criticizing her appearance," said Louise.

Matthew chimed in, "She's certainly brought some excitement here. A breath of fresh air."

"It's interesting to watch people's different reactions to the news about Henry's death." The innocuous comment came from Miles the next morning as he strolled with Brett across to the polytechnic. They were both walking slowly, for different reasons: Brett's leg was stiff in the mornings, and Miles seemed to get breathless quickly.

"Oh, when did you hear about it?" asked Brett.

"I guessed a long time ago."

"You knew?"

Smiling at Brett's surprise, Miles simply said, "Others suspected too, no doubt. Let's hope it doesn't cause any instability now it's out in the open."

"How would you assess people's reactions, generally?" Brett asked.

"Firmly lodged between apathy and indifference, as far as I can tell! Seriously, many seem upset, but I'm not sure if it's because he's dead, or the fact that they were kept in the dark for so long. But life goes on, people adjust to reality, and it won't affect most of the residents one way or the other, will it?"

Brett was taken aback by Miles' casual tone, but simply replied, "I suppose you're right. Do you think there will be some kind of memorial event to mark Henry's passing?"

"I'm not sure. Brigadier Thomas feels we should do something to acknowledge Henry's contribution to – to everything. His contribution–"

He was interrupted by Steve Brandon as they passed by the church. He called over to Miles and said, "Sorry about the news of your old friend. Thomas suggested a few of us get together to discuss a suitable tribute for Henry. We'll need to make an official announcement too."

"Check with Louise first. I imagine she's pretty upset about it all," advised Miles and he headed towards one of the bench seats under the trees. He removed his straw hat, placed his briefcase on the seat, sat down, and stared out to the glistening aquamarine sea in the South Bay. The sun was getting hotter as another perfect day became established in the small Zoo community. It seemed to Brett that Miles was waiting for something – or someone.

Turning to Steve, Brett said, "Actually, it's difficult to judge how Louise feels, although she is relieved that she doesn't have to maintain the pretence any longer."

Steve said, "Interesting. Thomas suggested a small memorial service. Let's see what she says. Can you join us sometime when I've had a chance to speak to her?" They agreed to consult Louise before making any arrangements. Later, Steve told the others he had spoken with Louise and she would like them to have tea with her the following afternoon.

Brigadier Ridge-Taylor, Reverend Steve Brandon, and Brett James visited Louise in her downstairs front room. After tea, and the ritual formalities, Thomas outlined their ideas. Louise shook her head. "No, we don't want a requiem do we! I wouldn't want it to turn maudlin. It's so long after the fact. In any case, Henry didn't believe in anything religious, so it wouldn't mean much."

Part 3: The Attack

"Memorials are mostly for the benefit of those left behind – to give them a form of expression of their grief and appreciation," explained Steve. "We ought to do something to recognize his massive contribution here in Kenya – and celebrate all he did in the Zoo."

Thomas insisted, "First we should issue a formal announcement. A simple letter will do. Mean-to-say, he was an important influence and a big man around here. Many people—"

"Shall I prepare the outline of a letter which can be printed off and put in all the pigeonholes and on notice boards?" offered Steve. The group agreed, then returned to their inconclusive discussion of a memorial event.

"What about a simple plaque, with his name and dates, which could be mounted in the entrance to the central buildings?" suggested Brett. They all thought that was a good idea, and asked him to draft some wording with Steve. He agreed, and then told Louise he would check it with her.

"Come for tea tomorrow Brett, and we'll go through your suggestions," she said. As they left, Steve offered to find someone who could make the plate and engrave the lettering.

The next afternoon, after his last class, Brett hurried across to Louise's cage. They sat outside, beside the desert rose bush, and had tea delivered there for a change. Brett showed her the wording he had suggested to Steve and Thomas. When she read what he had written, she gave a slight smile, sighed gently, and handed the paper back to him, saying, "That's lovely. I like it. Thank you." He felt relieved. She added, "By the way, 'spiegel' is spelt with ie, not ei." He grinned and corrected it.

"Otherwise, is it okay?"

"Perfect, thank you. Where do you plan to mount the plaque?" They discussed several possibilities, which Brett agreed to talk over with the others for their input. Although he had never met Henry, Brett felt an affinity towards him, and wanted to support Louise through the emotionally difficult time.

The next day, Coreene and Louise were sitting in the shade on the ocean-facing seat above the South Bay. Louise knew the clinic staff would find her if a problem developed. They were chatting about Steve's draft letter which Louise had approved. It was being typed and would be distributed within two days. Coreene asked about the suggested memorial plate for

Henry. "I'm pleased they have come up with that idea," said Louise, "as I didn't want to sit through a commemoration ceremony."

"Wouldn't you find that comforting, with people expressing their appreciation of Henry?" asked Coreene.

"Not now. If it could have happened just after his death, maybe…No, it's too late now. I've done my own grieving."

"Have you…" Coreene was interrupted by Kelsey as she walked past them towards the beach. The two seated ladies looked at each other and nodded in agreement that this was the time to speak with her about her clothing choices.

"Come and sit in the shade for a while, Kelsey. You'll catch the reflected rays, just as we are," called out Louise.

Kelsey joined them and they spoke of her time at the Zoo. She told them she had observed that Kenyans point with their chins, rather than fingers. She explained that Brett had set that as an assignment for her. The two ladies were impressed. Then Coreene said, "I hope you don't mind my mentioning this, but we feel that your clothes may be a bit too revealing for a public area. We are not judging you of course, but felt we should just mention it as several locals are commenting."

"Oh, sorry, I wasn't aware. I want to get brown," replied Kelsey, without resentment. "I guess this is a conservative area."

"Yes, that's true. You see, over the years, we have watched how the local ladies dress, and it is quite modestly, particularly compared to the tourist beaches."

Coreene added, "We have adopted the local ways because we do not want to cause any offence. We have to be careful what signals we send – particularly to the young men."

"Oh, sure. Customs that way are, like, totally cultural, I know. It's strange though, as I've seen a few local women dressed in real revealing ways."

"You are right, it's cultural, and the coastal people themselves have their own styles and customs, but they see white people in a different light. Just as long as you are aware…" said Louise.

"Thank you for being so gracious about it," said Coreene.

Kelsey said, "I sure appreciate you guys giving advice. It's been great -— you being so open and everything…" She stood up and headed towards the beach. "Don't worry, I'll keep this cloth wrapped around me till I'm by the sea."

"It's called a kanga. Many have ancient Swahili proverbs on them," noted Coreene.

"I've seen all the women wearing them. Kangas eh? Like sarongs. I want to take some back to the States with me. Pretty, aren't they?"

Several developments occurred in the days following Brett's discussion with Louise. Matthew told Steve he knew a sign maker in Mombasa, and he would be willing to drive down, select the plaque, and arrange for the engraving. Miles offered to accompany him as he had some business to attend to, and no longer had a vehicle. Kelsey McNeil had expressed an interest in visiting Mombasa, so the three of them arranged to go down together. Miles seemed reluctant to go with Kelsey in the car, but he needed transport to Mombasa, so he accepted the arrangements. Steve commented to Coreene, "An unlikely trio. Exuberant, youthful Kelsey; dour old Matthew; and positively ancient, sour Miles. I wonder what pranks they'll get up to, all compressed in Matthew's VW Beetle."

It was obvious, upon their return from Mombasa, that the long day had been a confusing blend of success and disaster for the three ill-suited companions. Steve heard the full account. Matthew and Miles had located the engraver, and ordered a suitable plaque. Louise had offered to pay for it, so they had chosen the best – and most expensive – option. Evidently, Kelsey had been a fascinating companion, generously offering her unique insights, instant opinions, and unrestrained comments on everything she saw and experienced. She had provided a stream of amusement, irritation, and embarrassment for the two unsuspecting, defenceless men. "She's quite a girl," was Matthew's summary of it all.

"What a day!" said Miles. "I'm glad I managed to accomplish something apart from being the impotent recipient of her unrestrained tongue."

Matthew added, "It was interesting to see things fresh through her eyes. For example, she was fascinated to see women washing clothes at the well beside the road and then draping them over bushes to dry in the sun."

"How did the plaque look?" asked Steve.

The Zoo

"I think you'll be pleased with it. We selected a formal but clear style of lettering too. It will be ready for someone to collect in a week. It's all paid for. On the way home, Kelsey treated us to her analytical views on the different ways human societies process the reality of death. Interesting, but not entirely helpful in our situation with Henry, I'm afraid."

Brett saw Peter by the office and told him about his recent trip to Nairobi. Peter asked, "Did you ever get your ordnance-survey map of this area?"

"No. Unfortunately they say it is unavailable now."

"That doesn't surprise me. I can show you the one Henry and I made all those years ago, if you like."

"Thank you, that would be interesting. Maybe I can compare it with the sketch I drew down at Mr. Sembhi's store. Can I bring it over sometime?" Just then, Kelsey McNeil walked by. Brett introduced her to Peter, and they chatted about her interest in the social norms and traditions of different cultures. Peter told her, "I know your main focus is the Zoo community here at the coast, but I wonder if you have spoken to any of the Kikuyu about their legends and historical background?"

"No. Are they, like, a different tribe from the Mijikenda around here?" asked Kelsey.

Brett and Peter outlined the many distinct tribes in Kenya. Brett explained that he had lived with the Kikuyu for only five years but Peter had been there for much longer. After several more perceptive questions from Kelsey, Peter suggested she speak with one of the Kikuyu staff, so they all arranged to visit Peter's cage for tea the following afternoon. Within minutes, Brett and Kelsey received another invitation, this time from Steve, to visit them for supper on the Saturday evening in their cage. "I expect you'd like a change from the cafe dishes. And Brett never misses the chance of a free meal!"

"Thanks. I am enjoying the food here, but it would be awesome to spend more time with you guys and meet the kids," Kelsey said.

Peter suddenly frowned. He had noticed a long black Mercedes coming along the driveway. "This is not good. It looks like Moshi," Peter said as he disappeared down the corridor towards the Executive Officer's office.

Part 3: The Attack

As the car stopped, Kelsey asked Brett, "What was that all about?" She had detected the concern in Peter's words.

"I'm not sure," he said, steering her away from the front entrance, towards the south. Imam Faiz walked by and Kelsey was introduced to him. He told Brett that, during his absence in Nairobi, the Facilities Committee had authorized a study to look at building a new water tower near the kitchens, and they had engaged men to work on some block enclosures and heavy wooden lids for the dustbins.

"What are dustbins? Are they, like, garbage cans?" asked Kelsey.

"Just like garbage cans," joked Brett. "I had recommended that we tidy those up a bit, so I'm pleased the committee is moving ahead on that. Thank you Faiz."

As Brett walked to the guest wing to collect Kelsey, clutching his sketchbook, he realized he had never been inside Peter's cage. That was true of many of his neighbours actually. He mentioned it to Kelsey as they walked to the northeast corner of the Zoo, explaining that most of the social activities took place in the central block which had been designed to facilitate group social-interaction.

She was interested in the original design concepts, and asked if it was still working well. Brett explained the many positive aspects to the Zoo structure and Kelsey analysed some of the issues and challenges from an anthropological perspective.

They greeted several neighbours and visitors as they wandered along. Brett pointed out the vegetable gardens and ornamental trees in the central area. A group of children follow them for most of the way, giggling shyly.

Kelsey asked, "Who are we going to meet this afternoon?" Brett explained about friendly Joram Mwangi, Peter's Kikuyu helper. When they reached Peter's cage, Brett was surprised, and pleased, to see Onesimus Njuguna there too, from the Ridge-Taylors' cage next door. Brett knew that Njuguna was Kikuyu also.

The Zoo

After formal introductions, and some initial awkwardness, Peter and Kelsey lit their cigarettes while Brett opened his sketch book to compare his map with the large one that Peter had spread out on the table. Everyone was fascinated to see the details, particularly commenting on the similarities between the two layouts. While Peter pointed out some of the northern coastal features, Brett ignored the discussion and feasted his eyes on the lower section of the map detailing the reserve area beyond the wall. Many trails and specific references to caves, shelters, and open areas were noted. Then, discreetly, he studied the sketches of Henry Emerson's hut and research laboratory. He recognized the main layout but was surprised at the amount of additional detail, along with outlines of buildings he had not noticed when he was there. He asked himself: "What is that?...a pair of parallel dotted lines, connecting two of the foundations..."

Noticing his intense interest, Peter quickly snatched back his map and rolled it up, declaring, "Well, you have come here to discuss culture, not look at old maps. Tell us, Bwana Mwangi, about the traditions of the Kikuyu. How did your tribe originate?" Kelsey took out her notebook and smiled disarmingly at both of the apprehensive old Kenyan men. Mwangi and Njuguna exchanged looks and then Mwangi began the story, with amplifications and fastidious corrections from Njuguna. Their two personalities were evident: Mwangi the voluble extrovert, with pedantic Njuguna speaking more slowly and earnestly. They described, at length, how the Kikuyu tribe began with the man Gikuyu who lived in the land below Kirinyaga, the large snow-capped mountain. Peter clarified for Kelsey, as she wrote, that Kirinyaga is the original name of Mt. Kenya, and the letters G and K are interchangeable in Kikuyu which explained the name Gikuyu. The story developed as their god, Ngai, supplied a wife for Gikuyu.

They were blessed with nine beautiful and wise daughters, but no sons. There were no other men around for the daughters to marry. Gikuyu explained his plight to his god who gave special instructions. Eventually, Gikuyu had made the required sacrifices beneath a special fig tree, and returned there alone at night. To his amazement, nine tall and strong young men stood beside the tree. He took them home for his delighted daughters who married them and they had many children, giving birth to the nine clans of the Kikuyu tribe.

Part 3: The Attack

Kelsey dropped her notebook on the floor and leaned forward, "Where *is* this fig tree!' she exclaimed, much to everyone's delight.

The two Kikuyus smiled happily and Peter explained, "That was a long time ago, but the sacred fig tree is still held in high regard and will rarely be cut down."

After further merriment, story-telling, cigarettes, and tea, they all parted, with McNeil expressing her appreciation for all of the insights. As they left, Brett told her the afternoon had made him miss the Kikuyu people he had met, and it had revitalized his plan to return to the Kikuyu region soon.

"Maybe, one day you can visit that area," he suggested.

"I'd love to. I'll try to come back," said Kelsey.

Having returned Kelsey to the guest house, Brett saw Louise and Coreene sitting outside on the benches again. He went and stood beside them, and Coreene related a funny story. Their youngest son, Graham, had come home that day, saying his friends had told him, 'You must tell Miss McNeil not to smoke. You tell her. She is from your tribe.' They all laughed.

As he left them, Coreene said, "See you on Saturday, Brett. Can you come a bit early? Ruth has some algebra homework she's struggling with." He agreed, and as he started to walk away, Coreene called to him, "By the way, Detective Ochieng spent over an hour interrogating Chengo today. Something's up."

Brett arrived at the Brandons' cage at 5pm on the Saturday and spent an hour with Ruth, answering her mathematics and science questions. Steve picked up her science textbook and showed Brett the place where evolution is presented as though it were an established fact. "I explained to our children that only one particular viewpoint is being shown, without acknowledging that macroevolution has many inconsistencies with what we observe. Also, no recognition is given to the belief of many people that God is the creator." Kelsey arrived just as Andrew dashed in, sweaty and sandy from playing soccer outside with his friends. "You smell like a damp camel," teased Steve. "Go and wash, so you will be fit for polite company with Miss McNeil here."

She said, "I've seen him playing out there. I guess both of your boys have good friendships with the local kids."

"Yes, we are pleased about that."

"I'm learning a lot about the societal norms and values in this culture," said Kelsey.

"Any surprises? Or challenges?" asked Steve.

Kelsey thought for a moment and confided, "One example is children stroking my blond hair. They like to do that. You know what, I don't mind. I love the kids, they are all so cute. But, guess what, I have been washing my hair more often than usual!"

"Have you found out the information about the Zoo that you wanted?" asked Ruth.

"Oh yes. It's been real interesting, like, the way things are run and the set-up you have. I'm still not clear on the financing and sources of funding, but I guess that's all confidential. You know what, I get that." Kelsey spotted Ruth's science textbook on the sofa. "Hey, I like science. I did that in school and had to cover some science courses in my undergrad programs." Steve asked if they were presented with a pro-evolutionary bias. "They were not biased. They just explained how evolution works," replied Kelsey. "You know, natural selection and how one creature evolved into another one. Survival of the fittest is the mechanism."

Steve responded with a careful description of why macroevolution is an unfounded explanation and then added, "I've started to write some notes on this, to clarify my own thinking. It looks as though it could be a long analysis." After further discussion, Kelsey was looking overwhelmed by the validity of Steve's reasoning, especially when he described the Cambrian explosion and the lack of transitional forms in the fossil record. She was relieved when Coreene announced that supper was ready.

As the children gathered around the small table, there was some jostling to sit beside Kelsey. The three kids were squeezed onto a bench seat next to her chair. Graham was pushed off the end in the struggle, landing on the floor. Brett said, "Never mind. That's *survival-of-the-fittest* in action." He continued, "You see, some have to drop over the edge. It doesn't seem fair, I know, but that's the way natural selection works!"

Part 3: The Attack

"Come down this end and sit with me," said Kelsey sympathetically, so Graham happily snuggled up to her for the rest of the meal. After Steve had said grace, blessing the food and giving thanks for their fellowship, Coreene served one of her most successful dishes, which was always a favourite: African chicken stew with peanut sauce and coconut rice. They all enjoyed that, followed by her experimental mango and pineapple pie. That dessert was much appreciated and pronounced a success. Graham was gobbling up so much that Kelsey commented, "He's shovelling it in like it's going out of style!"

During the meal, Kelsey described her family and home in Georgia, and they chatted about the children's school programmes, studies, exams, teachers, friends, and sports. Kelsey and Brett appreciated being part of a family again.

"I love your accents. They are so cute, and you all talk so precisely," said Kelsey.

The children giggled and Graham said, "We like your accent too."

Later, Coreene cleaned up in the kitchen with her maid and then joined in the discussion, while the children reluctantly worked on their homework. As the adults relaxed over coffee, they continued to discuss evolution, and then the conversation turned to religion. About twenty minutes later, Andrew wandered in, holding his mathematics book. "Can you help me with a problem please," he asked Brett.

"Sure, it will probably be easier than some of the things we're discussing!" Brett did not mind the interruption as he was wondering if poor Kelsey was feeling outnumbered. Glancing back at her, he concluded that she wasn't intimidated but instead was thoroughly enjoying herself. While looking at Andrew's work, he continued to half-listen to the adult conversation.

Kelsey said, "I've studied spirituality and all the major religions of the world, including animist teachings. They all help people deal with the world and their relation to it, and other people. I don't buy into any of it myself, but if it helps people, why not? Good for them. But I don't see any reason why one religion should force itself on the rest. It bugs me when one group gets all preachy and pushes their own opinion."

"If I share some good news with you – say, the local petrol station now has supplies – is that getting all preachy? Or a serious driving danger on the Malindi road, or sharks out on the reef, would you say I am I just pushing my own opinion of traffic safety or marine hazards?" Steve asked gently.

Coreene added, "Or would you say that we were sharing good news or a common concern with you in a natural, loving way?"

"Sure, but those are just practical things—"

"They are simple examples of how we share good news in a loving and concerned way."

"But sometimes your religious ideas come across as judgmental, or telling non-believers how they should behave."

"Sorry if it sounds judgmental as that's certainly not our intention. We simply try to present the truth for anyone to consider seriously," said Steve.

Andrew whispered to Brett, "What are they talking about? Do you understand?"

"Some of it, but not all," Brett admitted with a grin. He continued to catch fragments of what they were discussing.

Kelsey was stressing, "…everyone is searching, and essentially they all believe in one god. We just need to level the playing field. That's what I believe: all religions point to the same god."

Steve suppressed his frustration, and asked respectfully, "How can they? They all say *different* things about God! Each concept of god is incompatible with the others – some are totally opposite. In any case, you don't believe in God."

"No, but all religions point to something that other people think of as god. But, you know what, none of it has any credibility for me."

"Be careful not to reject what you do not know," warned Steve, with a concerned look.

"I just don't find any of the stories about Jesus convincing," admitted Kelsey.

"Tell me, which of the original eye-witness accounts you have read, do you find unconvincing?" said Steve.

"Well…I haven't actually read any," she laughed.

Part 3: The Attack

As Brett rejoined them, Coreene smiled, and patted Kelsey's arm, "Well, may I suggest you read them – start with John's gospel – and see if you find them convincing. We'll encourage you as you do that."

"Thank you for allowing us to discuss these ideas," said Steve.

"Yes, thank you. I appreciate chatting about these challenging ideas. You guys are real kind," smiled Kelsey.

"You have been gracious too. It's wonderful that we have the freedom to share ideas, isn't it? Remember, though, those freedoms are based on Judeo-Christian foundations that are fundamental to western civilization," Steve said.

Coreene emphasized, "Yes, it's only through the Christian background of North America that you have the freedom to express your opinions."

"I guess that's true."

"You know, Kelsey, in some quarters near here your life would be very restricted," Coreene said, glancing at the clock. "It's getting late, and we have services tomorrow. We have appreciated the frank sharing of ideas, thank you Kelsey. You have been a blessing to us."

"I loved the intellectual discussion, and the wonderful food, thank you," Kelsey replied. "I sure hope we'll have another chance to chat, although my short time here is almost over."

As they left, Steve invited them both to attend church the following morning, "I'll be giving a short meditation on the ways that God guides us."

"Thanks. Guess what, I just might show up. You've got me interested in some of these ideas. Lots to think about," said Kelsey.

"I'll be there. Thanks for a great evening," said Brett.

Brett was pleased to see Kelsey at the church service. She sat next to the principal's wife, Mrs Katana. Kelsey was impressed by the warm welcome from the Katanas and several other Kenyan ladies. They seemed to delight in taking her under their wings and making her feel comfortable. One lady admiringly squeezed Kelsey's chubby arm and whispered, "I like your shape. You are a well-fed lady. Your husband must be very rich." They guided her through the parts of the service that were unfamiliar.

Steve gave a homily describing the ways that God guides and directs our lives in the path He has chosen for us, if we follow His purposes. Kelsey was surprised to learn that a specific plan had been ordained by God for each of us. She had always thought that her life was under her control, and it was up to her to decide her own course of action. Steve said God has prepared, in advance, good works for us to do. The only way we can find true fulfilment is to be yielded to His will, as nothing else will satisfy our deepest longings. These were all new ideas for Kelsey.

Afterwards, she was introduced to several people she had not met previously. "Everyone is so friendly and happy, and there was a sense of – well – joy in the service. Quite an eye-opener for me," she told Brett afterwards.

Coreene spoke about the arrangement to get Kelsey to Malindi airport later in the week for her flight to Nairobi. Coreene said she would find someone to drive her, as she and Steve had an important meeting, and it was during Brett's busy teaching day.

The Brandons and Brett arranged a farewell dinner for Kelsey on the Tuesday evening. Louise joined them. At the last minute, Steve was called to deal with an urgent matter, so Brett found himself outnumbered by the women.

After the meal, and a review of her experiences and impressions of the Kenyan coast, Kelsey confessed, "It needs more than a one-month field trip. There is so much I still want to find out."

"Such as?" asked Louise.

Kelsey replied, "I've been thinking about what you told me of the religions here, Coreene. Of course, I don't believe in any religion."

Coreene said, "I've looked at this deeply by studying their texts – the books that summarize all the teachings. That allows me to respectfully find out what the various faiths represent." This generated further questions and frank sharing of beliefs on origins, the value of life, the erosion of sound moral precepts, and a weakening of the foundational role of the family.

Eventually, Coreene mused, "I'm not sure of this – Steve and I are still trying to sort out our thoughts – but our feeling is that some false ideology is just waiting in the wings for western democracies to become so weak morally…destroying ourselves from within, I suppose, that… I mean, if the Christian faith is weakened, then who will defend our values? I am beginning to see it all as interrelated." The others studied her serious face.

"This is all new to me," admitted Kelsey.

"But surely the churches are a strong defence against all these challenges," said Brett.

Coreene replied, "I hope so, but I feel that some of our western churches are adopting the same values as the surrounding society. It's less evident in Kenya, but we are in touch with a wide international community and—"

"But why are the churches compromising on their basic values?" interjected Louise.

"In an attempt to seem relevant and appealing I think…" Coreene began to say, when Steve joined them, after having spoken with Miles in the bar.

"I've been searching around for transport for you Kelsey but, as it happens, all of the people we asked have other firm commitments at that exact time, so I'm trying to dragoon Miles Jolly into the task! He says he has no means of transport." Brett immediately offered to lend him his pickup.

After the meal, Steve and Brett approached Miles. He again complained that he had no transport, but he was secretly remembering the stressful day with Kelsey and Matthew in Mombasa. Brett told him he could use his vehicle. Seeing that he was cornered, Miles put a brave face on it. "Okay, I'll drive her to the airport, but I won't be able to lift her suitcases, as I'm having difficulty with my heart and breathing these days. But I'll do anything to facilitate her departure. Just the thought that she is going thrills me." His ungracious response did not produce any smiles.

As with everything about Miles, there was more to the matter than he presented superficially. Miles displayed a facade of disliking Kelsey McNeil, but, in truth, he was disturbed by her. He found her objectionable in one sense but, at the same time, he was fascinated by her. He tried to reason through his thoughts as he drove over to collect her and her two cases. *I wonder if I see her as the daughter I never had? Could there be a form of latent filial affection?*

The tense trip to the airport did nothing to clarify his thoughts or improve their strained relationship. Kelsey was grateful for his help, but each time she tried to express something positive, it sounded hollow and left her wondering if she would ever be able to understand, or communicate with, this odd little man. Yet, she sensed a need in him, and a depth of hunger for a relationship that he appeared to be suppressing. She recalled that he had mentioned, very obliquely, a need for security, but he had clammed up the moment she had tried to explore that thought further.

It was a relief to both of them when the journey was over, although they parted on amicable terms. "Thank you for your help, Mr. Jolly," she said, shaking his soft hand.

"Have a good flight. Come back and see us some time." He could not bring himself to use her name, and he did not look back as he walked away from the line of people at the airline counter.

Climbing back into Brett's pickup, he thought, *Come back and see us. Now, why did I say that? It sounded like an augury.* Driving home, a disquieting thought struck him. *She is about the same age as the only woman I ever had a romantic relationship with…long, long ago. Am I feeling some form of atavistic warmth?* He dismissed the jumble of conflicting thoughts with, *Bah! Women are complicated creatures.*

As he entered his cage, Miles thought about Kelsey: *The real reason I don't like her has nothing to do with what she says, or how she looks. She seems to see through me. Do I want someone to understand me? I have built an effective shell that I can hide within – even from myself. That is what makes me uneasy.*

19

*"It's not a game. It's reality. Yes, the game of life.
My life. What's left of it!"*

Louise Emerson

Matthew collected Henry's memorial plaque from Mombasa. He and a craftsman mounted the brass plate on the wall of the central building, outside the main entrance door where everyone could see it. At one point, the policemen, Ochieng and Kinyanjui, stopped by to admire the work. They were on their way for another interview with the Executive Officer. Matthew whispered to his fellow workman, "Those two visiting Chengo again…I don't like the look of it." When they had finished the work, they made a temporary plywood cover to hide it until the unveiling ceremony on Saturday afternoon.

The official event attracted a large crowd. Brett was pleased to see, among many others, Dr. Patel and the Singh family from Mwakindini. Louise had not wanted any long speeches, but she agreed that Brigadier Thomas should make some opening remarks, and Peter offered to read out the words when the plaque was revealed. Miles then translated them into Kiswahili.

In spite of Louise's initial reservations, the occasion seemed to demand more recognition. Spontaneously, several key figures stepped forward and spoke respectfully of their appreciation for Henry and Louise Emerson.

It happened naturally, and Louise was visibly touched by the genuine expressions of sorrow and gratitude.

One man from the Sikh community spoke of the welcome his family had received and how well the purposes of the original vision had been accomplished. A Muslim man acknowledged the practical workings of intercultural harmony. He had been at the Zoo since the beginning and stressed how cross-religious friendships had deepened over many years. A Kenyan Christian echoed the thought, and expressed his appreciation of inter-religious harmony fostered during the joint community events. Steve Brandon spoke briefly of the mutual respect that had developed through honest sharing of information and ideas with Henry, and a common search for understanding and truth.

Eventually, Peter and the brigadier brought the gathering to a formal close, after which the guests came closer to inspect the plate, all expressing approval. It was mounted with four dome-head brass screws, and shone brightly. Simple refreshments were served on tables in the dining areas and along the corridor inside the central building.

When the crowd had dispersed, Louise was left with a small group around her as she carefully read the inscription:

HENRY EMERSON
'Cipher'
1908 - 1982
In grateful memory of his service
to his country and our community
Spiegel im Spiegel

Someone asked Louise, "What does Cipher mean?"

"It was Henry's code-name a long time ago," she stated briefly.

"And *Spiegel im Spiegel*? What's that about?"

She smiled and explained, "It relates to his life as the reflection of mirrors. It's a German expression he sometimes used. A mirror reflecting in another mirror." She held up her two hands with one facing the other.

Part 3: The Attack

The previous day, Louise had asked Brett if he was free to join her for tea after the ceremony. As they walked away, he asked, "How did you feel about the large gathering?"

"It was good. Very appropriate. Thank you for your contribution. I appreciated Dr. Patel coming, and Imam Faiz said some kind words of sympathy and understanding, bless him." They turned to see several small children touching the plaque.

"Soon it will be covered in tiny hand-prints," noted Brett.

"Good. It's theirs too. Henry would approve. Several people took photos of it when it was in pristine condition."

She ushered him upstairs to her upper living room, explaining, "There is something I want to show you." Mjuhgiuna brought tea, which they enjoyed, and then Louise said, "Come and look at Kismet Kantara from up here." They walked through the hallway to an open patio, with Kali following them. The outside veranda faced to the southeast, with woven panels hanging down to shield from the wind at the east and north. Across the wall, Brett noticed a crashing movement in the trees. He saw a group of monkeys swinging among the branches. He silently wondered if they were paying tribute, in their own way, to the man who had protected them. Pointing towards the south, Louise said, "The strong winds come this way so those walls fold out to give shelter, but most of the year I enjoy the vista across the roofs to the bay."

Brett admired the view, as Louise walked to a heavy door set in a solid frame at the eastern end of the patio. "This leads out to the walkway across our bridge of destiny. I lock it from this side as people have access up stone steps from the south, across the top wall."

"From which, interlopers down the other side can be spotted," he joked.

"And we hurl boulders and pour boiling oil on them," said Louise.

"So I got off quite lightly?"

"You surely did. Henry designed it this way to give us a means of escape if the stairs became blocked. He always liked an escape hatch. He would never place himself in a position where he did not have a second exit route. That strategy is built into all of this structure, along with some secret places."

"How can they be secret when the local builders knew, and the existing residents here would have seen it all being constructed?" said Brett.

"You are too sharp my friend. Come along now for more cake, and I'll explain."

As they left the veranda and walked back into her suite, Brett noticed Kali was limping. "Is she okay?"

"She's old, and has canine hip dysplasia. It's getting worse, poor thing." She patted Kali and told her, "We'll keep you going as long as we can, won't we, my poppet?"

She rang for Mjuhgiuna to bring a fresh pot of tea, and they sat down. Louise explained that, during the first few months of the Zoo's construction, they hired many local craftsmen, but for the building of the Emersons' cage, and their modest buildings over the wall where Henry did his research, they employed three Italian builders. "Henry met them while they were on holiday in Malindi and arranged for them to stay another three months to work on our construction here. They did all of the excellent marble tiling too. Also, Henry travelled over to South Nyanza to hire a large group of tradesmen to work with them. He did not want locals to know what he was building. Once the job was done he sent them all away – with a generous bonus to keep them quiet, I might add."

"Did it work?"

"What?"

"No one else knew about the secret construction?"

"No one. We needed our secret connections to the nature preserve."

Brett hesitated, and then said, "Faiz mentioned another way across to the protected area, to the north of the main gate in their sector."

She seemed shocked, but quickly said, "Did he? I thought only…" She quickly recover and casually added, "Of course, he knows about the gate on the north beach through to the reserve, beside the brigadier's cage. I imagine he's referring to that."

They chatted about Brett's time in Nairobi, McNeil's visit, and Louise's discomfort at some of the Executive Council meetings she had to sit through. "I got pulled in as Henry's understudy – an unwilling, nominal 'Emerson presence' when Henry was no longer available."

Part 3: The Attack

The conversation lapsed, and Louise thought for a moment. Then she stood up and walked over to the heavy wooden shelving unit behind the door. She lifted a box and asked, "Do you play chess?"

"Yes, but I don't think I have time—"

"No, not to play a game. I just want show you something," she said, handing him the delicately carved box. She dragged a nearby table across the floor. Kali made a brave attempt to get up and sniff it. Brett admired the table with its marquetry chess-board inlay on top. "We bought it in Sorento and had it shipped here," she said, opening the elaborate box which Brett recognized from the photo he had given to Sembhi. Two sets of chess pieces were nestled in velvet pouches on either side. "The white pieces are pure ivory and the black set is also ivory with black mahogany bands around the bases of each piece."

Louise selected a few pieces and placed them on the table top. She sat down opposite Brett and explained, "It's a special set that a friend gave Heinrick after a difficult project where he helped a wealthy family. It predates the ivory ban, so it's legal and I have the paperwork." While saying this, she was arranging several pieces on particular squares in the corner next to Brett. "Look at these. I have remembered these positions." She set several other chess pieces in plausible but, in Brett's view, random positions. "These three are the important ones. The others don't matter. Chess players call the column letters 'files' and the row numbers 'ranks'." She placed the black queen in the corner position a1, and the black rook on d4. She lowered the white king onto the c2 square and asked Brett, "Can the king move?"

He studied the arrangement and pointed out, "Only one square, diagonally to b3,"

"Anywhere else?"

"No. That piece can only oscillate back and forth between those two positions."

"But the piece can move? It's free to move?"

"Yes," he said.

"It's not check-mate, game over?"

"No."

"But very limited movement for the white king. Sort of...trapped?" she asked.

"Yes." He frowned.

Louise stared at the board and whispered, "That's me."

"Pardon?"

"That's me. Or it used to be. I am that white king She slid the piece from one square to the next, and back again. "Heinrick was the black queen controlling those vertical and horizontal lines and the diagonal, while Peter was the black rook, dominating the other ranks and files. I was trapped, but allowed slight movement. Or, at least, that's how it felt."

"Why were you trapped? There were no physical restrictions, surely."

"No. But I was trapped."

"By what?"

"By my knowledge."

Brett thought briefly, and responded, "You said something to that effect before – what was it? – held captive by your knowledge."

Louise stood up. "Exactly." She walked to the window and looked out across the shimmering sapphire ocean. Brett stared at the chess pieces. Kali stood beside Louise and glared at Brett as he leant back in his chair and looked down at the board.

After a moment, Brett said, "You're wrong, you know."

"What? Wrong?"

"You were wrong when you said only those three pieces matter. The others in the game matter too. Look at them – even in the arbitrary positions where you placed them. What do you see?" Louise strolled back and looked down at the randomly placed chess pieces she had casually set out.

"Black pieces, white pieces, here and there. None of significance to the point I'm making."

"Maybe not, but they *are* important to the point *I'm* making. Look again Louise. Are any on your side?"

"Well, the white ones, I suppose."

"And do you see any significance in their present positions, capabilities, and limitations?" She stared at the board. He spoke forcefully, "These are your friends. They support you. There is more to the game than this little corner here…" He encircled the three in the group near him with his finger in the air. "Bring in the other pieces. Don't fight the battle alone! Even a lowly pawn can take down a queen or threaten the king."

Part 3: The Attack

Louise stood still and looked down at the exquisitely carved pieces arranged on the finely crafted table. "I suppose you're right. But what about the black pieces? They are there too. Some of those are my opponents."

Brett didn't have a simple answer, but he voiced some impromptu thoughts. "It seems to me we have to accept everyone and everything as part of the total match we are engaged in – the game of life. We just take the configuration of the board we are placed on, and play the game from that time on, according to the rules – which often seem like restrictions, it's true." He sighed, and said, "I don't know, the analogy breaks down pretty quickly, doesn't it?"

They both looked at the board. Palm trees waved in the gentle breeze outside the open window. Brett moved his hand towards the board and Kali immediately stepped forward. Louise held her head. Brett said, "Forgive me for doing this, but the situation has changed." He respectfully lifted the black queen from its corner position and set it aside. "I believe you have more freedom than you think."

"But less than *you* think," said Louise, picking up several other black pieces and placing them in an arc around the white king. "There are other dark forces, I'm afraid. My knowledge is still entrapping me." She exhaled and said, "You are right, the analogy does break down." She scooped up the pieces and started to replace them in their pockets in the soft case, adding, "It's not a game. It's reality. Yes, the game of life. My life. What's left of it!"

Brett said, "I wish I could help. Please let me know if there is anything I can do."

She carried the chess set over to the shelf and placed it there, returned to Brett and laid her hand on his shoulder. "Thank you. There may be some things later." She lifted her hand and stood looking out of the window, far into the distance.

So much suffering. So many difficulties, Brett thought. *Louise, Peter, Miles, Chengo...Everyone is carrying a burden. I have been selfish. Just thinking about myself. All I have been concerned about was getting my questions answered.* In the stillness, Kali laid a paw on Brett's foot.

After several days, Brett found time to take his umbrella stand to Len's small workshop and grind down the sharp edges. He missed having it to hold the umbrellas, but he had developed love-hate feelings towards it. While at Len's cage, Miles returned from one of his fishing trips, but confessed to not keeping any of the fish his friends had caught. He told them he had located a pickup and was having the inspection and ownership transfers done in Malindi. Brett was puzzled. "Why Malindi? Can't they do the inspection in Mwakindini?"

"I'd rather use the mechanic that Peter knows. He'll do some small modifications for me."

"Such as adding a secret compartment like Peter has in his Land Rover," joked Len, but Miles frowned at him, and Len quickly changed his expression.

"By the way, I was called an angel yesterday," Miles beamed.

Len said, "Must have been a case of mistaken identity!"

"No, Coreene said I was an angel for taking Kelsey to the airport," boasted Miles.

He pulled down his straw hat and started to wander over to the main buildings, waving his driftwood stick and clutching his satchel under his arm. "Let's see what the postman has brought me," he muttered as he walked away.

"He's been acting a bit strange recently," Len whispered to Brett.

"Is that unusual?" scoffed Brett.

"Now now, nasty nasty," Len chided him.

"Sorry. I'm a bit cheesed off with him over his rudeness towards Kelsey."

"Forget it. That's Miles for you. She didn't seem upset. She just took it all in her stride."

"I suppose you're right. Thanks for the use of the grinder. That feels smoother now."

"And you'll be more careful about stumbling about your cage in a drunken stupor in future, I imagine," joked Len as Brett left.

On the way back, he saw Miles again, who was waving a couple of letters in the air. "Someone loves me," he shouted.

"That's unlikely. You must have got someone else's letters by mistake," Brett called back to him. They parted, laughing.

Part 3: The Attack

Several days later, Miles drifted over to his neighbour Len when he saw him sitting out on his patio. He stood lamely in front of Len and said, "I've received a letter from a woman."

"Are you boasting or complaining?" Len asked.

"It's a rather unusual experience for me."

"Why don't you sit down," invited Len.

"Sit down? That's bit energetic isn't it?" Miles said, smiling, as he flopped into the chair. He stared at the envelope he was carrying.

Len waited, but there was silence, so he suggested, "Now, why don't you tell Uncle Leonard all about it?"

"It seems strange, reading this…"

Len leaned back in his chair and squinted at Miles' slumped form. "Give me a few clues so I know whether to sympathize or offer congratulations."

"It's from McNeil."

"Ah, your favourite tourist. So, sympathy it is."

"No, this is surprising…"

"Come on, cut out the mystery, what's it all about? What did the elfin sylph write to you?"

"Stop teasing and listen, will you?"

"This is getting deep, you need a drink – tea, coffee, what?"

Miles looked up, "What? Oh, tea please."

Len called out to Marie-Anne while Miles handed him the letter, saying, "You read it."

"I don't think I should be–"

"Just read it," said Miles, waving a dismissive hand.

Uncomfortably, Len glanced at Kelsey's neat handwriting, and read a few thoughts from the script: '…writing like a petulant school girl… Sorry for the way I treated you…we are similar, you and me…single… both outsiders…the herd…introspective…Put on my analytical professorial hat… suggest you look deeply inside…An article that may help…respect and appreciation…Maybe you will be comfortable…writing your thoughts….'

When he had finished, Len looked up at Miles, saying, "She mentions sending you an article–"

"Yes, probably describing how to snap out of whatever condition she thought I was in – written, no doubt, by a currently-fashionable feminist author."

"Be kind Miles. She has gone to the trouble of contacting you. Obviously she feels some connection or affinity…"

Miles ignored him, and continued with his own mumblings. "When she was here, her eyes seemed to look through me and forced me to confront myself." Len said nothing and let Miles continue his introspections, which gradually took a different tack. "What's the meaning and purpose of it all? I've been selfish. I've survived, that's all. Simply survived. I've been dishonest. That's the whole point. Who am I? What have I accomplished in life?"

Len knew better than to attempt to reply to Miles' rhetorical questions, and he was relieved when the tea tray was delivered. Len thought, as he poured the tea, *Has Jolly been deceptive? If so, he's concealed it well. He is extremely bright and perceptive. I suppose clever deception doesn't equal intelligence. Is he selfish? In a way, perhaps. A complicated individual!*

Their conversation meandered along, with no further revelations or conclusions. As Miles eventually stood to leave, Len asked, "Well, what are you, selfish or an angel?"

Miles smiled sheepishly, "Something in between I suppose."

"And are you going to reply to her?"

"I don't know. What should I say? I'll think about it. It's a rather unusual experience for me."

"Yes, I think you mentioned that before," said Len, smiling as he patted Miles on his retreating back.

The next day, Brett walked with Miles on their way to the main building. Miles was just about to tell Brett that he was writing to Kelsey, when Grace dashed out of her office and told Miles, "Ochieng and Kinyanjui, they are on their way coming." Then she disappeared.

"Excuse me," said Miles as he followed her into the office. Brett assumed he was going to speak with Chengo. A turaco started to squawk in the palm trees above, as Brett entered the cafe.

Part 3: The Attack

After his snack, Brett almost collided with Kinyanjui in the corridor. He was carrying several boxes of files. The policeman attempted to shake hands while struggling to balance the boxes on one arm. Ochieng rudely marched past with other files and handed them to the driver beside the police car. He returned, and attempted to ignore Brett. When forced to acknowledge his presence, Ochieng simply stated, "This is not a sociable visit. We have serious matters at hand." Brett nodded to Kinyanjui and left. Outside, his path again crossed with Miles. "What's going on with Boniface Chengo, with the police and all that?"

"Difficult to say," Miles replied. He called back over his shoulder, "Difficult to say."

Miles headed over to the mailbox to post two items: a flimsy, pale-blue aerogramme addressed to *Miss K. McNeil* and another of his regular, insulting letters to his old insurance agent. He held one envelope in each hand, and seemed to be weighing them thoughtfully. He slipped Kelsey's in the box, and then hesitated, looking at the other envelope. On an impulse, he tore up the second letter. Suddenly it did not seem important any more. *It's so unnecessary and petty*, he thought to himself, stuffing the fragments of paper in his pocket. As he strolled out of the building into the evening warmth, it felt as though a load had been lifted from his shoulders. He relaxed and breathed with more ease. The relaxation was short-lived, however, because the memory of the visit from Ochieng to Chengo soon resurfaced.

Then, for some reason, Miles thought about Peter. Briefly, he wondered why he had not seen him recently, and then he remembered that he said he'd be away for his birthday. He had several days of medical tests in Nairobi at the end of November. *Never mind*, he thought, *we can endure a few days of separation from each other. No doubt of that.*

In early December, Miles and Brett drove south to Malindi to collect Miles' new pickup. They completed the paperwork and other formalities, including the mandatory vehicle inspection, and then left the vehicle with the mechanic for several days. They did some shopping in the town. Miles collected a bulky envelope from the photographer, and then Brett drove

The Zoo

home. He did not reveal that he guessed what the photographer's packet contained. On the journey, he tried to find out what modifications Miles required on the pickup. Miles was vague. "Just an extra little compartment – for convenience. A bit out-of-sight, let's say."

"Like Peter has?"

"Oh, I don't know about that…exactly…"

As Miles had stepped in to help by driving Kelsey to Malindi, Brett had been trying to think of a gift for him. "You know the oil painting I was telling you about – the one of the beach from my place – would you like to see it now it's finished?" asked Brett.

"Sure," said Miles. They drove straight to Brett's cage, and Miles admired the painting. He seemed to know about composition and colour techniques. "I like the way you've captured the form of the palm trees. I spend a lot of time appreciating them and their movements in the wind. You have recreated their structure perfectly, particularly the way the roots show above ground and the varying taper of the trunks. Good observation there!"

"Do you think you'd have a place for it in your cage?" asked Brett. "I'd like you to have it." Miles was genuinely pleased with the gift, and seemed touched at Brett's initiative in giving it to him. Brett drove him home with it. On the way, Brett said, "You seem quite knowledgeable about art and I think you mentioned you are interested in classical music."

Miles said, "I am fond of it, particularly opera. In my teens I was involved in an operetta, and other theatrical productions. I played the parts of a young priest, and a novice Friar. That was the extent of my theological training, I'm afraid! Then the war came along and it marked the final curtain on my promising theatrical career!"

As they stepped out of the pickup, Brett laughed and Miles added, "But I've been acting ever since." Brett continued smiling, but he noticed that Miles wasn't.

They carried the painting into Miles' cage and agreed on a suitable location on his living room wall. "I'll get Len to put up a screw there. Thank you very much," Miles said, in an almost boyish way.

Part 3: The Attack

A new day was beginning and, as it was a Friday, the early-morning assembly was to take place in front of the polytechnic. As he made his way across the compound, Brett looked around and appreciated, once more, the fresh morning vistas and aromas. He remembered his days commuting in the crowded and polluted areas around London. He thought, *How wonderful to be away from all that congestion and stress, and be living in a natural and fresh environment.*

All of the students, and most of the staff, were standing in front of the flagpole by 7:45am. Brett made a point of always being there ahead of time. He felt, as a foreigner, that it showed respect. The Kenyan flag was slowly raised. Its black, green, red, and white colours, emblazoned with the emblem of a shield, flapped gently in the breeze. The flag was an important and cherished symbol of unity in the country. Strict regulations were in force – and enforced – to ensure everyone respected the flag. For example, if a person was within sight of a flag that was being raised, it was imperative that one stood still and faced it silently.

Soon the students and staff would sing the National Anthem, a prayer, starting with *Oh God of all creation…* Then all present would say in unison the national pledge, either in English or Kiswahili. Brett knew it in both languages. In English, it was dutifully recited:

> *I pledge my loyalty to the President and the Republic of Kenya,*
> *My devotion to the words of our national anthem,*
> *My life and strength in the service of our nation,*
> *In the living spirit embodied in our national motto, Harambee,*
> *and perpetuated in the Nyayo Philosophy of Peace, Love, and Unity.*

The pledge, with minor variations, was routinely and respectfully said in all educational settings across the land. Thus began the day, with further announcements and dismissal to attend the 8am classes.

Brett felt he was now an accepted and trusted part of the community. He continued to enjoy his work at the polytechnic, his good working relationships with the other staff, and the commitment of the students. He admired the ingenuity of the students when preparing for a mathematics test. They were not permitted to enter the teachers' housing areas, so they would intercept one of the Brandon boys, Andrew or Graham, as they pedaled their cycles past the polytechnic. The students would write out a mathematics question on a scrap of paper, which the boy then delivered to Brett at his house. Brett would supply the solution and give it to the child, who would then cycle back to the students with the answer. This only happened for a short time, immediately before tests, and Brett did not mind as he was pleased that the students felt comfortable asking for his help. Also, it indicated the good relationship that the Brandon children had with the students.

Sometimes, when he was teaching, Brett felt a surge of profound awareness that he was doing exactly the right thing, in the right place, at the right time. He would glance out the classroom window, feeling the warm breeze across the dry gardens, shaded by the swaying palm fronds, catching the fleeting, distinctive fragrance from the frangipani trees, or seeing the flash of the iridescent back of a songbird feeding on the sweet-smelling flowers of the hibiscus trees.

He saw the students quietly copying down notes that he had given them on the board, having just explained a challenging topic that they seemed to have understood well. As a Christian, he recognized the deep satisfaction of following God's guidance and will in his life. Along with the precious expressions of appreciation from students, these frequent feelings of contentment helped to offset some of the frustrations, challenges, and problems that he had experienced within the Zoo. His fulfilling work helped keep his thoughts in balance.

The end of 1985 was approaching, so Brett began his annual report. In addition to a summary of his work, and the progress in the polytechnic, he described some economic, and political developments within the country. The continuing drought in some areas was causing stress, along with unemployment and the harsh economic conditions of many citizens. Tribal tensions were being exacerbated by economic realities. There were pockets of unrest, and increasing demands for multi-party elections to replace the single-party state which had existed until then. He was able to report that a new course in auto mechanics was in the planning stages, and would proceed once a new source of funding had been established.

Part 3: The Attack

Brett was pleased to complete, copy, and post his reports just before the Christmas break.

The exercise left him with an unsettled feeling which he could not define. To some extent, it continued during the holidays so he was grateful for the companionship of the Brandon family. After a supper with them on New Years' Eve, he strolled over to one of the small stone jetties projecting into the southern bay. He had lathered himself with mosquito repellent and decided to enjoy the sunset over the western hills. An orange light reflected on the delicate clouds as they offered themselves to the sun's dying glow. A few children played along the shore, making imaginary houses from the narrow rows of seaweed that the high tide had deposited. After some initial greetings and shy smiles, they ignored him. His introspective mood, and the rare solitude, allowed him to reflect on his time in the Zoo.

At one level, life was satisfying and his leg wound was healing. Yet the mysteries of the Zoo administration were still troubling: Boniface Chengo's evasiveness; the continuing police enquiries; and Miles Jolly's partial revelations, conflicting actions, and the violent side to his nature. There were Peter Lancaster's ongoing challenges and Louise Emerson's ambiguous references to dark forces. Brett thought, *There are hints of illegal activities beyond the wall, with so much intrigue below the surface. Will I ever know the answers to this riddle?*

On the other hand, as Steve Brandon had pointed out earlier, Brett was in a well-established role with good support and recognition. Steve was also pleased with the work at the church and the preliminary notes for his analysis of the social and religious situation in the country. He reminded Brett that, as outsiders, they were often treated as royalty, but constantly had to live with inner tensions and a panoply of ambiguities.

A fisherman walked past Brett as the sunset deepened. The man had been attending his dugout wooden canoe with its outrigger planks, bobbing on the gentle waves in the receding tide. The warm breeze from behind him kept mosquitoes away and Brett looked once more at the beautiful arc of the coastline as it swung south. He saw the rippled water in the bay and the white waves breaking across the fringing reef to his left. In the rapidly fading light, he admired the shadowy bulk of the rocky promontory sweeping to the east.

Half an hour later, the children had gone; the beach was deserted. He saw the buildings of the Muslim area set against the darkening sky, with a few faint lights shining through the gaps among the palm trees. Beyond the ruins of the ancient mosque, over the wall, he knew the darkness concealed the abandoned ruins of Henry Emerson's research station.

After a long while, in the gloom, he slowly walked up the beach, through the narrow laneway between the houses, and along the road in front of the central buildings. He soon arrived at his cage: his home.

BOOK TWO: The Zoo Revealed

Keith Brown's second novel dramatically describes shocking disclosures and disasters within the Zoo community and on the mysterious Monkey Island in the Indian Ocean.

During his time at the Zoo, Brett James had learned a lot about the history of the community from the long-term residents. Some of his questions had been answered, but there was still lingering doubt over the validity of the Zoo's finances. Also, his curiosity over the complex relationships between several prominent individuals was a long way from being satisfied. Would anyone reveal any more to him? And, in any case, how long would those who knew the truth be around?

The founder's wife, Louise Emerson, had been frank with him, but how much more was she able to draw him into her confidence? There was the ever-present clown, Miles Jolly, who had befriended Brett, but how far could Brett trust him?

Brett had not forgotten the warnings from Peter Lancaster, the no-nonsense security officer. He was friendly, but did not reveal much. Brett respected the Executive Officer – his Kenyan friend, Boniface Chengo. But even the affable giant, Chengo, was under police investigation, so how open would he be with Brett, the inquisitive foreign teacher?

Brett felt that his place in the Zoo was secure, but he had heard sufficient faint alarm bells to sensitize him to the dangers of probing too deeply into areas where his enquiries were not welcomed.

CPSIA information can be obtained
at www.ICGtesting.com
Printed in the USA
LVHW092127270521
688658LV00023B/114